NEMESIS IN LOVE

A PANTHEON LEAGUE NOVEL
BOOK ONE

ALSO BY MARIE K. SAVAGE

The Alchemist of Aleppo

The Trouble with Roommates

The Oracles of Delphi

&

THE SEEDS TRILOGY

The Sowing
(K. Makansi co-author)

The Reaping
(K. Makansi co-author)

The Harvest
(K. Makansi co-author)

NEMESIS IN LOVE

A PANTHEON LEAGUE NOVEL
BOOK ONE

MARIE K. SAVAGE

LAYLA DOG PRESS | TUCSON, ARIZONA

Layla Dog Press
Tucson, AZ 85719

Copyright © 2025 Marie K. Savage
All rights reserved.
(Marie K. Savage is the pen name for Kristina Makansi)

Publisher's Note: This book is a work of the imagination. Names, characters, places and incidents are either products of the author's imagination or are used fictitiously. While some of the characters and incidents portrayed here can be found in historical or contemporary accounts, they have been altered and rearranged by the author to suit the strict purposes of storytelling. The book should be read solely as a work of fiction, and no part of it may be reproduced or used to "train" generative artificial intelligence (AI) technologies to generate text without the author's express permission.

Thank you to everyone who takes a chance on an indie author/publisher like Layla Dog Press. We may not have the resources of a traditional publisher, but we've got big imaginations, we're dedicated to the craft of writing, and we firmly believe story has the power to change the world.

For information, contact:
Layla Dog Press
an imprint of Blank Slate Communications
www.kristinamakansi.com

Manufactured in the United States of America
Cover design by Kristina Blank Makansi
Cover images: Shutterstock and Wikipedia: *Wing of a European Roller,* a nature study watercolor by Albrecht Dürer
Set in Adobe Caslon Pro, Cormorant, and Gravesend Sans

Library of Congress Control Number: 2026904014
Print ISBN: 979-8-9912722-1-6
Ebook ISBN: 979-8-9912722-2-3

For all those who fight for truth, justice, equality, and the promise of a better tomorrow.

Democracy is only as good as the education that surrounds it.
—Socrates

The soul becomes dyed with the colour of its thoughts.
—Marcus Aurelius

There is no greater tyranny than that which is perpetrated under the shield of the law and in the name of justice.
—Montesquieu

A nation of sheep will beget a government of wolves.
—Edward R. Murrow

CAST OF CHARACTERS

THE HUMANS
and a couple of surprise demigods

Cyrus Horatio Bigelow, IV, one of the Bigelow Boys
Sybil Marie Bigelow, Cy's twin sister
BoJo Bigelow, Bonita Josefine Moreno Bigelow, Cy's wife
Sofia Marie Bigelow, Cy and BoJo's 7-year old daughter
Mateo Cardenas, one of the Bigelow Boys, former Navy SEAL
Mason Cox, one of the Bigelow Boys, former FBI agent
Brooks Paxon, one of the Bigelow Boys, engineer extraordinaire
Kenneth Lane, surgeon, NOT one of the Bigelow Boys
Inez Martin, Gerold Guerrero mistress
Gerold Guerrero, Governor of Arizona
Harold Jensen, Chancellor of The New America, world's first multi-trillionaire
Geoffrey Hunt, Jensen's personal physician and old friend
Pastor Erin Knight, Jensen's spiritual advisor
Julius Valentine, President
Alyssa Valentine, First Lady
Darryl Frazier, Vice President
William (Bill) Reynolds, Security Service Agent
Jack Dennehey, Security Service Agent
Helen Cross, Bigelow Enterprises corporate pilot
Kemal Dugan, Helen's business partner
Priests: Adam Diné and Eric von Hollen
Manuel and Annabelle, cabin groom and housekeeper
Hank and Tomas, cabin security guards
Uncle Jimmy, James W. Snider, former FBI HRT operator

THE GODS
Members of the Pantheon League

Nemesis, Goddess of Retribution and Vengeance, daughter of Nyx, Granddaughter of Kaos. Also known as Alexander Whitelaw and Hallelujah Delphinium Jones
The Erinyes or Furies, Chthonic Goddesses of Vengeance
   Alecto ("unceasing") - Ali
   Megaera ("grudging") – Meg
   Tisiphone ("avenging murder") - Tisi
Apollo, God of archery, music and dance and poetry, truth and prophecy, healing and diseases, the sun and light
Artemis, Goddess of the hunt, the wilderness, wild animals, transitions, nature, vegetation, childbirth, care of children, and chastity, and Apollo's twin
Asklepios, healer, son of Apollo
Chiron, Renowned teacher, known as the wisest and most just of all the centaurs
Dionysos, God of wine-making, orchards and fruit and vegetation, fertility, festivity, insanity, ritual madness, religious ecstasy, and theater
Hermes, Herald of the gods and protector of human heralds, travelers, thieves, merchants, and orators

Not Members of the Pantheon League:

Eris, Goddess of Strife, Discord, Contention, and Rivalry, daughter of Nyx, and sister of Nemesis
Ares, God of war, courage, brutality, and bloodlust
Atropos, "She who cannot be turned." One of the Fates, three goddesses who personify the inescapable destiny of man

FOREWORD

by Mnemosyne, Goddess of Memory & Storytelling

There are only three things that are absolutely true: 1) every story has a beginning and an end, except one; 2) the world is full of wonders beyond what humans can comprehend, and 3) every human story is about love—whether it's romantic, parental, familial, friendship, community, patriotic, or even the love of power, the desire for it, the loss of it, the fulfillment of it, or the fight for it. Love is the primary driver of human behavior.

Now, let's take those one at a time.

As incomprehensible as it may seem, especially to humans and their unwillingness to truly understand their connection to the universe, the story of creation—the story of Kaos—has no beginning and no end. Kaos is the beginning and the end. The creator, the created, and the consciousness of creation. The ouroboros of existence. The womb of the world. Whatever you want to call it. It's difficult even for us gods to wrap our minds around the idea of the boundlessness and the unity of Kaos.

Also, despite how often humans tell themselves that the gods are omniscient, omnipresent, and omnipotent, it's not true. We're not. There are limits to our powers and even if there weren't, Kaos and creation would remain behind the veil and beyond our ken. And that brings us to the second immutable truth, that the world is full of wonders beyond comprehension.

Among the infinity of things Kaos created are gods and goddesses. I am referring specifically to those of us directly descended from the primordial beings Kaos directly created in the beginning, namely Nyx, Erebus, Tartarus, Gaia, and, of course, Eros. From there, our family tree grows by twists and turns and gets more than confusing. Some of us can roam through the farthest reaches of space and time and some are more closely tied to Earth and its fate. It's hard even for me to keep straight, and it's part of my job. Needless to say, every human who has attempted to tell our story gets most of it wrong.

As for the heroine of this story, Nemesis, she is the daughter of Nyx alone, despite what some human historians say. Like many of Gaia's children, she was parthenogenetically conceived. If you find that strange or even impossible, I advise you to look it up. Creatures like her are all around whether you know it or not.

The gods are also confusing to humans because our names are time, place, and culture dependent. Humans may know us as Titans or Olympians, Vanir or Æsir, Trimurti, Ilhm or Elohim, etc., etc., depending on when or where the particular subset of humans came of age. (Note that for this story, I'll be using Greek patronyms because our heroine's Greek name has come to have significant meaning in human society, and it's the one I use most often in my own mind.)

But one thing is certain, we are not to be conflated with lesser magical beings such as fairies and witches or daemons and angels that are derived from and supported by our own power, like a table lamp plugged into the electrical grid. We are the grid. The table lamp is decidedly not.

And we are definitely not the same as the myriad nasty evil sprites that have been manifested into being by the malevolent energy of human hate. Those can be tricky and annoying little fuckers, but they are not very powerful and they're certainly not gods.

Which brings us to the third absolute truth, the one about love. Humans are just one among millions upon millions of creatures on Goldilocks planets scattered around billions of solar systems in trillions of galaxies and yet too many of them believe themselves to be at the very center of creation. This delusion, coupled with the desire for love in all its forms, practically guarantees trouble.

Brilliant. Ignorant. Beautiful. Hideous. Generous. Murderous. Humans can be courageously altruistic and deeply empathetic, but all too often are shallow, morally bereft, and astonishingly selfish. Our heroine knows this better than anyone. At the direction of Zeus and with the help of her friends in the Pantheon League—including the Erinyes, better known today as the Furies—Nemesis has spent thousands of years weighing their offenses and handing out appropriate punishments.

Note that although humans were conceived of by Kaos, they were ultimately fashioned by Prometheus and, in my view, therein lies much of the problem. Did I mention yet that gods are not perfect? Well, neither are their creations. In fact, we're all a mess.

Bottom line, there is no such thing as perfection. Or rather, only Kaos is perfect. Everything else is simply striving toward the asymptotic ideal of perfection. Like Plato's ideal forms, as gods we can imagine ourselves as representations of perfection, but we can never achieve it because we're not ideals of gods, we're actual gods. Guides and guardians. Protectors. Watchers. Teachers. Too bad we can also be arrogant, self-righteous, jealous, vindictive creatures endowed with enormous powers and all too often impervious to reason.

To complicate things further, we often play favorites and love too zealously. We have our own moral codes which, even by paltry human standards, aren't very moral. And to top it all off, we too often refuse to let well enough alone. Some even get a thrill out of stirring up trouble. Nemesis's sister, Eris, is a prime example of what humans often call a "shit disturber." Truth is, since Kaos set the laws of physics in motion and Prometheus formed the first humans, there hasn't been a lot for us gods to do except meddle.

And while the universe may be a big place, there is something compelling about the emotional contradictions of human affairs. I'm particularly fascinated by how so many humans go all in on worshipping our cultural aspects (that is, in how we present ourselves to them based on their geographic locations and history as a community, for instance an ocean god isn't going to do a tribe in the middle of the desert much good), and then ignore everything we tell them and do the exact opposite.

And then, of course, when things go wrong, they drop to their knees weeping, gnashing their teeth, rending their clothes, and begging forgiveness. Just look at what they call the Golden Rule. Every moral code incorporates some form of it, but most humans give lip service to the Rule while grabbing the gold. It's exhausting. But, it turns out, these contradictions are at the heart of human activity and, consequently, inform my role as a storyteller.

Plus, as if humans aren't fascinating enough, there are also the demigods to worry about. If a god mates with a human and a child is born, the child is a demigod. This happens more often than you might think because, well, when a god desires a human, there's no stopping them. And if a god actually falls in love with a human? Watch out.

Anyway, demigods can pose big problems because the powers a demigod inherits can range from zero to, well, a lot. But all too often, regardless of a surfeit or an absence of power, demigods have, shall we say, ego issues. Pride goeth before the fall and all that. It's a major problem with humans, but demigods? Hubris almost always comes with the territory.

Which brings us to this moment. This story. A story of hubris and hatred. Of revenge and retribution. Violence and sacrifice. A story of a goddess doing her duty and a demigod intent on saving his country, and, in the midst of terrible evil, discovering beauty, passion, and love. Most of all, love.

And it is with love, that I gift you this story...

December 15 | The New America

Sometimes even the most level-headed and brilliant humans do stunningly stupid things, especially when loaded up on testosterone and tequila. And that goes double for when said human is a demigod who has no idea he's a demigod.

Or that demigods even exist outside of myth.

The heroine of our story, Nemesis (or Nemi to those of us who have known her forever), was minding her own business enjoying a crystalline pink beach on a lovely little water planet in Canis Major, when she received a message from one of her oldest friends, Tisi, better known to all you geeky Greek history lovers as Tisiphone, one of the three Furies. Along with Tisi's sisters, Alecto and Megaera (or Ali and Meg), they'd all been using their particular attributes to try to prevent human societies of all sorts from descending into murderous hellscapes by punishing mortals for crimes against the gods and other humans. They'd had their share of successes, but their failure rate was astonishingly high. For that, they blamed Prometheus.

Giving form to humans by sculpting from clay in the likenesses of the gods, Prometheus inadvertently baked a number of serious flaws into human biochemistry. These flaws were amplified by the opposing forces of free will and the wiring of their brains which are bound, unlike the gods, by the laws of physics. Humans must consume calories for energy, defecate waste byproducts, rest and recharge their energy systems, and procreate and propagate their species. In other words, like all biological creatures based on the carbon form factor, humans must eat, shit, sleep, and fuck to keep their species alive. These flaws, along with the aforementioned desire for love in all its myriad forms, drive human behavior.

Demigods, of course, are much the same, even if they are sometimes blessed with legendary power and a few divine attributes thrown in here and there. So, while all this makes life on planet Earth fascinating, it also makes it unstable. And unstable systems tend to be volatile systems.

Which brings us to Cyrus Horatio Bigelow the IV, otherwise known as Cy. Cy first came to Nemi's attention seventeen Earth years ago when he threw himself over the edge of a cliff to save a friend during a rock-climbing incident.

Nemi just happened to be in Southern Arizona poking around some Hohokam ruins and reminiscing about old times when panicked shouts echoed around the canyon. Being one of the rare gods who is truly attuned to humans on an individual level, she immediately created a portal through which she could target and follow the sound waves to the originating location. With one look, she assessed the situation as life threatening and quickly manifested the guise of a magnificently fit human male forest ranger to help pull two men up to safety.

Turns out that Cy, along with his three best friends, had been rappelling down the face of a 120-foot cliff when the tree to which they'd tethered their belay rope was uprooted. Stupid, reckless humans.

It was monsoon season, and the ground was soaked from an overnight rain, so the tension from their weight eventually pulled the tree loose, roots and all, causing one boy to lose his footing and slip dangerously down the cliff face.

Despite imbibing too many shots of tequila the prior evening (did I mention humans are sometimes infuriatingly stupid?), Cy had immediately jumped into action, climbing down *sans rope* to save his friend. Knowing that's the kind of courageous and *idiotic* move a demigod would make, Nemi immediately paid attention. As soon as she got close enough, she could tell he had demigod vibes rolling off him. She could practically *smell* them. (Along with the stink of human sweat, beer, tequila, marijuana, and the clean fragrance of creosote because of the monsoons.)

Nemi knew full well that when multiple human boys—for they had been mere high school-aged boys back then—gather together and ply themselves with alcohol, idiotic behavior is likely to follow. (Same thing applies to grown men, if you want to be truthful about it.)

So, after Nemi had helped save the day and everyone was safe and on solid ground, she took stock of the situation and was struck by the fact that although all four boys were exceedingly handsome in their own way, Cy Bigelow was a breathtakingly beautiful specimen of humanity. Which, of course, made sense if he was indeed a demigod. And, after getting a good look at him, she was certain of that fact. She had no idea which god had fathered him, but she promised herself right then and there to find out.

Cy's beauty was almost blinding. Black brows and almost floridly luxurious lashes matched a head full of blue-black waves that he kept brushing off his forehead making Nemi think of an adorable little puppy with something sticky on its nose. She was struck by disconcertingly cerulean eyes rimmed in storm grey, a face that looked like it had been sculpted by the Prometheus himself, and muscles from here to eternity, despite the fact that he wasn't yet fully grown. And she'd been around for most of eternity, so she knew what she was talking about.

She knew that this boy was worth keeping an eye on, so she'd been watching over Cy and his friends—Brooks Paxton (the dangling man), Mat Cárdenas, and Mason Cox—ever since. Especially Cy.

Always Cy.

Anyway, back to the crystalline pink beach. Nemi had been dipping her toes in the deliciously warm, clear water when Tisi sent her an S.O.S: *We have a situation. You're needed back on Earth.*

Nemi ignored the message. After all, there's always a situation of one sort or another on Earth. It's just human nature.

Seconds later, however, her ears were ringing with what amounted to Tisi screaming at her: *Nemi, I know you're out there! Stop ignoring me!*

She sent back: *I'm relaxing. Stop bothering me.*

Nemi could practically hear Tisi snort at that. *We're gods. We don't get to relax.*

Isn't the point of being a god to get to do whatever we want? Right now, I want to bask on this beautiful beach.

No basking for you, Tisi sent. *We have a serious problem among the humans.*

Nemi hadn't dealt directly with humans in years. Hadn't even set foot on the planet in over an Earth decade. Of course, she kept tabs on her favorites, but she didn't need to be there physically to do that. In fact, she did her best to try to let them live out their lives without her interference. The last thing humans or demigods need is a goddess like Nemesis messing around in their lives.

You're a Fury, you handle it, she sent back.

We're trying, but things are getting out of hand, Tisi replied. *Remember the 20th century? Two world wars, thermonuclear bombs, millions dead through genocides, massacres, countless bloody regional conflicts, widespread famine, disease, displacement, religious strife, self-immolation, suicide bombers, etc., etc.? This is worse. Bottom line, the Nazis are back with a religious fervor. Everyone is being stupid and pushing everything to the brink.*

Okay, that got Nemi's attention. The gods had seen Nazis and their ilk come and go under different rubrics since Prometheus got his hands on that wet clay, but the twentieth century Nazis were particularly creepy. I mean, have you ever seen a photo of Joseph Goebbels? Seriously. If not, look him up, and you'll see exactly what I'm talking about.

So, Nemi said goodbye to Canis Major and headed back to the Milky Way.

Now, fast forward a week. Since Nemi had been back on Earth, her time had been filled with updates from Tisi and her sisters, Alecto and Megaera, and the others in the Pantheon League, along with various regional emissaries reporting in on who was doing what to whom, how they were getting away with it, and why they needed to be held to account for their cruelty and their crimes. Things had gone downhill dramatically since she'd last set foot on the planet, and the accounting was going to be ugly.

However, there was one interesting piece of news amidst all the bad. It turned out that her old favorite, Cy Bigelow, appeared to be right in the thick of things and, thankfully, on the right side of history. In fact, two of her friends in the Pantheon League had recruited Cy and his three best friends into the American Resistance Movement, or ARM, an underground group working to undermine the self-declared Chancellor of New America, or what was left of the old United States of America.

As for the Chancellor and his New America, known by the banal term "the Administration," they'd shuttered most of the departments, fired thousands of civil servants, seized resource-rich national and state parks, and had transformed the former proud democratic republic into a sleazy syndicate they tried to run as a for-profit business based on various flavors of cryptocurrency.

Needless to say, it wasn't working.

Several states had voted to secede only to be ruthlessly invaded by the Chancellor's private army, and the country had morphed into a violent anocratic kakistocracy run by puerile men of vast wealth, vaster egos, and an even vaster capacity for cruelty.

Worse yet, Administration leaders had destroyed old international alliances and cozied up to despots across the globe, cementing those new relationships by hiring out once respected American military forces as nothing more than mercenaries. Those in uniform who refused to carry out orders were simply court martialed and disappeared.

It was bad.

And then it got worse.

Nemi had been listening to Tisi rant about one particularly reprehensible CD, Chancellor's Decree, that mandated death by public hanging for any doctor caught providing illegal abortion services when she suddenly experienced the sharp jabby feeling she associated with Cy Bigelow.

Call it an acute awareness of danger. A warning signal of sorts. It's one of those spooky-action-at-a-distance things. The concept may be difficult for humans to understand, but the bottom line is that once a god is connected to another living thing, a sort of communications channel forms and they end up on the same quantum wavelength in the same quantum field.

Suffice it to say, once Nemi *felt* Cy, it was a simple matter of following the path of his energy wave to *find* him. And this time, the jabby feeling was warning her that the idiotic man had once again thrown himself, metaphorically speaking, off the edge of a cliff. Or worse, *not* metaphorically speaking. Her fear was that he was literally dangling by his fingertips above a 120-foot drop.

Fortunately, she was wrong.

Unfortunately, it was worse.

Cy Bigelow is one of those creatures with a viscerally robust sense of fairness and an out-sized belief in his ability to step in and right wrongs that occur within his sphere of influence which, in his case, is the Southwest region of what is still—despite multiple attempted secessions—part of Jensen's New America. More specifically, the southern Arizona town of Bigelow.

Today, Bigelow is a quaint old mining town founded by and named after Cy's great-great grandfather after he made his first fortune in copper and silver mining and before he made his second and third fortunes in cattle and cotton—and long before Cy's father nearly bankrupted the family backing one bad investment after another and spending extravagantly on one gold digger after another in the wake of his wife's untimely death from a sudden brain aneurysm while serving cake at Cy and Sybil's (his twin sister) kindergarten graduation party.

The twins had been six years old.

During Nemi's investigation into Cy's origins, she learned that the good people of Bigelow speculated that what made the twins so strange was the shock of watching their mother suddenly tip forward, hit her head on the corner of the outdoor dining table, and then crumple face-down onto the brick patio in a mess of red velvet cake, vanilla frosting, and blood.

Certainly, their father never recovered from the shock of his wife's death and his abrupt ascension into the role of single parent. Absent any grandparents willing to step up and help, it was up to the housekeeper-turned-estate manager, Mrs. C, and the ancient family lawyer to save the twins and keep Bigelow Enterprises from going over the brink into insolvency after their father skied into a tree on the slopes of some Swiss mountain—the old and vaunted Bigelow family would have been utterly ruined and Cy and Sybil would have inherited nothing but debt.

Poor Cy and Sybil, local gossips tittered with morbidly fascinated glee. They were never the same after that tragic day.

As they grew up, Cy strove to prove himself in every way—especially academics and athletics—and clung to his best friends as if they were lifesaving buoys in a stormy sea, while Sybil, already ethereally beautiful and old beyond her years at the age of six, became painfully strange and increasingly withdrawn. Especially after her third grade teacher revealed that she wrote out her book reports in dactylic hexameter.

"That girl's bound to be possessed by a demon or even by Satan himself," one nosy neighbor declared in a too-loud whisper others in the quaint coffee shop in which Nemi sat one day were sure to overhear. "Or she's a witch," the woman said with supreme confidence. "Amounts to the same thing as Lucifer is the lord of demons and witches."

Nemi's human instinct was to roll her eyes. Well acquainted with both Hades and Hecate, as well as with witches of every sort, Nemi was absolutely certain Sybil Bigelow was no witch. Demigod, yes. Witch, no.

Anyway, back to Cy. It turned out that the wrongs he was currently determined to right were connected to the same issues the Pantheon League was busy addressing—namely terrible people doing terrible things in the name of one god or another. Or in the name of their own greed and self-aggrandizement. Or, as was usually the case, both.

In this case, Cy was focused on rumors of mysterious deaths, disappearances, and abuses at the notorious Sonoran Desert Internment Center (or SDIC), just fifteen miles south of his beloved Bigelow.

And that's exactly where Nemi found him.

2

"Why do you even care about these vermin?" the man asked as he checked the IV in Cy's arm.

From Nemi's vantage point as a wisp of air hovering near the ceiling by the air conditioner vent, she could tell Cy, nude but for a single sheet spread across his hips, was trying to say something but nothing coherent was coming out.

"If you weren't so goddamned nosy, I wouldn't have to do this," the man went on. "Although I admit to fantasizing about getting rid of you, I didn't imagine I'd be able to make a profit in the process."

Wearing fashionable, black-rimmed glasses, he was, objectively, good looking, all fair haired and square jawed with a neatly trimmed beard and mustache. But Nemi knew that good looks didn't mean a damn thing when your heart was black as pitch. And this man's heart was black as black as black could be. The depths of Tartarus boasted more sunshine than this man's soul.

"But you never could mind your own business, could you? Always butting in where you aren't wanted. Sticking your nose in SDIC affairs. Acting all morally superior. And always trying to keep me away from Sybil even while Mason fucking Cox is mooning all over her. And you don't even see it."

Cy murmured something that sounded like *fuck you*.

The man smirked and put a stethoscope around his neck. "Yes, I know she swears she'll never marry me, but I'll make her come around." He barked out a laugh. "I'll make her come too. I suppose you don't like thinking of your twin spread out on a bed with me between her legs."

He laughed again and shook his head as if the hilarity of it all was too much for him. "I'm sure you hate the idea of me as a brother-in-law, but you won't have to worry about that because you'll be dead and gone. Bones incinerated to dust. I might even step in to help parent your mongrel daughter. Or, better yet, I'll figure out how to get BoJo and Sofia deported once and for all."

Daughter? *Since when did Cy have a daughter?* What had she missed by not paying closer attention while she'd been away? And who was BoJo? Was he married? Not that it mattered. She shouldn't care about Cy Bigelow's love life. It was irrelevant because unlike many of the other gods, she didn't make a habit of coupling with humans.

In fact, she'd been celibate since back in 1918 when she'd had a brief affair in France with Lieutenant Colonel Bill Donovan, long before he'd become head of the OSS. Of course, back then she'd suspected Bill was a demigod, or at least descended from a demigod, but she'd never tried to prove it since it didn't matter in the moment. He'd been attractive, compelling, and convenient, but it had just been sex. Of course, she'd hoped whatever demigod powers or talents he might have inherited would help his side in the conflict, but beyond that she didn't care. Demigods, as I already mentioned, are not exactly rare commodities.

Of course, Nemi was acutely aware that Cy was attractive and compelling too. But he'd never been convenient—until now.

"Just picture me as head of Bigelow Enterprises," the man went on, leaning over him to press the stethoscope to Cy's heart. "Won't be easy to get rid of your idiot friends, but I can probably manage to spin some yarn about illegal activities and get DICE to arrest and disappear them. Especially Mason Cox. I fucking hate that guy. There's something off about how Sybil talks about him. Sometimes I wonder if—"

Cy mumbled something as the muscles in his fingers and forearms twitched, like he was aching to wrap the good doctor's stethoscope around his throat.

"Anyway, Sybil will forget about Mason once you're all gone. Dead. Deported. Disappeared. Doesn't matter to me. I won't deny you've all done a fine job of rebuilding the family fortune after your father nearly bankrupted you, but now it's time for someone to step in and align it with Administration's goals."

Nemi could see the muscles in Cy's shoulders and abdomen bunch, as if he were trying to sit up. Whatever the doctor had dosed him with, it was effective enough to keep a demigod down.

"You have no idea how much Chancellor Jensen hates you—or maybe you do have an idea. Let me give you a hint. It's a lot." The doctor adjusted his glasses on his nose.

"Just imagine the scene: I'll tell him how I got rid of you and took control of Bigelow Enterprises and all those supposedly spent mines you control. He'll be so thrilled, he'll appoint me to some highfalutin job in DC. I'm thinking Surgeon General. I'll be sitting pretty as one of his most trusted advisors. Maybe run for president someday. Can you see your sister as first lady?"

Nemesis focused on Cy as he tried to say something. He twitched as the doctor leaned over, lifted one eyelid after another, to shine a penlight in his eyes. "Why aren't you out cold? I swear to God, I've dosed you enough to kill a goddamned horse."

Demigod. Damned things are hard to kill.

The man checked the pulsometer on Cy's finger. "I don't think I realized what a fine specimen you truly are. 6'3", 220. Not an ounce of fat. Muscles like they're sculpted out of marble. Pulse steady. Blood pressure perfect. Even under this stress. Whoever gets your organs will probably live to be a hundred and ten. At least."

The doctor shook his head and clucked. *Tsk. Tsk.* "Too bad it won't be you." He pulled on a pair of surgical gloves with a snap, but Nemi noticed he didn't bother with a mask. Then he picked up a scalpel and pressed it to Cy's skin. "Can you feel this?"

Kaos!

This was bad. She'd spent too much time watching and listening, and that meant she needed to stop floating around on the ceiling and do something.

Barely two seconds later, the door to the operating room flew open with a bang revealing a human male big enough to intimidate even a self-absorbed surgeon who probably wasn't quite 5'8" but had the bearing of a man who thought himself superior in all things—including height.

He whirled on her. "What the hell are you doing in here?"

Dressed in hospital scrubs, Nemi strode toward the operating table. *She was too late!* The asshole had already made an incision. Approximately eight long inches of perfect skin on Cy's lower abdomen had been sliced open. As a goddess, she was capable of many things, but she'd never trusted herself as a healer. Not for wounds like this. Not for a demigod like Cy.

She sent an emergency message to Dr. A to be on standby, vaguely wondering if the healer would recognize another son of Apollo. She almost laughed. Asklepios and Cy Bigelow. Half brothers.

"Get the fuck out of here or I'm gonna call security!"

Nemi's fleeting thoughts of Cy's parentage dissolved as the man growled up at her. "You're not going to call security because then you'd have to explain what you're doing," Nemi growled down at him. "Unless they're in on your nefarious scheme too."

"Nefarious scheme? What the hell are you talking about? I'm performing a surgery."

"No, you're harvesting this man's organs in the process of committing a murder. You need to step away from the operating table. Go sit in your chair like a good boy. Or else."

"Go sit in my chair?!" He looked at her like she was crazy. "Like a good boy?" He barked out an incredulous laugh. "Or else, what?"

Nemi did not have a problem dropping humans on the spot when necessary, but she generally tried not to draw too much attention to herself. Inexplicable occurrences of death or injury are just invitations to investigations. If you're a god in the modern world, you have to keep a low profile because otherwise humans get all riled up and you eventually get things like mysterious golden tablets dug up out of New England farms, weeping Madonnas in remote French grottoes, or sightings of Jesus on burnt toast or the sides of skyscrapers. Swindlers and grifters get involved and before you know it, entire new religions are formed and gullible humans are sending scads of money that ends up underwriting vulgar mansions, Gulfstreams, Lamborghinis, and triple-decker yachts with helipads and swimming pools. And more sexual promiscuity than Caligula and Nero combined.

She leaned down and snarled at him. "Or else I will be the last thing you see before justice is served."

Although in this form, Nemi had at least ten inches on the doctor, he glared up at her and spat out a heartfelt "Fuck you!"

Nemi wasn't a monster, but she took great pleasure in watching the reprehensible man drop as if a puppeteer had just sliced his strings. Generally, she tried to avoid usurping Atropos' role by cutting a thread of life prematurely, so she didn't kill the asshole. Not this time. But she did rejoice in the clanging noise of a metal tray toppling over and surgical instruments skittering across the floor as he banged his head on the way down. He would wake eventually and wonder where his patient had disappeared to.

In the meantime, she removed Cy's oxygen mask and his IV drip, left the pulsometer on his finger, picked up a few items from a nearby desktop, and slipped them in her back pocket. Then, with the sheet still draped over Cy's body, she reached both arms beneath him, picked him up like a baby, and vamoosed into thin air.

3

When Cy Bigelow finally emerged from his anesthetic fog, he was safe and secure in his own bed in his penthouse apartment on the top floor of the Bigelow Hotel. Nemi had piled blankets on top of him and lit a fire in the grate because it was mid-December and who doesn't love a cozy fire? On the bedside table was a selection of pain killers and an ice-cold bottle of water. On the floor next to the bed was a bucket. Dr. A told her some humans don't do well with anesthesia, so she wasn't taking any chances. The last thing she wanted was for Cy to cast up his accounts all over the carpet. He had good taste in carpets.

She watched as he blinked his way to awareness and pushed himself to a sitting position. What felt like a pile driver slammed into her breastbone as the blankets slipped down to reveal his solidly muscled chest, lightly sprinkled with coppery hair. Of course, she'd seen his chest before—when he was laid out on that operating table and when he was laid out in Dr. A's surgery. But previous exposure didn't seem to matter. Nemi felt the impact of his chest on display as if she'd suddenly come across a completely new habitable planet.

Did I mention that manifesting a human body does weird things to a god? It makes us *feel*. Things. Mortal things. All that adrenalin and dopamine, serotonin, oxytocin, and endorphins coursing through the human bloodstreams can be ... unsettling. (That's why I avoid it at all costs. I'm the goddess of memory and fervently wish I could forget the last time I took on human form.)

Cy looked around the room, narrowed his eyes at Nemi, tried to focus. "Who the hell are you?"

While she'd waited for him to emerge from his drugged sleep, she'd prowled around his apartment, looking at his artwork, his framed photos—including one with a tow-headed toddler sitting on his shoulders and one with his friends—Mat, Mason, and Brooks—all sitting on the edge of a cliff, legs dangling, with Brooks handling the controls of what was probably the drone that took the photo while hovering in midair. Then Nemi had found one of her favorite books on a shelf and curled up in a leather chair by the fireplace to read about wizards, humans, and the enchanting species Tolkien called hobbits. She loved stories where the good guys won despite the odds. And she adored dragons. Now, she closed the book and held his gaze. "How're you feeling?" She'd thought about how to handle the situation, but, honestly, that chest and those startling blue eyes, pinned on her, almost made her forget her plans.

"Like I've got a bad case of dry mouth and was punched in the gut." He ran his tongue across his front teeth and made a face, then reached for the bottle of water, and she watched his strong throat work as he took a long drink and swallowed. He set the bottle down and wiped the back of his hand across his mouth. "Why am I in bed?" He glanced out the window. It was full dark out. "What time is it?" He turned back to Nemi. "And you never answered my question. Who are you, and what are you doing in my bedroom?"

"That's a lot of questions," she replied. "You're in bed because you were unconscious, and it's 6:30. In the evening. Now, why don't you tell me about the last thing you remember." She'd managed to get him to tell her where he lived when he first started to emerge from the anesthesia, but then Dr. A had dosed him with something to put him back under for the stitching. Hopefully, he wouldn't remember any of that.

Nemi had no idea what gifts or powers, if any, Cy had inherited. Demigods were always wildcards. Cy's parentage had been a complete mystery when she'd first found him crawling down that cliff face fifteen years earlier. Since then, however, she'd done quite a bit of sleuthing and discovered that his mother, Madeline Marquez, the daughter of a Mexican oil baron, had been an extraordinarily beautiful and wild young woman with a passion for archaeology who had spent a month in Greece after she graduated from college and before marrying Cyrus Horatio Bigelow III. It had been an arranged marriage of oil interests and copper mining, and Madeline had only gone along with it to please her loving father. And by loving, I mean a man who had been sexually abusing his own daughter for years. So, marriage, for Madeline, meant escape.

But before her ultimate escape, she'd taken that trip to Greece which, of course, included a visit to Delphi where she met, you guessed it, Apollo. Taking on the aspect of a resident archaeologist at the Museum of Delphi, Apollo had given the lovely Madeline-soon-to-be-Bigelow a private tour, complete with all the perks of being in the company of a god with one of the biggest egos in the universe. Namely seduction, a magical aphrodisiac, a hazy recollection of torrid lovemaking, and a positive pregnancy test.

Madeline Marquez returned home, eagerly became Madeline Bigelow in a lavish ceremony, and gave birth seven months later to full-term twins—a preternaturally beautiful baby boy who latched onto his mother's breast with a voracious thirst for life and a similarly beautiful baby girl who entered the world with a worried look of stunned alarm, rejecting the breast and the bottle, and spending the first month of her life in a neonatal ICU with a feeding tube stuck down her throat. It was almost as if Sybil Bigelow spent her first month on Earth in protest.

Cy was the one protesting now. He pushed himself up again, settling back against the pillows. "My bedroom, my rules. How about first you tell me who you are and what you're doing here. Then, maybe, I'll answer your questions."

She set the book aside and stood. Slowly walked toward the end of the bed. "I'm not exactly a doctor, but—"

"What does 'not exactly' mean, exactly?" Cy looked her up and down, assessing.

Nemi wasn't manifesting as a ginormous man anymore. Didn't want to put Cy on edge. Instead, she'd taken on her favorite human aspect, one she'd used so often on Earth that she sometimes wondered if it's what she truly looked like. What she'd looked like at her creation. And maybe it is. I wasn't born yet. However, I know her mother loves beautiful things, and immortality can definitely mess with memory. Beginnings are so, so, *so* long ago.

Anyway, at that moment, Nemi was a flesh and blood woman wearing blue hospital scrubs—the same scrubs, albeit shrunken to her female form, that she'd worn when confronting that disgusting man at SDIC—and she was standing at the foot of Cy Bigelow's bed. "It means I'm here to help you," she said, the very picture of concerned caregiver.

"How and why, exactly, do you think you can help me Ms. Not Exactly a Doctor? And what do I call you while you figure out how to answer that?"

Over a hundred years ago, another human, grieving and desperate, had miscarried during the carnage of the Tulsa race massacre. Nemi had shown up at the scene to survey the damage and identify the miscreants at fault and had found the woman bleeding out amidst the still-smoldering rubble of her family's business. The woman's final words were to ask that she and her daughter—Hallie, short for Hallelujah Delphinium Jones—be buried together. Despite being enraged at the wreckage around them, Nemi had been charmed by the name and had since adopted it as her own Earthly moniker. Over the millennia, she'd gone by hundreds of human names, but this one was one of her favorites. Both mother and daughter were long gone, and remembering the senseless violence every time she used the name made her feel like she was honoring the innocent victims of that horrific crime. Plus, it was obviously much friendlier than introducing yourself as, "Hello, I'm Nemesis, Immortal Goddess of Divine Retribution and Vengeance." So, she answered with, "Call me Hallie. Hallie Jones."

"Hallie," Cy said softly, as if considering ... something. He looked her up and down again, obviously feeling better by the minute as interest flared in his eyes and the hint of a smile curved his full mouth up at one corner. Nemi knew what he saw. Cy Bigelow was looking at a beautiful woman. Perfectly symmetrical face featuring sun-kissed skin and characterized by startling dark eyes—a deep indigo, like the distant sky at dusk—with long black lashes and invitingly full lips coupled with a body of lush curves and luxurious auburn hair that shone with red and gold highlights, like polished bronze clinging to the nape of her long, elegant neck. Physical perfection.

Humans had been molded by the gods, after all. In recent years, more than one human had told her she resembled that old movie star, the one who'd starred in Cleopatra. Because she and the Furies often watched human movies in their downtime—especially historical dramas, to laugh at all the things filmmakers got wrong—she'd been delighted by the comparisons. Tisi always joked that Nemi's Hallie persona should have tried out for the starring role since Nemi had actually known Cleo back in the day. Nemi had even gone along on one of Cleo's river cruises when she was venturing up and down the Nile presenting herself as the goddess Isis incarnate. Those had been good times, long before that jealous, power-hungry Gaius Octavius decided to declare war.

The unfortunate truth is that demigods and humans appreciate physical beauty just as much as the gods, and no matter how pure of heart you are, a pretty face goes a long way toward getting what you want. It's unfair, but it's just the way it is. That giant male aspect Nemi used to confront that monster intent on murdering Cy down at SDIC was designed to get results through intimidation, but her favorite female aspect was designed to get results from the innate and intimate draw of beauty. From appreciation and familiarity. Nemi knew humans found her female aspect captivating. Intriguing. *Alluring*. She saw the spark in Cy Bigelow's eyes and knew he was no exception. He was, after all, a flesh and blood man with appetites and desires that ran demigod deep.

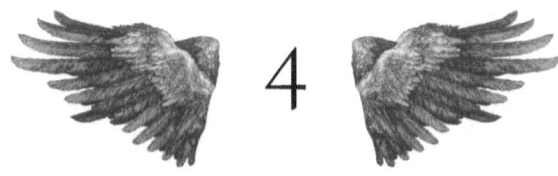

4

Cy's gut clenched. *There was a strange woman in his bedroom.* A stunningly beautiful woman named Hallie. He knew he'd never seen her before—*he'd definitely remember!*—but something about her spoke to him. She *felt* familiar. Certainly, she was gorgeous. Desirable. He imagined, to his shame, licking her. From the tips of her toes to the tip of her nose. He was a cad, yes, but he always tried to be honest with himself, and even if his brain wasn't always truthful, his dick was.

But there was also something reassuring about her. Which was a good thing because he was in dire need of some serious reassurance. He had no idea why he was in bed. Or how he got there. Or what time it was. Or why his side ached, and he felt like roadkill. He looked toward his bedside table. Where was his phone? And for that matter, where was his wallet and watch? Certainly, not where they were supposed to be.

His brain was fuzzy, and he closed his eyes and tried to think. She'd asked him about the last thing he remembered, and as he tried to concentrate, images flicked through his brain like cards being shuffled. *This morning. Mat called. He'd received bad news about ... something. I went downstairs. To the Saguaro Room.*

To meet ... someone. We're sitting in a booth. It's a man. It doesn't feel like Mat, Brooks, or Mason. It doesn't feel good at all. It's someone I don't like. Don't trust. Someone like ... damn. Ken fucking Lane. He'd been talking to Ken fucking Lane.

He remembered now.

Mat said he'd received a message from one of his ARM contacts. They'd gotten wind of some new horror involving missing children going on down at SDIC. Something beyond the usual horrors taking place on the swath of land the Administration had eminent domained away from his family and the local tribes. Cy's brilliant idea had been to invite Ken for a friendly cup of coffee and ask about the rumors since he was the chief surgeon at the Camp. He knew it wouldn't be a fun meeting since he truly loathed the guy and just pretended to be cordial for the sake of whatever weird relationship Ken and Sybil had going on, but if anyone knew what was going on at SDIC, it would be Dr. Ken Lane.

Still, none of that explained how he went from meeting Ken downstairs to being up here in bed with a beautiful woman sitting by his fire and watching him from across the room. Wearing scrubs. And apparently reading his well-worn paperback copy of *The Hobbit*.

He drew in a deep breath to steady himself and threw back the covers only to realize he was buck naked. And he had a large bandage on his abdomen. What the hell? When had he gotten hurt? He gently pulled the bandage away from his skin to see ... stitches. A good eight inches of stitches. *What the fuck?*

"Umm. Why do I have stitches and where are my clothes?"

The corner of her mouth tipped up. "It's a long story, but you were nude when I found you. And you needed stitches, so I—"

"Found me?" He cleared his throat. Took another long drink from the bottle of water on his bedside table. He was parched. Like he'd had all the moisture sucked out of his body. "I hardly think I was sitting in the bar in the buff. Regina would have kicked my ass. And why did I need stitches? Who stitched me up? What happened to me?"

He had a flash of memory. A man bending over him, a tug at his abdomen. The man was talking to … this woman. *The mystery man was talking to Hallie Jones about him.* The man had an accent. British? Maybe. It was a voice he'd never heard before. Was that who'd stitched him up? Had a doctor come to his apartment?

"Who's Regina?" the woman—*Hallie*—asked.

He wouldn't swear to it, but he thought he detected the tiniest bit of tension in her tone. He shot her a glance. "One of our restaurant managers."

"Ah, an employee." She nodded as if a great mystery had been solved. "At an establishment you own. And you remember being in this restaurant?"

"It's just downstairs, and yeah. It's the last thing I remember before …" He waved a hand down over his stomach. "Before I apparently had a run in with a carving knife."

He pushed his palms into his eye sockets as if the pressure would relieve the ache in his side and help him reconstruct what had happened to him. When had he been sliced open? Where? Not downstairs. All hell would've broken loose if someone had attacked him in the hotel he owned. So where had he been? Had he been taken to the hospital? If so, how did he get back here and why the hell didn't he remember?

Miraculously, there was a bottle of ibuprofen on the bedside table. He grabbed it, unscrewed the top, popped two capsules, and dry swallowed them. They didn't go down. He grabbed the water bottle and drained it in one gulp. Pounded a fist to his breastbone and coughed. Scrubbed a hand down his face and stood.

Damn. He was as dizzy and wobbly as a newborn colt. That wasn't good.

He braced a hand on the table until he felt stable enough to walk across the room to the closet. He could feel her eyes on him. *She likes what she sees. Despite the mysterious stitches. Good. That makes us even.*

He'd never been shy about his body and knew exactly what he looked like. Guys like Ken Fucking Lane and his little coterie of bullying sycophants had always hated him because he was a natural athlete and had been number one in their class every year since middle school. Never had to really try. Well, that and the fact that his family was wealthy. Or had been wealthy. Until his dad blew most of the family fortune up his nose. Or up some bimbo's nose. Or on some ridiculous scheme like pouring money into that AI company selling robotic maids designed to clean up "even the most disgusting messes in your home" but instead murdered the homeowners. (Well, actually, the homeowners *were* the ones who'd made the messes in the first place. At least that was the defense counsel's argument when the company was sued into oblivion.)

But Cy couldn't help how he was born anymore than he could have prevented his mother's death or his father's spiral into right-wing conspiratorial lunacy. And near bankruptcy.

Even his best friends—now business partners—ribbed him relentlessly. Sometimes he wanted to punch himself in the nose just to mar his face a bit. Give his features some character, a bump or a scar or something. Mat, who'd been a goddamn Navy SEAL, just shook his head and laughed whenever they worked out together. Cy had always been able to out wrestle, out run, out swim him. He could ride like the devil and shoot like he'd been born with a gun in his hand. Or a bow and arrow. Probably because he had 20/10 vision, uncanny hand-eye coordination, perfect balance, and remarkable speed. He liked rock climbing, skiing, and jumping out of airplanes, and had always been, quite frankly, bored with other sports. He'd left team sports behind in high school along with the lure of college scholarships because he'd always had only one goal in life: rebuild the family business.

His dad always said his abilities were a gift from God Almighty, and plenty of women had readily agreed over the years. But whether the *oh god oh god oh gods* breathed out in the throes of ecstasy were a testament to his physical appearance or to his relentless dedication to pleasuring his partners was unclear.

The last woman he'd slept with had compared him to a statue of Apollo she'd seen in Las Vegas. Or maybe it was a copy of Michelangelo's David. He hadn't cared. She'd been an effusive and enthusiastic lover, but once he realized she didn't have the information he wanted, he didn't give a damn about what came out of her mouth. All he cared about was what she *did* with her mouth.

He'd arranged to meet her because, rumor had it, she was Governor Guerrero's current mistress, and he'd hoped to at least learn where the man had disappeared to. But after more than a few drinks and even before they'd made it up to his hotel room at the Phoenician in Scottsdale, she'd slurred her way through a diatribe about how Guerrero had dumped her without explanation. He'd been a no-show at their last weekly rendezvous, and she hadn't heard from him since. His tryst with her had been over three months ago. Guerrero still hadn't been seen in public. And Cy hadn't been with a woman since.

Having a beautiful woman in his bedroom now was making him remember exactly how long it'd been. He waved a hand down his body. "You have me at a distinct disadvantage in both the clothing and information department, so how about you tell me what's going on while I get dressed."

"Be careful with your bandage. You need to keep it on for a few days to protect the stitches."

"I heal fast," Cy said, but he made sure the bandage adhesive was secure. "Start talking."

"Where do you want me to start?"

"Um, how about at the beginning?" He grabbed a pair of snug boxers and well-worn jeans from the built-in dresser in his closet and started pulling them on, keeping them low on his hips to avoid the bandage. "You can start by telling me why you, Ms. Hallie Not-Exactly-A-Doctor, care what's going on with me? A total stranger. What's your interest in my welfare?"

She leaned against the bed's footboard. "I can't tell you much, but I can tell you we're not total strangers. We've met once before. Years ago, although I'm sure you don't remember. I looked quite different back then."

That stopped him. "Different how? I'm pretty good with faces and"—he looked her up and down—"well, I would have remembered you."

"I suppose I should take that as a compliment," she said with a sparkling laugh he felt at the base of his spine. "Let's just say I was dressed as someone else at the time. As to the second part of your question, all I can tell you is that I work for an organization concerned about Administration activities in the area, especially what's going on down at the internment camp."

"And what does that have to do with me?"

She rolled her eyes and gave him a *Puleeeze, are you kidding* look.

Well, shit. Obviously, she knew at least something about his involvement in anti-Administration activities.

"Don't hurt yourself with that eye roll," he said. "Dad always told us that if you do that too often your eyeballs will stay that way. And that's not an answer. How do I know you're not working with the Administration yourself? Maybe you're trying to entrap me. You could be chummy with Chancellor Jensen for all I know. You look like his type." He buttoned his jeans and looked around his closet like he was trying to figure out what he was doing in there.

She huffed out a little snort. "Every woman able to stand upright and breed is his type."

He made a face. "Standing upright probably isn't a necessity either." He ran a hand over his chin. "So what's the name of this so-called organization you're supposedly affiliated with?"

"I can't tell you that just yet."

"Why am I not surprised? Okay. You said I was in my birthday suit when you found me and that I needed stitches, so you must know how I got this wound and who stitched me up. And since I know damn good and well I wasn't buck naked in the Saguaro Room, why don't you tell me where you found me and how I got back here."

Hallie ran a finger down one of the intricately carved bed posts. "It's complicated. But first, you said you remember you were in the restaurant. Were you with anyone?"

"I was having breakfast with an old friend—or rather, not a friend but someone I grew up with. I must've gotten sick or something. Did I fall? Stab myself with my butter knife?" He looked down at the bandage again. "This row of stitches looks suspiciously tidy, like I was sliced open with a scalpel."

"I believe your life is in grave danger." She couldn't believe she'd just blurted that out.

He coughed out a laugh. "That's hardly a surprise. But as much as I detest the guy, I don't think breakfast with Ken Fucking Lane is a life-threatening activity."

"Is that his name?"

"That's who I was with downstairs. Dr. Kenneth Lane."

"Describe him."

"Big guy. Well, a lot shorter than I am, but bigger around the middle. Burly, I guess you'd call it. Has a beard. Neatly trimmed but already going gray. Sometimes he wears black-rimmed glasses. Has a scar on his bottom lip from when my buddy Mat punched him in the eighth grade after the asshole made a remark about Mat's dad being a dead illegal. Just one of the myriad reasons he's not a friend."

Hallie nodded. "That's him. I believe he put something in your coffee."

"You think he roofied me?"

"Roofied?"

He narrowed his eyes at her. "A nickname for flunitrazepam. A date rape drug? It's a sedative that impairs your balance and speech. Makes you look drunk. Or knocks you out. And then, for good measure, messes with your memory."

"I see," she nodded thoughtfully. "Yes. I think you were roofied."

"Fucking hell." He pulled a white, button-down shirt off a hanger and stuck one arm through a sleeve. He stopped as he caught Hallie's intense gaze on him, raking over the muscles on his arms and chest, coming to rest on his bandage. Despite worrying about Ken Fucking Lane, Cy couldn't help a surge of satisfaction. If he didn't watch out, something else would be surging too.

Finally, her gaze met his. She swallowed. "Why don't you finish getting dressed. No one knows you're here, so we have plenty of time to talk."

He finished pulling on the shirt, leaving it untucked because of the stitches, and then slipped on a leather belt out of habit. "You say no one knows I'm here, but what about Mat? He always knows where I am."

"I have no idea. Did he know you were meeting with Ken Lane?"

"Yeah. He knew. He was the one who—"

"Who what?"

He wasn't about to tell her Mat was the one who'd received the tipoff about shit going down at SDIC. But now that his brain fog was starting to clear, he remembered Mat was going to try to meet with his informant. That's why he wasn't hanging around the Saguaro Room while Cy met with Ken. After all, no one thought Ken was a threat, especially in the hotel. There were security cameras everywhere.

He stared down at the closet floor. Where were his boots? His favorite pair? Wherever the hell his clothes were, he guessed. He yanked open a drawer, grabbed a pair of socks. Pushed the drawer shut, picked up a pair of old, scuffed-up boots, and went back out into his room. Sat on the edge of the bed and pulled on his socks and boots. Then, he slapped his hands down on his thighs. "Fully dressed. Happy?"

The woman slid her tongue over her bottom lip and scraped her teeth over it. And despite everything screwy about the entire situation, Cy felt his groin tighten. Damn. At least he knew *that* part of his anatomy was uninjured.

She gripped the bedpost and looked down at him. "Here's my theory. I think Ken Lane put something in your coffee, and when you appeared sick or unsteady or whatever, your friend escorted you out of the hotel and into his vehicle. I think he drove you down to the Sonoran Desert Internment Camp where I found you in the medical center. You were anesthetized and completely nude on an operating table with Ken Lane standing over you, totally decked out in a surgical gown, ready to cut you open. Before I could get to you, he'd already made an incision. So, I knocked him out and snuck you out of the facility. Made sure you were stitched up and then brought you here."

There was a weird ringing in Cy's ears. She couldn't be saying what she was saying. It was impossible. There were cameras all over the lobby, bar, and restaurant area of the hotel, so he'd have Brooks check the feeds. But … shit. Beyond that, how the hell was he supposed to believe this woman could knock Ken Fucking Lane out cold and sneak a 6-foot-3, 220-pound anesthetized man out of a heavily guarded facility?

The woman went on. "Your friend was preparing to murder you by cutting out your vital organs, selling them to the highest bidder, and then tossing your body into the camp's incinerator. Hence your stitches. He was starting with one of your kidneys."

The ringing got louder.

"And after you were dead and gone, he was planning to 'mourn' your death by comforting your sister and taking your place as head of your family. And I have the sneaking suspicion you're not the first person he's had on his operating table."

Like an idiot, he closed his eyes and banged the side of his head with his palm as if that would shake reality loose. It didn't work. When he opened his eyes, the strange woman was still in his bedroom saying ridiculous things that couldn't possibly be true. *Could they?* His fingers lightly touched his abdomen and traced the outline of the bandage under his shirt. He stared up at Hallie and, finally, let out a long exhale. "How do you know all this? And how did you find me if I was down at the Camp."

"I was tipped off and managed to get access to the room. I overheard your 'old friend' talking to you even though you were drugged and couldn't respond. He explained exactly what he was planning. Bragged about it. Even said he'd step in and act like a parent to your—and I quote—*mongrel* daughter. Or in lieu of that, maybe he'd get Sofia and BoJo deported."

5

Cy hissed out an impressive number of swear words and scrubbed both hands up and down his face. An almost violent gesture. Then he gripped his thighs so hard his fingertips turned white. He didn't move a muscle for a long moment. Just stared down at the carpet between his booted feet. Finally, he let out a long breath. "Holy mother of God."

"Precisely," she said, watching him take it all in.

"I need to make a call." He looked at his bedside table. No phone. No wallet. No watch.

"Is this what you're looking for?" Hallie strode back over to the chair she'd been sitting in and plucked up a cell phone, wallet, and wristwatch from the table next to it. "These were in the operating room. Figured they were either yours or your abductor's, so I pocketed them before we left."

"Thanks," he grumbled, grabbing them.

Her eyes crinkled at the corners when she smiled and offered a one-shouldered shrug. "Unfortunately, I forgot to rescue your clothes."

He stuck the wallet in his back pocket, slipped the watch onto his wrist and clipped the band closed, and keyed in his code to unlock his phone. He swore as he scrolled through his messages, then typed in a short text and hit send. Then he pressed another button and waited. After what seemed like forever, he spoke.

"Is Sofia with you?" He let out a long breath. "Thank God. Okay. Just keep an eye out for anything strange." He laughed. "Right. Anything stranger than normal strange. I know she's got the Christmas pageant at school next week, but—"

He paused, listened. Ran his fingers through his hair. "I don't want you to worry, but—"

Another pause.

"Yeah, I know. Listen, keep her the hell away from Ken Fucking Lane if you see him around town. And tell Sybil to stay the fuck away from him too."

Pause.

"No, I'm not just saying that because I can't stand the asshole. He's dangerous, BoJo. Ken may have convinced everyone else in Bigelow that he's a paragon of the community, but—"

Another long pause as Cy listened. "Well, do the best you can."

Pause.

A snort. "I may be older by eight minutes, but I think her spirit is older by about a thousand years. Jesus, I can't remember the last time I saw her let go. Really laugh."

A long pause.

"I know. I know. Listen, I gotta go. You feel like anything is off, you text me immediately, okay? And if you can't get me, text Mat or Mason. Brooks too. Hell, just text all of us, okay? Promise me."

He quit the call and stared down at the wallpaper photo on the screen.

"You're married?" Hallie said, her throat tight for absolutely no reason.

Cy nodded, distracted. Obviously worried. "Married my sister's best friend after a drunken and very ill-advised hookup. Our daughter, Sofia, is seven going on a hundred. Born on Christmas Day in '25." He smiled and touched a finger to the smiling face staring up at him. "Our little Christmas miracle. Now, she keeps us all on our toes. One minute playing dress up with her friends, the next dispensing wisdom like she's the goddamn Oracle of Delphi."

Sounds like the granddaughter of a god. "You're still married?"

He huffed out a harsh laugh. "Divorce is illegal without cause, so yeah. I'm not gonna cast the mother of my child to the wolves and put her at risk of deportation. But we don't live together. Never did except for show. We're more like siblings. In fact, she and Sofia live out at the Bigelow Estate with my sister. Whenever Sybil's around, I should say. Sybil's a bit of a wild card. Not wild, *per se*, but she inhabits her own world. She and BoJo are best friends and she loves Sofia, but she and I are ... well, we're like opposite sides of a coin. She has a seat on the company's board but doesn't want anything to do with the business." Cy had never understood his twin. Sometimes he wondered if they spoke the same language. "I prefer to live here," he said with a shrug. "The Bigelow Enterprises building is just down the street."

Good to know, Nemi thought. She wondered if his buddies—Mat, Mason, and Brooks—were still over there working tonight, wondering where their partner was. He probably had a dozen messages on his phone. "And you think this Ken Lane character will harm your daughter?"

"I didn't think so, but now..." He looked off into the distance. "He's always been obsessed with my twin. Since high school. Probably earlier. Something happened back then that Sybil won't talk about, but they have some weird connection that I don't like. For a long time, I thought he just wanted her money, but then we found out we didn't have any, so it's obviously more than that. Plus, he grew up a few doors down from BoJo and has always been an ass about it. And about me and BoJo having a kid together."

"Why is he an ass about something like that? And why did he call your daughter a mongrel?"

"Because although BoJo—her real name is Bonita Josefine Moreno—was born here and should be an American, her parents were from Nogales, so her citizenship was stripped after birthright citizenship was struck down. Her folks were deported, but we were able to keep BoJo here since we're married."

"I see." And she did. The Furies had told her all about the families that had been split apart because of the detention camps and mass deportations.

"Plus, I managed to get her a work visa." He wasn't about to admit the damn thing was a forgery. "She's smart as a whip and has worked in IT for Bigelow Enterprises since we managed to bring the company back from the brink. And she needs all the protection she can get."

"A marriage certificate and a work visa aren't enough?"

"Well, they are as long as she ... well ... as long as she...."

"She what?"

He drew in a long breath and let it out slowly. "The problem is, BoJo's not particularly interested in men, and since Obergefell was overturned, she'd be in danger if she was caught having a relationship with another woman."

"What's an Obergefell?"

Cy gave her a strange look. "Obergefell v. Hodges? Supreme Court ruling that legalized same-sex marriage?"

"Oh, right," Hallie said with a nod, like she could keep track of the inane human laws about who could love whom and how. "So, that was overturned?"

He narrowed his eyes and drew in a breath. "You been living under a rock?"

Mostly on other rocks, in other solar systems. In other galaxies. She cleared her throat and said nothing.

"SCOTUS overturned Obergefell in '28—two years before the Quiet Coup—and same sex relationships were fully outlawed in 2031. By CD. You know, Chancellor's Decree? Now, being caught in *flagrante delicto*, so to speak, is punishable by ten years hard labor. And that means slavery as inmates are hired out to landowners—or whoever can pay—for field or factory work. The promise was AI and robotics would replace manual labor, but that was just bullshit. All it's done is help roundup 'illegals' to go into the camps and then they're leased back out to perform the same manual labor jobs they did before. Only this time, they do them for no pay. The only ones making money are the private prison operators and good ol' Uncle Sam. Or, I should say, Daddy Jensen and his cronies."

"Daddy?" She suppressed a shudder.

"Bizarre, right? Grown men calling the head of the government, 'Daddy?' It's ... mind boggling."

The Furies had told Nemi her about what had happened in '29 when the Supreme Court rubber stamped one of Harold Jensen's first decrees as Chancellor. Apparently, as the world's first multi-trillionaire, Jensen had been able to bribe, blackmail, or buy off enough members of Congress and state legislators to easily rewrite and quickly ratify a new Constitution. Since he wasn't born in the U.S. and therefore couldn't run for president, Jensen's lackeys transformed the presidency into a symbolic office with the role of overseeing both houses of Congress while the Office of the Chancellor was created to actually run the government—and oversee the president.

And, voila, the law was written so only members of Congress could vote on who served as Chancellor. Since there were no term limits established, the New America—or rather, the territorial fiefdoms run by Jensen vassals—was stuck with Harold Jensen for the foreseeable future. For all intents and purposes, the man could hang around until Atropos cut his life thread. And only the Moirai knew when that would be.

"Anyway," Cy was saying, "BoJo and I spent exactly one night together because we were both drunk as fiddlers, and she was curious about what it felt like to be with a man. I happily obliged her, but condoms aren't foolproof." He choked out a laugh. "And because even a pharmaceutical abortion is considered first-degree murder and punishable by death, once she found out she was pregnant, I married her. To protect her and the baby." He swiped a hand down his face again. "Jesus, I don't know why I just told you all that."

Hallie knew. Because people always confided—*or confessed*—to Nemesis, the goddess. Even when they didn't realize they were doing it. She joked it was part of her charm, but her friends knew it was all part of a sort of spell she could cast on those she wanted to interrogate. Interestingly enough, she hadn't used that particular trick on Cy Bigelow. He just kept on talking, though. Like he trusted her without even realizing it.

"I fucking hate the idea of Ken Fucking Lane getting within a mile of Sofia. And calling her a mongrel?" He growled out another string of profanities. "What the hell is wrong with people like that?"

"Fear of the other," Hallie said. "Insecurity. A superiority complex. Narcissism. The need to assert dominance. I could go on and on."

Cy pursed his lips and shook his head at her. "It was a rhetorical question."

She turned away and looked out the window, over the charming streets and rolling hills of Bigelow. There was nothing rhetorical about the damage humans did to each other in the name of racial, religious, or cultural superiority. And the rules people made up about sex all too often had more to do with the need to grow more soldiers to fight rich men's wars than to any real issue with homosexuality. There were plenty of homosexuals in the Administration. Nemi's friends tried to keep track of everyone's secrets.

"Rhetorical or not," she said finally, "that kind of language is dangerous." Mongrel. Bitch. Witch. She could recite a thousand slurs from a thousand different languages used to describe those humans wanted to dehumanize. She let out a huff of frustration.

And she could never excuse a grown man calling a little girl a mongrel. It was inexcusable. Over the course of thousands of years, there were few things that incensed her more than crimes against innocents. Against children. Against animals. Against poor or elderly or infirm people who could not fight back.

And at that moment, the idea that this man's seven-year-old daughter might be in danger from a psychopath willing to harvest organs and kill for profit flooded her veins with a volcanic fury. She let it roll through her like Thor's thunderbolts, reverberating against her ribcage. Had to stop herself from shaking with the force of it. *Gods do not like it when their favorites are threatened.*

She walked over to the photo she'd noticed of Cy holding a little girl on his shoulders. "Is this Sofia?"

"Yeah. She was only four then. Why?"

"Because I want to know what she looks like in case my organization can help protect her from this despicable Ken Lane character."

What she really wanted was to meet Sofia and establish a communications channel with her. She would do everything she could to make sure Cy's daughter—*Apollo's granddaughter*—was never harmed. Speaking of whom, she should probably reach out to Apollo sooner rather than later and let him know what was going on. Or have Dr. A do it. Apollo might not always care to keep track of his progeny, but once he knew who they were, he always took an interest. And he had a soft spot for his grandchildren and great-grandchildren. Besides, she'd need to let Asklepios know how Cy's stitches were holding up. Strange to think they were half-brothers. Strange to think Cy had no idea who he really was.

Cy looked down at his phone, then back up at Hallie. "And how do you propose to protect her?"

"In any way necessary."

He appeared to consider that for a moment, then nodded, and opened his photo app. For some reason he could not explain, he trusted this strange woman. It made no sense, but he could feel the resolve and, for lack of a better word, *goodness* in her. And his instincts seldom failed him.

"I've got a million more photos." He scrolled through his photo folder, then held his phone out to show a beautiful towheaded girl with uncanny bright blue eyes. She was holding a fluffy grey kitten with ears tufted with fur so fine it looked like wisps of smoke. Hallie reached out to touch the screen then pulled her hand back.

She looked up. "You're dark, but her hair is practically white."

He laughed. "She looks like Sybil did at her age. My twin and I have always been polar opposites. Both Dad and Mom were dark. Dark hair. Olive skinned. Brown eyed. BoJo too. I've got blue eyes, but Sybil and Sofia are serious genetic throwbacks. Someone in our past was apparently a blondie." He smiled down at the photo. "Honestly, the kid's a wonder. Off the charts." His voice caught. "And *kind*. Genuine. Except when her sharp tongue gets going, then watch out."

Hallie could feel the emotion in his voice like a kick to her solar plexus. He would stop at nothing to protect his daughter.

"And here's BoJo." He thumbed to another photo, this time of a striking young woman with short brown hair cropped so close to her skull that her rich chocolate brown eyes and dark lashes stood out like beacons. There was a glittering determination in those eyes. In the grim smile on her full lips. Determination and disappointment. She was lovely. And she was his wife.

"Listen," Hallie said after a long moment. She planted her hands on her hips and sucked in a calming breath. "My informants tell me population in America has gone from 340 million in 2025 to 255 million today. Besides deaths due to lack of hospitals, doctors, and health care for the poor, skyrocketing infant mortality rates, eliminating vaccinations, new fast-moving deadly pandemics, stopping cancer research and treatments, and deporting non-citizens, I'm told there are thousands of political prisoners and non-violent criminals being held in camps like SDIC. I'm also told these people are being farmed out as slave labor to local businesses and farming concerns or simply disappeared into the global human trafficking network.

"My organization works behind the scenes to help stop these practices and to hold the people responsible accountable," she went on. "I believe your Ken Lane is involved. He was going to harvest your organs, and he wasn't going to just hand them over to someone who needed them. He was taking them to make a profit and to get rid of you in one fell swoop. I want to find out exactly what is happening and help you protect your loved ones. I want to help you, Cy."

He shook his head. "I still don't understand why me. This shit is happening all over the goddamned country. In the whole fucking world. We're just a little corner of it down here in Southern Arizona."

"Does that make your corner and your people less important?"

"Fuck no! Of course not, but—"

"You want to know why you? Because it's *what I do*, Mr. Bigelow." She couldn't tell him it was what she was created for. That it was her *raison d'être*. And that not only did she intend to put a stop to it in the here and now, she meant to make everyone responsible pay. For all eternity.

6

Because it's what I do, Mr. Bigelow. What did that even mean? Cy stuck his phone back in his pocket, crossed his arms over his chest, and leaned against the bedside table. "Before I say anything more, you need to understand that Chancellor Jensen would like nothing better than to nail me and my friends to the wall for treason. You talk a good game, and I'd love to believe every word you say, but I'm still not convinced you're not his tool sent to entrap us."

Her face was expressionless as she held his gaze. "I am no one's tool, Mr. Bigelow."

"So you say." He cocked his head and studied her. "It's strange ... I'm a pretty good judge of character, but I have been fooled before. That said, for some bizarre reason that completely baffles me, I'm inclined to trust you."

She looked up at him, the intensity of those big eyes nearly drilling a hole in his chest. "You're not wrong this time. There's no one in the world you can trust more than me."

He snorted a laugh at that. "Right. Sure. And I've known you for how long...? Even if that's the case, trust goes both ways. You need to tell me how you were tipped off, how you gained access to this operating room you say I was in, and how the hell a woman who looks like you managed to move a man who looks like me. Without being seen."

"I have my ways—"

"Or maybe you were seen. Maybe you had help. Maybe, despite my instincts, you're in cahoots with someone at the Camp. Maybe even Ken. Trying to worm your way into my life, discover my secrets to use against me. Although, I'm not sure he's smart enough to be that devious."

"In *cahoots* with a man like that?" She stared at him. Turned and walked away, then pivoted and strode back toward him, poked a finger into his chest. "Let me assure you that is *fundamentally* impossible. The mere idea goes against everything I am. I don't think I'm even capable of such a thing."

He had this sudden desire to grab her finger, capture it and press her whole palm against his heart. He wanted to know everything she was. *Fundamentally.* To understand her. More. To touch her. Hold her. Instead, he merely lifted an eyebrow and looked down at where her finger pressed into him.

She dropped her hand, obviously frustrated. "I wish I could tell you so you'd understand, but..."

"But what?" He tried to keep his voice calm. Why in the world did he want to trust this mysterious woman who'd appeared in his bedroom with such a cockamamie story? He *felt* like she was being truthful—certainly not forthcoming, but not dishonest, either. But could what she claimed about Ken actually be true? Could he have been in the process of murdering him? Harvesting his organs? Jesus. The mere idea ... but, then again, he'd heard terrible rumors of what was going on down at SDIC. And he did have a line of wicked stitches in his belly. He knew Ken was in thick with Administration functionaries and would do whatever he could to move up the power structure, but did that include murdering someone he'd known since kindergarten?

Probably. If Ken was intent on murder, was it his own idea or had it been an order from on high? Was the Administration finally determined to neutralize the Bigelow problem or was Ken running some organ harvesting operation on his own?

He'd made plenty of enemies in his lifetime, so he was always on guard and expected the Administration to target him physically eventually. And if he were in the crosshairs, it was inevitable that Mat, Mason and Brooks were right there with him. Sure, the Resistance had safeguards and backups in place, but taking out all four of them would significantly damage the movement and potentially put millions of people at risk. Including Sybil, BoJo, and Sofia.

So far, between targeted sabotage and political manipulation, they'd managed to keep the worst of the Administration's activities to the north and east. Since the second war of secession—this time against the United Alliance of Western States (UAWS, including California, Oregon, and Washington)—had turned into a nasty border war, Arizona was on the front lines. Mexico to the south and the breakaway states to the west. They all knew it was a dangerous business, but they'd tried to carve out a relatively peaceful zone in the desert Southwest where people could at least pretend to live normal lives. Pretend that not everything had gone off a cliff after the Quiet Coup of '28. A place where the worst of the atrocities happened elsewhere. Except that it did happen here. It was happening down at SDIC right now. And he knew the whole idea was a sick sort of NIMBY that they knew wouldn't hold. Eventually the Resistance would take down the power hungry, hateful, bloodthirsty bastards or the Administration would destroy them all.

The clock was ticking. The biggest danger now was the Administration finding out about the new nickel-copper deposits Brooks and the Bigelow engineers had found deep in mines long since deemed spent. And find out about the other project they were working on, the one that could tip the balance of power in their favor and power a new revolution. The few employees they had were loyal, but they also knew they weren't impervious to bribery or blackmail. Sooner or later, someone would talk and the news would get out. And when it did, Chancellor Jensen would take it all away. They'd all be marked men. Had that already happened? Did Ken Fucking Lane know? Was he responsible for the Administration's wet work? Assassination by physician?

"Look," he said, "I know Ken to be a narcissistic toady, but I don't know you at all. Bottom line is that as much as I want to trust you, I still find your story hard to swallow."

Truth was, Nemesis didn't have an explanation fit for either human or demigod consumption. She may have been keeping tabs on Cy for years, but he'd never seen her before. Except as a forest ranger. He was right to be suspicious. Still. She was an immortal goddess who had saved his life twice and his suspicion felt just a tiny bit ... hurtful. She swallowed. *It's just these damnable human hormones.* The emotions they triggered would get her in trouble if she wasn't careful.

"And even if you *are* telling even some small semblance of the truth," Cy went on, on a roll now, "how the hell could a woman who looks like you be strolling around down at that accursed camp in the first place? You say you were tipped off, but you won't say by who. You say you're not a doctor, but you won't say how you were able to get into the SDIC medical center to rescue me? You say you work for an organization interested in what the Administration is doing, but you won't tell me its name."

"Actually—"

"Face it, Ms. Hallie Whoever-the-Hell-You-Are, your story is for shit. Complete and utter BULLSHIT." Now he was mad. "So, if you're not willing to start from the beginning and tell me what's really going on, we're done and you can get out of my apartment and fuck all the way off."

Once upon a time, many thousands of years ago … Hallie sighed. Yeah, starting at the beginning was a non-starter.

"I'll tell you as much as I can," she said instead. "But first, you get something to eat. Your color has returned, but you're still not steady on your feet. And I'm surprisingly hungry too. I keep forgetting what …" She trailed off.

He narrowed his eyes at her. "Forgetting what?"

"Nothing."

"Right." He reached for the water bottle. Empty. He set it back down on the table. Hard. His throat felt like hard-packed caliche, like it would take a thousand-year monsoon to soothe it. He glared at Hallie Jones. Took a step toward her. Then another. Finally, they were toe to toe. He was taller, but he got the distinct feeling that nothing he could do would intimidate her. He didn't *want* to intimidate her, he just wanted to understand her. And he wanted her to understand him. She held his gaze as he searched her face, trying to see the truth of her. Trying to ignore the deep blue, almost violet, of her eyes. Like the Santa Rita mountains at dawn. Purple mountains majesty, indeed. There was something about the woman that felt majestic and fierce, but also safe. Like a fortress. Like a *refuge*.

"It's just that I forgot when I ate last." Or how human appetites work. She hadn't eaten much at all since she came to Earth. Gods ate and drank, of course, but mostly because they relished the ritual and abundance of banquets and the decadent flavors associated with the finest food and drink the planet could produce, not because they needed Earthly sustenance. Unless you took on a human form and then *all* appetites were, well, *godsized*.

And by saving this man—this magnificently beautiful demigod—she had worked up a terrible hunger.

7

Cy was still trying to figure out how Hallie had gone into his bathroom in hospital scrubs, with no purse or bag in hand, and emerged moments later wearing a pair of skin-tight black jeans, what looked to be wildly expensive black cowboy boots, and a turquoise camisole beneath a matching sweater and all topped off with an intricate silver and turquoise necklace and matching earrings shaped like intertwining undulating snakes eating their own tails. There was a name for that. Orobouros?

Didn't matter what you called it, this woman was fucking hot.

He'd gone in to take a piss after her she was done changing and her hospital scrubs were nowhere to be seen. Gone, as if they'd never been there in the first place. As they'd stepped into the elevator to head down to the Saguaro Room, they'd leaned back against opposite walls and stared at each other. After a moment, she'd raised her brows and given him a look as if to dare him: *Go ahead. Ask. You won't believe the answer.*

He didn't ask. He'd think about her quick-change routine later. Now, his side ached, his memory was for shit, and he'd apparently been almost murdered. Her clothes were the least of his problems.

They settled into his favorite booth near the back of the restaurant and soon Rosie appeared at the table and took their orders. "I'll have whatever IPA we've got on tap this week," Cy told her.

"No, you don't," Nemi chimed in. "The doctor said no alcohol for twelve hours. Until the pain medication wears off."

"Pain medication?" A worried expression drew Rosie's mouth down in a frown.

"It's nothing," Cy said. "Just a scratch and a few stitches."

"Okay," the girl said, reassured. "Just take care, Mr. Bigelow. We couldn't do without you around here." She turned and gave Hallie Jones an appreciative smile, commented on her *oh-my-god-those-are-so-amazing* earrings, and then headed back to the kitchen. That's when Cy's cellphone buzzed.

He pulled it out of his pocket, looked at the screen, then held a finger up in the "please wait one second" signal. With a wince, he scooted out of the booth, strode toward the end of the bar as a big man wearing a cowboy hat pulled down to shadow his face emerged from the restroom corridor. Cy placed a hand on the other man's back as they bent their heads together. Obviously, well acquainted, Nemesis thought it might be Mat, one of the trio of Cy's old friends—Brooks, Mat, and Mason. But with his hat low, she couldn't be sure. Plus, it had been years since she'd seen any of them in the flesh. Although she never forgot a face. Or a voice.

Even though she had amplified hearing abilities in her human Hallie Jones form, she had to concentrate to make out exactly what they were saying since both men had their backs to her and the music emanating from speakers around the room interfered with their sound waves. But she was able to hear the other man say, "I got your text. Where the hell have you been?"

"It's a long story. I'll tell you all later. What's going on?"

"Just got word," the man said. "Ken's apparently gone off the deep end." Something something something. A coarse laugh and more mumbling. Then the cowboy hat man pulled his hat down even lower and turned to look her way. She pretended to not notice but was now certain it was Mat Cárdenas. Cy took the man's arm and guided him back further into the shadow of the corridor. Hallie saw Cy pull his shirt up and, she guessed, peel back the bandage to show the other man his stitches. The man stared down for a moment, then whipped his head back toward her. "No idea, but I'm gonna find out if it's the last thing I do," Cy said and then mumbled something else. Hat man shook his head. "Things are escalating, and I don't like it." *That* had been loud and clear. And then he said something about inside sources being worried because "Ken's busy cursing you and your ancestors to kingdom come and back." Then more head shaking, more very colorful cursing, and a lot of mumbling she couldn't make out.

Nemi let out a soft snort of laughter. Ken Lane wouldn't be so eager to curse Cy's ancestors if he knew who they were.

Cowboy hat man squeezed Cy's arm, gave him a nod, cast one last dark look toward the booth where Hallie sat, and then disappeared back down the dark corridor from whence he came.

Hallie sipped her sparkling water as Cy slipped his phone into his pocket and slid back into the booth. She looked up innocently. "Everything all right?"

"One of my business partners," Cy said. He cast a glance back down the corridor. "Turns out he just shared some news you might be interested in."

"What's that?"

"Seems like our favorite surgeon is not very happy with me right now. Apparently *something* happened down at the Camp and our friend has gone a bit ... ballistic. So, it appears I'm going to have to take you at your word." He drummed his fingers on the table.

She couldn't help but feel a bit vindicated, but she'd learned long ago that telling a human *I told you so* or *You should have trusted me* was not a great way to engender good feelings.

"Until our food arrives, we can have a nice, friendly chat about how our mutual interests might align. Now that I have evidence—at least hearsay evidence—that what you told me is true, as unbelievable as it sounds, why don't you take it one step further and tell me who you really are and why you're here."

"I'll tell you as much as I can." Hallie was ready to spin a cover story that would satisfy even the most overly curious demigod. She'd done it hundreds of times before. Well, not always to a demigod, but certainly to humans with whom she wanted to work.

"My interest in SDIC and the other internment camps," she said, "stems from the fact that the global organization with which I'm affiliated is dedicated to punishing human rights violations and bringing perpetrators to justice."

"Good luck with that." Cy's voice was a low growl. "Since what's going on at the Camps is perfectly 'legal.'"

Hallie had rarely seen such angry air quotes and could feel the tightly contained rage roll off him. She leaned forward as if confiding a secret. "While my organization acknowledges a sovereign nation's right to codify 'the law of the land,' we operate according to, shall we say, a more *universal* code of justice."

Cy raised an eyebrow. "So, you're global vigilantes?"

Both Interpol and the International Criminal Court had long been ignored by the Administration, and there weren't any other global organizations, at least to Cy's knowledge, that could even attempt to hold Chancellor Jensen accountable for his crimes. The U.S. had withdrawn from NATO, and the United Nations had voted to kick both the U.S. and Russia off the Security Council.

In retaliation, the organization had been kicked out of New York right after the Quiet Coup and was now located in Brussels.

Chancellor Jensen had resorted to schoolyard bullying tactics and the rest of the world was both laughing and crying at the state of affairs in D.C. The name-calling alone was mortifying, and from what Cy could tell, the UN and the EU—along with pretty much every other nation or cooperative economic zone on the planet—simply tried to ignore the hot air emanating from Washington like so much putrid sewer gas. Everyone just hoped no one lit a match near Jensen or the whole world might blow.

Since she'd been back on Earth, Nemi had heard all about the rift between the UN and the Administration. Like petty tyrants throughout history, Jensen had declared the iconic building on the East River a monument to failed diplomacy and had ordered it razed to the ground. To top it all off, he then forbade anyone from rebuilding there. A modern-day salting of the earth.

The man had also erected an impressive edifice to the New America's glorious future right on the National Mall, where, from his expansive desk on the 13th floor—one floor for each of America's founding colonies—Jensen could look through his floor-to-ceiling windows and nearly peer into the windows of both the capitol building and the monstrosity that was the White House where the newly emasculated president, Julian Valentine, was still allowed to live.

"Global vigilantes. I guess that's one way of looking at it." Hallie shrugged and sat back. "Don't bother asking the name of the organization because I guarantee you haven't heard of it, and I'm not at liberty to tell you at this point anyway. Suffice it to say, it is immensely powerful and extremely well connected."

Cy gave a disbelieving snort. "If it's *that* powerful and well connected, it's gotta be as corrupt as hell. Everyone has a price, right?"

No, Nemi thought. The gods could be crazy, vengeful, and petty but they could not be bribed or blackmailed. If they truly wanted something, they could just take it and smite anyone who got in their way. That wasn't the way she and her friends worked, but there were other gods who had no qualms about smiting. And there were a few who liked to cause trouble for trouble's sake. Eternity is a long time and boredom can be, for some—including a couple of her own siblings—a good reason to stir the pot.

"You're wrong," she said. "This organization is absolutely incorruptible."

Cy barked out a laugh and then winced at the pain in his side. "Are you kidding me? What kind of fantasy world do you think we live in?"

His blue eyes took on a hard, glittery sheen, and the muscles along his jawline clenched. Anger. Disappointment. Despair, even. Nemi had seen the look a million times before. In throne rooms, on battlefields, and in quiet spaces as loved ones breathed their last.

"There is still good in the world, Mr. Bigelow," she said. "You know that."

"Oh, sure, Sam." He rolled his eyes. "And it's worth fighting for, right?"

"You know it is. Sam carried Frodo and the ring up Mount Doom when Frodo had all but given up, and isn't that what you and your friends are doing? And didn't they destroy Sauron in the end?"

"Technically, Gollum destroyed the ring." He let out a beleaguered sigh. Well, at least he knew she'd read Tolkien. He stared down at the table for a moment as if to ground himself.

"Look, I do know you're right. I have Sofia, after all. And she's definitely worth fighting for. But right now, we're living in the most dangerous and the most idiotic timeline," he went on.

"Shameless and shameful. And too many people have learned to adapt to it, like time and space have been stretched and warped into some nightmarish Dalí painting where everyone and everything is melting and no one cares. Hell, maybe most people don't even notice." He settled back in his seat with a shrug. "But one thing I'm pretty sure of is that there's not much on God's green Earth that's incorruptible."

She took a sip of her water and squeezed a bit more juice from the lime wedge she'd requested, biding her time. Trying to decide what to say. How much to reveal.

"Okay, enough of me up on my soapbox." Cy picked up his water glass and took a long drink. "So, how did this organization of yours help get me out of Ken's evil clutches?"

"I was alerted to a dangerous situation and was able to insert myself onto the premises. Once I was there, I found you in that operating room and heard Ken Lane talking to you. The things he was saying were despicable. I couldn't just leave a helpless man to die in such a manner, so I decided to do something." She gave him an electrifying smile that made her eyes twinkle like sunlight glinting off moving water. "After all, saving gentlemen in distress is just part of my remit."

One side of his mouth quirked up in an amused smile. "Wonder Woman herself," he said in a voice laced with skepticism. "Or maybe you're a magician." He arched a single brow. "Or a witch."

"A big believer in magic and witchcraft, are you? Djinn and magic lamps? Superheroes? Maybe get down on your knees and pray for a miracle now and then?"

"I would if it worked," he snorted. "Why don't we go back to how you discovered I was 'in distress.' Were you already inside the SDIC wire? Do you have a job there? Some sort of undercover role on behalf of your mysterious organization? Who tipped you off? How did you overpower Ken? How did you manage to get me out of there without being seen—*if* that's what indeed happened?"

Nemi started to open her mouth, but the pretty young server reappeared at their booth, this time holding two plates of food. "A Sonoran burger with fries for you, Mr. Bigelow, and an order of cheese enchiladas for you, ma'am."

"Thanks, Rosie," Cy said. "Just add it to my tab. And don't forget to give yourself a tip."

The server bobbed her head and gave Cy a radiant smile. Nemi supposed that was probably every woman's reaction to him—whether he was the boss or not. She should expect it. Accept it. Certainly not be annoyed by it. He was physically beautiful and there was no sense ignoring that fact. Well, she couldn't even if she tried. And besides, she was a goddess, so what did how humans react to Cy Bigelow have to do with her, anyway?

Nothing at all.

8

Cy dipped a clump of French fries in a little container of ketchup and held them up like a piece of evidence. "Best fries in town." The fries disappeared down his gullet and he grabbed more. "I guess being knocked out and nearly salvaged for parts makes a guy hungry." He'd barely finished chewing when he picked up his burger and took a huge bite.

Nemi picked up her fork and cut a tidy piece off the end of her enchilada. "What can you tell me about Ken Lane? Is he going to come after you again?"

Cy stared at his plate for a moment, his gaze going distant, as if trying to remember what the hell had happened to him. "My guess is yes. If your account of what happened has even a remotely tangential relationship to reality and he really did try to do me in, he's not going to stop at one failed attempt. But what I still want to know is why you or your organizations gives a damn about what happens to me."

She shrugged. "I told you. We don't like bullies—or people involved in crimes against humanity."

He set his burger down on his plate. Wiped his hands on his napkin. "So, you step in and save the day. If that were true, wouldn't there be a lot fewer crimes against humanity? Seems like those keep on happening on a daily basis, so your organization must not be very effective."

She sighed at that. "You're right. We are unable to prevent humans from being inhumane to each other. We do what we can, but we need human partners to step up and help."

"Human partners. That's an odd way of putting it."

She nodded, acknowledging the strange wording. "There comes a time when people must be held accountable, and people must be the ones doing the work of holding them accountable. Justice cannot simply be imposed from above. That way eliminates human agency and choice. Rather than being empowering, it is emasculating."

"So, basically, you're saying your organization wants people on the ground to help hold people in power accountable for actions that are, within the particular system, perfectly legal?"

"Harvesting someone's vital organs without express permission is not perfectly legal. Implanting tracking or augmentation devices in unsuspecting individuals is not perfectly legal. And holding family members hostage so individuals will work for slave wages or engage in unethical or illegal activities is definitely not perfectly legal."

"Everything else that goes on down there is. SDIC has *carte blanche* to do anything they want with those people. No due process. No accountability. Administration goons can just pluck anyone they want off the street and disappear them. Sell them on the global labor exchange and turn a profit in the process. American citizen or not, they can trump up charges and hold you until the proverbial cows come home. And that shit is legal."

"So, we hold people accountable e*specially* when their behavior is legal. When the laws have been warped to condone actions that in any honorable and civilized society would be forbidden."

He held her gaze. "Who are you really, Hallie Jones?"

"I told you."

"You told me shit. Some cock 'n bull story about a mysterious secret organization—"

"Look." She set her fork down on the edge of her plate with exaggerated precision. "You want to use profanity, I'll put it to you simply. My job"—*my entire existence!*—"is dedicated to making sure assholes who fuck around with other people's lives find out what justice really means. Assholes who take advantage of others. Who cheat and steal and rape and pillage instead of *serving* others. Instead of *caring* for others. Assholes who take and take and *take*. Who believe they're infallible. Invincible. And who set themselves up as godlike rulers and demand to be worshiped by 'lesser' humans or else."

If such an organization did exist, it would be a godsend. In Cy's opinion, what was left of the old United States of America—or, rather, of Jensen's New America—needed a good dose of fuck-around-and-find-out justice. He thought about the months leading up to the Quiet Coup and how it all happened with barely a shot fired. Except for the targeted assassinations and violent arrests and disappearances, there was little outright violence. For a while, he'd believed the people had a chance. There'd been thousands of peaceful protests, dozens of nationwide strikes, and hundreds of walkouts as college and university students took to the streets. When those didn't work, there'd been riots. And then there was the Taxation Without Representation movement that led to millions of people refusing to pay their federal taxes. That only led to all funding from D.C. to the states stopping abruptly, colleges and universities closed their doors, state capitols were occupied by DICE operatives, and the arrests, assassinations, and mass disappearances began in earnest. And everyone went dark. People stayed home. Locked their doors. The quiet before the storm. Except there was no storm.

It was energizing to think there were others out there actively pushing back. But was it true?

For years, powerful political leaders and wealthy business interests had spent trillions of dollars on classic mis- and disinformation campaigns so thorough and effective that regular citizens had no idea what to believe. Up or down. Left or right. True or False. Fact or fiction. The only thing that was *real* was that if you stood up or spoke out, you were punished. Locked down in camps like SDIC, transported to offshore prisons, or completely disappeared. And the only ones who could "protect the people" were the very ones who cultivated the chaos.

The war of secession of the United Alliance of Western States had been a welcome excuse for Jensen to send his military out in full force. Cy imagined the man breaking out the good bubbly the day the new UAWS Declaration of Independence was signed with pomp and circumstance in the governor's office in California. The Administration immediately sent in bombers to flatten Sacramento and put an end to all talk of secession. But the city had been emptied out days in advance and Jensen discovered, to his horror, that the signing ceremony had all been a stage set and the new UAWS cabinet was safe and sound in an unknown location. After that, the border war had gone on for years. Was still going on. The central states were desolate as farming dried up, and poverty, starvation, and disease ran rampant across much of the nation.

And the good old Stars and Stripes was back down to 45 stars since Alaska had been annexed by Russia and Hawaii had just declared itself an independent nation. Not that Jensen acted like he'd lost that battle. He didn't. He'd never admit defeat on any subject. No matter how small or petty. He still boasted of his power like he was Caesar Augustus himself. And now the man had his sights on Arizona. The state where copper was king, uranium queen, and silver, gold, lead, and zinc were members of the court, just waiting to be extracted. Extracted from land still owned by the tribes and by Bigelow Enterprises. Land Chancellor Harold Jensen coveted. Land he would gladly kill for.

As for Nemi, the Furies had shown her some of the television coverage of the Quiet Coup. It was nothing new. Nothing she and the other gods hadn't seen evil men do for thousands of years. The only difference was the scale. Swift, efficient, and global. Once America fell to fascism, despots and dictators around the world seized power seemingly overnight, wiping out or dismantling opposition leaders and organizations.

In America, Chancellor Jensen and his toady group of senators and representatives now accused anyone and everyone who spoke out against them of treason. Charges were leveled, properties confiscated, and people disappeared or hanged right there on the scaffolding on the national mall. *If you aren't with us, you are against us.*

Cy was most definitely against them. He wiped his mouth with his napkin, leaned back in his chair, and studied her face. *Considered* her.

"You claim your organization operates on a more *universal code* of justice, but under what authority do you operate? What gives you the right to hold these assholes accountable?"

Her eyes took on a determined glint and a slow smile took shape on her full mouth. "By our *own* authority. *Your* system of justice may condone their crimes, but that doesn't mean *ours* does."

"Hmm." Cy picked up his burger again. Chewed. Swallowed. Finished it off in just a few more bites, then picked up his napkin again. Wiped his mouth. All while staring at her. Suddenly, his gaze flicked up and off to the right, over Hallie's shoulder. He went still. *Damnit.*

Speaking of assholes. Two men stood at the threshold between the hotel lobby and the restaurant, one glaring down at the hostess while the other surveyed the room. Wearing red baseball caps and navy jackets emblazoned with the DICE logo, the Deportation and Internment Camp Enforcement goons loomed over the hostess, their thick necks and barrel-shaped bodies betraying the fact that they were jacked up on testosterone and other so-called performance enhancing drugs like, AIs, SERMs, hGH, and hCG. They were probably augmented too. Chancellor Jensen's HJBiotech had a contract to implant the latest and greatest brain, nerve, and muscle augmentation devices on all new DICE employees. As a signing bonus. That plus 20k in HJCryptoCoin and another 50k in government housing credits had led to a swarm of new recruits.

Their presence at the hotel was more than a little disturbing. To Cy's knowledge, no one from the Administration had set foot in the Bigelow Hotel in nearly a year, so why were they here now? Looking for him, no doubt. Had Ken Fucking Lane sent them? Had they been alerted to their resistance operations?

He pasted a smile on his lips and forced his gaze back to Hallie Jones. No way would he give them the satisfaction of even acknowledging their presence until absolutely necessary.

Hallie immediately sensed the tension in the room. Felt Cy go quiet. Noted where he was looking and stopped herself from turning around. Noted Regina, the bartender, had stopped chopping limes, the direction of her gaze alighting first on Cy, then on the kitchen door, then back down to the limes and the knife in her hand. Rosie, the server, carrying several plates of food out of the busy kitchen, stopped in her tracks then quickly eased back through the doors, disappearing from sight.

"What's happening?"

"DICE just arrived."

"Looking for you?"

"How the hell should I know? Maybe Ken sent them. Maybe they're after Rosie. Who knows. But it's never good when they show up. Last year they took half a dozen people from the hotel. All of them had papers. All of them credentialed workers sponsored by Bigelow Enterprises. All of them disappeared. And I couldn't do a damn thing about it."

"Tell you what," Hallie said, deciding to follow her instincts and gamble on the man sitting in front of her. "You interested in talking with them?"

"Are you kidding? I'm never interested in talking to those Nazis."

"So, how about we do a show and tell. I'll give you a quick demonstration of how I got you out of SDIC without being seen, and you tell me everything you know about the place, about your friend Ken, and about Administration's activities. *And* what you and your friends in the resistance movement are doing about it."

Cy's heart stuttered. He casually reached for his glass and took a drink. Set it back down. "What resistance movement?"

"I don't think an explanation is necessary. And since the mere arrival of these jackals has raised your hackles to red alert level, I'd say a quick exit is in order."

"A quick exit would be nice, but I don't think we can get out of here without them following us. Or, more likely, stopping us."

"Wanna bet?" Hallie smiled, a gleam in her eyes warming him all over as she reached across the table and wrapped her hand around his. The jolt of electricity he felt when they'd touched in his bedroom shot through him again.

And then everything went dark.

9

His stomach swooped, then dropped. Heart stuttered, stopped, then restarted with a sickening lurch. He stumbled. Swallowed the bile crawling up the back of his throat. Blinked through a wavery film, like he was swimming in a pond with his eyes open under water.

What the hell? How were they back in his bedroom? In his apartment? Upstairs? *How the...?*

"And that's how I got you out of SDIC without being seen," Hallie Jones said, a wary smile painting her lips.

Cy looked down at their still-clasped hands, then back up to her face. He dropped her hand and stepped backward. "Who the hell are you? Or better yet, *what* the hell are you?"

"To paraphrase Hamlet, there are more things in heaven and earth, Cy Bigelow, than you can dream of."

Now, that quip pissed him off. He grabbed her wrist and dragged her over toward the chair she'd originally occupied when he woke up dazed and confused less than two hours earlier. He pointed at it and commanded her like he'd command on of the family dogs.

"Sit."

He dragged the other chair by the fireplace closer and sat, his knees nearly touching hers. Leaned forward. "You have no idea what I can dream of." He shook his head. "My imagination is a *very* fertile field."

Nemi suppressed a smile. *I'd love to find out.*

"Let me see if I've got this straight so far. You work for a secret organization that metes out justice to bad guys. I have an old friend who tried to slice and dice me, sell me for parts, then take over my family. We both have, let's say, organizational interests in what the Administration is up to. Am I on the right track?"

She nodded. "Good so far."

"And you, apparently, are able to employ some sort of ... magic trick ... and have whisked me out of danger twice now. This little trick seems like a handy skill to have when trying to stay one step ahead of Administration enforcers, by the way, so I'd love to know exactly how you do it. Also, let's revisit the whole who-the-hell-are-you question."

"It's a long story."

"I don't care if it's fucking *A la recherche du temps perdu.*"

"*Remembrance of things past?*"

He snorted. "The longest fucking novel I ever tried to plow through."

"Is it worth reading?"

"Not even remotely as interesting or worthwhile as the woman sitting in front of me who also apparently speaks French. I have no idea why I brought it up. Now spill."

Remembrance of things past. How apropos. Hallie took a deep breath and turned toward the fire she'd built earlier. It was just glowing embers now. With hardly a thought, the embers brightened, and flames jumped.

Cy snorted. "Another magic trick. Nice, but it's not going to distract me. Start talking."

"First, I should tell you my name's not really Hallie Jones."

Cy's eyes widened in mock surprise.

"I can't tell you my true name, though because—"

"Your mysterious organization forbids it?"

"No. Because you won't believe it."

He leaned back in his chair. "Try me."

"Maybe someday. Soon even. Suffice it to say, Hallie is the name I prefer to use for now. Hallelujah Delphinium Jones. I borrowed it and I'm not giving it back, so that's what I want you to call me."

"Your real name is the least of my concerns right now. Tell me about this organization and how you're able to—what shall we call it? teleport?—from one place to another. With me in tow."

"It's all about the physics. Quantum physics, specifically."

"Last I heard teleporting multiple photons and electrons was Nobel worthy and here you are teleporting entire bodies all over the place like it's a walk in the park."

"A walk in the park is also all about physics."

Cy groaned as if he were in pain and ran both hands through his hair. "Holy hell. You're gonna drive me nuts."

"Well, it's true."

"I *know* how to walk in the park, but I *don't* know how you appear to be able to teleport like some Star Trek character. Or like it's magic, but since I don't believe in magic—"

"It's not magic. It just seems like it to you."

"Christ Almighty! This is getting us nowhere."

"*CYRUS BIGELOW, OPEN UP!*"

They both leapt to their feet as the main door to Cy's private apartment rattled in its frame. Someone out in the hall was pounding on the door.

"*DICE! WE KNOW YOU'RE IN THERE!*"

Hallie grabbed Cy's arm. "How do they know you're here?" She waved a hand and the fireplace went dark. Cold.

"They're bluffing," he whispered. "We monitor the hallways and public spaces and sweep them constantly for bugs and cameras. Especially up here. My suite occupies the whole floor so, believe me, they don't have eyes on this place. But those goons must have seen us downstairs and then … *poof*."

He moved quickly to his bedside table, slid open the top drawer, pulled out a gun and holster, snapped it onto his belt. Grabbed a small sheath with a knife handle sticking out and bent to clip it on his right boot. Pulled his jeans back over his boot and closed the drawer.

A man's deep voice came through the door. "We're investigating a murder, Mr. Bigelow, and you're wanted for questioning." More pounding. "You can let us in or we'll break down the door!"

Hallie went still. "Who was murdered?"

"How the hell should I know? I'm just glad it wasn't me."

"Can they break in here or question you without a warrant?"

Cy huffed out a laugh. "Warrants don't mean anything to this Administration."

The pounding and shouting out in the hallway continued. She flicked her hand again and Cy's rumpled bed made itself up, neat as a pin, half a dozen pillows plumped and in place.

Cy's eyebrows shot up. "You've got all sorts of tricks up your sleeve."

"You have no idea."

"Listen," he said, as he checked his watch for the time. "I have no intention of being questioned today. It never goes well, and I already have a headache and a bellyful of stitches. There's a secret corridor, hidden by a trap door at the back of my closet. We can go out that way, down the fire escape, or …" He held his hand out to Hallie and whispered, "Maybe you can give me another physics lesson."

Hallie nodded, took his hand in hers, and they were gone.

10

This time, Cy kept his feet under him. The physics, though, was giving him a helluva headache. His stitches throbbed like the devil, and his whole body felt … weird. Stretched. Compressed. Discombobulated. He was dizzy and more than slightly nauseous. He needed to sit down. He needed a lot more ibuprofen. He definitely needed a drink. Or three. And answers. He needed to know what the hell was going on, and he didn't think he was going to get a straight answer from this crazy, incredible, mysterious, miraculous woman any time soon. He'd used her for a quick escape, but now that she'd brought him here—*here! of all places*—he was more than a little freaked out.

He looked down at his watch, noting the time it took to get from his suite to this remote spot. His second hand ticked forward. *Holy fuck.* Less than a second. He tapped the watch face twice, waited, tapped again. Just to make sure it was still working. The second hand ticked forward. The watch wasn't broken, but maybe he was. Maybe he was having some sort of mental breakdown and was really back in bed, dreaming. He was having a difficult time breathing. He'd never had a panic attack, but there was always a first time for everything. He tapped his watch again, three times in rapid succession, then tried to marshal his thoughts. Control his breathing.

An owl hooted in the distance. The dusty scent of sandstone and shale waltzed with fresh pine and creosote on a gentle breeze. He looked around. The fire circle they'd built was still here. Undisturbed. The place brought back memories of a happier, more hopeful time. If this was a dream, it was hitting all his senses. If this was a dream, the SOS message he'd just sent to his partners wouldn't be real.

He needed to think. Regroup. Clear his head. Talk to Mat, Brooks, and Mason. Find out who was murdered. Why he was wanted for questioning. He cleared his throat. Tried to keep his wits about him.

"So, why did you bring me here?" He looked up at Hallie. She was studying him as if he were a fascinating lab rat.

"You recognize this place? Even in the dark?" She gestured up at the Milky Way arcing above them amidst a dark sky filled with stars, sparkling like tiny diamonds strewn on blue-black velvet. She knew it was just an illusion. She'd traveled amongst the stars, and knew the sparkle came from viewing them through Earth's atmosphere. In space they were hellish balls of roiling plasma too hot even for her to get near.

"My buddies and I used to camp here," Cy said. He'd had some of the best times of his life here. Sleeping in the open. Dreaming about the future. Wondering what was out there in the inky depths of space and having the kind of deep philosophical conversations that weed and mushrooms and beer could fuel for hours. "Did a lot of hiking and rock climbing in the area. More to the point, it's Bigelow land. My sister and I own it. The original homestead is less than five miles away." He narrowed his eyes at her. "But I get the sense you know this already."

He registered the surprise in her posture. In the way she cocked her head and looked at him. "I didn't know it was your land."

"Tell me why you brought me here." It was a command, not a question, and he held his breath, waiting for an answer. *How could she know this place?*

She hesitated, as if weighing her words and he took the opportunity to study her face. She was exquisite. Her bone structure, her perfectly formed nose, full lips, and those eyes ... he'd never seen anything like them and yet he couldn't have said what made them unique. Couldn't have said why her presence, so near he could touch her, pull her to him, made his heartbeats go all fluttery like a schoolboy with a first crush. The idea made him want to laugh. But he didn't. Whatever was going on—whoever and whatever she was—was no laughing matter.

"Did you ever have any accidents here?" she said. "Back when you were rock climbing, I mean."

"Other than Brooks almost slipping down the cliff face once, no. And that time, I climbed down to stabilize him, and we were able to pull him up safe and sound so one was hurt."

It had been a near thing, saving Brooks' ass. Their first real brush with their own mortality had sobered them up fast. Not that they'd been drinking while climbing, but they were all a bit worse for wear after a late night around the campfire polishing off the beer they'd hauled out to The Point.

"You did this by yourselves?"

"What do you mean?"

She cocked an eyebrow at him. "You three pulled your friend up to safety by yourselves?"

His eyes narrowed. His heart skipped a beat, then sped up. "Noooo." He said it slowly, dragging it out to multiple syllables. "This land abuts what was national forest back then, and a ranger happened to show up to help. Said he heard us yelling. Big guy.

Just appeared out of nowhere. Helped pull Brooks up over the edge."

A sly smile tipped up the corner of her mouth and one shoulder rose and fell in a nonchalant shrug. "I told you it's just a matter of physics. Quantum, I should clarify. Not Newtonian."

The muscles in his jaw clenched. He stared at her. Walked around her, slowly. Looked her up and down. His hands were actually shaking. His breathing shallow. "You're not trying to tell me that guy was—*no*."

"I told you we'd met before."

"Impossible. No. No. And no." She had to be insane to think he'd entertain something so outrageous.

"How can you say that's impossible when I just whisked you out of your bedroom in Bigelow to this very spot. In under a second."

"Because that's just … teleporting. Or whatever it is you do. This would be … this would mean … this would … no. No way you're going to convince me you were that man."

"So teleporting is suddenly not a big deal?"

"Jesus! Of course, it's a big deal, but—"

"But you can't separate a person's physical presentation—their flesh and blood and bones—from who they truly are on the inside. From their *mind*. Or their *soul*."

He planted his hands on his hips. "For fuck's sake. It's not like you lost a leg. Or had an arm amputated. It's a whole different person!"

"Humans are humans are humans, Cy. The packaging matters, yes, but it's not the most important thing. It's what's in here." Nemi tapped a finger to the side of her head. "And here." She pressed a fist to her chest where her human heart beat out a steady rhythm.

"Okay. I get what you're trying to say, and I agree. I mean, I understand your point. But your head and your heart are tissue and muscle run by electrical signals. It's physical matter that can't just be miraculously transformed from one thing into another."

"And how do you think I got you here? I didn't transform your physical matter from one thing into another, but I broke it down into its most constituent parts, transported it to a new location miles away, and put it all back together. If I can do that, what makes you think I can't put you back together in a different way using those same constituent parts? And that I can't disassemble my own physical self and put it back together in a different form?"

Cy was speechless. A rare event. And then he sputtered. An even rarer event. "But ... but..." He pressed his fingers into his temples as if he had a terrible headache. Which he did. "You being that *man*?" He shook his head and ran both hands through his hair as if he wanted to pull it all out by the roots. "It's just not possible." He drew in a long breath. Looked up at the star-studded sky. Then off into the distance. Then back at the woman. Or whatever she was. "I have no idea how you know about what happened that day Brooks almost died, but I can't wrap my mind around the idea that you were there. You want me to tell you why I don't buy it?"

He stepped closer without waiting for an answer. Frustration practically pouring off his skin. "Even disoriented and foggy from whatever the hell I'd been through, I was attracted to you from the first moment I saw you in my bedroom tonight. Viscerally. Yes, I was dumbstruck by how beautiful you are and by the shock of you being there, but it was more than that. More than just physical lust. It was like ... I don't know. Like my body *recognized* you."

"Maybe you recognized me because we'd met before. Right on this very spot."

He ignored that and plowed ahead. "And because I'm a red-blooded man in my prime, I imagined touching you."

He moved closer again, looming over her.

"Imagined licking you from the tips of your toes to the tip of your nose. Tracing your curves with my fingers, my lips. Exploring your most secret places with my mouth. And, forgive me, but I knew in that very first moment that I wanted to make love to you, hold you close and bury myself deep. I imagined it would be so good, like going home. Like finding peace." His voice was a low growl. "And even though I subscribe to the idea that love is love is love and don't give a shit about who fucks who or why—as long as everyone doing the fucking is a consenting adult—but I guarantee you that I did not have any lustful ideas about that goddamn forest ranger."

Well, that was ... blunt, Nemi thought, as her human body had a visceral reaction of its own. She suppressed a shiver as a hot rush of excitement alerted every hair follicle to stand to attention and await further instructions. She swallowed. Wet her lips. Looked up at him.

"You must be aware that sexual attraction can be due to many factors including appearance, personality, pheromones, social cues, cultural influences and individual biological preference, or a combination of all the above. Someone out there in the world might have taken one look at that forest ranger and thought, 'I want to lick that man from head to toe.' The desire to mate with a particular person can be a fickle thing among humans, so—"

"The desire to mate." He snorted. "Among humans. You say all that as if you're not one of us." Reaching out to run a finger along her jaw and down her neck, he whispered, "But you feel like flesh and blood to me." He pressed his thumb against her skin, felt the whoosh of blood through her carotid artery. "I can feel your heart beating." He looked down at her mouth, then back up to hold her gaze. Bent his head as if he might kiss her.

She braced herself. Waiting. Wanting, for the first time in over a century, to feel a human's lips on hers.

"Teleporting." He whispered, his breath heating her cheek. "Going into the bathroom in one outfit and coming out minutes later in another. Supposedly shape shifting between a beautiful woman and a man in a forest ranger uniform. Rescuing me from the clutches of a madman intent on murder."

He moved his hands to cup her face. Held her gaze.

"Talking about sex as if humans are an alien species." He traced both thumbs over her dark, perfectly winged eyebrows. "I'm a practical man, Hallie. Always try to collect evidence, weigh the facts, determine what's real and what's not. The Administration has spent years trying to get us to believe what they tell us despite what is plain as day right before our noses, and I've spent my entire adult life trying to fight that." He put his mouth next to her ear, his breath a butterfly kiss on her skin. "But nothing about you is plain as day."

She did shiver then. Tipped her head to give him better access to her neck, to her oh-so-delightfully sensitive human skin. "I'm not sure you're ready to hear the truth. You wouldn't understand," she murmured, her voice as sultry as a siren call.

He nipped her ear lobe then. Moved to touch his tongue to where his teeth had been. "Try me."

She clutched his arms for balance. She couldn't even remember when she'd last wanted a man to touch her like she wanted Cy Bigelow to touch her right then. But she couldn't just blurt out her real name. Or explain what she was. He wouldn't believe her. "Not yet."

He stepped back. Loosened her grip on his arms until her hands fell away. Hallie felt the loss of him like a phantom ache in a missing limb.

"Communicating is a two-way street," he said, voice tight, a pitying look on his heartbreakingly handsome features. He was angry. "You want me to share what I know about the Administration, but you won't tell me the name of the organization you supposedly work for or even who or what you really are. Until you're ready to be honest with me," he shrugged, checked his watch, and looked up at the sky, head cocked as if listening, "I guess we'll have to go our separate ways."

"I want to tell you, but it's complicated." Every part of her yearned to tell this man everything. That she'd been watching out for him, was connected to him, that she cared about him. More than she'd cared about another particular human in a long, long time. Many writers throughout history had speculated that Nemesis was not truly a goddess, but rather merely a human construct. A personification of ideas like hope and longing, retribution and revenge. Like justice. But she was real, dammit. With thoughts and emotions of her own. She was not just a vessel for others' feelings or a tool for others to wield. She was one of the earliest gods to exist in this universe, granddaughter to Kaos itself, and she was tired of not being recognized as such.

Cy took another step away from her, the space reverberating between them like an echo across a gaping chasm. Nemi felt the distance like a hand cracking through her ribcage and squeezing the muscle of her heart.

His voice was soft, but sharp-edged. "Life is complicated, Hallie. Every damn thing is hard."

Her arms fell to her sides, hands balled into fists. "I know that!" The heat in her voice scalded her throat. Of course, she knew that! Better than anyone. Better even than the rest of the gods combined. She had to understand love and hate, apathy and empathy, revenge and forgiveness, narcissistic jealousy and altruistic compassion. It was her burden to understand the whole complicated gamut of human motivations so she could deliver true justice. It wasn't just her job; it was who she was. What she was born to be. But how could she tell him that?

Then he looked up and she heard it. The thrum of a helicopter. Getting closer. Moving fast. A moment later, the wash of spinning rotors blew dust and grit into a whirlwind around them as a small four-man copter appeared overhead. They both watched, rapt, as a rope ladder snaked out of the passenger side of the open cockpit.

Cy grabbed it and put one booted foot on the bottom rung. He was drawn to Hallie Jones like an iron filling to a lodestone, but no matter who or what she was, she was hiding too much for him to trust her.

"I can't teleport," he yelled over the copter noise, "but I've usually got a handy means of escape nearby. Thanks for saving me from Ken Fucking Lane and the Administration's Gestapo. Now, it's time I make my own way." He gave the ladder a yank. "Maybe I'll see you around sometime."

Hallie shielded her eyes from the swirling dust and watched as the helicopter rose into the air, Cy dangling beneath it as he climbed the ladder as nimbly as a monkey up a tree. Despite everything, a wide smile formed on her lips as she bit back a giddy laugh.

"Orion's Belt!," she swore softly. Cy Bigelow was so more than she expected.

11

Cy climbed into his seat, clipped his seatbelt in place, and put on his headset. He gave Mason a thumbs up. "Thanks for the rescue. Glad you were at the cabin this week."

"That the woman Mat told us about?"

"The very one. We need to dig into her background. Says her name is Hallelujah Delphinium Jones."

Mason smirked. "That's a mouthful. Never knew you to need rescuing from a beautiful woman."

Cy shifted in his seat, adjusting his jeans so the waistband didn't bite into his stitches. "First time for everything, brother."

"So, who is she really, and how the hell did you get out to The Point without driving past the cabin?"

"I have no Earthly idea. Emphasis on the 'Earthly.'"

Mason turned and raised an eyebrow in question.

"I'm still trying to wrap my mind around everything that happened today, and I'd rather tell you all at once. Is Brooks still at the cabin with you?"

"Holding down the fort," Mason said with a nod. "And Mat was almost there when I left. Should be there by now."

"Why's he coming out? Figured he'd still be in Bigelow."

"We've all been busy monitoring Administration comms and gossip because shit has hit the proverbial fan."

Great. The last thing Cy needed was more shit flying in every direction since he already felt like a big steaming pile of it.

"After Mat saw you at the hotel," Mason went on, "he texted us and we pulled up the security cameras for the hotel. Saw DICE arrive. Saw you and your lady friend go *poof*. Figured it was time for a face-to-face, even if we had no idea where you were."

Mason glanced over at him. "I'm sure you remember Inez Martin."

Of course, Cy remembered her. Governor Guerrero's on-again, off-again mistress was the last woman he'd slept with, and although it had been an enjoyable physical release, she hadn't given him the information he'd wanted. "Yeah. She was a dead end on Guerrero's whereabouts."

Mason huffed out a laugh. "She's truly a dead end now. A kayaker found her body floating in the Salt River. Apparently been there awhile."

"Shit." Cy's head went back against the seat's headrest.

"They identified her by her dental records. First news reports claimed that her green card had been revoked so she'd apparently stuffed her pockets with rocks and drowned herself instead of getting deported to who knows where. But then some brave soul with a death wish —must have been a police officer or someone in the coroner's office—posted an enlarged photo of her face after it was pulled out of the water."

"And?" Cy had a bad feeling about what was coming next.

"It wasn't pretty. And, lo and behold, there was a tidy little bullet hole right between her eyes."

No wonder DICE was pounding on my door. Cy rubbed at his temples. "I made no secret of taking her up to my room that night, and everyone knows the Administration has cameras all over that hotel."

"Yeah, but remember that's why Brooks tapped into the hotel's security so we've got video of you taking her downstairs around 2 a.m. and of you leaving by yourself around 7:30 a.m."

Cy breathed a sigh of relief. His partners were the best. To the extent possible, they documented each other's whereabouts so the Administration couldn't pin any random crimes on them. Chancellor Jensen was notorious for leveling charges against or simply disappearing his political enemies for crimes his own thugs committed, and he probably got a boner every time he dreamed about taking the whole Bigelow crew down. In everyday parlance, the man was sick as fuck, and Cy and his partners did everything they could to stay out of his line of sight.

Of course, it wasn't always possible, but they tried. Luckily, they were pros at surveillance and always had each other's backs. Not only were they like brothers, but with Brooks' almost magical computer skills, Mat's experience as a Navy SEAL, and Mason's background as an FBI agent they were the perfect team. All Cy brought to the table was some scraped-together capital, the land, the old Bigelow Enterprises building and the historic hotel. And the name. And the name was probably more of a liability.

Rebuilding a business wasn't easy, but they were doing it together in the face of terrible odds, and Cy knew he couldn't do it without them. Especially since everything they were doing was illegal. At least everything they were doing below the surface.

He shook himself out of his reverie. "Any news on the missing governor?"

"No. It's like Guerrero disappeared into thin air. He's either got rocks in his pockets at the bottom of the Salt, he's rotting in the desert, or he's miraculously found a place to lay low. If that's the case, it's almost certain he had help. It's pissing me off that we still don't have a clue."

Maybe he's hanging around with Hallie Jones and her magical teleporting abilities. "Is he an official suspect?" Cy asked as he looked out the window into the darkness. Mason had his night vision goggles on, so he knew exactly where the landing pad was, but Cy was literally in the dark.

Mason shook his head. "Anything's possible, but from the chatter we're hearing, no. After Jensen practically accused the governor of treason for speaking out publicly against expanding the camps, Guerrero was under pressure to prove he was a loyal Administration soldier. If they aren't convinced, they may try to pin the murder on him whether they can find him or not. Or whether they already disposed of him or not."

"It's not healthy to suggest the Chancellor's wrong," Cy said with a disgusted snort. He trusted Mason's take. The man had gone straight from law school to the FBI academy, following in his Uncle Jimmy's footsteps. James W. Snider, a man all four boys had idolized, had been an agent and then a member of the elite FBI Hostage Rescue Team, HRT, before the FBI had been neutered and transformed into Jensen's personal national police force. Uncle Jimmy had been fired in the weeks after the Quiet Coup, in Chancellor Jensen's first purge of government employees. His offense was refusing to sign a loyalty oath. Mason had turned in his gold shield the next day, and both men had returned to Bigelow disgusted, angry, and ready to fight back.

Cy immediately offered Mason a stake in Bigelow Enterprises and Uncle Jimmy signed on as a trainer for anyone who wanted to know how to hold their own in a fight. Or jump out of an airplane. Or pilot a helicopter. Brooks, for his part, had been a partner for years, ever since he quit his engineering PhD program when his project's grant funding was cut and his advisor was arrested. And, of course, Mat joined the team not long after Mason. He'd completed his six-year commitment to the SEALS and was planning to reup when his commanding officer ordered him to sign the same loyalty oath to Chancellor Jensen that Mason and Uncle Jimmy had refused to sign.

In typical Mat fashion, he slapped his completed separation paperwork down on his CO's desk, offered the man a crisp salute, and told him to go fuck himself. And everyone thought Mat was the sweet one. Ha. His friends knew better.

Whereas Cy could be a little high-handed and imperious, always thinking he knew what was best for everyone, Mason was often too serious and overthought every decision, and Brooks was cocky and irreverent with a vocabulary that encompassed all manner of scatological and physiological impossibilities, Mat was as polite as you could get with all the *Yes, ma'ams* and *No sirs* that all the girls' mothers always loved. Plus, he had the face of an angel. Maybe a fallen angel, but still. Mat never had a problem getting a woman's attention, but now, his striking good looks and long hair had women in Bigelow swooning. After he'd said goodbye to the SEALS, he'd let his hair grow out in honor of all the men with Mexican or indigenous roots who'd served in the military, like his father, and who'd been deported or treated like a second-class citizens anyway.

Shortly after they'd teamed up to run the company, they were recruited as members of the American Resistance Movement by two others they only knew by code names: Chiron and Artemis. And how amazing was that, they thought, since they'd all devoured books about the mythology of the heroes and gods of the ancient world.

Even though things had looked bleak for the country, they'd toasted the future out on The Point, just like they'd done back when they were boys, spending weekends at the remote Bigelow Homestead and calling themselves The Four Musketeers. One for all and all for one. It'd been a joke when they were little, fencing with sticks and jousting with broken mesquite branches. Now it was real. Now it was life and death.

The family business may have been wrecked by his father's profligate spending and bad investments, but the four men were determined to build it anew. The cotton and cattle were long gone, and the mines had been shut down even before they'd been born, but Bigelow Enterprises still owned the two buildings downtown, the original homestead cabin, the family estate where Sybil and Cy had grown up, and the land and mineral rights upon which the original Bigelow fortune had built.

And although everyone believed the mines were exhausted, they weren't. That was one of the biggest secret the Four Musketeers protected. Bigger even than being involved in the Resistance. Chancellor Harold Jensen was obsessed with controlling every mine in the country. It was a matter of state security, he claimed. He'd hold press conferences and rant on and on about how modern economies and modern militaries needed the metals and minerals laying beneath American soil, and that he had the right to commandeer anything the Administration needed. And anyone who stood in the way was a traitor.

That's why he had his eye on Bigelow Enterprises and its four partners. To Jensen and his cronies, especially those industrialists in the Diamond Dome Consortium, it didn't make sense that the copper mines that had powered the American industrial revolution were tapped out. He was right, but no way Cy and his partners were going to admit it. Fuck Harold Jensen. And fuck all his rapacious billionaire buddies too.

They weren't about to bend the knee, even if the asshole was the world's first multi-trillionaire. None of them could understand how anyone could respect the man, let alone worship him as if he were some genius of unprecedented historical import. Besides, Jensen was a repulsive pig of a man who, along with his hair plugs, impressive paunch, and ego the size of the whole fucking outdoors, had a virtual harem of wives and lovers who'd produced enough children for his own personal army. It was medieval. Like the worst of the sultans from the ancient Ottoman Empire had been reincarnated and reinvented as the paragon of modern manhood.

They'd all spoken up publicly back when the First Amendment still meant something. Now, talk like that resulted in a hood over the head, handcuffs and leg irons, and a trip to ... well, no one knew exactly where. Nowhere good. Probably nowhere with oxygen.

As a result, their actions were thoroughly scrutinized, and Cy, as CEO of Bigelow Enterprises, was repeatedly threatened with arrest or blacklisting, which meant all sorts of dire outcomes, all of them bloody and most of them permanent.

Mason brought the bird down with a soft landing, turned off the rotors, and took off his headset. He looked over at his friend, narrowed his eyes. "You look terrible."

Cy drew in a breath and let it out with a harsh laugh. "It's been a helluva day."

"Mat told us about the stitches too. Still don't remember how you got them?"

"I don't remember a thing, although our mysterious Hallie Jones insists the man who did the slicing and dicing was none other than our old friend Ken Fucking Lane."

"Christ. I fucking hate that guy." Mason unbuckled his seat belt. "Let's get inside, and you can tell us all about it."

12

Asklepios, or Dr. A to many of his friends, looked up when Nemi appeared in the middle of his courtyard. He gave her a nod and a welcoming smile and then went back to crushing mint leaves in his mortar and pestle. The fragrance was soothing and made Nemi crave a cup of hot tea. Although Asklepios had been teaching medicine at University of Cambridge, under one name or another, for over a thousand years and had his own lab with state-of-the-art equipment, he still liked to do some things the old-fashioned way.

"I take it you got my newfound brother home safe and sound?"

"At 36 years old, he's hardly new." Nemi picked up a cup from a small serving table and dipped it into the courtyard's central fountain, burbling happily and providing an everlasting source of pure water. "I just stopped by to see what you thought of him."

"Considering he was unconscious most of the time he was here, we're hardly bosom buddies." The healer added more mint leaves. "I do find it invigorating to discover a new family member, though."

"Nyx hasn't produced any offspring in millennia, thankfully. I've got all the siblings a goddess needs."

"Yes, well, you're not a half breed like me and Cyrus Horatio Bigelow." He shrugged.

"You may have been born a half-breed, but since Zeus killed and resurrected you, you're as godly as the rest of us."

"That killing part was no fun, you know." Asklepios set his pestle aside. "And I had to promise not to bring any more humans back to life."

"Probably shouldn't have been doing that in the first place," Nemi said with a crooked smile. Then she paused, shuffled her feet. "What about Cy?" She tried not to be too obvious in her interest. "Do you think he could be immortal?"

"I admit I am curious about that myself. I've got DNA from when he was bleeding all over my examination table, so I was thinking I could run some tests."

Nemi stilled. Could Cy be immortal? If so, would that mean they could…? Was it possible…? Did she dare hope that…?

He glanced up. "How are his stitches holding up?"

She blinked. "They seemed fine. A little tender."

"The wound was already beginning to knit itself back together by the time you got him here, so I'd say the odds are good for immortality. Or at least for a very long lifespan." He watched Nemi's expression, her emotions moving over her face like she would never allow around mortals. "You were here and gone before I got the chance to ask if my father knows he's got another son."

Nemi swallowed and brought her attention back to her old friend. "I don't think so. I did discover Cy was conceived in Delphi. His mother was an archaeologist and, well, you know how it goes on Apollo's home turf." She shrugged. "Cy has no idea what he is."

"You mean beyond rich and handsome?"

Nemi laughed and then finished her water. "Not so rich anymore, but beyond that, yes."

"You want me to tell Apollo?"

"Maybe," Nemi said. "But not yet. I don't want him to show up and start trying to interfere in his son's life. Or his twin sister's. And Cy has a daughter. She's seven. The last thing they need is a bunch of long-lost family members arriving on their doorstep. Especially our kind of family. I'm not sure any human needs that. Especially when the poor guy's already got trouble on his hands."

Asklepios straightened. "Trouble how? Besides getting gutted like a fish, I mean."

"He's and his friends are involved with the American Resistance Movement. Chiron and Artemis's pet project."

"Working to undermine that pig Jensen?"

"Yes. That's why I'm back on Earth to begin with." She waved a hand as if to encompass the whole world. "As usual, I've been called in to try to help clean up a mess and hold people accountable."

"I fucking hate politics." Asklepios rarely cursed, so Nemi arched a brow at him. " How many times do we have to go through the same damn thing? What's the saying? History doesn't repeat itself, but it rhymes. Well, I think it's pathetic poetry written by weak, small-minded men, and I'm sick and tired of it."

"I couldn't agree more. Humans are exhausting."

"And yet we love them." He rolled his eyes. "Only the gods know why."

"We love some of them, at least," Nemi said with a laugh. "Anyway, Cy's involved up to his eyebrows, and I want to get a better feel for what's going on with him before we bring in the big guns. He deserves a fair warning, and your father has never been known for subtlety."

"It's Auntie Artemis and her temper that you have to worry about. My father may be the god of archery, but Apollo's just as likely to show up with a lyre in his hands and a tune on his lips, determined to soothe the world with a song, a poem, or a turn around the dance floor." He picked up the mortar and scraped the crushed leaves into a glass pitcher. "As the Brits might say, dear old dad can be a bit barmy." He made a show of looking up at the sky. "Sorry, but you know it's true."

Nemi set her cup down, looked around the beautiful courtyard at the center of Asklepios's Cambridge estate. "Go ahead and test his DNA. Given that someone just tried to murder him, it'd be good to know what he's really made of."

He cocked his head at her, seeing more than she was comfortable with. But what could she do? As one of her favorite people, Asklepios had always been able to read her. He turned and leaned up against his worktable. "I'll let you know as soon as the tests are done."

"You're the best. Now I best be off."

"You sure you don't want a mojito? I have fresh mint."

"Thanks, but I need to touch base with the Furies."

"Give them my love," he said. But Nemi was already gone.

13

When Nemi arrived, the Furies were watching an array of large screens mounted on the walls of their Pantheon League command-and-control center. More like a luxurious living room / movie screening room, Nemi thought of it as FAFO HQ. After all, despite their vaunted titles, they were all, essentially, the goddesses of Fuck Around and Find Out. Set up in the basement of the compound the three sisters—Ali, Meg, and Tisi—shared in Georgetown, conveniently close to the epicenter of Administration activities, they were watching Chancellor Jensen's annual American Christmas Extravaganza.

"You're just in time to see the lineup," Meg quipped, conjuring a glass of red wine and handing it to Nemi. "Besides the coats and ridiculous hats, Jensen's buddies all look like they're about to get their mug shots taken."

"Maybe because they're all criminals?" Tisi said with a disgusted huff of laughter.

Nemi took the wine and plopped down on the sofa next to Meg as the Chancellor's honored guests filed onto the front row of a viewing platform bedecked in thick garlands, red bows, twinkling lights, and dozens of American flags fluttering in the soft breeze. "Thank Kaos it's a mild day for mid-December. Although, I wouldn't care a whit if all those men died of hypothermia, it wouldn't be great for the performers and guests forced to attend."

"Are they forced to attend?" Meg asked. "Did someone put a gun to their heads? Or are they all going along to get along like happy little mindless sheep. Performing with smiles on their faces for the Fuhrer and his Friends while millions die or disappear."

Nemi raised a brow at her friend. "You're in a mood."

"We all are." Tisi waved at the bank of screens all tuned and merged to the same feed so the figures on the wall were larger than life. "Just look at Jensen posing in the middle of that ... what do you call them? Team of Tyrants? Retinue of Rulers? Delegation of Despots? Kaos, it reminds me of the old Soviet Politburo all lined up near the Lenin Mausoleum on Red Square." Tisi glanced over at Ali. "I'm glad you volunteered to go to Moscow last week. I hate that place. It's so dreary in winter."

"The last time that place wasn't dreary was when Catherine was in charge." Meg said. "She was a hoot."

"A hoot." Nemi nudged her shoulder into Meg's. "Is that what we're calling her now?"

"Well, she was a hell of a lot better leader than this crop of criminals. There's not a man among them worth his salt."

Nemi held her glass up in a mock toast. "Can't argue with that."

Jensen had taken to inviting his "kindred spirits" to D.C. in mid-December to enjoy his week-long pre-Christmas holiday extravaganza designed to mark the end of yet another year with him at America's helm, bravely and boldly steering the ship of state through treacherous seas into the glorious, shining future of peace and prosperity just waiting somewhere out there on the horizon. Oh, and also to celebrate the birth of Jesus Christ, his much talked about Personal Lord and Savior even as his troops are disappearing entire families. The leaders he invited and considered his bosom buddies were men just like him, tyrants who spent their days hoarding wealth and exploiting natural resources—including starving, poverty-stricken humans bought and sold on the GLE, the Global Labor Exchange. Of course, the leaders called it Maximizing Employment Across Nations For The Benefit Of All Economies," but Nemi and the Furies recognized involuntary indentured servitude when they saw it. GLE was just a shorter way of saying SLAVERY.

"It's like Circus Maximus," Meg groused. "I keep waiting for a *pollice verso* on a gladiatorial combat between the leaders' servile henchmen."

"Or between all those old men themselves," Ali said. "Imagine the Chancellor in a toga."

Tisi gagged and made a vomiting gesture. "Gross. Still, I'd watch. Every single one of those men deserves a thumbs up on the ultimate punishment. No mercy."

"They're going to get what they deserve." Nemi had a determined gleam in her eyes. "We're not going to rest until they do." She stretched out her legs and propped her feet up on the ottoman with a groan. It'd been a long day for her human body. "The question is how we're going to pull it off without causing even more chaos and carnage."

"I wish we could just smite them all and be done with it," Meg grumbled. "This latest breakout of measles has killed thousands of children in the last six months, and have you seen the numbers on polio and cholera? Cholera for Kaos's sake! I'm just surprised the Bubonic Plague hasn't made a comeback."

"That's what comes from banning vaccines. And rejecting science." Tisi said.

"That's what comes from being heartless bastards," Nemi added. "Dr. A could teach them a thing or two. I just came from his place, by the way. He used profanity. Twice."

All three sets of sisterly eyebrows shot up. "He never curses. Too much of a gentleman."

"I know." Nemi took another sip of wine, thinking she didn't mind a bit of cursing. In fact, she quite liked it and felt like some serious profanity was the only way to sum up the situation humans had gotten themselves into.

I've rarely known Asklepios to be in such a bad mood," Tisi said. Of the four friends, she had the foulest mouth. And the most tattoos, which was easy because the other goddesses had none. "Maybe at Trier or Bamberg. Or Nuremberg."

"It's the high cost of immortality," Ali said. "We keep watching the same shitty behavior over and over again. I don't blame him if he's ready to burn it all down."

"I get it too but burning it all down hurts the innocents more than the despots. They just dance in the rubble and blame the conflagration on the devil." As the goddess of vengeance, Nemi knew better than anyone that holding people accountable was a tricky business. When gods took matters into their own hands, things could go south very quickly. "Too many unexplained events and half the population of the planet is going to think it's the Second Coming. Then, watch out. Kaos only knows what kind of madness we'd unleash."

"Rapture smapture," Tisi snorted. "Between whatever John the Elder was smoking and John Darby was drinking, that bit of apocalyptic mumbo jumbo is going to get millions killed one of these days."

"It already has." Meg shook her head in disgust. "I wonder what Jesus would say if he knew his words were being twisted, again, into an excuse for slavery, oppression, and genocide. Again. Just like the fucking Crusades."

"Poor guy." Ali sighed. "I still think his lack of immortality was tragic. Son of the Dying and Resurrected God and yet poof. One spear to the kidneys and he's dead as a doornail. And all those people out there still waiting for his return."

Nemi looked around and whispered. "Dio's not here, is he?"

"No." Ali shook her head. "He went home this morning to check on something or other. Said he'd be back tomorrow."

"Remember Jesus's Sermon on the Mount?" Meg said. "We all had such hope for him. Especially Dio. Feeding all those people with just a few fish and only a basket or two of bread was such a Dio move."

"And turning water into wine at that wedding at Cana was definitely a trick he learned from his father," Tisi said. "Healing the sick and entertaining children wherever he went. And taking in that poor woman when everyone else treated her like shit. You can recite all the parables you want, model kindness all day long, and show humans a dozen 'miracles,' and they'll still twist your words to suit their own ends."

Nemi frowned. She knew Atropos had lamented doing her duty when Dionysos begged her to let his son live. But as one of the Moirai, "She Who Cannot Be Turned," she could not turn away from cutting a thread of life at the foreordained time. Even the thread of a beloved demigod. *No one can change his destiny,* she'd said as one of the Romans plunged that spear into Jesus's side. Spinning life threads, determining their length, and cutting them at the pre-determined time meant that the Fates were goddesses of death as well as life. It was not a pleasant existence and the responsibility of it all had worn the three down to mere shadows of themselves. More wraiths than gods. Being a god was not all it was cracked up to be.

"Still, Jesus tried to do good in the short time he had." Ali waved a hand at the main screen. "That, on the other hand, is what happens when bad men, no matter how gifted or talented, are worshiped like gods. Men who think they can do no wrong. Men who set themselves up to be followed by the masses with blind faith. Dangerous as vipers, every last one of them. But that's exactly what the Chancellor wants. To be worshiped like Jesus and feared like a poisonous snake."

"Albeit without the being nailed to a cross part," Meg added.

"Or the speared by a soldier part." Tisi frowned in disgust. "Remember when Harold Jensen threw himself to the ground like a scared toddler when a bird flew overhead during that speech on the Mall? So embarrassing. The only thing he's truly good at is convincing other people to hand over their money."

"And their freedom." Ali added.

"And their first born," Meg chimed in. "Well, technically, all their children. Membership in the Chancellor's Youth Brigade is now automatically conferred upon every child when they reach the age of ten, and indoctrination in the glorious precepts of the 'New America' begins in preschool."

"Are we sure he's not a demigod?" Nemi asked. Cy might have had demigod vibes rolling off him in waves, but not all of them did. Personally, she wondered if Eris wasn't lurking somewhere in Chancellor Jensen's family tree. It'd been her petty jealousy and that damnable golden apple that caused Athena, Hera, and Aphrodite to go at each other and eventually sweep all the Greeks into that dreadful war in Troy. So maybe she was behind this mess now too. If so, that made everything personal. Eris had always seen herself as the dark to Nemi's light, her penchant for chaos the opposite to Nemi's desire for order. They might be sisters, both daughters born of Nyx alone, but they were also opposing forces and their outlook on the world couldn't be more distinct.

As the idea began to take shape in Nemi's mind, her unease grew. Without their mother's power, none of Nyx's children could give birth to gods, but that hadn't prevented Eris from giving birth to countless imps and daemons and other assorted malevolent spirits. She thrived on preying on weak minds and sowing discord. If she was behind this mess, things could easily go from bad to worse. Her sister did not cause mischief out of any desire other than to cause mischief. And although she often hung out with Ares, she had no attachments to humans or any other creatures, but rather simply enjoyed the power of planting ideas in people's minds, pulling puppet strings, whispering in willing ears, and then watching what happened next. And if any of her minions chose to get involved and spin webs of deception or lure men into traps from which they could not escape, she wouldn't stop them. She would simply sit back and enjoy the show.

Ali sat forward. "The Chancellor is parading his kids out before the adoring crowds. Incredible. They're wearing matching costumes. This feels like North Korea or something. By the Seven Sisters, this is embarrassing. What year are we in?"

Meg shielded her eyes as if looking at the screen was painful. "Feels like about 970."

Nemi cut her a sideways glance. "We talking BCE or CE?"

"BCE. Remember Solomon and his 700 wives and 300 concubines, all pushing out babies at alarming rates? With his obsession with fertility rates and depopulation, I think the Chancellor's trying to outdo him." Meg groaned and rubbed her temples. "Wants to repopulate the Earth with his own seed."

"Stop!" Tisi put her hands over her ears. "Any talk of that ridiculous man's *seed* makes me picture, you know, him *doing* it, and that really is going to make me vomit."

Meg laughed. "I wonder if he takes off his fake hair."

"It's not fake anymore," Ali said. "He got hair plugs."

"Oh, vanity, thy name is Harold Jensen," Meg shuddered.

"How many children does he have now?" Nemi asked. "And does he have multiple wives too? And concubines? Like Solomon?"

Ali shook her head in disgust. "Divorce is against the law unless the husband initiates it, but having multiple wives is now perfectly legal. As far as kids go, there's probably some sort of royal registry. The man thinks he rules the world from on high like his own private kingdom."

"I still think massive amounts of money causes an epigenetic mutation in the brain," Tisi said with a wave of her wine glass. "I told Dr. A he should study that. Give him something productive to do."

Nemi raised a brow. "Training doctors and teaching medicine isn't productive?"

"He could do that in his sleep. He needs a new challenge."

"Right." Nemi laughed. "Be sure to tell him that next time you see him."

Nemi swirled the deep red wine in her glass. How had everything on Earth gone so far off course? Hadn't millions of humans recently died in two world wars and countless regional skirmishes over the right to govern themselves? Hadn't trillions of dollars been wasted on death and destruction? Hadn't democracy and equality been ascendant just a few decades ago? Oh, she knew there were still good, honorable people fighting for freedom from tyranny. People like Cy Bigelow and his friends. But they weren't winning. That was crystal clear from the spectacle playing out on the screen, a spectacle more ridiculous than one of those old sword and sandals movies they liked to watch. *Cleopatra. Spartacus. Hercules. Exodus.* Casts of thousands parading around in costumes designed to show off ample bosoms, muscled chests, and strong thighs. Those were fun. This was not. She wouldn't be surprised if the Chancellor appeared in public with a solid gold laurel crown on his head.

"Oh, look at that!" Ali said. "They're gonna sing and dance. Like in that movie based on that family. Remember? Where the Nazi has his kids sing to his dinner guests?"

"The von Trapps." Nemi said. "Remember, he didn't end up being a Nazi after all. In the movie he ripped the flag apart and even in real life, he got the nice girl in the end. Wanna turn up the volume. See if they're any good?"

Meg shook her head and put her hands over her ears. "No! I can't take it."

Still, Ali turned up the volume, and they watched the dozens of children fathered by the world's richest man sing and dance on the National Mall like little marionettes, as if their strings were being pulled by their own father. Which they probably were. Men like him felt the need to secure their line and prove their masculinity by putting their mark on everything. Like animals marking territory with urine and scat.

The whole event was a grotesquerie of narcissistic self-indulgence, but the gods couldn't just descend from on high and take over. That wasn't the way things worked. Humans were complicated and none of the gods—not even the high and mighty Zeus—were equipped to rule them like overlords. No. It was up to the humans—albeit, with a godly assist here and there—to solve human problems. Maybe that's why they never got solved.

Nemi took another sip of wine, settled back into her chair, and turned her thoughts to Cy Bigelow. She had the feeling he was the key. Or at least one of the keys. He was a man with unknown abilities and untapped strengths. Wealthy, yes, but not obscenely so, and not a man to hoard gold like a dragon in his lair. Unlike the Chancellor, and all his toadies. Cy was willing to share his fortune, to do good with it. For his friends and family, yes. But for his employees and for the people in Bigelow too. And he was obviously willing to put his body on the line if he was working with the Resistance.

She thought about Cy's strengths. The strength of his arms beneath her fingers. The breadth of his shoulders. His breath on her skin. The almost kiss. The absence of his warmth when he'd stepped away. And the challenging look on his face as he'd grabbed that rope ladder.

She could hardly wait to see what he did next.

14

Brooks, Mat, and Mason all stared at Cy as he finished his Unbelievable Tale of the Day's Misadventures and finally leaned back in his chair and closed his eyes with a long exhale.

"And that, my friends, is why my head aches, my stitches throb, and my brain is fried." He opened one eye to gauge their reactions, saw Mat get up to poke at the embers burning low in the oversized stone fireplace.

The cabin had always been more like home than even the estate in Bigelow or his penthouse at the hotel where he and Mat had across-the-hall top-floor apartments with gorgeous balcony views, Cy's looking out on the mountains and Mat's looking down into town and the valley below. While Mason lived in his parents' old refurbished historic house on the edge of town and Brooks had converted the top floor of the Bigelow Enterprises building into a loft, they all thought of the cabin as their refuge.

It was the original homestead built by Cy's great-great-grandfather and rebuilt by Cy's father back when he was spending money like he had an endless supply. It had always been a place where Cy and Sybil could take their friends to hang out, use as a home base for camping under the stars, and for doing stupid things like rappelling down cliffs after a late night of drinking.

Actually, Sybil had never had many friends and the ones she did have would have never done that last bit. In fact, she and BoJo, her best friend since childhood, had spent most of their time at the Bigelow Estate. Being around all that testosterone hadn't interested BoJo, and Sybil had her own issues hanging around her brother's friends.

With four bedrooms and en-suite baths, the cabin and its forty-acre home site had been transformed into a highly secure facility equipped with the most cutting-edge surveillance-blocking technology available, a landing site for a helicopter and a barn in which to store it out of sight, a stable with six horses tended by Manuel, a full-time groom, and his wife Annabelle who worked as the housekeeper. There were also two full-time security guards, Hank and Tomas. The staff lived in small well-equipped cabins on the property and were unswervingly loyal to Cy who had done his damnedest to keep Bigelow Enterprises afloat to protect those at risk of deportation.

"Teleporting," Brooks said, playing with the label on his beer bottle. He was the one with the engineering degrees and the multiple tattoos. Electronics, computers, programming, surveillance, fixing old mechanical equipment, he could do it all. Or knew someone who could. And who could be trusted. "It's just not possible. The technology doesn't exist."

"And yet ..." Cy offered an exhausted one-shouldered shrug.

"Buddy, I don't know what the hell happened, but you know as well as I do that teleportation is pure science fiction."

"And yet, I met Ken Fucking Lane for a drink and then somehow woke up in my bedroom with a bellyful of stitches and a hazy memory of ... a man with a British accent stitching me up somewhere? Then Hallie and I were eating in the Saguaro Room, DICE thugs showed up, and then we were suddenly back in my bedroom. Then they start banging at my door and, *voila*, we're out here at our old camping spot. Where she claimed she helped us drag your sorry ass up to safety all those years ago."

"I remember that day like it just happened," Mat said, looking at Brooks. "I mean, I was on leave from fucking SEAL training and was scared absolutely shitless when your weight on the rope uprooted that tree. It's one thing to go through hell in training and expect shit to come at you out of the blue, but it's another to have one of your best friends suddenly start going down on a day when you're specifically trying not to be on high alert. The tree went sideways, then started sliding across the ground toward the edge, taking rock and dirt with it like a big fucking broom. You called out something ridiculous like *Hey guys? I'm going down!* Trying to keep your cool as you slid down the cliff face. Cy, you disappeared over the edge like some freaking Spiderman, and Mason and I grabbed the tree and the rope before it all slithered over the edge and ... shit."

"And then that guy was suddenly there," Mason piped up, setting his empty beer bottle on the floor beside his chair. "Like he just appeared out of thin air. Always did think it was strange that he just happened to be so close. But he helped us save you both, and I guess we were all so hungover and hyped up on fear and adrenalin that none of us thought to question it. Like, where the hell was his truck? None of us even thought to look that gift horse in the mouth."

"Hallie Jones says 'it's just a matter of physics,' as if it's all some goddamn joke. As if it's perfectly natural that she's some freaking magical time-traveling shapeshifter like in those weird novels Sybil and BoJo devour like candy. Vampires, and werewolves, and witches, oh, my! Like some fucked up *Wizard of Oz* with hot sex thrown in on the side."

"Whoa, if there's hot sex, maybe I should read one," Brooks said with a snort. "I'm in a bit of a dry spell."

Mason drummed his fingers on the arm of his chair and pinned Cy with a penetrating look. "The question is, is hot sex on the menu for you and this Hallie person? You two were standing awfully close when I arrived at The Point."

"Christ." Cy laughed and drew in a breath. "If you must know, I told her straight out there's no way in hell I could buy the idea of her being that forest ranger because I wanted to fuck her as soon as I saw her, and I had zero thoughts of fucking that guy. Z.E.R.O." He pointed at Brooks with his beer bottle. "Even if he did help save your bony butt."

"And?" Mason said, "What'd she say?"

"She got offended! Like I'd insulted her somehow. Basically, took me to school on how an individual's worth and desirability is not tied to their gender. And what can you say to that? It's nothing I don't believe. But it also has nothing to do with who I, personally, want to fuck." He raked a hand down his face. "She's basically confusing and infuriating. And—"

"She's gotten under your skin," Mat quipped.

Cy shuddered. "As long as she's not *in* my skin."

Mason snorted, picked up his empty beer bottle. "So, what now?"

"We haven't talked about Jensen's Christmas shindig," Brooks said. "You still planning to fly out tomorrow?"

Cy grimaced. "One doesn't turn down an 'invitation' from the Chancellor himself, but I sure as hell wish he'd invite one of you jokers instead of always targeting me."

"None of us are nearly as pretty as you are," Brooks said with a laugh. "We may be Bigelow partners, but we're not Bigelows."

"Well, I'm just glad I didn't have to be there for whatever ridiculous show he put on for the opening ceremony. Mat and I will head out tomorrow afternoon and get checked into the hotel. Get a decent night's rest so we're ready for Monday. I think you two should stay here and do some more digging into what's going on down at SDIC, how deep Ken Lane is in it, and where the hell the governor disappeared to. Also find whatever you can on Inez Martin's murder and anything you can dig up on the mysterious Hallie Jones."

"After today's excitement, I'd like to make sure Helen and Kemal are on board with being backup, just in case," Mat said. Cy nodded in agreement and Mat pulled out his phone and started texting.

"I turned on the opening ceremony and then promptly turned it off." Brooks's lips twisted with scorn. "Jensen had his gazillion kids out there singing his praises like little Yes-Daddy-We Love-You-Daddy-automatons. Dressed in matching outfits. It was creepy as all hell."

"How can he be so weird and so revered at the same time?" Cy rubbed the back of his neck and sighed. "Sometimes I wish old Cyrus Horatio the First had stuck to ranching and never tried his hand at mining. Never found the motherload of copper deposits."

"But then you wouldn't be a near-bankrupt mining baron and need us to save your ass every other day," Brooks said with a laugh. "And how would we keep ourselves occupied?"

Although they were from very different backgrounds, the four men had grown up together in Bigelow, best friends through thick and thin. Brooks had moved to town when they were in middle school, but the others had been thick as thieves since preschool. The four musketeers. Or desperados. Or superheroes. Depending on the mood.

After his mother died with face-full of cake and blood, Cy's father had gone dark. He'd ignored his kids, and had wanted to send the twins back East to hoity-toity private schools, but Cy had refused. Sybil didn't put up much of a fight since she floated through life in her own world regardless of where she was, her surroundings barely registering, the people around barely touching her. But Cy wouldn't leave the boys he thought of as brothers. He couldn't imagine going on without them after losing his mom, so he played the guilt card. With aplomb. *Don't send us away, Daddy. Sybil will be lonely all on her own. Mommy wouldn't have wanted us to be separated.*

Luckily, their father had given up arguing, and eventually he had, for all intents and purposes, given up being on parenting. So, they'd all been raised, more or less, by Mat's mom who was the Bigelow Estate Manager. She was loyal to Cy and Sybil, and they were loyal to her—and to their friends. And when their father had died on some ski slope in Switzerland and Cy and Sybil had inherited everything, Mrs. Cárdenas had been the glue that held them all together.

For better or worse, they all belonged to Bigelow and to Arizona. To each other and to Mrs. C. The land and the people were in their blood, and they'd do everything they could to protect both. That's why Cy had to go sit in a room with some of the most amoral, murderous men humanity had ever produced. The company's land holdings made them all prime targets—for Jensen either to *win* over or *take* over. And to make sure neither of those things happened, they all had to play the game. But as CEO of the company, Cy was the one who had to do it most often and in public.

Mason yawned extravagantly, "I don't know about you guys, but this day has worn me out." He checked his watch. After midnight. "Brooks, I'll check in with Hank and Tomas if you double check all our security systems. Let's reconvene in the morning before Cy and Mat head to D.C."

"Let me look at those stitches, before lights out," Mat said as Cy stretched out his back with a wince. "Last thing we need is you with an infected wound. Then one of us would have to put on a monkey suit and go perform for the chancellor."

"Holy hell." Cy flinched as Mat pressed a gauze pad to the line of his stitches.

Mat rolled his eyes. "Quit whining, you big baby."

"Then stop trying to nurse me. I can do it myself and, besides, the stitches are healing fine."

"Better than fine." Mat kept dabbing at Cy's abdomen. "You've always healed faster than anyone I've ever known, but we still have to keep this sterilized to prevent infection."

"I've never had an infection in my life."

"There's always a first time." Mat turned and tossed the gauze in the trash. "Face it, buddy. You're a freak of nature." He replaced the cap on the bottle of alcohol and twisted it closed. "Emphasis on the freak."

Cy gave Mat a light punch in the arm then picked up his shirt and tossed it over the back of a chair. He plopped down and pulled off his boots, tossed them aside. Looked up as Mat headed toward the door.

Hand on the knob, Mat turned back. "You need anything else before I crash?"

"You saw her," Cy said. "In the Saguaro Room. Did anything about her strike you as off?"

Mat leaned back against the door. "Movie star gorgeous. But somehow still seemed approachable. An air of ... something ... about her. Like one of those people who walks into the room, and everyone stops talking. You just know something's different about them, but they don't seem like assholes." Mat snorted. "Sort of what a lot of people say about you, you know."

"I can't teleport though. More's the pity."

"Maybe she's an android or something. An AI robot. Maybe we've stumbled into some sort of alternate timeline. Or we're just realizing we're in the matrix."

Cy let his body sink into the chair. God, he was tired. Bone tired. Brain tired. But as wired as if he'd stuck a fork tine in an electrical socket. "Doesn't explain the teleporting because I'm pretty sure *I'm* not a robot."

"What'd it feel like?"

"Like ... I don't know. Disorienting. Like I'd been taken apart and put back together again. I was actually weak in the knees." He huffed out a laugh. "Like a fifth of tequila weak. Almost fell over when we ended up at The Point. Right there where we'd had so many good times." He inhaled a long breath and let it out. "I don't think I've ever told anyone about that place. It's *ours*. Like a secret clubhouse." He laughed at himself.

Mat nodded, a smile tipping up one side of his mouth. "And yet she somehow landed you right there."

"Seems impossible. And that business about the forest ranger? Jesus. I don't know what to think about that." Cy raked his hands down his face and stood. "Well, we might as well get some sleep. We're not going to find answers here tonight."

"Unless your mystery woman shows up in your bedroom."

"Maybe she's a genie, and I just need to rub a magic lamp to conjure her."

Mat barked out a laugh. "I have a feeling a lamp isn't what you'll be rubbing tonight."

A knowing smile bloomed on Cy's face. "Maybe if I say my bedtime prayers..."

"So, she's an answer to your prayers now, is she? A dream come true." Mat waggled his brows.

More like a wet dream.

Mat waved an arm toward the bed. "Best be gettin' down on your knees, then." And with that, he slipped out of the room leaving Cy with a ridiculous grin on his face as he pictured himself down on his knees with Hallie Jones's legs draped across his shoulders.

15

Nemesis showed her credentials to the Security Service gatekeepers and waited for the facial recognition software to confirm her identity. After the software dinged its confirmation, the SS agent ushered her into the high-resolution wave scanner to ensure she carried no hidden weapons. She dutifully raised her arms, keeping her body loose and confident even as she tried to keep the anticipation off her face.

Once she was completely cleared, she made her way up the blue sodalite marble staircase and into the Chancellor's Gallery, a round balcony situated above a main conference room and equipped with plush red velvet stadium seating sweeping up to a domed ceiling painted with historical scenes—a panorama of world-changing events leading right up to the moment Harold Jensen placed his hand on his family Bible and pledged himself to his country.

Today she was Mr. Alexander Whitelaw, CEO of Wave-Form Technologies, a secretive privately held company developing next-generation quantum computing and communications systems. Of course, Mr. Whitelaw, a tall, broad-shouldered, ruggedly handsome billionaire, existed only on paper—or rather in the digital world, which Tisi had hacked right down to its bytes and bones.

Despite the worry that she'd give off goddess vibes that someone might detect—especially if her sister Eris or any of her minions were lurking about—Nemi had decided to attend the opening session Chancellor Jensen's "Celebration of an American Christmas" in human guise. She needed to get close enough to see if Jensen *felt* like a demigod. And to see for herself exactly how Jensen, his buddies from abroad, and his Administration sycophants operated. Taking on a human aspect meant she could sit with other invited guests and overhear, or even be included in, nearby conversations. She could monitor it all as a wisp of air, like she'd done down at SDIC when Cy was laid out on the operating table, or through Tisi's systems from the comfort of FAFO HQ since she'd bugged the entire building, but being there "in the flesh" was preferable for the moment.

Plus, because Tisi had accessed the "invitation list," she knew one of those attendees would be none other than Cy Bigelow. And, feeling more than just a tiny bit mischievous—something she'd never admit to the Furies—she'd taken on the exact same male aspect she'd used that time she'd appeared as a forest ranger and helped pull Cy's friend Brooks to safety.

After what Cy had said about wanting to fuck Hallie Jones at first sight and *not* wanting to fuck the forest ranger *ever*, she'd decided to conduct a small experiment. Overall, human sexual desire was, in her considerable experience, better characterized as falling along a bell curve or a vast spectrum than as a binary choice, and she was more than a little curious to find out where the demigod son of Apollo fell. Despite what he said. Besides, the poor man had been so appalled at the idea of sex with that ranger, she was, quite honestly, eager to play a trick on him. She smiled. There was no helicopter or ladder to swoop in and rescue him from an awkward situation today.

A tingle of awareness danced along her spine, and, to her delight, she spied Cy on the other side of the horseshoe-shaped gallery. She quickly took a seat exactly opposite his and wondered how long it would take him to notice her or if he'd recognize her from all those years ago. And, if so, how he would react. She knew it was due to her human endocrine system, but despite where she was and why she was really there, she hadn't been this entertained in ... well, maybe in forever.

Cy filed in with a stream of other attendees and found a seat in the viewing gallery. The balcony was situated above the circular conference room in which the symbolically round conference table sat in the center. The Chancellor's Cabinet. The heart of American democracy. Yeah, right.

Since the new Constitution had denuded the president, the vice president, and both houses of Congress of any real power, this was where, supposedly, debate happened, and decisions were made. In reality, decisions were made in the Chancellor's head where Cy suspected there wasn't any debate at all. He doubted there was anything other than greed, lust, and a good dose of self-absorption lurking in the dark recesses of Harold Jensen's mind.

Some of the men in attendance—and they were all men—did have a modicum of influence on a regional or industry sector level, but once Harold Jensen spoke, that was it.

Cy had attended these types of events for the past five years, always coming when the Chancellor called, and he knew that what he was about to observe today was theater. Nothing more. Caligula and Incitatus came to mind. One of these days, Jensen would escort his favorite horse to the Cabinet room and expect President Julian Valentine to stand up and give the equine his seat at the table. Damn horse would probably be a better president.

He arranged his features to appear interested and engaged. Serious. Even though he hated feeling like he had to pretend to pay obeisance to this monster just to keep his family and friends safe.

He studied Jensen's cabinet of sycophants as they filed in and took their seats at the round table below. He shifted in his own seat, trying to get comfortable. It was going to be a long afternoon. Then the Chancellor strode in, and Cy choked on his own spit. Decked out in a floor-length purple velvet and ermine-lined cloak with silver and gold threads twining an elaborate design along the edges and accompanied by his own ponderous version of Hail to the Chief, Cy almost broke a molar clenching his jaw.

Holy fucking hell. He wanted to laugh, but this was definitely unfunny. Was Jensen posing as the fucking King of England? Pretending he was King Arthur taking his seat at his Round Table of Knights? Laying claim to the kingship of America? Or simply daring someone to point out that the emperor has no clothes. Or, rather, that the clothes he has are fucking ridiculous. Had Jensen finally gone over the edge and declared himself king or was that what this celebration was about? Announcing King Jensen. In All His Glory. Coming soon to a country near you.

Jesus.

He swallowed back a groan and a veritable boatload or profanities. He wanted to punch something. Preferably Harold Jensen. In the throat. Even rolling his eyes would probably get him arrested, though. He couldn't keep up with all the Chancellor's Decrees but groaning and eye rolling were no doubt considered treasonous offenses these days.

He took in a long breath, stretched out his neck, and tried to calm himself. Thankfully, the flight from Tucson to D.C. had been smooth and uneventful, and he'd been able to get some rest. Not that he'd really slept, but Mat had insisted he least try. After Mat pushed his seat all the way back and started snoring softly—the fucker could sleep anywhere—Cy had headed to the back bedroom, stretched out, stared at the ceiling, and thought of Hallie Jones.

Although Cy and Mat both (and Mason and Brooks) knew how to fly a plane thanks to Uncle Jimmy, they usually handed over the reins, so to speak, to Helen Cross, Bigelow Enterprises' on-call corporate pilot and all-round transportation expert.

They'd decided to get a small corporate jet of their own when three commercial airliners went down in as many weeks from bomb blasts, and the mysterious Helen and her partner came with the only plane they could afford. Well, she came with the plane because, in point of fact, it was hers and they didn't have to buy it or staff it or maintain it. They just had to pay her company to take care of the details.

When the company put out feelers through their channels to see about buying a plane, Helen had reached out. Said she and her partner were just getting established and would be willing to work at a reduced rate. Mason and Brooks did their due diligence, discovered that she and Kemal, her business partner, had stellar credentials and not only were they both crack pilots, but they were both experienced security professionals. Once they signed the contract, they discovered Helen and Kemal were always armed to the teeth and ready to jump in on any adventure, occasionally even joining Mat as additional members of the Bigelow security team.

In fact, Cy suspected that Mat and Helen had a more than professional relationship simmering below the surface—or maybe even below the covers. The woman had an otherworldly beauty and a steely competence that no doubt spoke to and challenged the former SEAL on every level. Cy noticed the way they looked at each other sometimes. Almost as if they needed to put on the gloves and climb into the ring. In a good way. In a I-want-to-rip-your-clothes-off-with-my-teeth kind of way.

Mat had never talked about the obvious attraction that crackled in the air around him and Helen, and Cy had never asked. In fact, he'd never had any deep conversations with Helen at all because, well, he was loathe to admit it, but she was intimidating as all hell. She generally kept him at a professional remove and he, in turn, did the same. Although, he'd been content to waggle an eyebrow a time or two when he'd caught Mat eyeing Helen's backside—or vice versa—but out other than that, he'd stayed clear of whatever minefields those two were dancing around on.

Today Mat was alone, waiting downstairs. All security personnel were forced to hang out in a waiting area outside the cabinet room, so Mat instructed Helen and Kemal to just stay put in their suite at the Waldorf. They had security cameras and sensors all over the plane's skin and interior that could be monitored from the hotel.

The Chancellor called the meeting to order, and everyone was asked to stand and repeat the new pledge. Cy moved his mouth, but he refused to say the damn thing out loud. Instead, he concentrated on the drone of voices filling the high-ceilinged room as the pledge was followed by a soaring rendition of the anthem blaring through the speakers. Finally, they were allowed to sit. Cy looked up to see the meeting's agenda posted on a large four-sided screen mounted high above the round table. He thought of the scoreboard at a basketball game and stifled a chuckle. Big difference was, this game was always rigged.

He pulled a small notebook from his suit jacket and clicked his mechanical pencil. The only way he could survive sitting still so long was to doodle. Circles within circles. Lines and cross hatches. Squiggles and little bug-eyed aliens with wiggly antennae standing guard in the corners. Little cats with fluffy tails and goofy dogs with long ears. He'd been doodling and drawing for as long as he could remember.

As a boy, his art teachers said he had a natural affinity for shape and form. Just like he'd had a natural affinity for the guitar and piano, instruments he'd learned without even trying and that had been extremely useful in getting pretty girls to sleep with him. Another thing Ken Fucking Lane hated about him.

The meeting started and Chancellor Jensen began droning on about the glorious progress he'd made in stamping out homelessness—mostly because the homeless were now housed in internment camps and used as slave labor or simply disappeared. Cy lifted his pencil from the paper, suddenly realizing he'd drawn a face. Hallie Jones. He smiled down at it. Not a bad likeness. He admired it for a moment, added some shading and a few refinements around her mouth and then....

And then his skin prickled with gooseflesh. Every hair on his body stood at attention. He held himself very still, like an animal just realizing it had become prey. But no. This didn't feel like danger. It felt like desire.

His grip on his pencil tightened, and he raised his eyes to survey the room. And there, right across from him, sitting on the opposite side of the viewing gallery, a man watched him.

Holy hell. Not *a* man. *The* man. The man from The Point. *The fucking forest ranger*. If the incident hadn't been on his mind, he probably never would have remembered his face. But ever since Hallie had suggested *she'd* been that man, he hadn't been able to stop thinking about what he'd looked like.

Now he knew.

Dark auburn, almost burnished copper, hair with a little curl at the nape of his neck. All swept back like some model emerging from the sea in a cologne ad. Or a vampire. Neatly trimmed beard with a hint of copper. Chiseled jaw, bright eyes. Strong neck and broad shoulders. Lean but obviously powerful. It was him. No question. And suddenly Cy wanted to see what he looked like standing up, all long legs and—

What in the everlovingfuck was going on?

Their eyes locked. And the man, the fucking forest ranger, broke out a smile so bright it felt like Cy had been tased. Like a lightning strike had slammed straight into his solar plexus. And then the man winked, tapped the side of his nose in an *it's our secret* gesture, and turned his attention back to the Chancellor.

And for the first time in his life, Cy thought he might faint.

16

Out of the corner of her eye, Nemi tracked Cy's movements. The man could not sit still. The look on his face when he'd recognized her human aspect and the fact that he'd spent the rest of the afternoon fidgeting in his seat gave her a deliciously satisfied thrill—another thing she would not admit to the Furies, especially Tisi who would tease her mercilessly.

Now, the session was nearly over, and several viewing attendees had already excused themselves, presumably to get ready for the state dinner to be held upstairs in the ballroom on the thirteenth floor, just above Jensen's twelfth-floor office. Nemi had attended thousands of banquets in the past, with pharaohs, emperors, kings and presidents. She'd even banqueted with Cyrus the Great. But never with Cyrus Bigelow.

Unfortunately, tonight she would be attending as Alexander Whitelaw. Damn. It would've been the perfect opportunity to wear a luxuriously sexy ballgown and to see the expression on Cy's face when he laid eyes on her. The invitation did allow for guests to bring a plus one, so maybe there was a way. Or maybe there'd be another opportunity. She did still have work to do. Conversations to eavesdrop on. New contacts to cultivate. And she'd have a better opportunity to do her job as a man than as a woman.

She hated that humans had willingly turned the clock back on women's rights, but that was one of the reasons Zeus had called her to Earth to work with the Furies. To hold these misogynistic, power-hungry men to account. Although he was the titular head of the Pantheon League and demanded justice for humanity's bad behavior, there was no denying Zeus was a terrible misogynist himself. She'd told him so innumerable times and in no uncertain terms. But he'd told her in no uncertain terms that *his* business wasn't any of *her* business. It wasn't her job to police the other gods; it was human behavior that mattered. So, while Zeus considered it *his* right to exercise extremely bad behavior, he wanted *everyone else* held to account.

Typical man. Typical god.

But, not Nemesis. She was incapable of not holding herself to account for her behavior. Judgment was in her godly DNA as the very essence of divine justice.

She turned as she saw Cy stand. He was looking straight at her. She glanced down at the round table below them. Apparently, while she'd been lost in her thoughts, the session had been adjourned. The Chancellor had closed the meeting, and his Cabinet members were gathering their things and following him and his ridiculous robes as they swept out of the conference room.

She unfolded her long legs and stood, now watching Cy watch her. She straightened her lapels. Smoothed out her suit jacket. On the other side of the balcony, Cy held her gaze. She gave him a curt nod and started toward the steps. Would he be waiting for her downstairs in the atrium? By the elevator? Outside? Beyond security?

Her lips curled in a smile. She'd find out soon enough.

Christ. There he was. *She* was? *Whatever!*

Cy surreptitiously wiped his sweaty palms on his pants. He looked off into the distance where he knew Mat was waiting. A text came through on Cy's smartwatch. *Don't worry. I'm here. I've got eyes on you.* Shit. He wasn't worried. He'd jumped out of airplanes and skied nearly vertical back country slopes and free dived in deep water, but he'd never been as antsy and, well, flabbergasted, as he was right then, as he stood outside on the National Mall and watched the goddamned forest ranger approach.

WTH? Cy glanced at Mat's last text and a bit back a grimace. No kidding, he wanted to text back, but he was out of time.

The man stopped an arm's length away and stuck out his hand. Remarkably, maybe on instinct, Cy took it in his and gave it a firm shake. His pulse pounded, and he wondered if the man could feel it in his grip. He let go. Stared for a long moment as the man said nothing. Waiting. Finally, Cy cleared his throat and said, with as much dignity as he could muster, "What the fuck?"

"Let me introduce myself," the man said with a confident—no, a *cocky* smile—and a whisky-smooth voice that resonated at at the base of Cy's spine. "Name's Alex Whitelaw. CEO of WaveForm Technologies." Alex offered another brilliant smile as he dug into his coat jacket and pulled out an engraved silver card case. He thumbed out a card and handed it over.

Cy glanced down at it. "CEO. Really." His voice was the very definition of sarcasm. "And I suppose you moonlight as a forest ranger. When you're not rescuing gentlemen in distress or developing ... technology." He flipped the card over, all suave and nonchalant. Trying to appear amused instead of freaked the fuck out. "Of course. Quantum computers and communications systems."

"Naturally." Whitelaw shrugged. "I have an affinity for all things quantum." Full lips quirked up in a rakish smile.

Cy swallowed, shook his head in wonder. "So, it really is just a matter of physics."

At that, Alexander Whitelaw, Hallie Delphinium Jones, Forest Fucking Ranger, or whatever this person's name was, threw his head back and laughed. Literally slapped his thigh. Put a hand on his belly as if trying to contain his mirth. Apparently, Cy was the most hilarious thing the man had ever encountered. When he was done, he wiped the corners of his eyes with long blunt-tipped fingers and huffed out a final soft laugh.

"I cannot tell you how delighted I am to see you again, Cy. That was worth the price of admission." He laughed again. "Tell me, will you be attending the state dinner tonight?"

"Is there a choice? I thought guest attendance was mandatory."

Alex Whitelaw shrugged again. "On penalty of death, probably. Or at least an uncomfortable number of questions about the wheres and whyfores of ignoring one's duty to one's glorious country. I hope you'll let me buy you a drink."

"I was hoping the drinks would be free at this shindig."

Whitelaw laughed again. "I was thinking now. Perhaps we'll be able to sit together tonight. Have a discussion about our many mutual interests, but I was hoping to spend a little time with you before we don the monkey suits and perform for the powers that be. By the way, how are your stitches?"

Cy sucked in a breath. *Jesus Christ, this is seriously freaky.* "My stitches are fine. I've always healed fast." He nodded toward the Old Post Office building in the distance, doing his best to appear nonchalant. "We could head to the bar over at the Waldorf. That's where we're staying."

"You and your security shadow?" Alex looked back over his shoulder to where Mat stood, watching the exchange with a strange expression on his face.

"The price of being so popular in D.C. We're practically joined at the hip. But I promise he's the very soul of discretion."

"Mateo Cárdenas." Alex mused. "Lifelong friend, business partner, and personal bodyguard. I believe he stopped by the Saguaro Room yesterday if I'm not mistaken."

Cy snorted. "You don't miss much do you, Mr. Whitelaw? Since we're all here, why don't we go ahead and take a walk over to Peacock Alley."

"Peacock Alley?" Alex looked around as if a peacock might come strolling by, fan spread for all to see. "That's the name of the bar?"

"Yeah. And you look so goddamned pleased with yourself, I think it is fitting."

Alex laughed again. Wrinkles rayed out from the edges of chocolate brown eyes as he swept out an arm, gesturing for Cy to lead the way. "After you."

"No fancy magic tricks today?"

"Since Jensen's Security Service agents are crawling all over the place, walking is a wise choice. Besides, I believe it's a familiar form of locomotion for people like you."

"People like me..."

"Indeed. Since you have yet to develop your own affinity for quantum mechanics." Alex cast a sly sidelong glance at him and swept out his arm again. "Shall we?"

17

"So, are you going to tell us what happened today or not?"

The three sisters were piled onto the king-sized bed in Nemi's suite at Pantheon League HQ as she emerged from the bathroom rubbing a towel over her short, wet hair. Steam billowed into the room. She liked her showers skin-peeling hot and now her normal Alexander Whitelaw olive complexion looked as though she'd spent the day on a sun-drenched beach rather than inside watching Chancellor Jensen's ridiculous show in his ridiculous legislative chambers—or whatever he chose to call it.

Tyrants were all alike, adorning themselves in uniforms with chests full of medals they didn't earn or robes of velvet and ermine as if those things proved their right to rule, all while surrounding themselves in gaudy gilt and imagining everyone around them would look on in awe and admiration. Unfortunately, Nemi knew, too many humans were too easily taken in by the trappings of power and privilege to look deeply at the men hiding behind them.

She adjusted the towel wrapped low around her hips and stared at her friends. Trying to decide what to say. "I bought Cy

Bigelow a drink today," she blurted out. "At the Waldorf Hotel bar."

"And?" Addi asked, hand circling in the air as if to say, *keep going.*

"He sipped mezcal. I had whisky."

"Fascinating," Tisi said with an eye roll. "But that's not what *we* want to know, and *you* know it."

"He's persistent, that's for certain. Says he won't stop digging until he finds out exactly who or *what* I am. Kept asking how I do it. Whisk him from place to place. Teleport like a Star Trek character. Change my form like some sort of shape-shifting magician. I told him I couldn't tell him—yet. But I all but promised I'd tell him soon. He was practically salivating by the end."

Meg huffed out a laugh. "Look at you in all your rugged Alexander Whitelaw glory. Any human with blood pumping in their veins would be salivating."

Nemi shook her head—or rather, Alex shook his head. "He made it quite clear he's not interested in men."

"Right." Ali rolled her eyes.

That's all Nemi was willing to say for now. She didn't want to admit that she didn't want to share what she and Cy had talked about at that bar. The Furies didn't need to know the details of Cy's life, and it wasn't important to their Pantheon League work. But it did give her new insights into Cy Bigelow, the man. The friend. The father and husband. Brother. The son he'd been to his messed-up father and long-dead mother. He had shared more than he'd intended to—she always had that affect on humans—but listening to him talk about his life made her ... respect him even more. That's all it was. Respect for a man trying to do his best when everything had gone to shit.

She stepped into her closet and returned with her neatly pressed tux. "Jensen is up to something." She draped the tux over the back of a chair and pulled the pants off the hanger. Dug a pair of snug boxers out of a drawer. "Don't ask me what because I'm not sure, but my goddess senses are tingling. And no—" she held up a hand for them to stop before they said anything more about Cy Bigelow making her tingle—"not just because he strode out in a king's cloak complete with the oh-so-original ermine lining."

"So trite," Tisi said. "I much prefer a man in a crisp uniform than a flowing robe. Or in nothing at all."

"I'm just glad most humans no longer feel the need to drape dead animals around their necks to prove their prowess," Ali said. "Remember Ashurbanipal and his obsession with lions? Or all the wolves and bears and panthers sacrificed for men's egos?"

"I wonder what Cy Bigelow would look like with a panther draped across his brawny shoulders and a leather skirt wrapped around his waist." Meg said thoughtfully, as if it was a serious question worth philosophical consideration or scientific study.

Alex shot her sidelong glance. "You all need to get out more."

Ali actually giggled. "We get out plenty, Nemi. You're the one traipsing around the stars while we're down here stuck on Earth interacting with humans."

"*Interacting*," Meg said with a cough. "Right. That's what we're calling it."

"Anyway, back to Jensen," Nemi said, trying to get the conversation back on track. Sometimes the sisters truly were like three old ladies gossiping and sharing stories of past adventures. "He seemed preoccupied. Edgy. I would almost say anxious, but that seems a stretch. You watched the proceedings remotely, so you know nothing substantive happened. No new policies announced. Just a lot of braggadocio about how great he is and how bright the future is for America. And no one sitting around me dared so much as murmur anything negative about any of it. It's either the happiest bunch of megalomaniacs or the most frightened. Honestly," he shook his head in disgust, "I wouldn't have been surprised if everyone in the viewing gallery jumped up and saluted Jensen with a crisp Sieg Heil."

Meg moved to sit cross-legged on the bed, plumped a pillow and placed it in her lap. "Even Cy Bigelow?"

"He may be working to undermine Jensen behind the scenes, but I'd wager he'd snap his arm up in public to save his daughter's life if he had to." Nemi paused and looked off into the middle distance. "And then he'd do everything in his power to destroy the man and burn everything he stands for to the ground. To bring every damn one of them down. I think that's what he and his friends are trying to do already. We just don't know how."

They were all quiet for a moment. "It's a dangerous thing for humans," Meg said. "Being a member of a resistance movement."

"Cy Bigelow isn't fully human," Nemi reminded them. "His anger is fathoms deep. Demigod deep."

"But his friends are human." Tisi said. "His wife is human."

"And he'll do everything in his power to protect them. Which reminds me." She turned to Tisi. "Were you able to change up the seating so Cy and I are next to each other at the same table?"

"Taken care of."

"Back to Jensen again," Ali said. "You said he seemed preoccupied. What did he do that made you think that?"

Nemi pulled on her pants, then sat, black socks dangling from her fingertips. "It was strange. He kept glancing furtively toward the doors to the meeting room. Like he was expecting someone. Or waiting for something to happen. It wasn't obvious and probably no one else noticed. I don't think Cy did. I asked him what his take on the afternoon session was, and I don't think he was even paying attention. Turns out he likes to doodle. Has a little notebook. Drew in it all afternoon." *Drawing and watching me*, Nemi thought. She put on her socks and shoes and then pulled on her crisp white shirt. "Think I should wear my Io volcanic rock cuff links?"

"Those or the pretty Europa stones," Tisi said. "They match Alex Whitelaw's dark auburn hair. Just makes me happy inside to think of you walking around wearing little pieces of outer space when all those jokers think the whole universe revolves around them."

"Did you sense any other gods or demigods there?" Meg said. "What's your verdict on Jensen being a demigod?"

"No, and I'm not sure," Nemi admitted. "I didn't feel anything, but I might just need to get closer to him."

"What happens tonight?" Tisi asked. "Besides eating, drinking, and dancing. I'm assuming the Chancellor is going to give a speech."

"He always does," Ali said. "The man cannot resist the spotlight. I just hope he doesn't dance. It's like he's never been introduced to the concept of rhythm."

"I want to know which wife he'll be parading around with," Meg chimed in again. "We've always had luck with disgruntled wives or concubines. We might have an in there. Or maybe a couple of his older children."

Nemi fastened her cummerbund in place. Turned and looked at her friends. "Why aren't any of you attending tonight?"

"I'll be there," Ali said, striking a pose and a bright smile. "Got my regular gig as a bartender. They're going to have eight stations set up around the perimeter of the room, but I won't be sure which one I'll be posted to until I get there. Still, you'll be able to find me easily enough. I'm going as Maurice again. Rich, powerful, white people will say absolutely anything around a Black servant. It's like we don't even exist."

"Meg and I will monitor communications and security systems," Tisi said. "We're already tapped into their systems, and we've got bugs in places even they haven't thought of. Anyone so much as texts or takes a cellphone picture to save or share, we'll log it."

"You are a marvel," Nemi said with a laugh.

"It's always fun to hack human tech. I've got to know what they're up to or one of these days they'll get the better of us."

Meg looked at her sister with a raised eyebrow. "Get the better of *us*?"

"Let's face it, if we're not careful, there's going to come a day when someone catches us with our metaphorical pants down. I'd like to put that off as long as possible. Besides, it's fun playing their games."

Tisi turned and looked Nemi up and down. "You do make a fine-looking man, Mr. Alex Whitelaw. I much prefer you in a kilt, though." She winked. "With a claymore strapped to your back and a sporran hanging right where it counts."

18

The glittering lights of D.C. and the majestic glow of all the monuments built to celebrate America's proud history—including the Lincoln Memorial, Washington's Monument, Jefferson's Memorial, and the World War II Memorial—could be admired through the floor-to-ceiling windows of the thirteenth-floor ballroom.

Designed in what some wag on social media had called "a mix of Soviet brutalist efficiency and Saddam-style elegance," Jensen's ode to himself was an assault on the senses. All dark marble and baroque embellishments. An edifice meant to intimidate with its power and (supposed) glory. To remind visitors of the strength of old empires and the implacability of new technology. And this ballroom was the worst offender of the Jensen Style, although the windows were a nice touch. Cy wondered what had happened to that snarky wag with the incisive wit. All their accounts had gone dark shortly after that post.

He stood in line to order a drink at the bar station closest to the main door and the hallway leading to the elevator bank. His tux was immaculate. He'd showered and shaved with care all the while wondering what had possessed him to practically pour out his life story to the person calling himself Alex Whitelaw who was somehow also Hallie Jones while poor Mat sat at the end of the bar nursing a tonic and lime and Kemal hung around in the lobby looking busy with his phone. The mezcal had lit a nice little fire in his belly that kept his tongue wagging non-stop. And since Alex refused to offer up any personal details or reveal anything at all about who or what he or she was and how they did the things they did, Cy had just rambled on and on.

Frankly, it was embarrassing.

"Good evening, sir. What can I get you?"

With Jensen being such a racist bigot, Cy was surprised the bartender was Black. But maybe all the cabinet members, congressmen, and their crowd of sycophants and invited guests would hardly notice anyone as lowly as a servant. For all Cy knew, the man might be indentured and forced to work for his keep or to prevent his family from being deported. *Or disappeared.* Still, Cy figured being invisible had its advantages. The man could probably listen in on all the best gossip and no one would even notice. Could possibly be a good source for intel.

"Think I'll start with some sparkling water. Cy leaned in. "Best to keep my wits at such an auspicious event."

"Would you like it over ice?"

"Sure."

"And would you care for a splash of lemon or lime?"

"Why not? I'll take the lime."

"Coming right up, Mr. Bigelow."

The bartender was all obliging smiles and innocuous small talk. He worked with smooth efficiency even as Cy wondered how he knew his name. He wasn't wearing anything so gauche as a name tag, but he noticed that the bartender was. He supposed all the servants wore name tags, so they could be easily beckoned with a single word and a snap of the fingers.

"Here you go."

Cy picked up his drink, took a sip, and tipped it toward the bartender as if in a toast. "Thank you, Maurice."

"My pleasure."

And then Cy moved away toward the door. He didn't want to look too anxious, but by now it was overwhelmingly obvious that Cy was fascinated with Alex-Hallie-Whoever-Whatever and that Alex-Hallie-Whoever-Whatever knew it. So, he might as well loiter by the door and wait for his-her arrival as loiter and wait anywhere else.

He took a sip, appreciating the delicious tang of lime and glanced back toward the tall windows as if contemplating something ponderous. Which, he supposed, he was. Mainly, what the hell had happened to the country his parents and grandparents—and all his relatives back to the first fiercely independent and ferociously driven Cyrus Horatio Bigelow the First who'd fled Scotland in the wake of the Clearances—had loved so dearly.

Had it always been this way? Had Americans always secretly longed for leaders like Harold Jensen? Men who rejected science and embraced idiotic and ridiculous conspiracies as if they were sacred texts long hidden away by demonic forces? Rejoiced in cruelty with a fervor that felt like a religious fever dream? Had he just been too white, too privileged, and too damned isolated to notice the true extent of the suffering around him?

Mrs. Cárdenas, Mat's mom, had been mother, father, housekeeper, estate manager, and guardian to four boys, one hauntingly strange girl and her shy, bookish best friend. Cy and Sybil's mom was dead, and their dad might as well have been too. Probably would have been better if he'd been the one to go early, so he didn't have a chance to almost bankrupt Bigelow Enterprises and send them all to the proverbial poorhouse. Mason's parents were divorced, his father was long gone, and his mother worked two jobs. Brooks's parents were always busy teaching or traveling. And BoJo was always around because, well, frankly, Sybil depended on her and she really didn't fit in anywhere else.

So, Mrs. C had done what needed to be done even as her own husband was deported and never heard from again. She'd raised them all to be empathetic and considerate. To try to put themselves in other people's shoes. To care about Bigelow, its people, and the land around them. And now, although he never knew what was going on in Sybil's head and he and BoJo's relationship focused on co-parenting Sofia, he and Mat and Mason and Brooks were doing their best to do ... *something*. Stand up against Jensen's cruelty and destructiveness and—

"You look like a storm's brewing inside your head."

The voice was a deep rumble. Soft, intimate. It sent a frisson of excitement up Cy's spine, which seriously disturbed him. He turned to find Alex Whitelaw standing at his side, drink in hand. Cy raised his glass. Alex did the same.

"To deep thoughts," Cy said.

"To deep thoughts," Alex repeated. "Any sign of the Chancellor yet?"

"No, but the President, VP, and most of the cabinet and congressmen have arrived." Cy kept his voice low, barely more than a whisper. "They're all in place, ready to bow down. The troops are assembled. We're just waiting for our glorious leader to appear."

As if on cue, a crisply uniformed bugler raised his horn and sounded out a single long note. When it faded, the chamber ensemble from the New America Marine Band began playing a string version of Jensen's revised *Hail to the Chief* as the Chancellor entered from a hidden side door and marched into the room as if he owned the place. Which he did, Cy guessed. Jensen had revised the score himself, or so the story went. Cy thought the man ought to have left dabbling in music to someone else.

Anyone else.

"And now the fun begins," Alex murmured.

"Or at least dinner will be served." Cy was glad Mat, Helen, and Kemal had already eaten. He'd ordered them dinner and had room service deliver it to their suite. Only Mat had accompanied him to the event, and he, along with the rest of the bodyguards and personal security personnel, had to wait in a lounge on the ground floor with the press corp. Only VIPs allowed upstairs.

"But not until Jensen has his say." Alex's voice was suddenly hard. Unforgiving. "The masses wait while the king opines. It's like the old days ..." He drew in a long breath. Let it out. "The City of Rome from its inception was held by kings."

Cy raised a brow in surprise. "Tacitus."

With an almost imperceptible nod of acknowledgment, Alex went on. "'He drew to himself the responsibilities of senate, magistrates, and laws—without a single adversary, since the most defiant had fallen in the battle line or by proscription and the rest of the nobles preferred the protection of the present to the perils of old.'"

"So, democracy and the ideal of a functioning republic is just some passing fancy," Cy mused aloud. "Perhaps because it takes too much energy to maintain."

Alex frowned, shook his head. "It's not a question of energy, *per se*. It's a question of empathy. Or rather, apathy. Small minds. Small men. It all breeds a lazy sort of cruelty and all cruelty springs from weakness."

"Seneca?" Cy asked. "You are full of Roman wisdom tonight."

Alex laughed at that. "It seems appropriate at an event like this."

"True," Cy said with a soft laugh. "I keep waiting for Jensen to demand his noble steed get a seat at the table."

"Caligula's reign is indeed an apt comparison for our times. How about this quote? 'I see the world being slowly transformed into a wilderness. I hear the approaching thunder that, one day, will destroy us too. I feel the suffering of millions. And yet, when I look up at the sky, I somehow feel that everything will change for the better, that this cruelty too shall end, that peace and tranquility will return once more.'"

"Sounds vaguely familiar. Who said that?"

"A young girl named Anne Frank."

"Shit." Cy lifted his glass to take a drink, acutely aware of the light glittering through the cut facets like prisms.

"Indeed. You and your people are truly in the shit."

Cy cast a sidelong glance at Alex, noting the distant *otherness* implied by his statement, and yet aware of the man's body next to his in a way that was definitely not distant. On the contrary, the man was too damned close. And Cy was doing nothing to increase the space between them. He set his glass on a passing waiter's tray. "Might as well take our seats before Jensen starts pontificating. I'm at Table 29."

"Isn't that a coincidence," Alex smiled. "I'm at Table 29 as well."

"Will wonders never cease." Cy rolled his eyes and gave Alex a lopsided smile as he led the way toward the table they'd both, by a coincidence Cy didn't believe in, been assigned. Then they both stopped. Turned their attention back toward the main doorway, toward what sounded like a scuffle in the hallway, near the elevator bank.

Automatically, they both moved toward the disturbance when a young man wearing the same uniform as all the other waiters—white shirt, black pants, black bow tie—started waving around … an ink pen? A member of the Chancellor's Security Service was grappling with him, trying to grab the pen and yelling for people to take cover.

"That's not a pen!" Cy said as the realization struck.

"It's a trigger," Alex said at the same time.

Instinctively, they both rushed forward even as the line of people at the bar nearest the door began pushing and shoving to get out of the way.

"Get down! Everyone down," Maurice shouted over the fray. "Behind the bar! Take cover!"

A woman in a lavender silk gown tripped and went down. A man, *her husband?*, bent to help her up and another woman tripped over him. People scrambled, panic-stricken, as a different SS agent tried to grab the waiter with the trigger.

Lunging, throwing punches, and flailing this way and that, the waiter was shouting now. Something about his children. His son. And daughter. Missing.

"I'm gonna pull your trigger, Jensen, but I know what you did. You already sold them. You already sold my kids!"

The waiter shoved and kicked, broke free of the SS agents and ran forward. One agent went down. Another pulled his service weapon. Pointed it at the waiter who was now pushing his way through the growing melee.

"Don't shoot!" Cy heard himself scream. "Too many people!"

A shot rang out and a woman in a pale, spring green dress with dangling emerald earrings and hair piled high spun around. Her eyes wide with surprise, she stumbled sideways. Fell against a table. A bloom of red spreading beneath her breasts.

"For god's sake, don't shoot!" Cy yelled again, plunging into the panicked crowd. Five hundred. There were five hundred people on the guest list, and they all seemed to be going in different directions. All of them in his way.

"You said you'd take care of them! Protect them if I did what you asked. But you lied. You already fucking sold them, you motherfucker!"

The man was struggling to get to the front of the room, pushing people out of his way, still yelling. On the dais, Valentine cowered as Jensen stood stock still, eyes narrowed. Not in surprise. In disdain. In hatred.

"I may die because of you, but I'm not gonna lie for you."

Alex was ahead of him. Cy watched as Alex launched himself forward. Practically flying through the air. Saw him grab the waiter around the waist. Saw them both go down in a sea of chairs and tables, plates and glasses, gleaming silver flatware. And screaming people.

Another shot rang out. Cy felt the impact of it in his shoulder. He kept moving. Another shot, and he spun around. Shit. He'd been hit in the arm. The pain was more theoretical than real, but he knew this was not good. Still, he got his feet under him again and kept moving. Yelling for people to get down. Take cover. Shoving guests and servers and chairs and tables aside to get to where Alex now had the man with the trigger pinned to the ground.

Cy went to jump over a fallen chair only to feel a hand grab his injured arm and pull him backwards into the hard body of a man at least six inches taller.

Holy hell, that hurt.

The grip on his arm was like a steel vise, and Cy craned his neck up only to meet the blank-eyed stare of a thick-necked, wide-shouldered SS agent. And then he felt the barrel of a gun dig into his ribs. *What the fuck?*

"Hello, Mr. Bigelow," the man growled. "I've been assigned to take care of you, and now's as good a time as any."

From the look in the agent's eyes, Cy knew the *care* this man was assigned to give him would land him six feet under. Which really and truly pissed him off. He'd just met Hallie. Just met Alex. Life was getting very interesting and he wasn't going to let this asshole ruin it.

Time seemed to slow as he made a show of struggling against the giant's grip to get a sense of him. His arm was weak from where the second bullet had hit him and his shoulder throbbed from where the first bullet was still embedded.

"I'm honored. Was Jensen willing to stage a terror attack just for me? Surely there are easier ways to kill me."

The whole room was in chaos. Screaming. Sobbing. Another shot rang out. But the man pulled Cy closer, seeming in no hurry to complete his task.

"Don't flatter yourself, Bigelow. You're less than a gnat on a monkey's ass compared to what Jensen's got planned."

Cy twisted, sneered up at him. "Oh, I'm sure the Chancellor shares all his secret plans with geniuses like you."

The killer didn't seem to mind the insult. Or maybe the big oaf didn't understand irony. He jammed the gun into Cy's side again, bent down, and whispered. "Just like Jensen, I'm a true believer. Willing to die—and willing to kill— for a new life. Are you?"

No, Cy thought. He wasn't willing to die for any nutcase religious belief. He was willing to die for the people he loved, though. And the democracy he was fighting for. But he was not planning on doing it today.

So, in a blaze of movement the agent never could've seen coming, he gouged two fingers into the man's eyes, grabbed the man's wrist, twisted away from the pistol, and yanked until the giant bent over and the gun skittered across the floor. Then he grabbed a gleaming steak knife that had fallen to the floor, jammed it up into the man's throat, and drove his knee up to smash the man's nose. He staggered back, fell, and didn't move again.

And then the floor shook. The windows cracked and rattled. Debris rained down from the ceiling. And everything went dark.

19

For a single moment, everything stopped.
Then, emergency lights flickered on, and Cy was moving again. Climbing over the body of his would-be assassin. Crawling forward. Head pounding, blood in his eyes, he scrambled to his feet and, through the dust and rain of plaster, saw SS agents leaping frantically over broken furniture and broken people to reach the dais at the front of the room where Chancellor Jensen, President Valentine, Senator Parker, and a few cabinet members crouched behind their overturned table. Other agents threw furniture aside and picked through the wreckage, trying to get to the dead and injured as people called out for each other, in turns weeping in grief or relief, moaning in pain, or staring in blank-eyed shock.

Someone just tried to kill me. In the middle of all this, that man was going to kill me and it would've just explained away as tragic collateral damage.

Cy set the thought aside and pushed his way toward where a mangled body lay scattered in pieces on the floor and, *oh holy fucking hell,* a man's head looked like it had been ripped right off at the neck, like a soda bottle shaken so hard the cap had popped clean off. The bomber. Decapitated. Someone moved a piece of a chair, and the head rolled over, eyes now staring up at the damaged ceiling. A man in a tux, a legislator who looked vaguely familiar, turned away and vomited. A woman screamed. Another fainted.

Cy swallowed hard. His ears rang. Sound around him was muffled as he pushed broken chairs and tables out of the way, clawing through the wreckage. But there was no sign of Alex. No pieces of him. Nothing. It was like he'd vanished into thin air. He hoped to god he'd employed his fucking physics trick and that he was in one piece somewhere safe. The idea of losing him—*or her*—after just meeting them hurt more than Cy could imagine.

So, he didn't imagine it. Alex was alive. He had to be. He wasn't here, so he had to have teleported out of the room as soon as he realized the bomb was going to detonate. He was safe. God, please, he had to be safe.

But whatever was going on here needed his full attention. He'd been shot twice. An SS agent—or at least a man dressed like an SS agent, had stuck a gun in his ribs intending to finish the job. A man's head was rolling around on the fucking floor. Dust and debris filled the air. People were in full panic mode. Screaming. Crying.

Where was Alex?

He righted a chair and stepped up on it. Turned in a circle, surveying the damage. It was bad but definitely could've been worse. The windows held. They were cracked but not shattered. Looked like there were hundreds of badly shaken people, many of whom were injured. But from where Cy stood, he didn't see too many bodies. Of course, one was too many. But thank god, there weren't more. Maybe a dozen. Apparently, the bomber wasn't wearing enough explosives to bring the place down.

"Where is he? That poor man. I saw him!"

Cy turned toward the voice and stepped down from the chair. The First Lady, Alyssa Valentine, breathing heavily and gesturing wildly, grabbed a passing agent's arm. She held her other arm close, tucked under her breasts, but Cy couldn't see a wound. It was probably broken or dislocated. At first he couldn't understand what she was saying. Her voice reached him as if he was under water.

"I saw him try to save us all!" she gasped. "He practically flew through the crowd to throw himself on the bomber! He was a hero."

She was talking about Alex!

"But where is he? *He's not here!*" Her voice got higher and higher with each word.

Alex isn't here, and I just killed a man.

Cy'd been in plenty of fights over the years, but he'd never killed anyone. Strangely, it didn't seem strange. It'd been kill or be killed. Survival instinct. Still, maybe that man had a family who depended on him. Maybe he had a daughter like Sofia. Or a son who looked up to him. A wife who loved him. Maybe he did what he did because he had no other good choices. He said he was a true believer, whatever that meant. Maybe he thought killing Cy Bigelow was somehow part of his salvation. If so, that was some fucked up religion the guy subscribed to.

No. Didn't matter why he did it. Killing people on command was still murder. And people who did that were assassins. And killing an assassin before he killed you was nothing to feel guilty about. He needed to snap out of it. Start thinking. Find Alex.

Alyssa Valentine's entire body was shaking. "*Oh my God! He's been disintegrated!*" She was fully hysterical now, and the agent pulled over a chair and gently pushed her down to sit.

"Put your head between your knees, Mrs. Valentine. Or you're going to pass out. I'll send your husband over in just a moment."

The agent turned and touched Cy on the shoulder. Cy winced, remembering he'd been shot. Twice, goddammit. The agent nodded toward the front of the room where the Chancellor and President Valentine, now surrounded by men bristling with weapons, had their heads bent together as if telling secrets. Which they probably were.

"I'm Supervisory Security Service Agent Reynolds, attached to Chancellor Jensen's personal security detail. Follow me, Mr. Bigelow. The Chancellor wants to speak to you."

The last person Cy wanted to talk to was Harold Jensen, but he wiped the dust from his face with his left arm and followed. Moments later, Chancellor Jensen extended his hand, and Cy had no choice but to take it. He stuck his hand out and everyone looked down. It was covered in blood.

"You're injured, Mr. Bigelow." Jensen's voice was even higher and whinier than usual. "In all the confusion, I didn't see what happened, but you must have gotten hit by flying debris. It's a miracle you survived."

"I'm okay," Cy said. "Just a scratch." He didn't want to deal with this man. He needed to find Alex.

"My agents tell me that you and Alexander Whitelaw bravely stepped into the fray, warning fellow guests of danger. It was a heroic thing you two did tonight, and I wanted to thank you personally for helping to save all our lives." He nodded at Valentine who was still looking down at Cy's hand with distaste.

Cy had met the chancellor, but he'd never met the president in person. "I only acted on instinct, sir. But if I helped save even one life, I'm glad of it. Unfortunately, President Valentine, I believe your wife may have been injured."

That seemed to snap Valentine out of his trance, and he looked out over the room then started moving.

"Sir," Agent Reynolds said, "Mr. Bigelow obviously needs medical attention. I think he was shot in the shoulder."

Jensen nodded like a wizened old sage. "Shot. Of course. How terrible. And yet he's still upright. Must be made of sturdy stock. My personal physician will take care of him." He turned Cy as if he had all the time in the world. "We've got a state-of-the-art surgical unit in the building so we can get you patched up faster than trying to get you to a hospital. They'll all be packed anyway."

Mat had enough medical training to tend to any but the most dangerous wounds, and Cy would rather his friend dig a bullet out with a spork than let Jensen's quack anywhere near him. "Thank you, sir, but I'll be okay. I just need to get to my security team. We travel with a medic, and he'll be able to fix me up. I need to let them know I'm safe."

"Cell service has been knocked out, I'm afraid. I've got my team working on it."

"I can walk. I'll be fine taking the stairs."

"No," Jensen said, his tone emphatic. "You're *not* fine. In fact, it's a miracle you survived. You can notify your men when you go down to the medical suite, but I want my team to keep an eye on you. You and Mr. Whitelaw are national heroes, and I'm going to make sure everyone knows it."

Jensen's eyes were assessing as his gaze flickered over Cy's shoulder to take in the disaster behind them. "Unfortunately, it appears Whitelaw was one of the casualties. Agent Reynolds informs me that no one has found his body."

Cy's heart pounded under Jensen's intense stare. Alex had to be fine. *But where the fuck was he?*

"Such a tragedy," Jensen went on. "Especially since the bomber is dead. Pieces of his body strewn everywhere."

Just like you wanted me dead. "I saw Mr. Whitelaw tackle the bomber and then ... well, then everything went dark. Maybe he was able to roll under one of the tables strewn around the room. Maybe he's passed out or dead under the debris."

Jensen nodded, considering. "Are you and Mr. Whitelaw well acquainted?"

"I met him for the first time just today, after the session. We were headed in the same direction, so we shared a drink at the Waldorf. That's where I'm staying."

"And where is—was—Whitelaw staying? If he traveled with a staff, we'll need to notify them. And his next of kin."

Cy cleared his throat. "I have no idea, sir. As I said, I barely knew him."

"Well, let's get you downstairs where we can see to your wound and monitor you."

Monitor me, my ass. "But—"

"I insist, Mr. Bigelow. It's the least I can do for such a brave patriot." He looked at Agent Reynolds. "See to him." And then he turned away and stepped back up onto the dais. Apparently, the man was going to make a speech after all.

"Let's go," Reynolds said, taking Cy's good arm and guiding him back toward the main doorway and the bank of elevators.

Out in the hall, more security agents were trying to contain the chaos. "The Chancellor's private elevator and stairwell is this way," Reynolds said, leading Cy past the crowded stairwell other guests were using to make their way downstairs.

As they passed the men's bathroom, the door swung open and Maurice, the bartender Cy had met, stumbled out.

"Oh my god! Help, please! There's a man in the bathroom. Injured. I think it's the one who tackled the bomber. His leg isn't working right, and I can't manage him myself. We need to get him to the hospital."

Cy shook off Agent Reynold's arm and rushed into the bathroom where a badly disheveled Alex Whitelaw sat propped up against the wall, legs outstretched. Head back. Eyes closed. Under the soft glow of a row of emergency lights and covered in dust and debris, it was impossible to discern how—or even if—

he was injured. Cy hoped it was all a ploy just to ensure he made an appearance after the bombing, but he couldn't know for sure. Jensen was obviously already suspicious of his disappearing act, but it would be worse if he was seen hale and hearty right next to a bunch of the bomber's dismembered body parts.

Cy dropped to a crouch and Reynolds joined him. Maurice stood over them, his voice high and agitated. "I found him when I came in to see if we had running water," he said, plowing his hands back and forth over his head as if he didn't know what else to do with them. "To help with the injuries, you know? He was unconscious. I checked to make sure he was breathing. And then he woke up. But he's hurt. See? Drifting in and out."

Alex coughed. Shifted and opened his eyes slowly, long lashes fluttering. Coughed again. "I managed to pull a table down over me just as the bomber hit the detonator." His voice was a rough croaking whisper. "I blacked out from the blast. Thought I was dead. Someone must've dragged me out to the hall where I came to but was almost trampled to death. I crawled in here. Safer than…" He waved a hand toward the hallway. Gasped for air. Coughed again. Gasped again. "Out there."

Reynolds stared at Alex for a moment, then stood. Cy followed suit. "How you holding up, Bigelow? Your shoulder."

Cy saw Alex's eyes flare in worried surprise. "Hurts like hell. Bullet didn't hit an artery, though, or I'd already be bleeding out." He didn't feel the need to inform the agent he had more than one bullet wound. Or that one of his colleagues had intended to murder him in the melee. He didn't want the man knowing anymore about him than necessary.

"You three stay here," Reynolds commanded. "I need to let the Chancellor know that Mr. Whitelaw has been found. Alive. And I'll be back with more help to get you both downstairs." Reynolds turned on his heel and hurried out.

20

"Damn it, Cy. I could feel you were in pain, but I didn't realize you'd been shot," Alex started to get up, but Maurice put a hand on his shoulder and pushed him back down.

"Stay down. The show must go on, and you need to look like you just barely survived a bomb blast in case someone else comes in." Maurice dropped back into to a crouch beside Alex, suddenly not sounding very panicky at all.

"Okay, you're right." Alex looked up at Cy who was pale, but still on his feet and pushed himself up against the wall, disheveled and covered in dust, but otherwise hale and hearty. "Tell me where you were shot. Your hand is dripping with blood, so … your arm?"

"Christ Almighty," Cy ground out, looking back and forth between Maurice and Alex. "Who the hell are you two?"

The bartender gave him a grim smile and touched a fingertip to his forehead. "You can call me Maurice for now. At your service, Mr. Bigelow."

Alex's eyes raked over Cy's body. "Later with the introductions. The SS shot you?"

"I was screaming at them not to shoot, but they opened fire anyway. I saw a woman take a bullet right in front of me. At first, I thought, what else were they gonna do? Just let a suicide bomber stroll in and take Jensen and Valentine out? And all the members of Congress? But then some bruiser tried to murder me."

"What do you mean?" Alex's voice was sharp. "You were shot intentionally?"

"My shoulder and my arm may have been random. Line of fire. But then this guy grabbed me, shoved a gun in my ribs, and said, 'I was assigned to take care of you, and now's as good a time as any.'"

"Well, that's rude," Maurice sniffed.

"Fortunately, I killed him." He tried to keep his voice from shaking. "Shoved a steak knife in his throat."

"Whoa. I am impressed," Maurice said with a whistle. "I take it Jensen wants to eliminate you."

"He wants Bigelow land. He looks at me and sees copper. Uranium. Gold."

Alex did a little whirly motion with his finger. "Show me." Cy turned in a circle giving Alex a look at his back. "Looks like you were hit in the bicep, but the bullet went straight through. Probably just a flesh wound. But you've still got a bloody bullet in your shoulder. You still steady on your feet?"

"Hanging in there."

Alex snorted. "First a scalpel, now two bullets. You're living dangerously, Mr. Bigelow."

"Tell me about it," Cy groused.

Alex looked up at Maurice. "Find Mat Cárdenas. I'm sure he's in a state of panic. Probably trying to make his way up here. Let him know he's going to be fine."

"Mat Cárdenas," Maurice said with a nod. "Probably best to take him with me back to HQ. And I'll tell Dr. A to meet us there."

"Thanks," Alex said, and then Maurice was gone. *Poof.* More physics, Cy figured as the hair on the back of his neck stood up. These last two days had been a wild ride, and he figured things were about to get wilder.

"Dr. A is our family doctor," Alex said, pulling one leg up and propping an elbow on his knee. "He'll take care of you."

"Family doctor," Cy said. "So, Alex the billionaire and Maurice the bartender are related?"

"I promise I'll answer your questions. Soon. But the most important question right now is how a suicide bomber got through a high-resolution wave scanner, a hands-on pat down, and two checkpoints with bomb-sniffing dogs and half a dozen of Jensen's hand-picked Secret Service personnel if he was wearing a vest full of explosives."

Cy locked eyes with Alex. "He didn't. He put the vest on *after* he was in the building. It was all a big show."

"That's my guess. Assassination by performance art."

"For what was purpose? Who was the target?"

"You? Some other poor soul Jensen had a quarrel with? Maybe no one in particular. Maybe he was just sending a message. Tyrants are maestros at wielding violence and threats of violence for their own purposes. I'm certain there were plenty of people in that ballroom Jensen would be happy to be rid of."

"And the bomber?"

"If he was a willing martyr for the Jensen cause, his family will be well rewarded for his sacrifice. If not, they're probably already dead. Or soon will be."

"Holy hell." Cy sunk down to sit against the wall and then remembered he'd been shot. He hunched forward and rested his bleeding arm in his lap. "Now what?"

Alex's lips quirked in a grim smile. "Now it's our turn to perform. And then we'll talk. I'll introduce you to my family. And yours."

Cy jerked his head up. "What the hell is that supposed to mean?"

"You'll see."

By the time Agent Reynolds and his colleague, Agent Dennehey, maneuvered the two so-called national heroes down the stairs and into the waiting room of Chancellor Jensen's medical suite, the doctor was already seeing other injured patients. One of whom was First Lady Alyssa Valentine, the new Alexander Whitelaw superfan, who had several broken ribs and a punctured lung. A nurse came out to tell Reynolds that the First Lady was stable, but that the wife of a senator had gone into premature labor and so the wait for Cy and Alex to be seen was going to be longer than expected since neither had gone into shock or were losing blood by the bucketful. And that gave them the perfect excuse to leave.

"But the Chancellor insisted you wait," Reynolds said, looking like he'd be more than happy for the two men to be on their way.

"Senator Parker's wife needs the doctor's attention more than I do," Cy said, his patience at the ragged edge of playing polite. "I told you I've got a medic on staff who can get this bullet out of me, and while I may be still standing now, I don't think I'm going to last much longer."

"I'm afraid I can't just let you—" Reynold's hand came to rest on his holster.

"Look, Agent Reynolds," Alex said, drawing himself up to his full height and peering down at the man. "We are leaving now because this man needs medical attention, and as gracious as the Chancellor's offer is, I don't believe he'll want the news to spread that an SS Agent held tonight's heroes at gunpoint while the man he thanked personally for saving countless lives—in front of witnesses—bled out on the carpet in the doctor's waiting room."

Reynolds' fingers flexed on the butt of his gun. "Fine," he said with a huff. He moved his hand from his holster and stood back so Cy and Alex had a clear path to the door.

"Give Chancellor Jensen our deepest regards," Alex said. "I believe I can speak for both of us, when I say that we are more committed than ever to being of service to this country." And then they shuffled their way toward the medical suite's door.

Reynold's caught Agent Dennehey's eye. "Follow them." The man nodded and slipped out behind Cy and Alex who pretended to hobble through the lobby and out the door where Mat and dozens of other assorted security personnel waited for their principals. Red and white lights strobed from police cars, ambulances, and fire trucks as first responders worked to triage and treat guests still straggling their way down the stairs and out the door.

Mat rushed forward and put an arm around Cy's waist. "Jesus! What happened? Are you okay? What do you need? Some guy showed up and said you'd been shot, but that you were still upright. I wanted to come up, but they're not letting anyone in the building."

Although he was putting on a good show, Cy's legs were far from steady, and he was glad of the familiarity of Mat's support. "Maurice found you?"

"Yeah. Said he saw the whole thing and talked to you. Insisted I go with him, but I told him to fuck off. I wasn't going anywhere until I set eyes on you."

Cy looked over at Alex. "Guess it's time for formal introductions. Mat, meet Alexander Whitelaw, aka, the Fucking Forest Ranger. Alex, meet Mat Cárdenas. I'm sure you already know all about him."

"Yes, I believe we've met before," Alex said with a knowing smile.

"Fuck me sideways," Mat muttered, shaking his head. "I couldn't believe my eyes earlier, even though Cy said it was you, but holy shit."

"Holy shit is the least of it," Cy said with a grimace. "I killed a man tonight, Mat. Or at least I think I did."

"What the fuck? How? What happened?"

"Well, he was trying to kill me first, so…I'll tell you all about it later." He turned to Alex. "Do you really have a car waiting?"

Alex snorted. "Now why would I need a car?"

Cy and Mat just stared at him. Then Cy nodded.

"Okay. Are you able to take Mat with us?" Feeling precariously close to crying for the first time since his mother died, Cy took a breath. He felt like he was about to step off a precipice into the unknown. Plus, the trickle of blood down his arm and back was making him woozy. "I *need* him with me."

"No problem," Alex said. "First, turn off your phones and hand them over. We want to avoid any chance of the SS tracking us."

Mat dug into Cy's jacket pocket and pulled out his phone, then pulled his own out and handed them over. Alex dropped both into a small opaque bag that he produced out of nowhere and that then, just as quickly, disappeared.

"Okay, let's go. We can't do this in plain sight." Without another word, they made their way to the curb and Alex led them between two idling firetrucks where they were out of view of the crowds swarming the Mall.

"Hold on." Alex held his hands out, palms up. Cy put his non-bloody hand in one and motioned for Mat to do the same. Alex closed his fingers over both hands and gave them each a reassuring squeeze.

Not ten minutes later, Supervisory Security Service Agent Reynolds snapped his head up from reading something on his tablet. "What do you mean, they disappeared?"

Agent Jack Dennehey waved an arm out toward the Mall. "I followed them like you told me to. Another guy joined them just outside, and they all headed toward the street. They were moving slow. The big guy—or rather, the bigger guy—Whitelaw, was leading the way. The third guy must've been one of their bodyguards. Almost as big as Whitelaw. He was helping hold Bigelow up. I watched them step between two firetrucks parked along Consti—I mean, along Jensen Avenue—and went around the far end of one of the trucks to wait and watch as they crossed the road. The street was packed with emergency response vehicles, but I didn't see any private car waiting for them. I hesitated for just a minute or two and when they didn't cross the street, I circled back around and peeked in between the vehicles. They weren't there. If they'd gone back to the Mall, I would've seen them. But they were gone. I swear it."

"People cannot just fucking disappear into thin air, Agent Dennehey," Reynolds smirked and looked at Dennehey like he was a blithering idiot. "Go back out there and look again. Do your job. Ask questions. Find me some answers. And don't come back until you have something more believable to say. Imagine me telling the Chancellor that three grown men just disappeared into thin air. Like that." He snapped his fingers. "I'd lose *my* fucking job. And *you'd* lose your fucking head."

Jack Dennehey straightened his shoulders. He didn't sign up for this shit. He didn't put on a suit everyday only to be constantly berated by a sycophantic supervisory agent who drank too much, cheated on his wife, and couldn't hit a target at twenty feet, let alone a hundred. He hadn't gone through the FBI Academy only to have his career disrupted, told to sign a loyalty oath to a loathsome toad of a man with hair plugs, and then required to follow orders from his imbecilic henchmen.

But damn it all, he needed his paycheck. His father's cancer treatments had nearly bankrupted the whole family already. He couldn't let his parents lose their house. Or let his sister's girls grow up in a government camp for the homeless where who knew what kind of shit went on. He wouldn't do it. He refused to let petty tyrants like Reynolds or Valentine or Jensen win.

But maybe they'd already won. Maybe he was a fool. Maybe he should just give up. Like his father wanted to. Stop treatments. Let the cancer win. The cancer in the old man's colon and the cancer in the country.

No! He wasn't about to let that happen. He gave Agent Reynolds a sharp nod, turned on heel, and went back out the way he'd come in.

21

Cy knew to brace himself, but Alex held on to Mat as they arrived. Alex told him not to worry, that first timers often fell over and threw up. Second timers were often dizzy and disoriented. Even third timers could be unsteady on their feet. It takes a while for carbon-based life forms to acclimate themselves to the physics of teleportation. Having your cellular structure disassembled, shot through a wormhole at faster than light speed, then reassembled into its previous state isn't for the faint of heart.

"You okay?" Cy wobbled, shook his head as if he had water in his ears. Turns out third timers who were bleeding from multiple bullet wounds didn't fare too well either.

"Been better," Mat choked out, sitting hard in a chair that seemed to have materialized out of nowhere. He put his head between his knees. "Room's spinning. How're you holding up?"

"Still here. Bit woozy. Think I need a nap."

Mat risked raising his eyes, glanced around the room. "Nice place. Comfy. You, in contrast, look like utter shit."

They were in someone's swanky living room, full of fine art on the walls and thick rugs on the tiled floor, low tables set amidst arrangements of comfortable chairs and couches and adorned with vases full of fresh flowers. And what looked like a bank of large television screens mounted on the far wall. They were all playing different news feeds of the disaster on the Mall, but they were all on mute.

Mat looked up as Alex produced a glass of ice water as if by magic and gave it to him. "Where the hell are we?"

"As I told Cy—and as I'm sure he told you—I'm part of an organization dedicated to global justice. This is our main headquarters in the U.S."

Mat took a long drink. Wiped his mouth on his sleeve. "So, you're like, what? INTERPOL? International Court of Justice or something?"

"Or something," Alex said. "Because we're global, we have places like this all over, but some of my closest friends and colleagues live in this house much of the time, so it feels like a home base. We'll explain everything soon. I promise you won't leave here without the answers you need, but first we need the doctor to—"

"Glad you made it in one piece." A dapper, classically handsome man with a touch of steel grey at the temples and a smooth British accent walked into the room rubbing his hands on a white cloth. "I was just prepping the operating room." He reached out to hold Cy steady. "Whoa, there. I understand you've got two bullet wounds this time. Not to worry. I'll get you fixed up in a jif. I want to check on those stitches too."

"Wait. I remember your voice." Cy wobbled again. Mat was on his feet to help him, but Alex got there first.

"I've got him, Mat."

Mat shot Alex a dark look but sat back down hard as the room decided to go for another spin.

"Indeed?" The doctor looked at Cy appraisingly. "I thought you were unconscious most of the time."

"But that was in Arizona and we're in ..." Cy looked to Alex and then swayed again. The teleportation had given him a headache and made him feel hollowed out. Plus, his shirt was sticking to his back, his left shoulder was throbbing like a drum line in a marching band, and he couldn't feel his right arm. The only things he'd had since breakfast were a few pretzels, two mezcals, and a sparkling water. He swallowed against a wave of nausea, everything finally catching up to him.

Alex gripped him around the waist. "We're still in Washington. Or, rather, Georgetown."

"You haven't traveled far this time, my boy," the doctor said. "But I didn't stitch you up in Arizona. Nemi brought you to my surgery in Cambridge."

"Cambridge?" Cy rubbed his temple. "Massachusetts?"

"No. UK. I've nothing against Massachusetts, but I don't think I'd like to live there. Too cold."

Cy squinted up at him. "UK as in England?" He tried to rub his temple, but his extremities had apparently gone on strike, and he felt like his head might explode. *No. Better to not think about exploding heads after seeing that bomber's head rolling around on the ballroom floor.*

He tried to focus on Alex. "Who the hell is Nemi? Another one of your names?"

Before the Alex could answer, Cy's knees decided to buckle. His eyes drifted shut as Alex supported him around the middle. Dr. A was right there beside him, and Mat was moving too.

"Nemi, get us to the OR," the doctor said, and suddenly they were all in an operating suite and Alex and Mat were lifting Cy onto an operating table.

Dr. A took Cy's wrist in one hand, checked his pulse. Produced a pen light and opened first one eyelid and then the other.

"He'll be fine," Dr. A reassured them. "I'm going to need to cut off his clothes. Want to help?"

"I've got medical training," Mat said. "Special forces."

"Then you know what to do. Go wash up, grab a mask, gloves, and a gown, and let's get down to business."

Forty-five minutes later, Alex lowered himself into a chair across from where Mat was sitting, head tipped back, gaze focused somewhere in the middle distance. "How're you feeling?"

Mat shifted, looked over at Alex. "I think I've completely lost my marbles."

Alex chuckled. "We'll help you find them. I promise."

Mat was quiet for a long moment, studying Alex like he was trying to take his measure. "Cy said he'd killed someone," he said finally. "What happened?"

"An agent—or someone posing as an agent—grabbed him and shoved a gun in his ribs. Right after the bomb went off. Told him he was instructed to 'take care of him.' Thought the chaos of the moment presented the perfect opportunity. Cy apparently took umbrage at that and took him out instead. A steak knife to the throat."

"Jesus." Mat blew out a breath. "Jensen's after Bigelow land."

"That's what Cy said."

Mat held Alex's gaze. "Cy's never killed anyone before."

"He's got you to talk to if he needs it."

Mat nodded. He knew what it felt like, that first kill. No matter how justified, the first time was hard. The sense of relief that you'd survived the fight still standing was both euphoric and draining. But it was the sense of power that was dangerous. Some could control it. Wield it for good. Some let it control them. Those were the real assholes. And he'd known plenty in his time on the Teams. On both sides—enemies and friends. "You said there's a guest room I can use?"

"Yes," Alex stood. "And your phone in your room, along with Cy's. You can talk freely as any communications going in and out of this location are completely invisible to Administration eyes and ears. We sent someone to the Waldorf to get your bags, so you should have everything you need. Helen and Kemal know you're here. I'm going up to shower and change so I'll show you the way. And where the kitchen is, in case you're hungry."

Mat made no move to get up. Instead, he cocked his head sideways and let his eyes run up and down Alex Whitelaw's long frame as if assessing him for hidden weapons. "So, we're just supposed to trust you. After everything."

Everything like throwing myself on a man with a bomb and saving your friend's life again, you mean? Nemi was truly glad Mat was not just taking her at her word, but still. It did grate a bit on her human ego.

"I know it's hard for someone like you, but I believe your instincts are telling you that we truly are on your side. We know you're involved in the Resistance. We know you're keeping secrets from the Administration, and we want to help you keep them. We want to help you keep the people you care about safe. Just trust me for a little longer. Until Cy wakes up, and we can explain everything. Then you can decide if you want to work with us or not. It's your decision."

Mat took in and exhaled a deep breath, then pushed himself to his feet. "I suppose that has to be enough for now."

"Let's shake on 'enough for now.'" Alex stuck out his hand and Mat took it, gave it a bone-crushing squeeze that made Alex smile. "You're safe here and on the grounds of the compound, but don't try to go back to the Waldorf without letting anyone know."

"I'd never leave without Cy."

Alex smiled at that. "You wouldn't get far anyway. The perimeter is booby trapped."

22

Cy blinked awake. For the second time in as many days—had it only been two days? Or was it three?—he was in a bed with Hallie Jones sitting across the room, a book in her lap, watching him. Hallelujah Delphinium Jones. That's what she'd said to call her. That was before she'd teleported him all over the place and turned into Alexander Whitelaw, a.k.a. the Forest Fucking Ranger, a.k.a. quantum communications entrepreneur, a.k.a. the man who threw himself on top of suicide bombers to save lives.

His life. Again.

And, he remembered through the waking haze of a deep sleep induced by pain meds, that he'd killed a man. With a steak knife and a well-placed knee. And he remembered that the doctor had called Alex—called him? called her?—Nemi. *Nemi.*

He tried to scoot up against the pile of soft pillows behind him. He'd obviously been given some excellent drugs because he couldn't feel any pain in his left shoulder or his right arm, although he realized his right arm wasn't quite operational yet. Which, he supposed, was normal if he'd had a bullet dug out of it. Or maybe the bullet had just whizzed right through muscle and bone. He had no idea. He was still foggy, but all in all, he felt remarkably good for having been sliced open, teleported all over the place, flown across the country, shot, shot again, blown up, and teleported again. And operated on.

He twisted so he could use his left arm to reach for the bottle of water beside the bed, situated just like back at his apartment in Bigelow. Took a long swig. Swallowed. Cleared his throat. Quirked a smile at the woman watching him and said, "Hello, Hallie. Nice of you to stop by for visiting hours. Or should I call you Nemi?"

She ignored that. "Glad to see you're among the living."

"Hmm. Maybe I've died and gone to heaven. Or I'm dreaming, and I'm really back home on familiar territory with a strange woman who enjoys lurking in bedrooms and rescuing gentlemen in distress."

No matter where they were or who this person really was, she was beautiful in a way that made something inside his chest feel all twisted up. Bruised. Like he'd suffered a bad heart sprain. Maybe he needed to ice it. Or was it heat? Or maybe he should just embrace the pain.

She smiled. "Everyone's here. They're waiting for you. You feel ready to get up or do you need more time?"

"Define everyone."

"Friends. Family. Colleagues."

"Sounds like too many everyones. Might need a couple decades to feel ready." He scrubbed his left hand down his face. "What time is it and where's Mat?"

"It's still early. Just after five a.m. You slept through the night. Mat's still here. Impatient and demanding answers."

Cy snorted. "Is he ordering everyone around yet?"

"I wouldn't call it 'ordering' exactly. But he's made his thoughts clear where you're concerned. I imagine that's how all your friends are. Mat. Brooks. Mason. They take care of you."

"We take care of each other." He felt the scruff on his jaw. Maybe it was time to grow a beard again. "I guess your super secret organization has dossiers on all of us."

"We don't need dossiers."

"Memories like steel traps, huh?"

"Something like that." Hallie stood, picked up a bundle of clothes off the floor beside her chair, and approached the bed, setting them in a pile on the mussed duvet. "By the way, we're national heroes. The bombing is the only thing on the news, crowding out stories of women and children disappearing from internment camps, murdered women turning up face down in rivers, and governors disappearing into thin air. There's video of the heroic and elusive Alex Whitelaw throwing himself on the bomber, and—"

"Does the video show him disappearing into thin air?"

"Not surprisingly, it goes dark for a few critical seconds, then when it comes back online, it shows the handsome millionaire from Arizona being led by an SS agent up to meet Jensen and Valentine after taking a bullet to protect them. Apparently, the Chancellor and President wanted to thank him in person."

"Millionaire, huh? More like thousandaire."

"Mat has talked to Helen and Kemal at the Waldorf, by the way, and called your friends and family at home to let everyone know you're okay. You can speak to them when you're ready, but I suspect you might want to wait until our Q & A session is over. And before any of that can happen, you need to get up and get dressed. We got your bags from the Waldorf."

"How efficient you are." With his right arm feeling floppy, he grabbed the covers with his left and threw them back. Well, well. He smiled up at Hallie. "This is getting to be a habit. Me naked. You ... well, you know. Not naked."

She laughed at that. "I'm not complaining."

"Oh, but I am."

"Mat told us you sleep in the buff, so ..." She shrugged and let her eyes drift up and down his body.

He waved a hand at himself. "Feels like an uneven playing field. Like you should at least sacrifice a shirt or something. You know, in the interest of fair play and all that."

"Maybe someday we'll have to do something about the playing field, but right now, people are waiting and Dr. A has a nice fire going because he said you might be chilled after surgery. It's not every day you get a bullet dug out of your back. The bullet that hit your arm is apparently lost amidst the rubble. He just had to do a bit of repair work and give you another shiny new set of stitches."

He tried to lift his arm, but it was as responsive as a wet noodle.

"He's got a sling for the arm, but since you heal quickly, you'll be operational in no time."

"I take it my tux is toast?"

"Mat and I cut it off you. So, unless you want to keep it as a souvenir, yes."

"And a bathroom? I've gotta piss like a racehorse."

"How charmingly eloquent you are first thing in the morning, Mr. Bigelow." She gestured to a door behind her. "You can take the clothes in if you want some privacy while you get dressed. Or I can wait outside."

He raised a brow. "Seriously? You've already watched me get dressed once. We're not plowing new ground here. Yet."

Still, he disappeared into the bathroom while Nemi's human brain got busy flooding her system with dopamine, oxytocin, and endorphins and her ovaries and adrenal glands happily pumped out enough estrogen to float a trireme. When he emerged a few minutes later, face and neck scrubbed pink and hair damp as if he'd put his head under the sink's faucet, she was still standing smack in the middle of the room.

"Thanks for setting out my toiletries. Especially the toothbrush." He made a face. "Mouth felt like a lab for testing poisonous gas." He walked straight toward her, still buck naked, a lazy smile on his lips that sent a bolt of heat straight to her center.

She let her gaze drift over him again, soft as a feather's touch, and pretended to be completely unaffected by his body, now close enough—*how was he suddenly so close?*—that she could feel the heat of him and run a finger down his muscled chest. Trace a line around his stitches, healing remarkably well. And drift lower. If she wanted to, that is.

But she didn't.

At least not right this minute.

She swallowed. *Stupid human hormones.* He was recovering from surgery, for Kaos' sake. And the others were waiting just down the hall. She rolled a hand in the air in a hurry up motion. "Well, Mr. Buck Naked. Better get moving. Answers await just outside your door."

"Wanna help me get dressed?" He pointed to his right arm, hanging numbly at his side. "I'm a little short-handed."

Her mouth went dry. "Maybe I should get Mat to help you."

He tilted his head. "Hmm. Let me think. Would I rather a beautiful, mysterious woman help me put my pants on or a big hairy guy I've known since we were in diapers?"

"Fine." Hallie rolled her eyes and grabbed his boxer briefs to hold them out for him to step into.

"A little lower, please. I'm not some high stepping Lipizzaner." His voice was laced with suppressed laughter.

Her mouth twisted into a smile as she bent to hold the boxers lower and felt his hand land on the back of her head for balance. The pressure from his hand pushed her head down ever so slightly until she was eye level with his stitches—and that line of dark hair that arrowed straight toward his ...

Well. That's impressive.

"I'm trying to think of cold showers and icebergs and glaciers and all things freezing and shrinking," he said with a laugh, sticking one leg and then the other into the boxers while trying to keep his balance. "Unfortunately, looking down at the top of your head positioned just so, it's not working."

"I guess I should be flattered, although what I know of anatomy is that any woman in this position would garner the same physical reaction from a human male."

"Human male." He barked out a laugh. "Oh, Hallie, you are a delight."

"Kaos! Quit wobbling." She tugged the snug briefs up his legs until... "You're going to have to tuck that thing in while I pull up the waistband."

"Oh, all right." He let out an exaggerated sigh and took himself in hand. Thinking of cold things had not helped. His cock had more interesting things in mind. Snug, warm, wet things.

Hallie tried not to laugh. "Move your hand, damn it."

He did. Circling his thumb and forefinger around his shaft, he moved his hand up and down. "This is a little awkward because I usually do this with my right hand."

"Not like that!" *Was she actually giggling.* "Stop it or I'm going to get Mat to finish this."

"Okay, okay." He was laughing now too. He couldn't remember the last time he'd been so irredeemably delighted. If that was even a thing. Despite all he'd gone through, he couldn't stop the joy welling up inside him like a fucking geyser. His eyes were watering, and his chest felt full to bursting. Like his cock.

"The idea of Mat in here is definitely deflating." He held his throbbing dick against his body so she could pull the waistband up. She released it with a snap. "Ow."

"Pants next. And no funny business or we'll never get you dressed. Everyone's waiting."

"Fine," he said with mock contrition. "I promise I'll be a good boy." He stepped into the pants she held out.

"I'm not asking for a miracle, just a bit of cooperation." She pulled them up and stood.

"Ah, so you like the idea of me being a bad boy?"

"I'd like it if you kept your mouth shut until we're done here. Can you manage the zipper?"

"I can think of a few ways you can shut me up. And no, I'm gonna have to rely on your nimble fingers to zip me up."

There were other things she'd like to do with her nimble fingers, but she zipped and buttoned him up. Then held out a well-worn cotton button-down so he could lift his right arm and slip it into the sleeve. And then he stuck his left arm into the other sleeve, and she checked the bandage on his shoulder before adjusting the collar. "Hold still, I need to button this."

He watched her fingers patiently work the buttons down the front of the shirt. "Don't forget my cuffs. Or better yet, just roll them up." He held out his left arm. "You'd make a good valet. Maybe you could prepare my bath next. Give me a close shave."

"You're enjoying this too much."

"You have no idea. I think getting shot, twice, was worth this little interlude of ours. I might have to throw myself in the line of fire more often."

"Don't even joke about that." She finished rolling up his cuffs, leaned forward and pressed a quick kiss to his lips. She heard him suck in a breath as she picked up the socks.

"What was that for?"

"For you not dying. You want these on?"

"I'm happy I'm not dead too. And of course. I want to see you kneeling before me."

"You are incorrigible."

He sat down on the edge of the bed and stuck a foot out. "All just part of the charm."

Back at the New America Building, SS Agent Bill Reynolds held the Chancellor's narrow, steely grey gaze and waited. One. Two. Three seconds. He flexed his fingers. Clasped his hands behind his back. Four. Five. He was starting to sweat. Or sweat more. He'd already been sweating as he descended the dark staircase to the Chancellor's underground bunker. Or the Liar's Lair, as he knew some of the agents called it. The agents who didn't value life, liberty, or the pursuit of happiness. Agents he'd happily bribe, blackmail, or throw underneath a bus if needed.

And then, Chancellor Jensen stood up from his chair. "What *exactly* do you mean they disappeared? Both of them? Do we have CCTV we can check? Drone footage? Eyewitnesses? Anything to establish where they *really* went since Agent Dennehey appears to be a complete idiot?"

"I'm afraid not, sir. I made sure Agent Dennehey interviewed the first responders and guests who were milling around that area of the Mall, and no one reported seeing anything strange. No one remembered seeing the men at all. Of course, most people were still in shock and worried about their own safety."

"Worried about their own safety." Jensen repeated, the words slow and deliberate. The Chancellor took a deep breath. Stepped around his desk until he was toe-to-toe with Reynolds. They were about the same height, but the similarities ended there. Reynolds was trim and fit, a man who worked out not just because it was his job, but because it was his nature. Jensen was a study in muscle gone to flab, his scent eau de flatulence, his breath as rancid as leftovers left too long in the back of the fridge.

Reynolds wouldn't allow himself to flinch. He stood at attention, not a single muscle even so much as dared to twitch or quiver. Jensen's shoulders hunched forward like he was missing part of his spine. And maybe he was. Sometimes he hardly seemed human. Like right now when his face was a sort of mottled color, as if a two-year-old had played patty-cake with his food and mashed his yams and beets together in a bowl then smeared it on himself.

"*WHAT ABOUT MY SAFETY? WHAT ABOUT THE PRESIDENT'S SAFETY? CABINET MEMBERS? SENATORS? REPRESENTATIVES?*"

Reynolds didn't dare wipe the spittle from his face. But he wanted to. Oh, he definitely wanted to. In fact, he would've paid good money for the privilege to spit back, right in Harold Jensen's twitchy little eye. But he didn't. He had too much to live for.

"I'm sorry, sir. Of course, we'll keep looking for them. And we'll find them. I can promise you that."

"Or I'll have Dennehey's head on a platter, Reynolds. Mark my words." Jensen shambled back behind his desk and sank down into his chair. "You tell him that's a direct quote." The outburst seemed to have cost him. "Now get the hell out of here."

As Reynolds crossed the large expanse of carpet toward the door, he heard the Chancellor grumbling under his breath. "Only four dead. Jesus, what a disaster. And that stupid baby. Shit. Parker's going to be even more of a problem now. I'm surrounded by fucking idiots."

23

"Where's his sling?" Dr. A asked Nemi as she led Cy back into the main gathering area of the Pantheon League's American headquarters, now full of people.

Nemi unrolled the soft blue mesh sling she'd tucked under her arm and held it out. The doctor took it, chuckling and looking Cy up and down. "You managed to get him dressed, didn't you? I'm sure you're perfectly capable of helping with his sling, Nemi."

"*Nemi* does have a deft touch," Cy said with a smirk. "But she once told me she's not *exactly* a doctor, so I insisted on leaving the sling to you." He looked across the room where Mat was pouring himself a cup of coffee. "How you doin', buddy?"

"I'm still here, wherever here is. The more important question is how are you?"

"Think I'll live."

Mat finished pouring and nodded. "Good. Brooks and Mason would kill me if I brought you home in a box, and I wouldn't ever be able to face Sybil, Sofia or BoJo again, so you better keep it that way."

"I'll try to stay alive for your sake."

Mat held his gaze for a moment, then nodded, raised his cup. "Coffee?"

"That'd be great. Thanks."

Cy's gaze swept over the others in the room as Dr. A adjusted his arm and made sure the sling's strap wasn't touching the incision on his shoulder. Who were these people and why were they here looking at him so ... expectantly? He wanted answers, but this seemed like some kind of setup.

Whatever it was, he didn't think he'd ever seen a more beautiful group of people gathered in one place. It was like he'd stepped into a magazine photo shoot complete with mood lighting and a prototypical roaring fire in an impressive stone fireplace in the background. *Vanity Fair Georgetown Edition* or something. He knew he was well put together and Mat always turned heads, but these people? Wow. Even the doctor looked like he'd just stepped off the page of some fancy *GQ* menswear ad. *Bespoke suits for the man who has everything.*

His gaze snagged on the woman who'd told him to call her Hallie Jones. Was her real name Nemi? Or Alex? Was she a she or was he a he? Or a they? Did it matter? He knew Hallie would say it didn't. And maybe it shouldn't, but he'd much rather imagine running his tongue along Hallie's warm, wet, welcoming cleft than along Alex's ... whatever.

He wasn't going to let himself think about that possibility, especially now that she was right here, flesh and blood and within arm's reach. She was the most beautiful person in the room and catching her eye made something in his chest bloom with a powerful feeling of *rightness*—if that was a word. Especially after their silly shenanigans. He suppressed a smile.

Yes, he wanted answers, but he also wanted to replay that little kiss she'd planted on his lips. Take it deeper. Pull her to him and bury his face in the crook of her neck. Feel her pressed against him. With everything terrible going on in the world, he longed for a simple moment of closeness with this woman. And if she was somehow also Alex Whitelaw?—although it didn't seem possible, it did appear probable, and he couldn't conceive of an alternative explanation—well, what then?

The doctor took Cy's elbow and guided him toward an chair with a padded back.

"Thanks," Cy said, settling into the divinely cushioned seat.

"Mat's already met everyone," Hallie/Alex/Nemi said. "Well, I should say that preliminary introductions have been made, but everyone's been waiting for you to tell you both who we really are."

Cy glanced over at Mat who gave him an *I-have-no-fucking-idea-what's-going-on!* shrug.

"So let me introduce you to our crew. First," she waved at a trio of women who all smiled and waved from their places on one of the couches. "This is Alecto, Megaera, and Tisiphone, or Ali, Tisi, and Meg to their friends. They're also known as the Three Sisters, the Erinyes, or the Furies. They're the owners of this beautiful home, the founders of the The Philology League, the front organization we've set up at this address, and they maintain all the services we rely on to do our jobs in the human world."

"We hope you both feel at home here," Ali said with a mischievous smile. She looked to Nemi/Hallie/Alex and gave her an exaggerated wink. "We have a sneaking suspicion we'll be seeing a lot of you in the future."

"Don't let them sidetrack you, Nemi," Dr. A said. "We've got a lot of territory to cover, and no matter who he is, Cy's body still needs to rest and recuperate."

No matter who he is? Cy wondered who they thought he was supposed to be. He was a freaking open book. Everyone knew who he was. That was the problem. Even fucking Chancellor Jensen knew his family history and what kind of man he was.

"Yes, well, okay. Here we have Dio." Nemi said as a deeply tanned man with a boyish look, a roguish smile, and a mop of wavy sandy blond hair stood and shook Cy's hand with gusto. He looked like a surfer who'd just thrown on some casually fashionable and very expensive clothes after stepping out of the waves. His hair even looked artfully windblown.

"It's a pleasure to meet you. Been looking forward to it ever since we found out. My job here is to keep the whole crew in wine and food and music. Help make sure we don't forget the finer things in life while we attend to everything else. We even play a mean board game every once in a while."

"Nice to meet you, Dio, but ever since you found out what?"

"Nemi should be the one to tell you."

"Tell me what, exactly, *Nemi*." This was all getting supremely aggravating.

"Let's get introductions out of the way first," Nemi said.

"Fine," Cy ground out. He had absolutely no clue what was going on, but if Dio was in charge of the liquor, he'd take advantage of that. "Got something to go in my coffee, Dio? An Irish coffee sounds good about now, if that's your territory."

The doctor shook his head. "No alcohol until the pain meds wear off."

"You're no fun," Dio frowned. "No booze, I'm afraid, Cy, but I can manage some food for you."

As if by magic, a large plate laden with slices of cheese and fruit and several beautiful pastries—smelling like they'd just come out of the oven—appeared on the table next to his chair. No one in the room seemed to think it unusual for food to magically appear. No one except Cy and Mat, of course.

"Next," Nemi went on, completely unfazed, "is Hermes. He's in charge of communications for our organization. Always flitting here and there, making sure messages are delivered securely whenever we can't rely on other means of communications or we need to communicate with someone outside our organization. Our systems are the most reliable and secure in the world—Tisi, our tech guru sees to that— but sometimes a face-to-face chat is the only way to make sure a message is delivered correctly."

Hermes tipped his head in a nonchalant nod then uncrossed and re-crossed his legs. He was wearing a chocolate brown V-neck sweater that showed off a series of gold chains against tanned skin, black skintight leather pants, and fringed leather ankle boots with cowboy cut heels. A black leather biker jacket was draped over the back of his chair and a black helmet decorated with flaming wings sat on a side table. A bit flamboyant. Cy wondered what kind of motorcycle the guy was into. He and Mat had probably already had that conversation.

"And last, but not least," Nemi said, "are two people with whom you've already communicated but who never revealed their true identities. You know them as the founders of the American Resistance Movement: Chiron and Artemis. They're the ones who initially reached out to recruit you to ARM."

Cy and Mat looked at each other sharply and then at the two people they'd only ever known by code names.

"As you may have already guessed," Nemi went on, "our organization and your organization are, in essence, one and the same. Honestly, I've wanted to tell you all along, but it's usually a bit much for the humans we work with to take in."

There was that 'humans' thing again. What was that all about? Cy pushed to his feet as the two stood and approached him, looked him in the eye. Cy was 6'3", but Chiron towered over him by at least another five inches. The man's skin was olive-dark, his features broad and strong, his eyes grey and penetrating, and his black hair, glinting in the lamplight with streaks of amber gold, was long and tied back in a thick braid that hung down his back.

Artemis, on the other hand, was shorter but still probably close to six feet. Her features were finely drawn, her golden hair pulled back in a bun at the nape of her neck, and her skin so fair it glowed as if lit from within. He imagined her draped in fabric and posed on a plinth in a museum or sculpture garden somewhere.

"I'm honored," he said, reaching out to shake Chiron's hand first. With a sideways glance toward Mat, who had always wanted to pretend they went to school in a cave with Chiron the Wisest and Justest of all Centaurs as their teacher, he said, "Your code names are certainly spot on."

"It is indeed a pleasure to finally meet you in person," Chiron said in a voice that was as resonant and melodic as it was deep. "Your father will be very proud to know you."

Chiron took Cy's hand, wrapped it in both of his and held him tight for a long moment. Cy started to say that his father, now dead for almost a decade, had been a profligate, self-centered bastard, but suddenly Chiron released him and went back to his place, leaning against the fireplace mantle, and the awkwardness of the moment passed.

Artemis, in contrast, cupped Cy's face in both hands and kissed him full on the mouth. It wasn't a sexual kiss. More like some sort of claiming. An acknowledgment. Or something. Hell, he had no idea. He just stood there, one arm starting to tingle in its sling, the other limp at his side.

"We need to tell him," she said, looking over at the doctor. "It's past time."

"Soon." Dr. A nodded.

"Tell me what?"

"Not you," Artemis began. "Well, you too, but we need to tell your—"

Dr. A lifted a hand and Artemis stopped mid-sentence.

Cy sank back down in his chair. "Look, all this *wink wink nod nod* shit has to stop." He pinned Hallie/Alex/Nemi/Whoever with a hard gaze. "Who are you really? More to the point, *what* are you? Why are you taking care of me, and why have you brought Mat and me here? To put it in layman's terms, *WHAT THE ACTUAL FUCK IS GOING ON?*"

"Bravo." Tisi clapped slowly and gave him an approving nod. "I knew I was going to like you."

Nemi took a deep breath and pulled a chair close to Cy's. She sat. Leaned forward. "I warned you that you wouldn't believe me if I told you my real name, but here goes…"

Cy waited. Glanced at Mat, then back to Nemi.

Nemi swallowed.

Everyone in the room held their breath. Dio stopped swinging his leg. Mat and Hermes leaned forward in anticipation. Ali, Meg, and Tisi tensed, on the edges of their seats.

"First, let me preface all this by saying that everyone in this room is a part of the organization I told you about. We call it the Pantheon League, and we're all dedicated to the same ideals of justice. Ideals I have served my entire life. As have Ali, Meg, and Tisi. And my name is…well." She wet her lips. Drew in a long breath. Sat up straight. "I am a daughter of Nyx, primordial Goddess of the Night, and my true name is Nemesis, Immortal Goddess of Divine Retribution and Vengeance."

A long moment of silence. Then Mat snorted. Cy choked out some sort of sound, half laugh and half cry. Nemi went on.

"My oldest friends call me Nemi. Dr. A's full name is, simply, Asklepios of Epidavros, the most famous healer in human history. I took you to him in Cambridge the day I found you at SDIC because he's not only a great physician, he's your half-brother."

"Holy hell." Cy ran his hand through his hair and sought out Mat. Their gazes locked.

"Half-brother?" Mat growled. "You have *got* to be kidding me. I've known Cy my entire life!"

"Let me finish. You both wanted the truth, and I'm giving it to you even though I know full well it will be difficult to hear."

She leaned forward, took Cy's left hand and held it tight. Pinned her gaze on him. "After I met you during that climbing accident in Arizona, when Brooks nearly fell to his death, I suspected you were different. I *felt* you were different. So, I did a little digging and discovered the truth."

"Which is...?" In for a penny, in for a pound. Cy was going to push this to its logical—or illogical—conclusion.

"Your father was not Cyrus Bigelow. He was—*is*—Apollo, son of Zeus and Leto. You and your sister are demigods, children of an Olympian and a mortal woman. You were not conceived in Arizona after your parents' wedding, but in Delphi when your mother visited Greece just before your legal parents were married. I have been keeping track of you and your friends since the day of that accident. It's how I knew taking you back to that site would be important to you. I hoped you would remember me. Remember what I looked like. How I helped you then. And that you would know—*in your heart*—that I want to help you now."

"Cy, this can't be real," Mat managed to choke out.

Cy tried to pull his hand back, but Nemi held on to him.

"I knew you were in danger down at SDIC because we are connected. Since that day on the cliff. And when you were on that operating table, when that monster was going to cut you open for your organs, I could *feel* your anger. Your fear. So, I acted. I've shared all this with my friends. Your half-brother. Asklepios. Your aunt, Artemis. And we are all in agreement.

"We believe you are a man destined for the history books. All of you. You and your friends are all extraordinary. Honest. Brave. Intelligent. Resourceful. Loyal to the oaths you took, and to the country you believe in. You refused to bend the knee to a tyrant. You have been true to each other as friends. As brothers. You care for each other and for your community. And we believe you are destined to overturn Harold Jensen's evil regime and establish a new era for American democracy. And we want to help."

24

Cy's brain function stuttered and then came to an abrupt stop. For a moment, everything went blank. *Tabula rasa.* Then the gears reengaged, and he realized he was so fucking furious that he had to blink back blinding tears. And yet, he wanted to howl with laughter. Double over, slap his thigh, and literally laugh his ass off. This farce was so ridiculous that half of him wanted to go along and see how it played out while the other half wanted to weep. The beautiful woman who had so captivated his imagination was mad. A raving fucking lunatic. Everyone in the room was a complete nut job, and he had put Mat at risk by wanting *her*, trusting *her*. By trusting Alex Whitelaw ... *wait.*

WAIT.

What if...?

His gut clenched in rebellion at the thought, but what if he was the one who was mad? Because what about Alex Whitelaw? Where was he? How did he survive that bomb blast? And what about the forest ranger? And all the teleporting? And what about all those times he healed so fast and why had things always come so easily to him—the music, the athletics, the academics. What if he wasn't just some gifted prodigy like his father boasted, but was something more ... s*omething different?* What if Sybil's strange behavior was not a function of a mental illness, but a function of being the daughter of a god? What if her episodes and headaches really were visions of other people and other places and other times like she claimed when they were little? What if their father's casual cruelty and ultimate disregard wasn't rooted in his narcissistic personality, but in the suspicion that his betrothed had cheated on him? That his children weren't really his?

"Prove it." Mat stood up and glared down at everyone in the room. At six foot four, he was the tallest and broadest of the four friends and knew that he cut an imposing figure. He could loom and intimidate with the best of them—it was part of his job, after all—and right now he damn well wanted to do both.

He strode over to stand beside Cy's chair. Put a possessive hand on his friend's shoulder. "We have a lot of friends who put on their Sunday best and attend church every week. My mother, who basically raised us all, believes with her whole heart that God Almighty and Jesus, his only begotten son, and all the angels and saints and demons from Hell are real and at work in the world. So the idea of gods being real is not foreign to me. But now you're saying that this man—" he squeezed Cy's uninjured shoulder—"a man I've known all my life, is a demigod. A child of Olympus. I know my Greek mythology." He nodded over at the man with the long ponytail still standing by the fireplace. "When we started first grade, I got down on my knees and prayed that our new teacher was Chiron and we could all go to school in a cave. She wasn't and we didn't. We went to Bigelow Elementary and none of us was raised a fool. You've been kind. Taken care of Cy. So, I'm telling you to prove what you're claiming right now or I'm taking Cy and we're leaving."

"Bravo," Dio said with a slow clap of appreciation. "I wouldn't believe such a load of malarky without proof either." He stood and started to meander around the furniture. "So, how do you propose we prove it? Turn water into wine? Multiply loaves and fishes? Conjure my *thyrsos* and crown of ivy out of thin air?" He snapped his fingers. "Done."

Mat gasped. Cy choked.

Striking a pose, Dio stood before them with a Greek *himation* draped across his shoulder and wrapped around his waist, a pine cone-tipped staff in one hand, a golden chalice in the other, and a circlet of ivy set atop his sun-kissed curls. "Dionysos at your service." He laughed and spread his arms wide. "Easy peasy, as they say." He turned to Ali, a sparkle in his eyes. "Now, you go."

"Always with the dramatics," Hermes muttered, rolling his eyes.

Ali jumped up from the couch. "This is sort of like reverse charades! Okay. Let's see. Don't blink or you'll miss it!"

Mat's fingers dug into Cy's shoulder as they stared at Maurice the bartender, decked out in his black pants, white shirt, and black bow tie. He gave them a deep bow, and said, "Good evening. What can I get you?"

"He really is the best bartender in town. Knows all the gossip."

That voice was familiar. As if synchronized, Cy and Mat's heads swiveled to see Alexander Whitelaw sitting where Hallie/Nemi had just been. Their mouths gaped open.

All easy grace and casual elegance, Alex sat back and crossed his legs as if he'd been there all the time. "We don't call them miracles, but as gods we intuitively know how to manipulate the laws of nature. So, you see Cy, it really is just a matter of physics."

Cy's face had gone bleach white.

And then Alex leaned forward and took Cy's hand in his. Just as Nemi had held it moments earlier. "And I am *me* no matter what form or name I take in the moment. I'm always me. I knew you were someone very special the first time I laid eyes on you, and in knowing you even a little better, I am more convinced of that than ever."

25

Mat stood outside on a wide brick patio. Collar up, hands tucked in his coat pockets, he stared into the light and shadow of the surrounding garden. Cy was inside talking to Nemi, Dr. A, and Artemis, trying to figure out how to tell Sybil about their father. Thinking about what to tell Sofia and BoJo. But Mat needed fresh air. Time to think of what all this meant.

It was still early. Back home, he'd be getting back from a run. Getting ready to start another day doing whatever needed doing in his multiple roles at Bigelow Enterprises. Doing whatever was needed to keep his mother safe. His friends. His *family*.

Thinking about Helen Cross and how she was doing holding down the fort back at the Waldorf. Wondering what it was about her that piqued his interest. Wondering why she kept him at arms length after that one almost kiss that he couldn't stop thinking about. It wasn't because she wasn't interested. He was sure of that. Not because he was some great catch, but because she sent such mixed signals and kept saying how yes, she admitted she was attracted to him, but no she couldn't go there because her life was a mess. That she carried around baggage she couldn't tell him about. Baggage he wouldn't like. But everyone had secrets, didn't they?

But this secret? Cy and Sybil, fucking demigods? Jesus. How would Sybil react to the news? She'd always been fragile. And little Sofia? And what about Mason and Brooks? How would any sane person react to news like that?

The things he'd seen and heard were ... well, they were unbelievable. And yet, he believed them. And why not?

His mother had gone to mass twice a week her entire life and still believed a god—the creator of the entire universe who also knew the number of hairs on your head—had inseminated a virgin who had given birth to a man who was crucified, went to the underworld for three days, and who then miraculously came back to life, rose to heaven to sit at the right hand of his father, and would someday come back to Earth again and take all the believers up to the clouds to live in mansions on streets made of gold. She believed in Lucifer the fallen angel who ruled over Hell, which was somewhere deep in the bowels of the Earth, and in all the demons and the saints and the angels and threw salt over her shoulder and refused to walk under a ladder and wouldn't have a black cat in the house. So why not believe the things he'd experienced this morning were real?

A door shut behind him. Footsteps approached.

"How you doing, big guy?"

Mat turned to see Dio—he couldn't bring himself to call him by his real name. Their nicknames made them more approachable. More real. Otherwise, he felt like he was occupying the pages of his old, well-worn copy of *D'Aulaires Book of Greek Myths*.

"Honestly?" he said. "Struggling with all of it."

Dio huffed out a soft laugh. "I'd be worried about your sanity if you took it all in without question."

They were quiet for a moment. Dio reached out and drew a finger along the leaf of a mountain laurel and a white bloom appeared in the wake of his touch. "Looks like it's going to be a beautiful day. I know you had coffee earlier, but I'm going to make me a nice hot mocha. Want one?" He smiled. "I'm a bit of a chocoholic, I'm afraid."

"That'd be great."

"Coming right up." Dio gave Mat's arm a reassuring squeeze and headed back inside.

"Wait," Mat called out. Dio stopped, turned. "Earlier, I asked why you all don't just teleport here and there and conjure everything you want like magic. You'd said *When in Rome*, but I still don't get it. Like why can't you just get rid of murdering tyrants like Jensen and protect all the children who are scared and starving and lost and why are you going to walk back into the house right now and make coffee like one of us mere mortals? Why not just conjure a coffee the way you like it right here?"

"Ah," Dio said, his voice a whisper. He looked down at the white bloom now fully flowered. A siren in the distance penetrated the quiet. Life went on all around them as the city woke to a new day.

"Eternity is a very, very long time, my friend," Dio said. "For primordial gods like Nemesis, the universe is available for them to explore, but some of us are tethered to the Earth. Stuck here. Forever." He shrugged. "Or at least for another five or six billion years. I don't hold out much hope for our sweet little planet surviving when the sun runs out of fuel in its core and slowly enters the red giant phase. So, what are we to do with all that time? Even the god of wine, ecstasy, and theater cannot party or playact 24/7. I spend much of my time performing my duties as the dying-and-resurrected god of agriculture and fertility, and in that role, I go by many names, but ..."

He trailed off and was quiet a moment more. Mat waited.

"But why not spend some time strolling in the garden to fill the time?" he said finally. "Stopping to smell the roses, so to speak. To *feel* things. *Experience* things. To embrace pain and joy and *love*. Why not take the time to make love to a beautiful woman or a handsome man. Or make art. Music." His lips quirked. "Coffee."

Mat nodded thoughtfully as Dio turned and headed back inside. He knew Dio was supposed to be the party boy of the gods, into wine and fertility and ecstasy, but he'd seemed to get what Mat and Cy were going through this morning. Almost more than the others.

Dr. A. had Cy's physical health to think of, plus the fact that they were apparently half-brothers. Hermes seemed like a self-important ass, Chiron wasn't half horse-half man as he'd always imagined—or at least he hadn't appeared so this morning—and Artemis was, well, intimidating. Goddess of the hunt? Of wild animals? Diana herself? Christ Almighty. Ali, Meg, and Tisi seemed almost normal in comparison, but they were the fucking Furies, so all in all, this was fucking insane.

As for Nemi, well, she was obviously focused on Cy. Mat smiled at that. It was obvious Cy felt the same. They seemed *attuned* to each other, like there was an unseen connection binding them together. He'd never seen his friend look at another woman the way he looked at her. The word *besotted* came to mind and Mat almost laughed at the romantic notion. He knew that the whole Alexander Whitelaw thing had thrown Cy for a loop. He'd said as much back at the cabin when talking about the *forestfuckingranger* he would never dream of fucking. So, how the hell was it all going to play out? Who was the real Nemesis? And did it even matter?

Footsteps again and Mat turned to see Dr. A approach. After a few moments of comfortable silence, Mat said, "Can I ask you a question?"

"Of course."

"How old are you?"

"Well, the answer is that I don't know exactly. At least, I can't name the year I was born. I remember I was still a young man, under thirty, when word of my sanatorium truly began to spread. Suddenly people were coming to Epidavros from all over. It had already been known regionally as a place of healing but eventually became famous throughout the ancient world." He smiled. "You could say I hit the big time around 600 BCE."

Mat considered that for a moment. "Over 2,600 years ago."

"Yes."

"And your mother was a mortal?"

"Yes."

"But Nemi said you're a god now. Immortal."

"I wasn't born this way, but yes."

"What about Cy? Will he be"—Mat choked on the words—"immortal too?"

"I don't know. Some demigods are and some are not. Some are born immortal, some are made so, and some die like a mortal. But we are all blessed with very long lives—unless, of course, the Fates determine otherwise. When Nemi brought Cy to me straight from that camp in Arizona, his belly sliced open by that monster Ken Lane, I took a sample of his blood. I'm running it through some tests in my lab now. It's a bit tricky, though, identifying the genetic markers for immortality amidst what many scientists still call 'junk DNA', but I hope to have the results back soon. Maybe even by tomorrow. One of my research assistants will let me know."

Mat sucked in a deep breath and let it out slowly. "I don't … I can't … I mean … I don't know what to say to him now. We were born in the same hospital just a day apart. My mother was head of housekeeping at the Bigelow Estate back then, but she's managed the whole place for years. We've been … well, we're all brothers. Raised together, basically. Through thick and thin. And yet, we're going to grow old and die and he's going to just …"

He choked back a sob. Squeezed the bridge of his nose. "Keep going."

"Mateo." Dr. A's voice was soft, soothing. "He's your *chosen* brother. Your *chosen* friend. Nothing's changed on that score. We may be blood relatives through Apollo, but you're his true family. You've got to look after him. And his sister. And his daughter. We've kept knowledge of their existence from Apollo so far, but once he finds out he has another son, another daughter, and another grandchild, he's probably going to want to meddle. Exert his influence. We'll all help, but it's up to you and your friends to keep Cy sane and centered because, well, Apollo is a bit much. Quite eccentric, to put it mildly."

"Eccentric," Mat mused. "I always read that he was the most beautiful of all the gods, so that explains Cy's looks." He laughed. "And yours."

Dr. A chuckled. "My father knows it too. Modesty is not in his godly DNA."

"That's one thing Cy did not inherit from him, then. The guy can be a bit cocky—like the rest of us—but he's not arrogant. Never been an asshole."

"No wonder Nemi is so attracted to him. If there's one thing she absolutely cannot abide, it's hubris."

"Ha! Between me, Brooks, and Mason—and his sister Sybil and her best friend, now Cy's wife—the poor guy's ego was never going to have a chance to run amok. If hubris is a common demigod trait, it skipped Cy. Of course, there were a couple of times when we were growing up that it took more than a joke to put him in his place."

"Took him out behind the barn and taught him a lesson, so to speak?"

"Mason mostly. He's the one who always calls us on our bullshit. Besides, I was a late bloomer. Didn't grow until high school. Almost college."

Dr. A nodded. "Apollo doesn't always take an interest in the children he fathers, but I think Cy will catch his attention. Once he finds out about him."

Mat drew in a fortifying breath. "This is all..."

"I understand."

"Tell me more about Apollo. I grew up with Cy's dad and Mason's Uncle Jimmy as surrogate fathers since my own was deported when I was little. Haven't seen or heard from him since I was two. Don't even know if he's still alive. Cy's dad was a first-class ass, but Uncle Jimmy is a man's man. Took us camping and taught us how to ride and hunt. Shoot a gun. Gave us all puppies from the same litter." Mat shrugged.

"Apollo may meddle, but he is not a doting father. He did instill the love of healing in me. Gave my life purpose and direction. He's also the god of music and dance, truth and prophecy. He can't best Artemis with a bow, but he doesn't care. Doesn't need to be like Ares or Poseidon. Doesn't need to prove his masculinity. He's a poet at heart. A true romantic, always falling in love. Passionate to a fault."

"You admire him," Mat said.

Dr. A shrugged. "Hard not to. You'll see."

"I'm not sure I'm up to meeting Apollo. Chiron and Artemis were ..." Mat shook his head and huffed out a soft breath. "My ears are still ringing from Chiron's diatribe about how careless Americans have been with the democratic ideals first nurtured in Athens, and how we have learned nothing, how we are a petty, small people, completely ignorant of history, and how we truly do not deserve help from the gods. How Athena herself is so ashamed of us, she won't lift a finger to help."

Dr. A smiled at that. "He can't help himself. Just wait till you meet Zeus. Not all the stories about him are true, of course, but Cy's grandfather is not warm and fuzzy."

"God," Mat said on an exhale.

"Exactly. But Nemi will help. Honestly, she's the best of us. And since she's older than Zeus and our entire messed up family tree, she has no compunction about putting him in his place if push comes to shove. Or any of the Olympians, honestly."

Mat tugged his hands from his pockets and scrubbed them down his face. "What about this sister Nemi was telling us about? Eris."

"Eris is an epic bitch. As Nemi said, none of us would be surprised if she wasn't behind all this. Jensen. Valentine. The corruption and cruelty. The undermining of democracy in the West. Well, all over the world, really. When she gets bored and decides to cause trouble to liven things up, everything can go sideways in a hurry. A lot of humans have blamed Ares for wars and conflicts Eris is ultimately responsible for. Ares has a code of honor that he always lives by. It may not be pretty—in fact, it may be quite bloody—but there is a logic to it. Eris does not have that. Bottom line, she is trouble simply for trouble's sake."

The door opened again, and Dio appeared with two oversized mugs. "A mocha for you, my friend."

Mat took the proffered mug in both hands, brought it to his nose and inhaled. Took a sip and closed his eyes as the flavor hit the back of his tongue. "This is perfect."

Dio gave Mat a slight bow. "There is one other thing I want to say, Mateo Cárdenas. You are not 'mere'. No mortal is, but especially not someone who has dedicated his life to protecting his country and the people he loves. That is a rare. And the gods know it and honor it."

Mat held Dio's gaze for a moment and then gave him a nod. "Thank you." He sucked in a breath. "So, what happens next?"

"I'm just in charge of food, drink, and merrymaking and Dr. A is in charge of patching people up."

"In other words," Dr. A said, "your guess is as good as ours."

26

"Cy, wake up."

Cy swallowed. His mouth was dry, his pillow was wet with drool, and he had no idea where he was. He opened one eye and rolled over onto his back. *Ow!* Okay. He might be a demigod, but apparently his injuries were not going to magically heal themselves overnight.

"Hey, man. Take it slow." Mat was sitting, elbows on his knees, in a chair next to the bed. "Remember you got shot yesterday. Twice."

"Don't forget the blown-up part. Or the sliced open bit."

"The sliced open bit was two whole days ago." Mat scrubbed a hand down his face. "Your stitches still healing okay?"

"They had to slice me open to dig out the bullet in my shoulder too," Cy groused. But he sat up, pulled up his shirt—his right arm seemed to be working now—and peeled back the bandage taped to his belly. "Lookin' good. Probably don't even need this anymore." He pulled it off, dropped it onto the bedside table. Cleared his throat and swung his legs over the side of the bed. "What time is it?"

"Just after five. You crashed for three hours."

"Dr. A gave me something for my headache at lunch. You'd think my arm or my shoulder or even my side would hurt, and they do. But it's my head that's really causing trouble."

Mat laughed. "Makes sense. It's probably a mess up there after learning you're, well, you know."

Cy rubbed his eyes. "You know what I'm most worried about? How the hell am I supposed to tell Sybil that after all these years she was right about everything? Her dreams being real. Her premonitions coming true. All that gobbledygook I never took seriously. Shit. I feel like the worst brother ever."

"No one in their right minds could have ever suspected you're both demigods, for Christ's sake. She'll understand."

At least Mat hoped she would. Mat had never understood Sybil. At all. In fact, she'd always wigged him out a bit. And he'd never understood Mason's infatuation with her. An infatuation Mason had only ever admitted to Mat and Brooks once and had then sworn them both to eternal silence on the subject on threat of slow evisceration and sudden immolation. After that, Mat and Brooks had never mentioned it outright. Oh, they'd alluded it to it when they were by themselves, but that was as far as they'd ever gone. Evisceration and immolation might have been an exaggeration, but they'd seen the pain in Mason's eyes and they all respected pain.

"Listen, I woke you up because we've got trouble."

Cy groaned. "Ya think?

"More trouble." He scooted the chair back to give Cy room to get up. "You know how you were a hero this morning? Well, Jensen is holding a press conference right now saying that despite what the press was reporting this morning about the suicide bomber's motives, the claim he was angry about his family's disappearance, investigators have talked to his family members and they're all fine and dandy. Of course, he hasn't trotted said family members out so anyone else can question them, so no one knows if they're dead or alive or rotting away in one of the camps.

"Anyway, he's now got you and Alex in his crosshairs. Saying that although you were injured in the bombing and offered medical assistance, you both refused and then, shortly thereafter, you disappeared along with a third man. An accomplice. I guess that's me."

"Well, fuck me sideways."

"Yeah, he's suggesting that you either planned it all or at least knew what was going to happen and had an escape plan in place. That's why you were neither one seriously injured. He's, you know, not *officially accusing* you of anything. He's just *asking* questions."

Cy groaned. Reached down to put on the shoes he'd taken off for his nap.

"Now we're all 'persons of interest,'" Mat went on, "wanted for questioning in the attempted assassination of everybody who is anybody."

"This is bad."

"No kidding. Good thing Alex put our phones in a signal blocker bag last night so we can't be traced because Jensen sent SS agents to the Waldorf looking for you."

Cy's eyes went wide. "We need to—"

"Don't worry about Helen and Kemal. They have it covered. I told her to cooperate and give the SS permission to search the plane if they insist, but to make sure she or Kemal go along so they don't trash it. Meg volunteered to go as a random Bigelow employee, in case the team needs to be extracted quickly."

"But what about—"

"Tisi can apparently whip up any kind of documentation Meg would need. Also, Helen and Kemal are not allowed to leave the hotel for now, and all their communications are being monitored, so the Furies and their magical teleporting abilities will serve as our communications channel for now."

"Christ..." Cy went into the bathroom to piss while Mat stood in the doorway.

"Wait. It gets worse," Mat went on. "Just got done talking to Mason and Brooks, and Cy, the SS is at your house. At the Bigelow Estate. They showed about thirty minutes ago demanding to be let in. Said they had a warrant to search the place in connection with the bombing and in connection to Governor Guerrero's disappearance and Inez Martin's murder. With a warrant in hand, the security staff had no choice but to comply. And it looks like the agents are not going anywhere, either."

"Shit." Cy swore as he zipped up and grabbed a washcloth to scrub his face and hands. "Are Mason and Brooks still at the cabin?" He grabbed his toothpaste and toothbrush and started brushing as if he had a grudge against enamel.

"Yeah, but out of an abundance of caution, they've closed up the cabin and have decamped to the Basement."

Cy closed his eyes. Braced himself on the bathroom sink. *The Basement.* Holy shit. That meant they'd activated what they jokingly called Operation Deep Throat, otherwise known as *Take the elevator down the shaft*—lovingly known as the throat because the shaft was long and narrow and the car was shaped like a cylindrical capsule—*and get in the fucking Basement now.*

They could last down in their emergency hideaway for months if they had to, but both Cy and Mat knew their friends would not be content doing that. From their setup in the Basement, they had eyes on all Bigelow properties and could monitor Administration communications, but it would make them crazy to just sit there. They'd want to get topside and do something.

The Basement was part of a maze of tunnels initially constructed over a hundred and fifty years earlier, back when Arizona copper was king and the Bigelow family owned several of the richest mines in the world. The place was a labyrinth that the four friends had spent years exploring, mapping, and then bringing in trusted teams to build out and reinforce. There were new hidden doorways, expansive sleeping quarters on several levels, space for dining, food storage and prep, and wiring, servers, power systems, and backup batteries to power sophisticated communications systems connected to the outside world by a series of relays that allowed their signals to anonymously piggyback on existing satellites.

Plus, it housed a lab and a clean room where they tinkered with "the toys" they hoped would one day soon power the whole place and give them leverage over Jensen—and any other wanna-be tyrant that came their way. And it was all screened from LIDAR by some fancy blocking gadget Brooks had come up with.

It was while building out the Basement complex that Bigelow's chief geophysicist—Brooks's own mother—had discovered a new nickel-copper deposit she suspected was larger than anything Bigelow mining had ever worked before. A deposit that only a select few Bigelow loyalists knew about and that every despot on the planet—including Jensen—would gleefully kill to get their hands on.

"And there's one more thing," Mat said, watching his friend carefully. "Ken Fucking Lane showed up at the estate with the SS agents. He's moved in. Claims he's there to look after the girls' interests. Protect them from you."

Cy spit in the sink. "Fuck me sideways." He grabbed the towel Mat held out to him and wiped it hard down his face. Tossed it on the counter. "Okay. First things first: how are you?"

Mat shrugged. "Running on pure adrenaline, strong coffee, and volcanic fury."

Cy gave his friend a grim smile and nodded. "Where's Nemi?"

"Fuck Around and Find Out HQ." He smiled. "Nemi's name for this whole place, but mainly the room with the monitors. Come on. It's gonna be a helluva day."

27

Less than an hour later, Cy and Nemi appeared in the Basement's communications center in the tunnels beneath the Bigelow homestead, nearly scaring Brooks and Mason to death—even though Mat had warned them to expect Cy to show up "out of the blue." The explanations that followed were met with wide-eyed open-mouthed incredulity laced with some serious swearing (from Brooks), lots of pacing (on Mason's part) and a *well shit, that explains a lot* attitude from both of them.

"I always did think you were a bit of a freak," Brooks finally said with snort.

Cy groaned and rolled his eyes. "Thanks a lot, buddy."

"Well, just look at you," Mason chimed in. "You were nearly divested of a kidney and then shot twice and you're still walking around like it's a regular Monday."

"It's Tuesday, asshole," Cy said.

"Whatever." Mason stopped pacing and plopped down in one of the chairs in front of the bank of screens and computer consoles. "Okay, we need to focus on Sybil, Sofia, and BoJo. Make sure they're safe since Ken is literally in the fucking house." He pinned Nemi with a skeptical look. "So, what are we supposed to call you? Hallie Jones or Nemesis the Goddess or Alex Whitelaw?"

"My friends call me Nemi and you can call me that too. But when I'm around humans who don't know who I really am and I'm in this female form, Hallie is best. When I'm in the human form that Cy knows as Alexander Whitelaw, obviously, you should call me Alex. We've set up complete identities with foolproof backgrounds for Hallie and Alex, so those names can be checked out by the security services. Nemi is, of course, off the books."

"Riiiight," Brooks groaned. "And you say this Tisi person—oh, sorry, I mean *goddess*—can get our systems securely connected to yours without hopping on any Jensen satellites? You can get around all the AI crawlers searching their systems for intrusions?"

Nemi's lip quirked up in a smile. "The Pantheon League doesn't need the kind of satellites you use, and, well, let's just say that human-designed *artificial* intelligence is not a threat to *our* intelligence."

"Let me guess," Cy quipped, "it's all about the physics."

"Well, yes, as a matter of fact. And the fact that we don't operate on or iterate within a 'garbage in – garbage out' artificial intelligence system that can be easily manipulated by a psychopath and a few lines of code. We may not be omniscient and omnipresent, as so many humans believe, but our intelligence is not artificial. It's not tied to all the trillions of bytes of data fed into an algorithmic system by humans who somehow think more data means true data. I mean ... seriously?"

"Nice. The goddess is an AI skeptic," Brooks said with a laugh. "I like her already."

"As far as the satellites go, we're able to work with physical laws at the most elemental quantum levels. Waves and particles, gravity and wormholes, up quarks and down quarks, spin and entanglement ... all of it. It may look like magic to you, but it's more like harnessing nature to do what needs to be done. Not to say we don't manipulate things here and there when we need to," she said with a mysterious smile, "but think of it like this: Homo sapiens existed for a very long time without electricity, but it was always there. You just had to discover how to harness it before you could use it for your own purposes."

Mason swiveled in his chair and looked at Nemi as she pulled up another desk chair. "If you can do all this"—he waved a hand at, well, everything—"then why can't you just take out Jensen and restore at least a semblance of democracy in the country? Why can't you manipulate things here and there to make civilization just and fair?"

"Because that's not the way it works," Nemi explained. Again. "We can meddle in human affairs, but we can't control them. Or we could, but you don't want us to because we'd be really bad at it and humans would definitely not like it. Besides, if we did that, we'd be taking away your free will and self-determination. And we aren't built to be mired down in the day-to-day running of a government."

She looked up at Cy and then around the room the friends had created as a safe space. "And, believe me, not all of us care about humans in the same way or are as benevolent as Pantheon League members. There are some, like my sister Eris, who love nothing more than sowing discord and strife. Human suffering means nothing to her because humans are nothing more than toys to play with when she gets bored. Trust me, the gods are not all humans think—or hope—we are. Yes, we were created first, and yes we're immortal and we definitely have more power, but that doesn't make us better."

Cy leaned back against a computer desk, arms crossed. "What if Zeus appeared at the UN and declared himself god of all mankind? Some would bend the knee, some would denounce him, and some would declare a holy war and start throwing nukes."

"And what do you call him," Nemi said. "Jupiter, Thor, Indra, Amun-Ra, Baal, Jehovah, Anu, Enlil, Marduk, Ishtar? How would Jews, Muslims, and Christians react? How about the one billion Hindus, the 500 million Buddhists, and all the Baha'is, Confucianists, Daoists, Jains, Shintoists, Sikhs, Taoists, Wiccans, Zoroastrians, etc., etc., etc.?"

"Okay," Brooks said on a exhale. "We get your point."

"Here's what I don't understand." Mason popped up to start pacing again. "If you think America is worth saving, why didn't you step in earlier and help us avoid this shitshow in the first place. You said you've seen the rise of fascism many times and it never ends well, so what gives? Why show up now when the fascists are already in power?"

"We hoped humans had learned the terrible lessons of the 20th century, that 120 million dead or wounded, tens of millions more displaced, and over $8 trillion wasted would drive the terrible cost of tyranny and fascism home. We were wrong. We've been wrong before too."

"So, if the gods can be so wrong and can't foresee the future, what *can* you do?" Mason's voice was deadly calm. "Besides your magic tricks, how does the Pantheon League help us fight back right now?"

Before Nemi could answer, Brooks spoke up. "Magic tricks got Cy out here without being seen, so I'm all for them. But here's the immediate problem." He picked up a pen and started chewing on the tip. "I'd bet good money that within the week, we'll learn Jensen has uncovered 'evidence' that proves Cy Bigelow and Alex Whitelaw planned the bombing, that Cy murdered Inez Martin, and that he's responsible for the disappearance of Governor Guerrero. They'll get warrants to crawl through the company's financial affairs on the pretext of discovering who we're in league with. And while it might take them awhile to discover what we're sitting on here and learn about our toys, it's going to come out sooner or later, no matter how much we try to keep it quiet. And how are we supposed to counter that?"

Nemi's gaze sharpened. "What do you mean 'discover what we're sitting on here'? What toys?"

Cy let out a long sigh and started doing some pacing of his own. After a moment, he turned to Nemi. "When I inherited the company, I needed to understand just how big of a hole we were in. Brooks joined me when his PhD program was shut down, and the first thing we thought of was mining. Copper got Bigelow started, so maybe copper could help us resurrect the business. With new technologies, we decided to figure out if the mines really were tapped out or not.

"We decided to bring in a couple of trusted experts and start exploring, and during the process, we began reinforcing and building out these old tunnels. As the situation in the country deteriorated, we began thinking of the tunnels as a just-in-case hiding place, and that's when we started calling it the Basement. Ultimately, what our experts discovered is that we're sitting on a previously unknown copper deposit that dwarfs what's already been mined in Arizona. And it's not just copper. We've got nickel, cobalt, silver, and magmatic platinum metal deposits. A little gold. Uranium. And a lot of lithium."

Nemi's eyes went big. "Who else knows about this?"

"Counting you, now nine people. Mat plus the three of us, Bigelow's chief mining engineer, and his three closest advisors. Others know a little, but no one else knows the full extent of the deposits. And I trust all of them with my life."

"How can you be so sure?" Nemi said, stunned by the revelation. "Humans are easily corruptible, and entire wars have been fought over less."

Brooks spoke up. "Because Bigelow's chief mining engineer is my father, and his closest advisors include my mom, our geophysicist, my sister, a ridiculously brilliant physicist, and my little brother, a geochemist who is equally brilliant and not a little unhinged when it comes to rocks. It's basically my whole family. They've traveled a lot in the past, but they're basically here now. And on the Bigelow payroll."

"I had no idea." Nemi wondered how she'd missed this. She knew Mat's mother managed the Bigelow estate and that Mason's Uncle Jimmy was a mentor to all the boys. And now this. It's all just one big Bigelow Enterprises family.

"Brooks's family moved from Australia to Arizona when the university expanded its mining program," Cy went on, "and his mom and dad were recruited to manage the demonstration/classroom mine. It's on the east side of town, in one of our small, easily accessible mines. The university rents the space from us."

Brooks picked up the story. "I met Cy, Mason, and Mat when were assigned the same fifth grade teacher. They were thick as thieves and when Ken Fucking Lane and his friends started making fun of my accent, they stood up for me. I was even scrawnier than Mat back then, and he was a puny little runt. Anyway, we've been 'all for one and one for all' ever since."

"My theory is the Paxons are secretly descended from dwarves," Mason quipped.

"At least that explains that scruff on his face," Cy agreed.

Brooks rubbed his thick, neatly trimmed beard. "Still jealous that I had to shave before you?"

"Always," Cy said with a laugh.

"Anyway, although I opted to study computing and electrical engineering, mining still fascinates me," Brooks said. "We all rely on the stuff we dig out of the ground, and yet it's a destructive and dirty business. Our goal, as a business, is to figure out how to do it as responsibly as possible—and still make a mint. And we've got an ace up our sleeves that we're working on."

"If we can play that ace, we're golden. But we have to do it quietly and keep everything under the radar and out from under

Administration control," Mason said. "Which means the whole making a mint thing is still just a dream."

Brooks nodded. "While we're confident no one who knows what we've found or what we're working on will tell another soul, there are still risks to keeping it a secret. Our production and processing facilities are all small scale and everything is done robotically underground and powered by our own systems. The ace we're talking about is part of our project to power everything ourselves. But it's hard to make money that way because we can't sell product directly into the market. Maybe the time for laying low is past, though. Maybe, with the Pantheon League on our side, it's time we go on the offensive. Time to go public."

"What's the ace you're talking about?" Nemi asked.

"It'll be better if we show you," Cy said. "But we don't have time for all that now. Let's deal with the immediate situation before we start reviewing our long-term strategy again."

"No matter what, we certainly can't just be reactive any longer," Mason said, turning to Cy. "Not with Jensen sending goons to assassinate you in public. Not with Ken Lane and more goons in your house breathing all over Sybil, Sofia, and BoJo."

"Agreed," Cy said with a decisive nod.

Mason plopped down in his chair again and pointed to one of the screens. "Let's get that link established with your crew in Georgetown and determine how to approach Sybil and BoJo at the estate. It's one thing to monitor the house, another to communicate with the people in it."

Cy leaned forward. "Let's do a check on the estate's cameras and make sure all our systems are operational. We need to give the Pantheon League access to everything so that you two aren't the only ones keeping an eye on the place. I don't want to miss anything when it comes to their safety. BoJo's got a good head on her shoulders, but you know Sybil. She's often living in her own world…"

Brooks shot a surreptitious glance at Mason. Anything to do with Sybil was a minefield for Mason, and the pain in his eyes was clear, although he was doing his best to hide it from Cy.

"I promised to do everything in my power to keep your family safe." Nemi's voice was soft but edged with determination. "It will help if I meet them in person, though." She turned to Brooks and Mason. "Making a personal connection enables me to create a two-way communications channel. Even if the human doesn't know the channel exists, I can usually sense emotions and state of mind. Especially fear and danger. It's how I found Cy down at SDIC."

Cy held her gaze, considered their connection, considered everything he'd learned about her. His feelings were growing stronger with every single moment they spent together and yet it was still sinking in that she was a goddamned goddess.

It suddenly hit him that he would never truly know her. She would always be beyond his reach—*beyond his comprehension*—no matter who he was or how he felt about her. He swallowed the pain of that knowledge, and it felt like swallowing molten lava. It filled his throat, and for a moment, he couldn't breathe. His fingers burned, hot with the need to touch her, to verify she was real.

"So, all you need to do is meet them?" Mason asked, interrupting Cy's thoughts.

"Yes. Hopefully. Although—"

"Although what?" Mason pinned her with a hard stare.

"Dealing with demigods is different from dealing with humans. And every demigod is different, so there are no guarantees."

"Fuck." The tension on Mason's face was clear in the fine lines around his mouth.

"Let's go ahead and get connected to the Pantheon League," Cy said. "I want Mat on screen."

Brooks got busy and by following Nemi's instruction, the secure connection was quickly completed.

"Hey guys," Mat said as soon as the two-way screen went live. "All's well out there?"

"As good as can be expected," Cy said, "but I need you to call your mom. We need to get a message to Sybil and BoJo, and I doubt the SS will be bugging the estate manager's phone."

"Probably not, since she's just the help."

"Who runs the whole place. She'll be around today?"

Mat snorted. "Unless you fired her."

Cy rolled his eyes. "Fat chance. Call her now. We'll wait. If by some stretch of the imagination, the Administration tracks the signal, it will simply be a son calling his mother."

Mat pulled out his cell and dialed. They all waited. He held up one finger. "Mom, don't say anything. We know the SS is in the house. We're all fine, but I need you to listen." Pause. "I have you on speaker phone now. Don't say anything more, just listen to Cy and respond when prompted."

Cy glanced at Nemi and was surprised when she reached out and grabbed his hand and squeezed. Strength, reassurance, and something more coursed through his bloodstream.

Cy turned back to the screen. "Mrs. C, can you hear me? Just say yes or no.

"Yes, yes." Maria Cárdenas' voice filled the room. "Of course."

"I need you to find Sybil and BoJo and get them alone. Make up some excuse. Groceries or the dogs or whatever works. Once you're alone, tell them that I know a secret way to sneak into my bedroom suite without being seen."

"But there is no—"

"Mom!"

"Okay. Sorry."

"Tell them they need to go in there, better yet, go tell them to go into my bathroom in thirty minutes. Together. You'll need to keep Sofia occupied. Take the dogs out or go feed the horses. Whatever. Just keep her away from Ken Lane and tell Sybs and BoJo I'll be there waiting for them."

"I tell them, Mr.—"

"Mom!" Mat barked out again. "Don't say what you were going to say."

"Okay. Got it. Roger. Over and out."

Mat stared at his friends through the screen, a bemused look on his face.

"And don't tell anyone else about this call," Cy went on. "We'll explain it all later. But the bottom line is we're trying to keep you all safe—especially Sofia. Rumors are that camps like SDIC are trafficking women and children on the Global Labor Exchange."

"I must take the dogs out now. Goodbye." And then the woman, all business, cut the call.

Mat quirked his lips in a smile. Maria Cárdenas may look like a softie, but the boys knew she was sharp as a cut diamond and as strong as graphene. One arched eyebrow could make four rowdy boys stop in their tracks. And when it came to keeping her girls safe, especially little Sofia, Mrs. C would lie, cheat, steal, and kill.

They all would.

28

"Nice place," Nemi said, turning to take in the expansive bathroom. Looks like early Charles Le Brun or late Saddam Hussein with a little Peter the Great thrown in for spice. Or maybe Leo X was in charge of decor."

"No idea what you're talking about. Leo who?"

"Pope from 1513-1521 Did you know you can get heatstroke if you gild your body in gold? The gold prevents your pores and sweat glands from helping regulate body temperature."

"I thought that was just something made up for James Bond."

"Well, you don't suffocate from it, like in the movie, but Leo once had a little boy painted in gold and made him march in a parade. He overheated in the Italian sun and died soon after. So did Leo's pet elephant."

"He painted it in gold too?"

"No, he made it *eat* gold."

"Jesus, why are people so weird?"

"A question for the ages."

Nemi reached across the black marble sink and turned one of the gold faucets on and off. Then on and off again. She realized she was anxious about meeting Cy's twin. Another grandchild of Apollo. What would she be like? In all her years of keeping tabs on Cy, she'd paid scant attention to his sister other than knowing where she was.

She now knew Sybil had majored in creative writing at the university up in Tucson and had worked at the bookstore on campus. After graduation, she'd gone on to grad school to get an MFA in poetry, still in Tucson. They'd all gone to the University of Arizona, even staying to pursue their graduate degrees. Even BoJo who'd studied library sciences. Nemi wondered if Sybil and BoJo—best friends since high school—had socialized with Cy and his friends, like a big Bigelow pack.

"My dad remodeled it years ago," Cy said, looking around the gaudy room, walls clad in gold-veined mirrors. "After a winning trip to Vegas. I only stay in here because Sofia's taken over my old bedroom. Sybil still prefers her own rooms, and BoJo claimed the guest suite closest to Sofia, so I'm in here. When I'm here." He shrugged. "I've never had the energy or the money to renovate the place."

Nemi dragged a finger along the rolled rim of the oversized claw-foot tub situated on a raised platform in the middle of an alcove fitted with expansive bay windows and a view out toward the mountains. It was a spectacular view, and she felt the beauty of the craggy range and the unforgiving desert landscape in her very bones.

She'd always been drawn to places like this, places where adaptation was essential to survival. Where flora and fauna had to evolve or die. A hawk floated on a current in the distance. A predator. She wondered if it was stalking prey or simply enjoying the sensation of being alive. Of being free.

She sat on the lip of the tub—big enough for two—and caught Cy's gaze. "Love the tub." Her voice dropped. "And the mirrors."

His skin practically ignited. If we were covered in gold, it would be melting about now. He took a step toward her. "Nemi, I can't ... you're...."

His body knew what it wanted, but his brain stuttered. Stopped him from moving closer. He'd imagined kissing this woman, touching her, making love to her, but how could he hope to satisfy an immortal goddess? How was he worthy? He wasn't.

She reached for his hand. Opened his palm and pressed her lips to it, touching his hot skin ever so lightly with the tip of her tongue and sending a bolt of heat straight to his groin. "Right now, I'm just a flesh and blood woman who hasn't been kissed in a very, very long time. A woman who would very much like to be kissed now. By you."

Cy took another step forward, his dick saying, *Well, when you put it like that.* He looked down at her, pulled her to her feet. Cupped her face in his hands. Bent to brush his lips across hers. Slide his tongue into the welcoming warmth of her mouth. But suddenly that wasn't enough. He enveloped her in his arms, one hand moving around to cradle the back of her head, the other sliding down to cup her bottom and press her against him.

She snaked her arms up around his neck, pulled him even closer, opened to him as he took the kiss deeper. Then deeper still until he growled with the need to fill her completely. To join his body to hers no matter who or what they were. The need was blinding as she moaned into his mouth. "Yes, Cy. This is what I want. What I've dreamed of."

"Jesus, Nemi. I—"

The soft snick of a door latch in the bedroom made them both jump back. Cy's heart thudded in his chest as he stepped away, his hands dropping to his sides as if they didn't know what to do with themselves now that they weren't full of goddess.

Through the open bathroom door, they watched the bedroom door slowly open. Sybil. She was early. She stepped inside, shut the door quietly, and then rushed across the carpeted expanse of the room to the bathroom.

"Oh, my god!" She flung herself at her brother and wrapped her arms around his neck. "We've been so worried! What is going on? Why does Jensen think you tried to kill him? And since when is there a secret passage to get in here?"

Nemi watched as Cy pulled his twin in for a long hug, and then dragged her arms from around his neck and stepped back. In contrast to Cy's dark hair and tall, broad-shouldered build, Sybil was a fair, almost otherworldly female miniature of their father. Nemi was certain Apollo would recognize her as his daughter at first glance.

Side by side, Sybil barely came up to Cy's chin, and Nemi remembered that she'd spent the first month of her life in an incubator connected to a feeding tube. With thick sun-gold hair caught up in a messy bun that reminded Nemi of a peony in bloom, she was barefoot and wearing stretchy yoga pants and a baggy University of Arizona hooded sweatshirt. Wide-eyed, she appeared as delicate as fine bone china, but Nemi sensed an untapped strength beneath the fragility. This was a woman who had been underestimated her entire life. A woman who'd lived in the shadow of her big, beautiful, vibrant brother. A woman who knew more, understood more, *saw* more than anyone gave her credit for.

"I've got a lot to tell you, but first where's BoJo?"

"She's right behind me. We didn't think it would be a good idea to come tromping in here at the same time. The agents are watching us like hawks." She looked over Cy's shoulder. "You going to introduce me to your friend?"

Cy reached for Nemi's hand and drew her up beside him. "Sybs, this is Hallie Jones. Hallie, my twin, Sybil."

Nemi moved first, extending her hand. "Your brother and I first met about fifteen years ago and only recently reconnected.

I'm here to help you both and am very glad to finally meet you in person."

Sybil took Nemi's hand. The handshake was brief, cautious. "This is the first I've ever heard of a Hallie Jones. Where did you meet?"

"It's a long story," Cy broke in. "I'll explain when BoJo gets here."

At that moment, there was a soft knock on the bedroom door. The knob turned. Sybil grabbed Cy's arm. They both went still as statuary.

BoJo slipped inside and quietly shut the door behind her. "Sybs?" she whispered. "You here?"

Sybil stepped out into the bedroom and motioned for BoJo to hurry. After another quick hug and quiet introductions, BoJo hopped up onto the counter and Sybil sat on the toilet lid as Nemi leaned against the lip of the tub.

"We're here because you're in danger," Cy began.

"We're in danger?" Sybil interrupted. "*You're* the one wanted for terrorism and murder."

"They don't have any evidence because I'm not guilty."

"Since when has lack of evidence hindered Harold Jensen?" BoJo scoffed.

"I can take care of myself. You're the ones with Ken Lane and SS agents watching your every move. That's the real danger."

"They're only here because they think you'll try to contact us, and lo and behold..." BoJo spread her arms out as if to say, *See? They were right.*

"That's not the only reason they're here." Cy pulled his shirt up to display the arc of neat stitches, now mostly healed. "Ken Lane did this to me. Three days ago. He drugged me while we were having coffee at the hotel, then he dragged me down to SDIC with the intention of harvesting my organs—starting with my kidneys—before tossing me in the camp incinerator."

"What the hell?" Horrified, Sybil shrank back, then reached out to let her fingers hover over her brother's abdomen. She looked up at him. "How do you know it was Ken if you were drugged?"

"There was a witness. Someone who helped get me to safety and get me stitched up. Now, Ken is literally in the house, and you're the ones in danger. He's a madman, Sybs. He's always been obsessed with you. He—"

"I know, Cy. I'm not a child."

"Jesus, I know you're not a child, but—"

"Do *not* go all big brother on me again, Mr. Eight-Minutes-Older. If you must know, I did sleep with him a couple of times. Years ago. When I was young and stupid and very, very angry."

Cy wanted to ask why she'd been so angry, but now was not the time for a heart-to-heart.

"It's not just you he wants. The witness overheard him talking about taking control of the company and getting BoJo and Sofia deported."

"What? He couldn't do that!"

BoJo smacked both hands down on the sink beside her thighs. "Of course, he could do it. He'd like nothing better."

"But—" Sybil cast a pleading gaze at her best friend, but BoJo was having none of it.

"Look, I know you and Ken have a history and I know you've never been honest with anyone about what all that entails, but you've got to take the fucking blinders off. He's worse than you want to admit. And the idea of him hurting Sofia should make your blood boil."

Sybil closed her eyes and took a long breath. Her hands fisted in her lap. "It does make my blood boil. The idea of him hurting Sofia or you, but you're right. Ken and I do have a history, and I've always given him the benefit of the doubt because of it. I've turned a blind eye, but lately ... lately, he's been acting weird. Weirder than normal."

Cy pinned his gaze on her. "Weird how?"

"Like I turn around in the coffee shop and he's there. I went to the grocery store with Mrs. C a couple of days ago, before all this stuff with you and Jensen started, and he was in his car in the parking lot when we came out. I've never seen him at the Safeway before in my life. And ... then, the other day, I came out of the library, and he was standing across the street. Watching me. I don't think he knew I saw him because he was standing back in the shadows, but I knew he was there. I could *feel* him." She shuddered.

BoJo hopped off the counter. "Jesus, Sybs! He's stalking you! Why didn't you tell me?

"And then the asshole moved in to 'protect' you," Cy said on a growl. "If I'd known, I would've—"

"Would've done what?" Sybil stood and faced him. "Asked Mat to shadow me? I'm a grown woman, and we're right here in our hometown where everyone knows me. I *hate* it when you and your friends treat me like I'm a child!"

"They're your friends too," Cy shot back.

Nemesis was glad she'd created a sound barrier around the room because this exchange was rapidly increasing in volume.

"No, they're not!" Sybil shouted and then took a deep breath. Her voice lower, but just as harsh, she said, "They've never been my friends. They are loyal to you. To each other. They will always pick you over anything else. It's like I'm invisible. Or worse, untouchable because of you."

He ran a hand over his head, grabbed a fistful of hair, and stood there for a moment. Staring at his twin. Still as a statute. Finally, he blew out a breath. "Okay. I'm sorry. I deserved that. We all deserve that. Sometimes I'm a domineering asshole. Maybe we all are, but it's only because—"

Sybil poked a finger into her brother's chest. "I don't want to hear your litany of excuses again. You've always treated me like

I'm breakable. But I'm not. Not anymore. So, why don't you get over yourself and tell us why you and this woman are here, and what's really going on in D.C. I know you're working to grow the company and keep it solvent, and I support that. But I also know you're all up to something more. The way you act as if you're sitting on some giant secret, like you're building the atom bomb in the basement or something. I don't ask questions, because, frankly, I don't want to know, but BoJo and I are not stupid."

"God, I know that. I'm sorry if we ever made you feel—"

"Whatever. Get on with it. Why are you here when you know this place is being watched? Also, how did you get into the house without being seen? I know there are no secret passages. Believe me, I've looked."

"Okay, okay. We are in trouble. Jensen's put a target on Bigelow Enterprises. Our theory is that he wants our land and mineral rights, but there's more to it than that. For the past couple of years, the guys and I have been working with the American Resistance Movement. If he suspects or finds evidence of our involvement, we could be arrested and tried for treason."

"Oh, god," Sybil buried her face in her hands and collapsed back down to sit on the toilet lid. She looked up at her brother, her face white. "You could all be executed!"

"I know and I'm sorry. But that's why we couldn't tell you or involve you. We wanted to keep the people we love safe. You and BoJo and Sofia. Mrs. C. Everyone we care about." He paused and glanced at Nemi. "But that's not all."

"Jesus, Cy." BoJo rubbed her forehead as if she had a splitting headache. "That seems like plenty. So whatever you're going to say next, don't sugar coat it because you're trying to shield us. Just spit it out, for god's sake."

Cy nodded and knelt down in front of his sister, took her hands in his. "This is going to be hard to believe, but knowing this—*believing* this—will help keep you safe."

And then, with the mother of his child looking on, he told his sister the truth. About their mother. About their father. Their *real* father. And about Nemi. With a quick-change demonstration transforming herself into Alex Whitelaw and back into her human female form while they watched—wide-eyed and speechless—both women were finally convinced.

"Holy hell," BoJo whispered. "You're telling me I gave birth to the granddaughter of a real-life god?"

"So, I'm not crazy." Sybil said after a long moment of staring down at the floor, breath held. "All those years. Everything I felt and thought ... the visions. The premonitions. The feeling like I wasn't always present. Like I was somehow somewhere else. And how everyone treated me like I was a freak. Like I was too weird or too fragile or too ... whatever. Too *much* to deal with. And every time Dad looked at me, it was like seeing me *hurt* him. Physically. As if I was an injury he couldn't quite remember how he got. Mostly, he ignored me. Both of us, but he was particularly shitty to me. A son like you he could at least relate to. But me? He had to suspect he'd been cuckolded. Look at me. I am nothing like the Bigelows. And neither is Sofia."

"And no wonder Sofia is the way she is," BoJo said. "My god, it's impossible to take in, but yet it explains so much."

Sybil looked down at her hands as if they were new appendages. As if she were wholly new to herself. Then up at her brother. "Mason? Mat and Brooks? They know?"

"Yes."

She closed her eyes for a long moment. Drew in a deep meditative breath. Let it out slowly. "Good." Then she opened her eyes and looked at Nemi. "I want to meet him. Our father. Does he even know we exist?"

"I don't think so. Artemis and Asklepios will be the best ones to figure out how we handle all that. They can arrange a meeting, but right now—"

Just then, a small blonde dynamo swung open the bedroom door and swept into the bathroom, launching herself at Cy. "Daddy!"

"Shush, sweet pea," Cy said, lifting Sofia into his arms and burying his face in her shining golden hair. "It's a big secret that I'm here. No one else can know. Just us."

"I've blocked the sound from this room. No one else in the house can hear us," Nemi assured him as BoJo hurried into the bedroom and shut the door to the hall. Locked it.

"I'm good at keeping secrets," Sofia proclaimed.

"Where's Mrs. C?" BoJo asked.

"The bad men made her make them food. She told me to stay with her in the kitchen, but I said I had to go to the bathroom and then I came here."

Cy glanced at Nemi. "How did you know where we were?"

"I don't know." Sofia shrugged. "I just did."

What does that mean?

The little girl pulled back, rested two small hands on either side of Cy's face, and looked him in the eyes. "I don't like those men because they aren't nice to Mommy or Mrs. C." She turned to look at Cy's sister. "And Dr. Lane is *too* nice to Auntie Sybil."

"I don't like them being here either, but there is one new person I hope you'll like very much." He shifted Sofia and set her down gently so Nemi could step forward. "This is my friend Hallie. She is a *very* special person who is going to help us. She's sort of like a secret agent. Like from that movie you've watched a thousand times, *The Incredibles*."

Nemi crouched down to Sofia's level and held out her hand. "I'm very happy to meet you, Sofia. Your father has told me that he's very proud of you and that you're very smart and very brave."

"I *am* brave and smart," Sofia said, her chest puffing out just a tiny bit. "Do you have a mask? Do you really have superpowers? Can you make all the bad men go away?"

"I would like nothing more than to make all the bad men in the whole wide world go away and keep children like you safe always and forever. I can't do that, but I am going to do my best to make sure that you, your mother, and your aunt are safe from the bad men here."

"And Daddy. You'll keep him safe too, right?"

"And your daddy, of course," Nemi said, her voice catching.

There was a loud knock at the door. "Sofia? Are you in there? Sybil? BoJo? Where is everyone?"

Ken Lane. Knocking on his bedroom door. Rattling his doorknob. Cy clenched his jaw tight to keep from saying something. Then Nemi touched his arm and suddenly he, Sofia, and BoJo were behind some sort of shimmering curtain of invisibility. Still in the room. Still right there with Sybil. But cloaked, as if they were transparent as air.

Sybil blinked. Swallowed. Gave her brother a quick nod, then slumped her shoulders, went to the door and pulled it open just in time to see Ken gesture for the two heavily armed SS agents standing with him to break it down.

"JESUS!" Ken jumped back, then caught himself. "Sybil, sweetheart," he said, collecting his wits. "What are you doing in Cy's room? I was worried! Mrs. Cárdenas didn't know where you were."

Sybil made a grand show of wiping her eyes. "I'm just so ... upset. What if he tries to come home? What if Cy tries to hurt us? Oh, Ken! What are we going to do?"

Ken pulled her to him and wrapped his arms around her, one hand sliding up and down her back, making Sybil's skin crawl like it was covered in stinging scorpions and making Cy want to put him in the ground.

"Don't you worry, sweetheart. I'm going to protect you from your brother and his friends. As long as I'm around, they won't be able to reach you."

From behind the curtain of invisibility, Cy struggled to tamp down his emotions, tried not to explode.

Sybil answered with a delicate whimper. "Just get me out of here, Ken. It's too painful to be in his room. Oh, Cy ... What are we going to do?"

Cy wondered the same damn thing as Sybil maneuvered Ken Fucking Lane out of the room, shutting the door behind her.

"You all need to stay together as much as possible," he told BoJo and Sofia. "And help keep an eye on Ken. We've got the whole place monitored, but if you need to contact us, have Mrs. C call Mat. We've got a place where we can all stay together and stay safe, but we can't disappear you right now without putting everything else at risk."

He pulled BoJo in for a hug, then gave Sofia a kiss on the top of her head. "Hallie and I have to leave right now, but I want you to be brave. Mason and Brooks are watching and listening to what's going on in the house. And Hallie's *Incredible* friends—are watching over you too."

"And Mrs. C too?"

"Of course. And you need to be a brave girl for Mrs. C because she's worried about Mat."

"He's with you, though, right?"

"Yup. Just itching for another chance to beat you at chess."

Sofia giggled. "He always lets me win."

"Cy..." BoJo started. Then stopped. She swallowed. "Take care of yourself. Sybil and I can handle things here. And our brave girl is going to help too, right Sof?"

"Don't worry, Daddy. We're going to be fine." Sofia turned and crooked a finger to Nemi and Nemi crouched down to hear her. "I knew you were coming today," Sofia whispered. "I saw it in my mind. And I know you love my daddy, so ..." She reached up and pressed a kiss to Nemi's cheek. "Come back for us soon. I'll be waiting."

29

Cy and Nemi made no pretense of hiding how they got in and out as they disappeared from Cy's bathroom and reappeared in the Basement's control center. He was getting so used to teleporting that he barely stumbled, although his brain still did a dizzied lurch like some sort of phase change in his biochemistry had his neurons and synapses firing out of sync. And his stomach responded with a now familiar but thankfully not violent, flip flop.

Mason swiveled around in his chair. "How's Sybil? How'd she take the news about, you know ... And Sofia and BoJo, how're they doing?"

Cy took a seat in one of the swivel chairs and ran his fingers through hair, messing it up more than smoothing it down. "Sybs took it surprisingly well. Like it explained things about herself that fit, made sense to her and how she is in the world. The crazy dreams and premonitions I never took seriously. Probably took it better than I did."

"Not probably," Nemi said with a smile.

Mason let out an obviously relieved breath. "Good. I'm glad for her. She"—Mason swallowed hard—"deserves some peace."

A strange memory tugged at Cy's brain then, something about Ken leaning over him, going on and on about Cy sticking his nose in SDIC affairs and ... about Mason and Sybil. About how Cy tried to keep Ken away from Sybil but ... *shit*. About how Cy never even noticed Mason mooning after her.

And then it occurred to him, hadn't Sybil asked about Mason first too? When she'd asked if the guys knew about the demigod thing. Did his twin and one of his best friends have a thing for each other? He'd thought so once or twice back in high school. And maybe for a while in college it seemed like they might be attracted to each other, but he didn't think anything had ever happened between them. Surely, he'd know. Surely, one of them would have confided in him. Right? Surely he wasn't that wrapped up in his own head or that blind.

Sybil wasn't attracted to guys like Mason. She'd never wanted to hang out with Cy and his friends. Too much testosterone, she always said. They gave her a headache. She dated seriously intellectual types. One guy was doing his thesis on Plutarch, another studied Chaucer like he was the most fascinating thing in the history of the world, and yet another spent all his free time making Risograph-printed zines of his poetry and sketches.

Not that there was anything wrong with any of that, but given that those were the kind of men his sister gravitated toward, he couldn't see her and let's-go-jump-out-of-a-plane-before-chasing-bad-guys-through-back-alleys Mason together. Although Mason could be serious as hell and single-minded to a fault, he was just as big an adrenalin junkie as the rest of them. And if there'd been anything between him and Sybil, wouldn't one of them have said something when Mason left to join the FBI? Or when he came back?

But, what was it Sybil just said? That the guys were *his* friends, not hers. That they'd all been *loyal* to him. That she'd felt *invisible*. Well, shit.

"We saw Ken and his shadows head down the hall," Mason was saying. "They were just about to knock down your door when Sybil opened it. She put on a good show to draw him away."

Cy heard it then. Clear as a hammer and gong. The tension in Mason's voice. If Mason really did have a thing for Sybil, he must be worried as hell about Ken Fucking Lane being in the house with her. He tried to catch Mason's gaze, but his friend turned toward the door.

"You're back." Brooks sauntered into the room with two glasses, wedges of limes floating in ice water. "Everything okay?"

"As well as can be expected," Cy said. "I take it you saw the Ken and Sybil show."

"Yeah, asshole was going to have his goons break down your damn door." Brooks handed one of the water glasses to Mason. "Mason tell you we're supposed to ping D.C. when you got back? Although"—Brooks looked at Nemi—"Mat also said you lot can just mind talk or something? Communicate telepathically? No secure comms link required."

"It's true," Nemi said. "But we can also block each other when we want some privacy." She cast a knowing glance at Cy. "Communicating, as some wise person once told me, is a two-way street."

Brooks laughed at that. "Cy Bigelow, a font of wisdom. Who knew?" He held up his glass in a mock toast. "Anyway, while Mason fires up our super-duper secure Pantheon League connection, why don't you tell us what you already know and us mere mortals are about to find out."

Nemi nodded and pulled out a chair. "Jensen put out a statement saying he's not going to let an act of terrorism stand in the way of his beloved National Christmas Celebration and is going to address a special session of Congress to announce the latest news in the bombing investigation. Since the New America Building is a crime scene, the session will be on Capitol Hill."

Nemi worried her bottom lip with her teeth, a simple, human gesture that warmed Cy's blood. He ignored the sensation as Mat appeared on the screen, the Pantheon League's meeting room in the background.

After a quick recap of what went down at the Bigelow Estate, Cy mused, "seems like the perfect opportunity to make some sort of symbolic statement since tomorrow's special session is going to be in the capitol building. You all have any ideas?"

"Are you kidding?" Mat laughed. "This crew is full of ideas and intel. Some they've shared with me and some they haven't. Here's what I know so far. Chiron and Artemis took off shortly after you two left and Ali and Meg are scurrying here and there to get their plan in place. What that plan is, I'm still not sure."

Cy felt a surge of adrenaline and saw a slow smile take shape on Nemi's face.

"Whatever the plan is," Mason said, "I'm in."

"Damn right." Brooks echoed.

"Then Cy Bigelow and Alex Whitelaw need to get their asses back to D.C. pronto," a woman's voice offscreen said.

Mat scooted aside so a sable-haired woman with dark, sparkling eyes and a mesmerizingly devious smile could join him on screen. Although she looked like some sort of nymph straight out of a mythology picture book, Cy now knew Tisiphone cursed like a sailor in multiple languages—some long dead—and worked the Pantheon League's control center like a technical magician. Which, Cy supposed, she was.

Brooks turned to Cy, waggled his eyebrows, and mouthed, *Who the hell is that?*

"I'm Tisiphone Erinyes," the woman said as if reading Brook's mind. "One of the legendary Furies and let me tell you that we are indeed furious. So, here's what we have in mind for tomorrow's festivities. Jump in if you see a problem or have a better idea."

30

The next day, Cy and Alex stood side by side in the men's bathroom down the hall from the chamber in which members of the House of Representatives met when in session, which was now for only one month each quarter. Now, as they prepared to take their seats in the gallery, Cy's heart thudded in his chest.

"Don't worry," Alex said. "I've got us cloaked and no one in this building knows we're here. Jensen's paranoia has convinced everyone we've gone on the run because he's a coward and that's what he'd do."

Reflexively, Cy checked his watch and adjusted his tie. "Invisibility is a nice trick. And I'm not worried."

"Sure. Most people think we're national heroes, after all."

"Right up until the moment we're not."

Alex ran his fingers through his hair and straightened his lapels. Their eyes met in the mirror above the row of sinks, and the corner of Alex's full mouth quirked in a smile. "I can hear your heart beating."

Cy blew out a huff of laughter. "Well, if Tisi's intel is correct, we're in for a helluva day."

"We'll get through it." Alex placed his palm on Cy's chest. No other words were needed. Just a touch. Just the warm pressure of reassurance. But it was enough to make Cy want to find out what leaning in and kissing Alex would really be like. How the length of this man's well-muscled body pressed against his own would make him feel.

Cy pressed his palm over Alex's, then stepped back, wiped his hand down his face. *Get it together.* The last thing they needed was to be caught in *flagrante delicto* in the halls of Congress just before Jensen planned to call them out as terrorists in front of the entire world. Especially since homosexuality was a fucking crime.

Alex grasped his arm and gave it a squeeze. "Ready?"

Cy drew in a breath, held Alex's gaze, and exhaled slowly. He nodded. "Let's do this."

Back at Pantheon League HQ, Tisi made sure her communications with Brooks back in the Basement in Arizona and their eyes and ears on the Bigelow estate were safe and secure—for about the millionth time in the last hour. Not that there was any risk of their systems being compromised, but still. Then she double checked her link to Chiron and Artemis, who were getting their part of the plan in place, and with Ali, who was at the Waldorf with Helen and Kemal. Everything was secure.

Mat, along with Mason and Hermes, waited in the rotunda along with other bodyguards and security personnel because weapons were not allowed in the Chamber itself. Dio and Dr. A were still at HQ, hunkered down with Tisi and ready to watch the fireworks while Sybil and BoJo were in the small theater in the basement of the Bigelow estate, preparing to watch Jensen's speech while Sofia played a video game on her tablet nearby.

Everything was in place and would go according to plan, Mat reassured himself. He patted his pockets. Yes, he had plenty of ammunition if things went sideways. He knew Mason was similarly equipped. They both wore microfiber graphene vests that were as thin as a fine silk shirt and tough enough to repel a rocket-launched grenade. Well, Hermes had teased, maybe not quite that strong, but strong enough for anything Jensen's men could shoot at them. And they had backup weapons strapped to their ankles. Just in case.

It was certainly convenient to have gods who could teleport men and materiel around the country without the hassle of flying, even if flying meant transport by private jet with a compellingly attractive, smart-mouthed pilot who never took shit from anyone who couldn't take it right back. He rubbed the back of his neck and tried to not think about Helen Cross sitting in a hotel room just a few blocks away.

After breakfast, Hermes had gone to Arizona to get Mason, and Ali had transported Mat to the Waldorf to brief Helen and Kemal in person. Mat hadn't had a chance to be alone with Helen in what seemed like eons, but she didn't seem to care. Which was fine because Mat didn't know how he felt about her anyway. At least that's what he told himself. It was best to stay professional. And because she kept him at arm's length, he didn't have much of a choice.

Mat checked his weapon and watched as Mason followed suit. Hermes watched them both with an amused look on his face. The god was probably bored. Or entertained by their mortal failings. But no. Maybe he deserved more credit than that. He wasn't quite the ass Mat originally thought he was. More like he was jaded and sarcastic, but it seemed his heart was in the right place. He didn't have to work with the Pantheon League. He could be off doing godly things with other godly types on some sacred mountaintop in Greece or racing around on his custom-made, one-of-a-kind, electric, 0-180 mph Wraith motorcycle delivering important messages to who knows who. But he wasn't. He was here with them.

Hermes was supposed to be Alex Whitelaw's bodyguard because no billionaire worth their bitcoin traveled without one. Mat knew Nemi would take care of Cy, but he also knew his job was to stick by his friend no matter what. And Mason was acting as another Bigelow bodyguard because, given his degree in criminal law, he'd be close by and ready to step in as Cy's attorney if necessary. *When* necessary, more like.

He glanced at his watch. Almost showtime. From what intelligence the PLeague, as Mat had taken to thinking of it, had gathered on Jensen's plans, the shit should start flying in about fifteen minutes, give or take.

He pictured Helen sitting in front of the television in her room. Wondered if she ever thought about him. Wondered why she didn't seem alarmed by the sudden comings and goings between the PLeague HQ in Georgetown and the Waldorf in the District. Neither Helen nor Kemal seemed surprised. And that was surprising. He exhaled. Frowned. He hated surprises.

Nemi would have loved to thread her fingers through Cy's as they sat in the lion's den, cloaked by a shield of invisibility and silence and waiting for their plan to unfold. But as Alex Whitelaw, she kept her hands to herself. No one could see them or hear them until she dropped the shield, but she wasn't sure Cy would welcome Alex's touch. There had been a frisson of connection when she'd put her hand on his chest in the bathroom, but that wasn't enough.

She still had no idea what Cy's demigod powers were, other than an ability to heal quickly from physical wounds and to be preternaturally good at everything. Academics. Athletics. Music. What else was he capable of? How far could he be pushed before any latent powers manifested? Did he even have any latent powers?

And what about Sybil and little Sofia? Sybil had apparently been plagued by visions and dreams her whole life, so she'd clearly inherited Apollo's powers of prophecy, but was that all she'd inherited? And what about Sofia? How had the little girl known where they were in the house, and how had she seen so clearly into Nemi's heart? *I knew you were coming today. I saw it in my mind. And I know you love my daddy, so ...* How had she known something Nemi hadn't even admitted to herself?

The music started and the Senators and Representatives—all now directly appointed by their respective state legislatures which had been gerrymandered to the point that elections were strictly pro forma—jumped to their feet, clapping and whooping like giddy teenagers in the presence of their favorite rock stars.

When the noise got nearly unbearable, the double doors at the back of the room opened and Chancellor Jensen, President Julius Valentine, and Vice President Darryl Frazier all paused a moment for dramatic effect before striding in with the Justices and Cabinet members close behind.

Cy groaned and rolled his eyes and Alex frowned at the spectacle. It was embarrassing to see grown men bowing and scraping to such opportunistic, narcissistic grifters. The Cabinet members took their reserved seats in the front row as Valentine and Frazier followed Jensen to the podium. They gave the sycophants in the crowd hearty waves and took their seats behind Jensen who stepped up to the microphone and gestured for everyone to sit.

"Yes, yes," Chancellor Jensen said, basking in the applause and adulation. "Thank you! Please sit. Thank you. I would say Merry Christmas to you all, but this nation has been through a horrific experience—an experience that has bound us even closer together—and I'm beyond relieved to see so many of you here today. Standing up to terror. Showing the world that American patriots will never be intimidated by cowards and their dastardly deeds."

"Dastardly deeds? Who writes this drivel?" Cy muttered.

Jensen kept going, his voice finally hitting a crescendo. "We will *never* bow down before the weak and the woke. We will *never* bow down before those who want to drag America back to the failed past! And we will *never* bow down before anyone who tries to take away our freedoms!"

The men went wild. Stomping their feet and drumming their hands on their desks, drowning out Jensen's words. He held up both hands and the crowd quieted as if choreographed. He looked around the room, those beady eyes catching and holding the gazes of the several hundred men gathered before him. Then he looked directly into the camera.

"Governments must go on in the wake of terrible tragedy. It's our God-given sacred burden. Our sworn privilege to serve our motherland and to guide it forward with hope in our hearts and determination in our spines. We will never stop. We will never rest. But now, before we go on with our agenda for this session, I'd like for us to all bow our heads and offer up our thoughts and prayers for the dead and injured."

He made a show of wiping his eyes and sniffling and Cy noticed Alex's fingers go white on his chair's wooden arms. Then Jensen lifted his face again to the crowd—and to the teleprompter—and, in a somber and resonant voice, he read off the names of those injured and lost to the bombing, ending with, "And last, but certainly not least, let us remember Senator Parker and his lovely wife who lost their precious unborn baby. Senator, I swear to you—to all of you—America will never forget your sacrifice!" His voice rose again. "Nor forgive those responsible!"

31

"Cutting away in three, two, one," Tisi said.

In the Basement back in Bigelow, Brooks watched the live feed from the floor of the House of Representatives go dark, flicker, and then, less than a second later, viewers across the country and around the world were looking at a slight, disheveled boy with big brown eyes and dark brown skin. Next to him was a rail-thin young girl of about nine or ten, her hair in pigtails and dressed in a white dress with pink roses at the collar and flounces at the hem trimmed in pink ribbon. Hollow-eyed, she squinted into the dim light of the camera. Their fingers, nails blunt and grimy, grasped the galvanized wire of their cage while dozens of children in similar cages looked on.

The boy, who couldn't have been more than twelve or thirteen, looked straight into the camera. Voice shaky and reedy thin, he nodded to someone and began to speak.

"My name's Martin Collins. This is my sister, Addie. One day she found a book in Daddy's closet. It was about a girl named Addie Mae Collins, exactly like her own name. In the book, Addie Mae Collins and her three friends were killed by a bomb in a church a long time ago. It was a Black church, and the bomber was a White man. We'd never heard this story before, so Addie took the book to the factory school and showed her friends. Her teacher took the book and told the headmaster. And they pulled me from my class and called Daddy in. They said having the book was a crime, but I defended Addie and Daddy defended both of us. He said it was just an old library book and besides, it shouldn't be a crime to know your own family history. The factory superintendent said it was a banned book. That it was against the law for a parent to allow their children to have it, and so they took him away and then ... after awhile, they brought us here."

"Where were you before here?"

"I don't know. But there was no windows. Just that man. And he ..." He shook his head as if he couldn't even contemplate the words.

"Do you know where you are now? Or how long you've been here?" the voice behind the camera asked.

Martin shook his head. Like his sister, he had an intelligent air about him. His hair had probably been cropped closed, but now it was thicker, sticking out in tufts that gave him a mischievous ragamuffin look. He had a high forehead, large almond-shaped eyes, and thick, curled lashes. A wide mouth that should have been smiling.

"They put us on an airplane," he said, "but it wasn't like in a movie. There weren't no seats or nothin' fancy like that. We was loaded up in a big metal box and locked in. And then they unloaded us here. I know the season has changed since we got here, but we got no idea what day it is. It was hot then, and it's cold now. And we don't have good blankets."

"Where is your mother? The rest of your family?"

"Gone. Dead. Sold." He shrugged. "It was only ever us."

"Did you hear what happened in Washington D.C. two days ago?"

"They told us there was a bombing. Some people died. A baby was killed."

"Did the guards tell you who the bomber was?"

"They said it was Daddy, but we know they was lyin. He'd never hurt nobody."

"Even if he was desperate to save you?"

"How could he save us?" Addie Mae spoke up this time. She had an elfin-like face that should have been bright and shiny and happy. Intelligence nearly shone in her eyes. Intelligence and anger. Her fingers were clenched around the wire.

"That man already hurt us. Told us he'd hurt Daddy too. He already made us—" She looked away, shuddered. "Besides, I don't think we're even in America anymore. Most everyone grownup speaks a different language. Kids too. Most times we don't know what anybody's saying."

"Have the grownups hurt you?" The voice behind the camera was soft now.

The children looked at each other, then Martin waved his hand around the big room. A mid-sized warehouse of some sort. Shelving stacked with boxes lined the perimeter. A couple of forklifts sat near a tall, roll-up door, a sliver of light visible along the bottom where it didn't quite meet the floor. Where cold air billowed in from outside. And rows of cages filled with children.

"They take us to the back. It's like a different place. There's couches and smaller rooms. Some with beds and some with..." He shook his head. "Sometimes one at a time. Sometimes in groups. Boys and girls. They touch us. Make us do things to them. To each other." The boy's eyes shone with tears. He choked back a sob as he dropped his head and stared at his hands on the fencing. Tears tracked down his cheeks.

Addie's eyes were dry as she looked beyond the camera, up at the person holding it. "I don't know how you got in here, but can you get us out? Take us away from here? Can you save us?"

Then another child called out. And another. "Can you save us? Please help us!" More cries. A hundred voices begging. In a dozen different languages. Louder and louder. Rattling their cages. Sticking thin arms through the bars, reaching out toward the hope of freedom.

Then chaos.

None of the guards could see Chiron and Artemis, standing just outside the cage recording Martin and Addie's statement with their own camera technology and beaming it directly to Pantheon League HQ where Tisi had hacked into the video feed from the Capitol building. But the guards had heard the children talking, then crying. Then calling out. And that was absolutely not to be tolerated.

Bright lights flickered on in the cavernous room and armed guards rushed in yelling. *TIKHO! STOY! NE RAZGOVARIVAY! Quiet! Stop! No talking!*

But the children just got louder. And louder. And then shots rang out and Addie Mae Collins was blown backward, her white dress with pink ribbons blooming red with blood.

Then the feed went dark, so no one saw Chiron sweep into the cage, gather Addie Mae into his arms, and disappear.

And no one saw the guards crumple to the ground, their life threads sliced clean through. Or watched the locks on the cages spring open. Or the children pour out—one hundred and thirty-seven in all—and gather around Artemis who stood with her arms open as if she could embrace each one. No one saw Martin take her hand. And no one saw the children vanish. Or the building explode.

No one except Brooks, deep in the Basement beneath the Bigelow homestead, and Tisi, Dio, and Dr. A in Georgetown, all of whom had been monitoring other Pantheon League cameras placed within the building as well as the drone hovering high overhead. And it wasn't even a heartbeat later that Dr A disappeared from the room in Georgetown. Gone, Brooks hoped, to save that little girl.

Brooks's skin felt too small for his bones. His face was hot with rage. His eyes brimmed with tears. His body nearly vibrating with the need to do violence. He thought of his friends—old and new—each playing a role in the unfolding events. He checked the feed showing the small theater at the Bigelow estate and saw Sybil staring into the distance, eyes wide, as if she were watching something else, somewhere else. He saw Ken Fucking Lane standing, gripping the door frame, eyes bulging in disbelief. And he saw Sofia gathered into her mother's arms, both weeping.

And then the feed went live again.

Arizona Governor Vincent Guerrero, a man who had been missing for over four months, sat on a folding chair at a small wooden table in a nondescript room that could be anywhere in the world. He held a photo in his hand and appeared to be considering it. After a short pause, he looked up and addressed the camera.

"My name is Vincent Guerrero, and I am the duly elected governor of the great state of Arizona. I disappeared 142 days ago because if I had stayed in Phoenix, my life would have been forfeit. My crime? Speaking out against expanding the DICE camps in Arizona, the most notorious of which is the Sonoran Desert Internment Camp just south of Bigelow. Chancellor Jensen didn't appreciate my public rejection of his plan to expand the camps, and he sent his minions to tell me, in no uncertain terms, that I was to retract the speech or face the consequences. And that I was to sign a new loyalty oath—not to the Constitution he rewrote. Not even to the Jensen Administration. But to Jensen himself. I had 24 hours to decide what to do. Keep my position as governor, retract my statement on the camps and sign a loyalty oath, or pay the ultimate price for treason."

He drew in a breath. "I swore an oath to serve the people of Arizona, not to imprison them. And I swore an oath to uphold the law, not to prostrate myself before a dictator. My wife is dead. I have no children. So, I refused. And I fled."

He pushed himself to his feet. "Now, I am going public and declaring that I will no longer be a silent witness to the crimes of this Administration. Now, I am telling each of you watching that if we all stand up, if we all speak out, and if we all fight back, we can win. I am now working with the American Resistance Movement on behalf of everyone who has had their jobs or their homes or their savings or their loved ones ripped away just because the world's first trillionaire said so.

"I am standing up and speaking out for Martin and Addie Mae Collins. And for their father, Reginald, a man who was given an impossible choice: pretend to attempt to assassinate Chancellor Jensen in a suicide bombing and die with the promise that his son and daughter would be safe. Or refuse and die anyway, knowing that his son and his daughter would suffer unspeakable horrors.

"Well, now we know what happened. Jensen sold those innocent children to monsters just because that little girl read a book. And then his guards taunted Reginald with that knowledge. And that's why that desperate father did what he did. Reginald Collins was a man without a choice. Jensen has a choice. And he chooses cruelty. Every single day.

"And right now, on Capitol Hill, Jensen is still speaking to a joint session of Congress. He thinks he's still speaking to all of you out there watching. But because he's so fearful of being recorded, mocked, and undermined, he never allows electronic devices around him, and that means he has no idea that the feed from the Capitol has been hijacked. He has no idea that you just watched that interview with Martin and Addie Mae Collins. That you saw those cages with all those other children.

And he has no idea that I'm going to tell you exactly what he's going to do next.

"So, when you watch the next few minutes of his speech, you'll see exactly what kind of man he is. I have it on good authority that he is about to claim that the two men he praised as heroes yesterday are about to be arrested today. He's going to claim that Arizona native Cyrus Bigelow and a man named Alexander Whitelaw are behind the suicide bombing he himself orchestrated. He's going to claim that they recruited Reginald Collins to do their dirty work and to undermine the Jensen Administration.

"But I tell you that Bigelow and Whitelaw are innocent of this crime. Cyrus Bigelow was shot twice by Jensen's security forces while trying to save lives. Alexander Whitelaw threw himself at Reginald in attempt to disarm him. These men really are heroes. And yet, mark my words, they will be dragged away by SS agents in the next few minutes. Right before your eyes."

"So, I'm standing up for Reginald, Martin, and Addie Mae. For all those other children whose names I don't know. And for Cyrus Bigelow and Alex Whitelaw."

Guerrero looked down at the photo in his hand and then held it up to the camera.

"And I'm standing up for Inez Martin, a kind and generous woman who ended up with a bullet between her eyes, shot by Jensen's men while they were looking for me."

He paused, put the photo on the table. Then looked back up at the camera.

"Who are you willing to stand up for?"

32

As Chancellor Harold Jensen droned on and on about dangers around every corner and conspiracies and internal threats to his Glorious New America, Alex and Cy sat in a back row of the gallery, wrapped in a cocoon of silence and invisibility as they watched Tisi's feed on Alex's smart watch which, of course, was designed to pick up signals directly from the Pantheon League comms center. As soon as Governor Guerrero went dark and Jensen reappeared, Alex turned his watch's video feed off and dropped the shield. The whole thing took just shy of five minutes.

But it had been almost a full minute into the hijacked feed before a Security Service agent on the outside realized what was happening and contacted an agent on the inside. Another thirty seconds for the team in the building to decide what to do. At the three-minute mark, SS Agent Reynolds yanked the door open to the media operations center where the feed from the cameras in the press gallery still displayed Jensen speaking at the podium on all the screens.

Startled at Reynolds' interruption, the techs leapt from their chairs, demanding to know what the hell was going on. They had no idea their feed to the world outside the capitol building had been hijacked. And no one inside the chamber had any idea what was happening.

Because no one dared defy Jensen's hard and fast rule that all electronic devices had to be turned over to security or turned off while he was speaking so no one would be distracted from his brilliance—or capture and distribute unauthorized audio, video, or photography of his numerous gaffes—no one on the inside received any messages from friends or family on the outside. And that meant the minutes ticked by before frantic men behind the scenes—men who were sworn to protect the Chancellor's physical safety—finally realized the real danger was on the airwaves.

Meanwhile, Jensen droned on. He took a sip of water and prepared for the best part of his speech.

"To keep our nation safe, we must not give any quarter to men who would sow division or attempt to tear us down. And that is why I have issued arrest warrants for Cyrus Bigelow and Alexander Whitelaw, both suspects in the terrible attack against our institutions and our leaders. To the untrained eye, it may have appeared that the men were heroes—and I, myself, was initially fooled—but they were prepared to act heroically because they were behind the bombing in the first place. My personal security services are searching for these two men even as I speak. They may think their wealth and privilege will protect them, but it will not! I don't know where they are hiding, but"—and here he looked into the camera again—"I promise you, we will find them and hold them accountable."

"You don't have to look far, Mr. Chancellor."

Cy's voice rang out in the chamber, a resonant declaration that had everyone in the room standing, turning, craning their necks to see where the voice came from. State-endorsed journalists in the press gallery swung their cameras around to search out the speaker as Jensen's head jerked up and his beady eyes scanned the gallery.

Cy stepped out of the shadows and into the aisle and walked down to the railing. Alex was right beside him. "Because, unlike you, we have nothing to hide."

President Julian Valentine and Vice President Darryl Frazier were on their feet. Eyes wide. Taking their cues from Jensen's stunned face, they pointed up at Cy and Alex. Waved their arms and began screaming. "Arrest them! Terrorists. Traitors!"

Some men in the chamber stood open mouthed, unsure what to do or think. Others immediately joined Valentine and Frazier. Soon the chanting took on a religious fervor—*Terrorists! Traitors! Make them pay! Terrorists! Traitors! Make them pay!*

Cy's heart thudded against his ribcage, and Alex's little finger stretched out to touch the back of Cy's clenched fist. A soothing balm. Cy forced himself to relax. Took in a breath, let it out. Made sure that the world saw a supremely confident, self-assured man. *I'm a fucking demigod,* he told himself. Although, even thinking the words still bordered on the delusional.

But he believed in Nemi. Believed in Alex. And Dr. A and Tisi and the rest of the Pantheon League. He wasn't in this alone no matter what Harold Jensen wanted him to think.

The crowd quickly arrived at the frothing-at-the-mouth stage, and he had no doubt that just a few hundred years earlier, he'd have been dragged out and hanged, burned at the stake, or guillotined on the spot.

A man wearing a suit, a sidearm, and an earpiece stepped up beside them. "I'm SS Agent Jack Dennehey, and I'm going to handcuff you both now and escort you out." He pulled Cy's hands together behind his back and clicked the metal bracelets closed. Did the same to Alex. Head down, he leaned in and whispered. "For your own safety, don't trust anyone, but know you have allies. You are not alone here."

And then Agent Jack Dennehey jerked the two men around and marched them up the stairs to the sound of thunderous applause.

33

Jensen stood still as a stone sentinel watching the playback on the screen in his private apartment beneath the New America Building.

He hit rewind.

Again. And again.

He'd watched it dozens of times already, sickeningly mesmerized. Looking for some clue as to how this disaster had unfolded. Who was behind the camera. How they'd found those kids. How they'd accessed the warehouse. Only a few trusted men on his personal staff knew about those kids and that fucking children's book the girl had taken to school.

Or the deal he'd made with their dad.

He would never even have known about those kids if it hadn't been for the factory superintendent—one of the many employees who owed his wealth, health, and happiness to Jensen—bringing the thing about the book up as an excuse for why he was late to their quarterly board meeting. Like a sniveling idiot, the man had paraded the kids in front of the board to prove he had a iron-clad handle on the factory school and that he was a big enough man to push a bunch of little kids around like some fucking king.

But there was only one ruler in America, and Jensen had taken one look at that little girl and known he wanted her. Known she'd make him feel like a king when she was on her knees, his cock in her pretty little mouth. And the boy too. All wide-eyed innocence. It hadn't been hard to convince the superintendent to put Collins and his kids on the next flight out to DC.

Poor guy. Jensen actually felt sorry for Collins. But it was the man's own fault for keeping contraband books in the house where children could find them. So, he'd given the man a choice: Walk in with a bomb and die knowing your kids would be cared for. Or refuse and know your kids would be fucked six ways to Sunday for the rest of their lives. And die anyway.

The question was, who'd told Collins that the kids had already been sold? He'd had them down here with him for a month before he'd sent them away. Not because he was done with them, but because he refused to get attached to anyone. Even such beautiful children with such soft skin and pretty eyes. It made him vulnerable. He knew he couldn't let anyone get close. Couldn't trust anyone.

Jesus. Did he have a spy on his team? Had someone sold him out? Had the Russians turned on him? The Chinese? The Koreans? Venezuelans? Brazilians? He had more enemies than he had friends, that was for sure.

He'd canceled the evenings' formal dinner and retreated to his chambers to sulk and brood and worry. And then he'd sent a loyal crew of SS agents to the temporary weigh station at Guantanamo to interview every fucking guard and cook and secretary and janitor on the entire fucking island.

The place was supposed to be as secure as Fort Knox. And ever since Jensen had taken over the entire island and quarantined the few Cubans left, he'd been assured it was *more* secure than Fort Knox. It was the perfect place to hold the product until the deals went through. Foreign or domestic, no buyer got their hands on the women and children until their payment was in his pocket.

But someone had found them.

Then they'd taken this goddamned video and broadcast it to the world. How had they cut into the government media feed? And where in the fucking hell was Vincent Guerrero hiding?

He'd ordered Cy Bigelow and Alexander Whitelaw taken into custody for suspicion of murder even though he knew they were innocent. Knew with a certainty since he was the one who'd sent one of his personal SEALS to take out Guerrero's bimbo, and he'd been the one who'd forced Reginald Collins's hand. Jensen might as well have strapped the explosives on Collins himself. But he'd had one of his SEALS do it. The same SEAL he'd paid handsomely to kill Bigelow in the melee. But somehow, Bigelow survived and his indestructible SEAL was dead.

He didn't even know the man's name. Went by Bruiser or some idiotic nickname. Seemed like everyone on the Teams had a fucking nickname. Didn't matter now. If he couldn't get a job done right, Jensen would find someone who could.

He knew he couldn't hold prominent men like Bigelow and Whitelaw for too long without significant blow back, but he'd make them sweat for as long as he could. He figured 24 hours ought to be fine this time around. Although he'd long had his eye on Cy Bigelow, he knew very little about the mysterious Alexander Whitelaw—other than he was apparently some physics genius developing quantum computing and communications technologies and had somehow made a mint even while flying under the radar. But he suspected both men were up to their eyeballs in the resistance, and he was hellbent on proving it. And making them pay. Permanently. Sooner, rather than later.

In the meantime, they could sit in their cells and wonder about their fates.

He scrubbed a hand through his hair. Still kept it thick and dyed black. Maybe he ought to add a touch of silver to his temples. Give himself a distinguished air. He was getting closer to eighty ever day, after all.

He knew people made fun of him now. He'd gotten lazy. Put on weight. Even with all the injections and procedures, he had trouble keeping the weight from creeping back on and his face was getting jowly. His ankles swelling. His hands had fucking age spots. Jesus Christ. That's why he always insisted on controlling the cameras. Having the press in his pocket.

Getting old sucked, but he was still twice the man Julian Valentine was. Fucking president was a sniveling ass-kisser. Always had been. He could call him up out of the blue right now and tell him to jump and the man would ask how high and thank him for the privilege.

And the vice president? Darryl Frazier was even worse than Valentine. A spineless shadow of a man. He wondered if Frazier could even get it up for that pretty wife of his. She was more masculine than he was. Probably had to shave every morning unlike Darryl whose face looked smooth as a baby's behind.

He ran a hand over his own chin. Used to need to shave twice a day. Now, it was maybe every other day, even with the testosterone shots. Too bad testosterone had never helped up top. He'd had a receding hairline even in his teens. People had made fun of him back then too. The seventeen-year-old with the big nose, weak chin, and terrible acne.

Fuck them. His daddy had been rich, so he'd ignored the taunts. He knew the world was a jungle, so he'd leveraged his daddy's money, transformed himself, and become king. He'd had the money for hair transplants, facial reconstruction surgery, and dental implants so why not? And now he was getting monthly augmentations that would keep him strong, sharp, and extend his lifespan.

And why not? Women did it all the time and no one thought the worse of them. Fake smiles. Fake boobs. Fake butts. Fake affection. He wasn't stupid. He knew women slept with him because he was rich and powerful. Strike that. Because he was *the richest and most powerful* man on the whole goddamned planet.

And still, somehow, someone had been able to make a fool of him today. He'd find them and make them pay. That was for damn sure.

There was a soft knock at the door. He could barely grind out the words, *come in*. But a moment later, Dr. Geoffrey Hunt, his personal physician—one of the few friends he had from before he'd plotted his rise to power and the only person to have unfettered access to him besides his pastor—poked his head around the open door.

"Harold, you're setting off every alarm bell on my remote sensing monitor. You need to calm down."

"Fuck you, I need to calm down," he growled, waved his hand at the TV monitor. "How the fuck am I supposed to calm down after everyone on the whole fucking planet has seen this shit?"

The doctor did not have the heart—or the courage—to tell him that not everyone tuned in to every speech he made.

"You've weathered worse. Scandals blow over, but if you stroke out on me, it won't matter. You have to take care of yourself. Your blood pressure is off the charts right now."

"You're going to be off the charts if you don't leave me be."

The doctor waited. His old friend was the loneliest person he knew and sooner or later, he'd start talking. He didn't have anyone else. He even kept his wives at arm's length.

"Did you watch it? Did you see what they said about me?"

The doctor didn't answer. He didn't have to. He knew Harold wouldn't listen to anything he said anyway.

"Basically, said I planned the bombing. Accused me of murder. As if I'd need to stoop to that."

Geoff Hunt knew exactly how low Harold Jensen would stoop. He'd seen him stoop so low, the hairs on his head wouldn't touch the ceiling in the deepest circles of hell.

"Said it to millions of people as if my followers would believe it. I'm the most popular politician in history! I won in a landslide with the biggest margins since George Washington! Who the hell do they think they are speaking out against me like that? I'm the richest man in history. Richer than fucking Midas. And they think a couple of kids in a cage and a loser in hiding can touch me?" Jensen ran his hands down his face and turned to face his doctor. "What the fuck do I do now, Geoff?"

"You take your meds and go to bed. If you don't take better care of yourself, that idiot Julian Valentine is going to be sitting behind your desk, and you'll be in a box six feet under."

All the fight seemed to go out of the Chancellor, but Geoff knew the man was most dangerous when you least expected. "Here," he said, holding his palm out with a few pills in it. "Take these and go to bed. If anything happens, I'll wake you personally. I promise. I'll sleep in my office tonight, so I won't be far."

Jensen took the pills and threw them back, dry swallowing them. "You promise you'll stay close?"

Geoff handed him a bottle of water. "I always keep my promises."

Jensen drew in a long breath. "I know, I know. You and Erin are the only ones who still believe in me. The rest pay lip service because I've got more money and power than they do."

Geoff suppressed a grimace. Pastor Erin Knight was about as distasteful a person as he'd ever met. The woman actually made his skin crawl with her exaggerated plastic features, holier than thou attitude, and sycophantic fawning. He'd tried to warn Jensen about her when she first appeared on the scene, but the man had been entranced. For all her talk of Jesus and salvation, Geoff knew she and Jensen had been fucking for years. The mere idea disgusted him, but he was practiced at keeping his thoughts to himself and his features neutral.

"I know exactly who you are, old friend," Geoff said. "Now, I don't want to sound like a mother hen, but you need to brush your teeth, wash your face, and go to bed. Otherwise, you won't be able to do what needs to be done tomorrow."

"Fine. Just make sure you're the one to wake me if I'm needed."

"Of course." Geoff set a bottle of pills on the desk beside the water. "Just in case you wake up. Take two and call me in the morning."

"Ha," Jensen said. "Always the joker. Now get out of here."

"I hate this," Geoff Hunt said when he closed the door to his office. "I don't want to hurt him."

The man sitting behind Geoff's desk scoffed. "But you're okay with him hurting millions of other people? In just the past few days, he forced a man to kill himself, shot a child, and arrested two innocent men."

"What child? He didn't shoot anyone! He was right here. You know that."

"Oh, right. He didn't actually pull the trigger. How astute of you to point that out."

"Why are you torturing me like this! I've known Harold since we were kids. He trusts me. I'm his goddamned doctor!"

"That's exactly why I'm here."

"But I don't even know who you are! Why won't you tell me your name?"

"You're joking, right?"

"Give me something. Tell me I'm doing the right thing! I swore the Hippocratic oath."

"Spare me."

"You come and go like you've got the keys to the fucking kingdom. You're like a wraith I can't even touch, so how can I hurt you? I'm doing everything you tell me to. I'm monitoring his health. Physical and mental. I'm giving him the drugs you tell me to give him. I'm in this as deep as you are."

"Hardly."

The mysterious man stood. He was handsome. Distinguished. Spoke with a foreign accent Geoff couldn't quite place. British and something else? Two years ago, he'd started appearing in Geoff's office at random times, but Geoff had no idea how he was getting past security without them even knowing he existed. He was a ghost, never appearing on any security footage. It was freaking him out. Now, he could smell his own fear as the man walked around the desk and leaned against it as if he owned the place.

"I already told you why I'm here."

"But it doesn't make sense!" Geoff sputtered. "I never hurt anyone."

The man huffed out a laugh. "Let me spell it out for you one more time. You betrayed a friend of mine. You spoke out against a good man who never betrayed his oath, never broke a law. You maligned him, dragged his name in the dirt, lied about his work and his motivations. A good man who'd saved millions of lives with his research and could have saved more if he hadn't been thrown in prison and left to die. I'm here because you are a pathetic toady who not only betrayed the Hippocratic Oath but betrayed all concepts of ethical and moral human behavior. I'm here because I'm going to haunt you until you atone for your sins."

"I'm atoning! I'm trying, I swear!"

"You've got a long way to go."

Geoff ran both hands over his head, back and forth until his hair was standing on end. "Give me a name at the very least. Make something up, I don't care. At least give me something."

"Fine." The man walked to the office door, pulled it open, then turned back to Geoff. "You can call me Asklepios."

As soon as the door clicked shut behind *Asklepios*, Geoff pulled out his phone and dialed security. "I just heard something in the hall outside my office. Check the cameras and tell me what you see."

"Pulling it up now, Doctor."

Geoff waited, sweat beading on his skin.

"Nothing, sir. Everything's secure. Maybe it was a heating vent?"

Geoff slumped down into his chair and squeezed his eyes shut against his pounding headache. "Okay, thanks. Must be hearing things."

"No problem, sir. I'll send a technician down to check the HVAC system."

34

Agent Bill Reynolds, the man they remembered from the night of the bombing, was waiting for them when they arrived at Security Services headquarters escorted by Agent Jack Dennehey and several other beefy men in dark suits and earpieces. Alex and Cy were stuffed into separate holding cells and told to be prepared to be interrogated about their roles in the bombing. Agent Reynolds informed Cy that he was also a suspect in Inez Martin's murder.

No surprise there.

Dennehey removed Cy's handcuffs and then locked the door to the cell as he left. He hadn't said another word about trust or allies or not being alone. Cy figured that even if the guy was sympathetic, he couldn't afford to say more when there were listening devices and cameras all over the place. One thing the Chancellor and his goons excelled at was paranoia.

Cy heard the lock click on another cell door and figured Alex was not far. He loosened his tie and looked around. Luxury accommodations. A tiny sink and matching stainless-steel toilet. Concrete walls and a matching concrete bench. All the comforts of home with everything color coordinated in the same dull shade of Cool Concrete. Or was it Evening Shadow? Maybe Dove or Silver, or more likely Gun Barrel Grey.

Sybil and BoJo would both have opinions on the name of the color. Last time they'd picked paint for a bit of redecorating, they'd been in stitches making up paint color names. God, he hoped they were still safe. Brooks would be watching out for them. And everyone at Pantheon League HQ. It had only been a few hours, but it still made him itchy to not be able to contact them, especially since Ken Fucking Lane was preying on Sybil.

He crossed his legs at the ankle and leaned back against the wall. Closed his eyes. Thought about Nemi. Wondered how she felt about being locked in a cell and having to pretend to be Alex Whitelaw, human terrorist suspect. A faint smile tugged at the corner of his mouth as he wondered what she'd experienced over the, what, hundreds of years? Thousands? *Millions?*

He couldn't even begin to conceive of all the things she'd seen and done. How she'd spent her time. Where she'd been. Who she'd known. What it was like to be a god. To be immortal. The limitations of his own mind reminded him of the vast gulf between them. She was a freaking goddess, for god's sake. CAPITAL G, goddess. The word would never have a generic connotation for him again.

They all claimed he was a demigod, but he didn't feel like anything special, so how could they be so sure? What did it really mean? Had his mother known there was something different about the "archaeologist" she'd banged in Delphi all those years ago? Had he seduced her like a regular human or had he shown her something more about himself? Had his father—Cyrus Bigelow—really suspected he'd been cuckolded? Had he been suspicious when the twins were born early? Cy knew Sybil had always been different, but besides healing quickly, did he have any powers? If so, what were they? How would he even know? And how the hell were these gods real in the first place?

Your thoughts are very loud.

Cy nearly jumped out of his skin. He blinked. Looked around. He was still alone. And yet that was definitely Nemi's voice. *In his head.* As clear as if she were sitting next to him. He felt ridiculous saying it out loud, even moving his lips, but he whispered anyway. "How can I hear you? Are you in my head?"

Not technically, as I assume it would be very crowded in there. Remember I told you how I found you at SDIC, when you were on the operating table? This is the same kind of thing. We've got our own private communications channel because we're ... well, connected. Entangled. And this is only possible because you're a demigod and can respond to me. Humans can't do this.

"So, I can talk to you in my head?"

Yes. Which is why you don't need to whisper. Or move your lips. Just send your thoughts to me.

"Okay, but does this mean you can read my mind? Because, um, that would be embarrassing."

Well, now I'm curious, but the answer is no. I mean I could, but I won't. I can access people's minds, but it's an invasion of privacy that I don't condone. Besides, you can easily block me.

"So, I just think at you?"

Yes, but you're still whispering. I can hear you. And not just in my mind. And that means that, depending on the sensitivity of the listening devices on this floor, the SS agents monitoring your holding cell can hear you too. And most likely, they've decided you've slipped a gear.

Cy pursed his lips together and deliberately sent a thought to Nemi. *Roses are red. Violets are blue. I feel ridiculous talking to you ... like this. Did you get that?*

You're no Homer, but yes, I got it.

A smile broke over Cy's features. He scrubbed a hand down his face to wipe it away. He didn't want to look giddy while in custody for suspicion of terrorism and murder. But holy shit.

Could I communicate with Sofia or Sybil like this?

I'm not sure. But it'd probably be a good idea to talk to them in person about all this before you try.

Nemi hadn't told Cy what Sofia had said to her at the Bigelow estate, about how she knew Nemi was coming to help and that she knew Nemi loved her daddy. That had been startling. Not because a granddaughter of Apollo had the gift of sight or prophecy, but because she saw something in Nemi's feelings about Cy that Nemi hadn't yet been willing to examine so closely. Of course, she loved Cy. She loved all her favorites. She cared deeply about all the humans and animals of Earth. Even the ones she had to punish. Well, most of them. And yet...

Cy bent forward, elbows on knees, and stared at the floor. Best to keep his face down and away from the cameras because he wasn't confident in his ability to keep a poker face while communicating with Nemi like this. So, he sent, *What're you doing over there?*

Talking to you.

Cy bit back a smile. *I can feel you smiling. Are you smiling?*

I'm smiling on the inside.

Cy snorted. *Now I can feel you laughing! Shit. This is hard. I'm staring at the floor so the cameras can't tell I'm trying not to laugh. We should talk about something that's not funny. Like have you ever been locked up before?*

Many times. But never for long. It's the physics, you know.

Guess I should've majored in physics instead of history and business.

I believe you have an intuitive understanding of the way things work. You just need to get in touch with the knowledge buried deep inside and take some time to get a feel for it. Although there are more demigods running around than you might expect, learning that you're one of them is not something that happens every day. Some have tremendous power and some have none. Some sense they are different, and some don't. Sometimes, a baby is born and the gods are drawn to it immediately, like a beacon. Some humans say these children are born with 'old souls,' and, in a way, that's true. But most demigods never find out the truth, and their powers remain hidden. Undeveloped.

What about Sofia?

Well, okay, if Cy was willing to go there, it was time for Nemi to tell him. *Listen. I didn't tell you earlier, but I believe your daughter inherited her grandfather's gift of sight. She told me she knew I was coming and knew that I was there to help. She said she'd seen it. You know her better than I do, so if you want to try to communicate with her through your connection, I'm not the one to tell you to wait. But—*

A noise. Outside Alex's cell. Nemi's voice in Cy's head again: *Looks like I'm about to be questioned. I don't know if you'll be able to hear through our connection or not. But Artemis is on her way to record it.*

In case we need to broadcast the truth?

That, or good old human blackmail.

35

Alexander Whitelaw looked up when SS Agents Reynolds and Dennehey opened the door and stepped inside his cell. He stood, looking as fresh as if he'd just showered, shaved, and dressed in his impeccably pressed and what appeared to be outrageously expensive suit. With a cryptic smile, he extended his hand like he was welcoming them into his private office. "Hello, gentlemen. What can I do for you today?"

A disgusted scowl painted Agent Bill Reynolds' lips as he glared down at Alex's hand as if it was covered with warts oozing deadly poison. Dennehey, however, took the hand and gave it a firm shake, earning a dark glare from his boss.

"This isn't a social call, Mr. Whitelaw," Reynolds nearly growled. "No need to pretend otherwise."

Alex shrugged and settled back down on his concrete bench. "I'm certainly aware of your intentions, Agent Reynolds, but I've always believed good manners are a sort of baseline marker of civilized society."

Reynolds didn't take the bait, but Alex saw Dennehey's lips twitch. "You are a bit of an enigma, Mr. Whitelaw," Reynolds said. "You appear to have come out of nowhere. Your company is involved in what I suspect is very expensive, cutting-edge research and yet you've applied for no government grants or subsidies, so we have no idea how your work is funded. No one in law enforcement has ever heard of you. Your record is clean. We have no fingerprints on file."

"Well, I certainly hope not. I've never even had a parking ticket."

"Exactly. Strange, isn't it? I mean, everyone gets a parking ticket at one time or another."

"Not when you employ a chauffeur. Honestly, I can't remember the last time I drove myself anywhere."

In fact, Nemi had never driven a car. Why would she need to? Now, she'd driven plenty of horse-drawn carriages and ridden plenty of horses, camels, and even elephants over the millennia, but cars? They'd only been around since the 1880s. Carl Benz had once given an enthusiastic young engineer going by the name of Alexander Wolf a ride in his motorwagon and then let him take the steering stick in hand, but that was about it.

"Well, I guess wealth has its privileges, but you have certainly flown under the radar."

That much was definitely true. Alexander Whoever-it-was-at-the-moment always got a gloriously human rush from piloting human-designed flying machines. But obviously, that wasn't what Reynolds was driving at.

Alex cocked a brow. "And your point is?"

"My point is that no one knows anything about you."

"Did you visit my website? WaveFormTechnologies.com? Everything you need to know—including my curriculum vitae—is on the site. I believe in transparency."

She wished she could go transparent right now just to watch Reynold's reaction. Men like this were tiresome bullies.

"Your profile is complete. I don't dispute that. We've got a birth certificate, a drivers' license—even though you say you don't drive—and a passport. We know you've never been married. You graduated at the top of your class in physics from University of Cambridge and went on to do your graduate work at the same institution. Your company does have a website, but you don't have any social media accounts and, apparently, never have. Your life is perfectly accounted for, and yet no one knows you. At all."

Alex huffed out a soft laugh. "Are you looking for personal references? Do I need to call a few old friends and have them attest that I am who I say I am? Maybe a few college chums?"

A muscle in Reynold's jaw clenched and unclenched. "How did you receive an invitation to the Chancellor's Christmas festivities?"

"The same way everyone else received the invitation, I suppose. It arrived in my email inbox. I accepted."

"You've never attended before."

Alex flashed a smile. "Perhaps my net worth finally met the elusive Jensen threshold that put me in the rarefied category to merit the Chancellor's attention. The company did quite well last year."

"What do you know about Reginald Collins?"

"The bomber?"

"The terrorist who blew himself up while targeting the leaders of our great nation."

"I never saw him before he rushed into the room yelling something about his children. Honestly, it was quite chaotic, and my first thought was to try to disarm him."

"Fancy yourself a hero, huh?"

Alex's eyes narrowed. "I *fancy* myself someone who cares about the welfare of others. I was in a position to help, so I did. I believe my actions saved lives."

"But *why* did you do it? Surely you knew you were risking your own life."

"Why does a perfect stranger leap into the water to save a drowning man?"

"I honestly have no idea," Reynolds said with a huff of exasperation.

"Not much of an altruist, are you?" Alex leaned back and crossed his arms over his chest. "Or maybe you don't believe altruism exists. Perhaps I could recommend some books on the topic. It's a fascinating concept, philosophically speaking."

Reynolds let out a frustrated sigh. "Do you understand how much trouble you're in right now?"

"Why should I be in any trouble? My understanding is that there were approximately five hundred people in that banquet room and that's not including bartenders, servers, or security personnel. I believe six people were killed, including the bomber. One died by gunshot, for which your own security service is responsible."

Another died when Cy Bigelow took out his own assassin, but Alex wasn't going to mention that.

"Fewer than twenty had to be hospitalized," Alex went on, "three of whom remain in critical condition. And, of course, one stillborn baby. As for me, I suffered multiple bruises and lacerations from the blast. If I had not knocked the bomber to the ground and prevented him from charging to the front of the room where Jensen, Valentine, and Frazier were on the dais, the impact of the bombing would have been dramatically worse. And yet, here I sit, in custody for putting my life on the line to save those men. I wonder why that is."

"How do you know Cyrus Bigelow?"

"I knew of him, of course, but we met for the first time on the day of the bombing, after the afternoon session. We had a drink at the Waldorf and then met again at the banquet."

"And yet you left together. After you refused medical treatment from Chancellor Jensen's personal physician."

"Because others were more gravely injured, we both opted to receive care from our own personal physicians. We told you this repeatedly. Perhaps your memory of events is unreliable. Were you injured in the blast? Perhaps you're suffering from a concussion."

"My memory is perfectly fine!" Reynolds gritted out. "I sent Dennehey here"—he waved a hand toward Agent Dennehey—"to follow you both, and he swears you simply disappeared after you left the Mall."

"Indeed?" Alex turned to Agent Dennehey. "If I'd known you were following us, I would have been more deliberate about getting Mr. Bigelow and his bodyguard into my car and getting out of the area. As it was, we hurried as fast as we were able to keep the street clear for emergency vehicles."

Dennehey held Alex's gaze. "I didn't see a car."

Alex gave Dennehey a generous smile. "I'll tell my chauffeur to drive more slowly next time."

Alex could smell the anger pouring off Reynolds. The man was as furious at Dennehey as he was at Alex. As for Dennehey, he was obviously sharper than he let on. What did he suspect, and could he really be a sympathetic ally?

"I'm wasting my time talking to you, Whitelaw. Think I'll go ask your friend Cy Bigelow some questions now. See how he likes being in custody."

Alex stood. "Give him my regards." He winked at Dennehey. "And ask him if he'd like a ride when we get released. My chauffeur will be waiting."

Cy was still processing the idea that his little Sofia had inherited the gift of sight from Apollo. That was going to take some getting used to, and he didn't want to try to contact her mind-to-mind or ask her about it until he'd seen her face-to-face. Until he tried to explain what was going on. How do you tell a kid that they're descended from an actual real-life god? He choked back a hysterical laugh. Jesus. As if life wasn't already complicated enough.

He heard what he figured was Alex's cell door click shut and steeled himself to be next. He hadn't been able to listen in on Alex's interrogation, figured he needed more practice with the whole entangled communications thing. In fact, he nearly jumped out of his skin when he heard Nemi in his head again. Would he ever get used to his new reality?

You're up next. They don't have anything on us, but Dennehey followed us the other night on the Mall and apparently figured out we simply disappeared. He's clearly not sure what to make of it so watch out for him. Reynolds, on the other hand, is just a run-of-the-mill bureaucratic bully.

The lock to his own cell clicked, and Cy watched the door swing open as SS Agents Reynolds and Dennehey stepped inside.

Cy, do not, under any circumstances, close this link or block me from listening. I can't disappear from here, but I need to hear what they say—or do—to you.

Cy swallowed. *I don't know how to close or block the link, so ... here we go.* He felt a new presence in the room but couldn't see a soul. He reached out again to Nemi. *Is someone else in here with me?*

Nemi responded. *It's just Artemis. In case your interview goes south.*

I hope it doesn't go too far south. That sounds painful.

If you're in real danger, we'll get you out of there. In the meantime, smile. You're on candid camera.

36

Agent Reynolds closed the door behind him and leaned against the wall. "How're you doing, Mr. Bigelow?"

"Fine and dandy. You?"

"Fine. Just fine. Ever been arrested before?"

"I'm sure you already know the answer to that. But as I was never read my rights nor formally charged, I don't believe I'm under arrest now."

"Yes, well, let's just say you're not under arrest *yet*. Although I must say it is surprising that a man such as yourself would stoop so low as to resort to bombings and murders. Chancellor Jensen has had his eye on you for awhile, and it appears you've been a model citizen. Good student back in the day. Respected member of the community. Benefactor to those less fortunate. Might be a bit of a womanizer, but I can't fault you for that."

Cy's eyes went wide as if in surprise, and he touched a hand to his heart. "Why, thank you for that recitation. I didn't know you were a fan."

"A fan of yours? Don't flatter yourself."

Cy gave him his most charming smile. "Ah, well. Maybe we just need to get to know each other a little better."

"You appear to be enjoying yourself," Reynolds said. "I take it your accommodations are to your liking? Anything we can get to make your stay more comfortable?"

"Bread and water, perhaps? A bit of gruel?"

Reynolds rolled his eyes. "Very funny."

Cy shrugged. "A little laughter is good for the soul. Increases endorphins, is good for your blood pressure, and even your stress response. Maybe you should try it."

"Causing a mass casualty event and murdering an innocent woman are not, in my view, laughing matters."

Cy's expression went hard, and he pierced Reynolds with an icy glare. "On that, we agree. That's why you should be out following leads and collecting evidence to reveal the person who blackmailed Reginald Collins with threats to his family and who arranged to put a bullet in Inez Martin's brain for who knows what reason instead of hanging around here harassing me and Alex Whitelaw."

"Is it true you had an affair with Inez Martin? Perhaps you killed her because of a lover's quarrel?"

"I'm not answering any further questions without my attorney present." Cy leaned back against the wall and crossed his legs at the ankle again. "I know my rights."

"Your rights are whatever the Chancellor decides they are."

Cy raised a brow. "Have you forgotten the Chancellor swore an oath to the Constitution? As did you, I assume."

Reynolds sighed. "The *new* Constitution. Not the *old* one."

Cy mimicked Reynolds' sigh. "Even the new Constitution guarantees the right to legal representation and due process." Cy looked Reynolds up and down and then slid his gaze over Agent Dennehey. "Perhaps you're not quite as familiar with the law as you think you are."

"And perhaps you're not quite as clever as you think you are," Reynolds said with a smug snort. "It appears you've forgotten that in times of national emergency the new Constitution gives the Chancellor unilateral power to override Fifth Amendment concerns regarding compelled self-incrimination, Sixth Amendment rights to counsel and Fourteenth Amendment rights to due process. I'm just hazarding a guess, here, but it seems like targeting the entire leadership of the government—*and their wives*—with a bomb qualifies as a national emergency."

"Has the Chancellor formally declared a national emergency?"

"The Chancellor is taking all pertinent steps to protect the people of this great nation."

To protect his own ass, more like. "So," Cy mused, a finger tapping his chin as if he were in deep thought, "the answer is ... no. A declaration has *not* been formally made, although I do wonder why not. Perhaps the Chancellor is not particularly worried about another bombing. Whatever his reasons, that brings us back to the question of my incarceration and my attorney. Who is obviously not present."

Reynolds ignored that and plowed on. "Why don't you tell us how you knew a bombing was about to happen when Collins first entered the banquet hall."

Cy raised a brow. "What on Earth makes you think I knew? Because I happen to have good reflexes? Because an angry man pushing his way through a crowd holding what was obviously a triggering device looked dangerous? Because security guards yelling and trying to tackle someone was clearly suspicious?"

"I'm the one asking the questions."

Sitting up straight, Cy shook his head and looked back and forth between the two agents. "So, what? You think I organized a bombing and then shined my shoes, put on a tux, and went to the scene of the crime so I could potentially be blown up along with the bomber?"

"I *said*, I'm the one asking the questions." Reynolds growled.

"And you think Alex Whitelaw threw himself at the bomber thereby putting himself in grave danger just to look like he wasn't in on the whole thing? That instead of attempting to disarm the bomber, he was in league with him all along?

"Mr. Bigelow, I'm the—"

"And you think I screamed for people to get down and take cover and then put myself in the line of fire because I wanted to get shot?"

"MR. BIGELOW!" Reynolds was red in the face.

"Do you think your colleagues were in on it too?" Cy plowed on. "Have you interrogated the agent who shot the woman in the green dress? The woman I saw die right in front of me? And what about the ones who shot me? Was it one agent or two? Want to see my wounds?"

Cy's hands went to his tie as if to loosen it when his head snapped back and bounced against the concrete wall as Reynolds plowed a fist into his jaw. Hard.

Holy. Shit. That hurt!

His ears rang and his eyes watered with the impact of the blow. He drew in a breath and shook his head as if to rattle his brains back in place and then reached around to touch the back of his head. His fingers came away red and sticky. He held them up hoping Artemis got a clear view. "That's gonna leave a lump. Might need more stitches."

"This interrogation is over," Reynolds declared, gripping one hand in the other. "But don't go anywhere," he sneered. "I'll be back."

"With my attorney?" Cy winced at the pain. "Since you confiscated my phone, perhaps you can call him for me."

Not content to let Cy have the last word but not wanting to leave any more visible marks on the man, Reynolds took a step forward, bent down as if to whisper something, and drove his fist right into Cy's gut.

Cy doubled over, head between his knees, as Reynolds turned and strode out the door. Dennehey hesitated for a moment, then turned and followed in Reynolds' wake.

"Fuck," Cy gasped out, sucking in a lungful of air. "That wasn't very nice." He felt the sensation of a comforting hand on his back. Artemis, he supposed. His aunt. And fuck if that wasn't weird.

You okay? Nemi asked.

Fine. Jaw's gonna bruise, my head's pounding, and he hit me right where Ken Lay cut me open, but he's got a weak punch for such a big man. You know what they're doing now?

Probably going to tell Jensen to declare a national emergency.

Cy laughed at that. *I doubt Jensen listens to anyone, let alone a man like Agent Reynolds. How long do you think they'll keep us?*

Artemis says Mason is outside right now finishing up a press conference. Flanked by Mat and Hermes, he announced that he represents both of us and demanded that we're either charged or released as there is no evidence to warrant holding us. Apparently, the big money on the online betting sites says we'll be out before dinner. And Artemis says that if Jensen goes live to announce a national emergency, Tisi will cut in and run the interrogation video instead.

Cy snorted. *Oh, that'd make Jensen happy.*

The Pantheon League aims to please. Nemi sent the message with a sensation of warmth.

I thought you aimed to punish.

Sometimes it feels like the same thing.

Cy could almost sense the one-shouldered shrug and see the sly smile on Alex Whitelaw's handsome face. And on Nemi's beautiful, full lips. A warm glow starting somewhere in the vicinity of his heart heated his blood, and it felt natural to open his mind to allow the feeling to flow down the connection.

37

Mat and Mason looked up as Cy and Alex, released after a mere five hours in custody, pushed open the doors of the Security Services headquarters and stepped outside. Hermes had disappeared somewhere, promising to return if needed. How he'd know if he was needed or not, neither Mat nor Mason had any idea. Godly telepathy, maybe.

Hurrying up to meet them on the broad stone stairs, Mat said, "Hermes told us Reynolds smacked you around a bit, but holy hell, you've got blood all over your collar."

Mason turned Cy around to look at the back of his head.

"Don't be Mother Hens," Cy said. "Heads bleed like crazy, you guys know that."

"If you were a normal person, I'd say you'd need stitches. But since you're you, well...." Mason gave him a slap on the back.

Cy rolled his eyes. "You two get a good look at Reynolds and Dennehey when they came out?"

"Reynolds looked pissed as hell, but Dennehey almost looked like the cat that ate the canary."

"Interesting," Alex said. "When Dennehey escorted us out of the chamber, he whispered, 'For your own safety, don't trust anyone, but know you have allies. You are not alone here.' I get the distinct feeling that Reynolds is not a fan of Dennehey's. And vice versa. We need to dig into their backgrounds. I think there's tension there we could exploit."

"We've got a car waiting," Mason said, waving toward a sleek black SUV parked at the curb with an even sleeker black woman—dressed in figure-hugging black pants, black jacket with a zipper that cut a slash across her breasts, and black combat boots—leaning against the bumper. "Hermes said we needed a chauffeured limo waiting, so Helen will get us all out of here, and then while we disappear back to PLeague HQ, she'll take a nice long drive around the city and give the goons something to do with their evening."

"I'm sure they'll love that," Alex quipped as they approached the vehicle.

"Alex," Mat said, "meet Helen Cross, pilot, chauffeur, all-round Bigelow transportation expert."

Helen gave Alex a quick nod. "You're looking quite fine these days, *Mr.* Whitelaw."

"I could say the same to you. Love the platinum blonde look, by the way. Very glamorous."

Mat stopped in his tracks. "Wait. You two know each other?"

"Our paths have crossed now and again," Helen said with an enigmatic smile as she opened the back door and gestured for Alex to get in.

Mat, Mason, and Cy all stared at each other and then at Helen. "So, you know who this man really is?" Cy said.

Helen shrugged. "Mysterious quantum physicist, billionaire inventor, etc., etc."

"Old family friend," Alex added.

"Estranged."

"That was your choice."

"And that's a conversation for another day."

Mat looked hard at Helen. "What kind of family friend?"

"As I said, that's a conversation for another day. Hop aboard, gentlemen, before Jensen's goons get antsy."

"Geoff Hunt is wound tighter than a Gordian knot," Dr. A was saying when Alex, Cy, Mat, and Mason appeared in the room. "He's believes he's being tormented by a ghost, like some poor Dickensian character. Wanted to put a name to his tormentor, so I told him to call me Asklepios. If he's caught and he gives that name up to an interrogator, he's likely to live out his days in a rubber room. If he lives, that is."

"Cold," Hermes said with a nod of approval. "You're usually the one advising empathy and understanding."

"Not in this case." Dr. A gestured for Cy to sit and bend forward so he could examine the back of his head. "Your hair is a matted mess. Doesn't look like you'll need stitches, but why don't you shower, and I'll take another look when you're cleaned up."

Cy stood and looked down at the dried blood on his fingers. "Okay, but first, what's the latest on Sybil, BoJo, and Sofia?"

"Brooks and Tisi are keeping an eye on everything," Dr. A said. "Nothing to report as far as I know."

"I'll call Mom and let her know you've been released." Mat pulled out his phone. "I think that's the best way to communicate with the girls for now. But first"—he shot a dark look at Alex—"I want to know how you and Helen know each other."

Dr. A laughed and offered Mat a kind smile.

"What?" Mat's eyes narrowed. "You know her too? Christ Almighty."

"Families are complicated," Dr. A said, laying a placating hand on Mat's arm. "Helen's story is her own to tell. For now, suffice it to say our familiarity with Helen is just another way through which the Pantheon League and you lot out in Arizona are connected."

Mason rolled his eyes. "Probably woulda been nice to know she had an in with the gods when we brought her on board. When it comes to security, we don't like surprises."

"Did you send Helen our way?" Cy asked Alex. "To avoid Jensen blowing us out of the sky, we wanted our own plane but couldn't afford anything decent. All the sudden Helen turns up with a sweet Bombardier 9000 and an offer we couldn't refuse."

"I had nothing to do with it. I only realized she was your pilot when you arrived here in D.C. The Furies knew I was interested in your welfare, so maybe one of them is responsible."

Positioned in front of the bank of computers and screens, Tisi swiveled her chair around to face the group. "I did it. While Nemi was off doing her thing, I kept tabs on the Bigelow crew. I saw you were looking for a plane, so I suggested Helen contact you." She shrugged. "Turns out it was a good fit. You're safe. She's safe. Everyone's happy."

"Wait." Mat glowered. "What do you mean, 'she's safe'?"

"You'll have to ask her."

"But—" Mat started.

Tisi held up a hand. "If you want to know more about Helen's situation, you need to talk to her. By the way, I've routed all your cell calls through the servers at the Waldorf and the nearest cell tower, so if anyone tries to trace your location, it'll look like you're at the hotel."

Mason watched Mat pinch the bridge of his nose and pace around the room, obviously not satisfied with Tisi's answer. "Good idea. Thanks," he told Tisi, nodding in acknowledgment. "In the meantime, I'm starving. You people—or rather, you gods—eat real food?"

"It's one of our greatest pleasures and, speaking of, dinner's almost ready," Dio announced, coming into the room. "Artemis came and went and now she and Chiron are off doing something with Ali and Meg—I think they're getting all those children settled at Chiron's place. So it's just us. Let's meet in the formal dining room and celebrate the release of our returning heroes."

"Count me out." Tisi stood, stretched her back, and rubbed her eyes. "I'm going to make a quick trip to meet with Brooks. I've got some suggestions about how we can better monitor the Bigelow estate and improve your overall communications systems. Get them more closely integrated with ours."

Cy arched a brow as he, Mat, and Mason all looked at each other. Tisiphone was going to Arizona? If there was a womanizer among the four friends, it was Brooks Paxon, and his friends knew that if the nymph-like Tisiphone with her brains, beauty, and smart mouth showed up in the Basement with Brooks there all by himself, sparks would likely fly. They all hoped the sparks wouldn't start an electrical fire.

Remember that I said dealing with the limitations of occupying a human form can be inconvenient for a god, but we do it when we want to form closer ties, share experiences, and in the hopes that we don't totally freak out every human we deal with. It's a bit like that old saying that a person can't understand another without walking a mile in their shoes. Also, when interacting with human technologies, having a human aspect—including hands and fingers—is often unavoidable. And of course, it's essential when one wants to interact *with* another human body. In the flesh. Something in which Tisiphone, like many of the gods, takes great pleasure.

Dio glanced at the clock on the wall. "Dinner will be served in thirty minutes." He turned to Mason. "We've got a guest room set up for you. Next door to Mat's so he can take you up and show you where to go if you want to clean up before we eat."

Turning to Cy, he added, "Nemi can show you to your new room. We moved your things out of Dr. A's infirmary and into a guest suite upstairs. Figured you'd prefer not to sleep in a hospital bed after the day you've had. And," he addressed everyone, "for those who want a drink before dinner, we've got sparkling water, the wine is decanted and ready to pour, and anything else one might want is at my fingertips. I've got my homemade ouzo for anyone wanting a taste of Greece, or ..." He smiled, snapped his fingers, and was suddenly holding a bottle of 30-year-old Highland single malt.

Three hours later, Cy pushed back from the table, full and bizarrely happy considering the events of the past few days.

Before dinner was served, they'd all watched Artemis's interrogation videos as well as video of Mason's press conference on the steps of the Security Services Building. Cy had shaken his head in disgust at the questions the bought-and-paid-for press had lobbed at Mason as he'd demanded his clients be afforded their Constitutional rights and stated that he was being denied access to them while they were in custody.

"They're all just Jensenian sycophants," Mason had groused. "Not a damn one of them asked a single question that betrayed a shred of independent thinking."

Hermes snorted at the idea while leading the group into the dining room. "Independent thinking? AI bots write all the articles anyway. Transcribers just slap their byline on a few paragraphs of text and call it reporting. Where are the Ida B. Wells or Nellie Blys of today? Or how about Hannah Arendt? Or Breslin, Pyle, or Lippmann?"

"Journalism in Jensen's New America is a lost cause," Mason said, taking his seat at the table. "As is the concept of truth."

"What do humans know of truth?" Hermes scoffed. "Too many of them mistake their own ill-informed opinions as god-given truths. What's worse is that their opinions are warped by the fact they drift through life half asleep, either willing to be swept here and there like a fallen leaf riding the currents in a running stream or determined to dig in their heels and ignore what's happening around them because it contravenes their supposed truths."

"They're not all like that," Nemi protested. "The Pantheon League has always been able to find humans with whom to ally, including those at this table."

"Yes, of course," Hermes dismissed her comment with a wave of his hand. 'Not *all* humans are unthinking drones. Just 99 percent of them. The other one percent is made up of tyrants who systematically take advantage of the drones—men like Jensen and Valentine or Hitler and Stalin—and those few brave souls with both brains *and* backbones willing to stand up against them. The rest are no more sophisticated than frightened children."

"Tyrants do love casting themselves as parental figures," Mason said. "I remember something this guy named Erich Fromm said. He wrote somewhere that most men are suggestible, half-awake children willing to surrender their will to anyone who threatens them or sweet talks them."

"It's classic gaslighting," Mat added. "Every tyrant uses the brutality of the stick and the reward of the carrot to psychologically manipulate the masses into believing that what they experience is not true. And when the 'free press' plays along, the outcome is almost always foreordained."

"That's why tyrants like Jensen control the press," Cy added. "He doesn't even trust Valentine or Frazer to deal with media outlets—or their owners."

Mason laughed. "The Chancellor doesn't trust anyone, *especially* the president and the vice president."

"He trusts Geoff Hunt," Dr. A said. "The doctor's the only

person who has nearly unfettered access to the Chancellor—and the only person Jensen really listens to."

"What about that spiritual advisor of his? Pastor Erin Knight?" Mason asked. "She's always given me the creeps."

"We need to find out more about her," Hermes said. "I'll take that task. Charlatans are a pet peeve of mine."

Conversation continued, ebbing and flowing as both gods and humans demolished serving after serving of spiced lamb meatballs dipped in tzatziki, fresh pita bread, Greek salad with vine-ripened tomatoes and slabs of feta, and baklava still warm from the oven. Dinner was paired with a dry, full-bodied Agiorgigitiko red wine from Nemea in the Peloponnese and dessert came with Dio's own homemade ouzo and small cups of Turkish coffee.

Cy couldn't remember when he'd had a better time or a better meal. Of course, he missed having Brooks with them and kept thinking of Sybil, BoJo, and little Sofia stuck in the house with Ken Fucking Lane hovering and SS agents watching their every move. And he was distracted by the sight of Nemi sitting across from him wearing a wine-red, curve-hugging, cashmere sweater with a plunging V-neck, and a drop necklace with a chain of cabochon rubies dangling between her breasts and knowing the rest of her was encased in skin-tight black leggings and knee-high black leather boots with kill-me-now heels.

But other than those things, he was, for the first time in a very long time, content.

"If I'd known I was half Greek," he said, pressing a finger into a stray bit of phyllo and honey left on his plate, "I'd have been eating like this all along."

"Feels like coming home, no?" Dio asked. "The honey is from Attica, from my own bees on a farm I keep there. Perhaps you will all visit someday. We can swim in the sea and drizzle sun-warmed honey on our lovers and lick it off under the shade of a plane tree." His words drifted off as the temperature in the room seemed to rise by several degrees.

Cy caught Nemi's gaze as he sucked the sticky honey from his fingers.

Mason cleared his throat and threw a meaningful glance at Mat. "It's time for me to hit the hay."

Mat stood and stretched out his neck. "Think I'll go up too," he volunteered as Mason pushed himself to his feet. He turned to Cy, his eyes flicking between him and Nemi. "At least *try* to get some rest, brother. Who knows what tomorrow will bring."

"Yes, yes," Dio said with a wave of his hand. "Everyone off to bed now. Tomorrow is another day."

"Okay, I'm out of here." Hermes stood and whipped his leather jacket off the back of his chair. "Places to go, people to see and all that." And then he was gone.

"And I'm off to Cambridge for a few days," Dr. A said. "So, no more injuries, Cy. Doctor's orders. Artemis and I are going to talk about the best way to approach Apollo, so he doesn't storm in here and start ordering everyone around. Or show up at the Bigelow Estate causing an uproar. In the meantime, try not to get murdered and let me know if someone else needs stitches. Or a bullet removed."

Then, he too disappeared.

38

"Cy looked across the table at Nemi. "Would he just show up in Bigelow? Without us knowing?"

"Don't worry. That's never going to happen." Nemi stood and absently tugged at the hem of her sweater, pulling it tight over her breasts. "I told you I would keep your loved ones safe, and that means from your enemies as well as from a meddling father."

Cy's throat went dry at the thought. Apollo. His father. Sofia's grandfather. A fucking god. It still didn't seem real. Of course, Nemi was a goddess too, but she wasn't part of the Olympian pantheon, so she seemed different. She and the Furies. Even though he now knew they were older than the Olympians, somehow they seemed more approachable. Maybe because he hadn't grown up with stories about them fucking and fighting their way through the ages.

"In the meantime, let me show you the way to your suite." Nemi's voice was soft and low, like a cat's purr, and it raised the hairs on the back of Cy's neck and reverberated all the way down to the base of his spine.

"Good idea. Wouldn't want to get lost."

He walked around the end of the table and held his hand out to her like some eighteenth-century courtier. "Lead the way, Nemesis, Immortal Goddess of Divine Retribution and Vengeance."

She took his hand, gave it a gentle squeeze, and guided him out toward the grand staircase sweeping up in an elegant arc from the gleaming, marble-tiled foyer. "Sometimes," she said, "the Immortal Goddess of Divine Retribution and Vengeance would prefer to simply be plain old Nemi."

"Ah. Well, you may be old, but there's nothing plain about you. And the more I know about you, the better I like you just the way you are—even if I feel unworthy of you."

She squeezed his arm. "I understand what you're saying, but I'm not sure you understand *what* I am or what it means."

"I know you're a force for good in the world. I know your friends love and respect you. I know you've saved my life multiple times, and I know I can trust you. Whether you're Nemi or Hallie or Alex."

"Changing human aspects is like changing clothes. It doesn't alter who or what I am. I can't change my nature, nor would I want to. But it can be ... lonely."

"You have Tisi, Ali, and Meg. Dr. A and Dio. Hermes and Artemis. You have family and friends to keep you company."

"I love my friends, but my close family is an unmitigated disaster of Earth-shattering proportions and someday many of my friends will be dead and gone as they are tied to the fate of this small, blue planet. The idea of losing them makes me lonely now, even though that day will be millennia in the future."

Immortality stretching out in front of her forever and ever in an expanding yet slowly dying universe was more than exhausting. Not that gods get tired in the way carbon life forms get tired—unless we're manifesting the physical body of a carbon life form and even then ... well, it's not the same.

She stopped in the middle of the foyer. Drew in a breath, let it out slowly. Turned to face him. Touched a fingertip to his cheek, traced the line of his jaw.

"I know this is all difficult for you to take in."

"I admit the last few days have felt like a blow to the head, and"—he looked away, as if searching for the right word—"I still have no idea what it all really means or that it's not some strange fever dream. I keep expecting to wake up safe and warm in my bed back home like Dorothy in the *Wizard of Oz*."

Nemi smiled at the reference.

"Only if that happened, there wouldn't be a beautiful woman sitting in a chair by the fire waiting for me. And that would be a crying shame."

She pressed her palm against his cheek. "This is not a dream. When you wake, you will still be a demigod, son of Apollo and a mortal woman, and I will still be Nemesis, daughter of Nyx alone, a primordial goddess."

He shook his head, still stunned at the mere idea of it all. Primordial goddess? Demigod? It sounded ridiculous.

"Your body may appear to be human," Nemi went on, "but you know intuitively that it's more than that. Dr. A ran some tests on your blood. On your DNA. The tests are new and complicated, and he hasn't got the results in yet, but there's a chance you could be immortal, like your father."

"I can't wrap my mind around that possibility right now. It just doesn't compute."

"I understand," Nemi said. "But are you beginning to accept that you are different?"

He shook his head again. Blew out a breath. "Yes? No? Maybe? I have no fucking idea."

"Think about it. You are preternaturally beautiful."

He started to protest, but she pressed a finger to his lips to stop him.

"You've grown up knowing that you're highly intelligent. Academics were easy for you. You were an outstanding student athlete. A daredevil who relished pushing boundaries. When injured, you heal quickly. Your reflexes are lightning fast. I would wager you have heightened hearing and excellent eyesight. Thinking about it in these terms may be new to you, but I believe your body has long known the truth. Think of how you dispatched the man who tried to kill you at the banquet. Tisi showed me the video. You moved like a god. So fast the camera couldn't capture it. You were a blur and then the man was dead."

His brow furrowed. "Jensen will see that? On the video?"

"No." Nemi said. "Tisi saved a copy and then corrupted the Administration's version."

"Ah, okay. That's a relief." He ran a hand down over his face. "Now let me ask you something. What does it feel like to be an immortal goddess in a human body?"

She smiled. "I feel all the things a human feels—or at least how I think a human feels. My body experiences the same sensations, urges, and desires a human experiences. It needs food. Sleep. Shelter." She looked up at him, a smile curving the edge of her mouth. "Sex."

He laughed, a deep throated sound that made her human toes curl in her boots. "You have no idea how delighted I am to hear that."

She sobered, brows bunching as she frowned. "But despite all that, I can never forget who and what I am. And you shouldn't let a pretty face make you forget either."

"How can I forget? I've seen you as a man. I've experienced you teleporting me all over the place. I've communicated with you telepathically."

"Those are things I can *do*—change my physical form, move through space and time, manipulate entangled particles. But it's not *what I am*. We rarely show humans our true forms because, well, sometimes we're not easy on the eyes. But I want you to see me. I don't want you or Sofia to be surprised—or worse, yet—scared of me."

"I would never—"

She let go of his arm and stepped back to stand in the middle of the softly lit foyer. "I am a daughter of the night, a tool of Kaos the Creator, born bearing the golden wings of justice, destined to help keep the world in balance."

The foyer lights flickered as glowing wings slowly unfurled behind her, casting flashing shadows and shimmering like golden fire, reaching half again Cy's height and nearly encompassing the full width of the entry hall.

His blood thudded in his ears, and he wanted to fall to his knees, worship her. Prostrate himself at her feet. But instead he braced his legs and held her gaze as she stretched out her arms, the rubies sparkling between her breasts, the red cashmere and black pants and boots dark as blood and soot against the brilliance of her feathery wings.

She was awe-inspiring. Stunning in her power. Her breathtaking beauty. But if she'd meant to scare him, it wasn't working. Instead, something inside him awakened, and his need—*his hunger*—for her detonated. From the heat of passion that had burned hot as glowing embers to a conflagration of desire that seemed to consume him from within.

"I wield the scales of justice in one hand and the sword of retribution in the other."

Cy's heart pounded as his gaze tracked between the weighted gold scales that appeared in one hand and the gleaming and very lethal-looking long sword that appeared in the other.

"I am bound by my very nature to exact vengeance for crimes against the gods, for the senseless suffering caused by human hate and self-aggrandizement, and for the harm and destruction wrought by arrogance, hubris, and vanity."

Every muscle in his body taut, hard as forged steel, he was barely able to form a coherent thought aside from his primal need for her. He was parched earth soaking up summer rain. He was the roll of thunder and the bolt of lightning, finally released in the heart of the storm. *Finally*, his body rejoiced. *Finally*, his mind cried out as recognition ripped through him. *This* was what he'd been waiting for his whole life. This winged creature. This primordial goddess. This woman.

"This is who and what I am," she said. Slowly, her wings curved over her, tucked in tight at her back, and then disappeared completely. "And yet, in all my history, in all my experiences on this lovely little blue dot, my most cherished moments have been when I've been valued as a friend. An equal. By my fellow gods and goddesses. And by the humans I've come to know over the ages. Not as someone to fear or placate or beg forgiveness from. Not as a goddess descended from on high to pass judgment and deliver justice. But as a being with thoughts and feelings of my own wrought from lifetimes of joys and sorrows and loneliness. And longing."

She smoothed back her hair, a few strands of which had blown into disarray by the unfurling and furling of her wings. Touched her necklace as if it gave her comfort.

He reached out to take her hand, squeezing her fingers and swallowing back the emotions threatening to choke him.

"Excepting Kaos the Creator," she went on, "all matter and every animate and inanimate thing in the universe was created by something else. The nitrogen in Earth's soil and the nitrogen in human blood is no less worthy than the nitrogen created in the hearts of stars. I say this because I want you to understand that a god is not more worthy than a human—or any other creature—just because one was created prior to the other. That would be like saying a parent is more worthy than a child because the parent is older.

"Of course, not all gods believe this." She twined her fingers with his. "But if I were to speak for my friends—the Furies, in particular—I'd say that because of what we are, we know that empathy and goodness and sacrifice and love are just as essential to the character of a human as they are to a god. As instruments of justice in the universe, we are uniquely positioned to see the good and evil in all creation."

She brought his hand to her mouth and pressed a kiss to his palm.

"I've seen true evil in gods and humans. In both cases, it is an utter void. An emptiness. A lack of caring, of listening, of understanding. I see it in my own sister. And I see the opposite in you. In you, I see empathy and understanding. Fierce love. Caring devotion. Kindness. These attributes are fundamental to who you are. And I am drawn to you because of it. You are worthy, Cyrus Bigelow. Never, ever doubt it."

His eyes flicked down to her mouth and then back up to hold her gaze. The words he wanted to say stuck in his throat. How could it be possible that this woman—this *goddess*—was drawn to him?

Your thoughts are very loud. She sent the message through their shared connection, then stepped closer, reached up and drew a finger down the center of his chest. *I want you, Cyrus Horatio Bigelow, the Fourth. Everything I just said and showed you—and I know it was a lot—was the long way of saying I desire you as a human desires another human. As a lover desires a beloved. As a goddess desires a mate.*

His thoughts stumbled over themselves as he sent them, like rocks tumbling in a raging river. *But I'm just ... I'm not ... And you've had ...*

"No," she said out loud. "You're not *just* anything. Whether or not you're a son of Apollo, you're a good man. A worthy man. And I haven't even had *all* that many men before you."

His eyes narrowed in confusion.

"Oh, don't get me wrong. I've had lovers, yes. In both my female and my male form. Many times. And I am *very* old and have not been celibate like Chiron. But neither am I a wanton like Aphrodite. Or even Tisi, who definitely takes delight in her human body. Why have one if you're not going to use it is her mantra."

Then she looked up at him with an almost shy smile. "It has, however, been a long time for me, over a century, so perhaps we should go slow so we can savor every moment."

His mind almost blanked at the thought that this was actually going to happen. He was going to make love to a goddess. He was going to fuck Nemi. Hallie. Alex. He didn't fucking care what form she took. He needed Nemesis like he needed oxygen. Now.

"Slow. Ha." He huffed out a laugh and started walking again, practically pulling her up the grand staircase. "You might as well have set a lit match to my blood. I actually think I have a fever. Like I'm literally on fire. You reveal your most fundamental self to me—glorious golden wings and all—and then say we should go slow when all I can think of now is ... well ... I don't think I can even spell the word 'slow' right now."

"Slow is a relative term."

"More like an incendiary term."

"We better hurry, then, before we set the house on fire."

39

In the next instant, they were in his room, pressed up against the closed door, her wrists clasped in one of his hands and raised above her head. He held her gaze with an intensity that set her blood rushing straight to her core.

"I've wanted you since I first blinked awake and saw you sitting by the fire." He touched his lips to her neck, just below her ear, and the hair on his body stood to attention as she moaned and tilted her head to give him better access.

"Since you first waltzed toward me and told me to call you Hallie and declared that you're 'not exactly' a doctor." He outlined the edge of her ear with his tongue and blew softly on it. "Since I first touched your hand on my bedpost and felt a spark of electricity ignite my blood."

"You weren't so eager when you discovered I was also the forest ranger who helped save Brooks."

"Even then." He lowered his mouth to hers, traced his tongue along the seam of her lips, and then delved deeper as she opened to him. Together, they explored each other like they were discovering new worlds. Lips. Tongues. Teeth. Breath. All mingling and tussling for dominance as the kiss went deeper still.

She pulled back and murmured against his skin. "You sure didn't act like it."

"I was an idiot." Alex is you and I want you."

Her body arched toward him as his fingers started exploring. "After that display with the wings, my mind keeps torturing me with images of us fucking in the air. Or on the moon. Covered in the red dust of Mars. Me on top. You on top. Floating through Saturn's rings. Holy hell, the possibilities are infinite. I think you've hijacked and rewired my brain."

"The only possibility I care about is right now."

"And right now, I want you naked," he rasped. "Except for that necklace. That stays." He followed each link of the chain with his lips down to where the last ruby sat in the valley between her breasts.

She leaned her head back and threaded her fingers in his hair. "It's one of my favorites."

"Why rubies?" He asked as he kissed his way back up, and along the fine bones of her clavicle.

"I love the vibrant color. Rubies, sapphires, emeralds, amethyst, topaz, opals. So many to choose from. Like rich flavors. The spices of the Earth. It's not that I don't like diamonds, but …"

He let go of her wrists and slipped his hands between them, to the hem of her sweater. She looked up at him through thick lashes as he pulled the sweater up over her head and tossed it to the floor.

His breath hitched as his eyes fixed on her full breasts, encased in ruby red lace. "We're you hoping to kill me tonight because I'm not sure I'm strong enough for this? How do goddesses discard the bodies of the mortal men they destroy with their feminine wiles?"

She laughed. "Feminine wiles?"

"Feminine wiles in fucking spades. And if you're wearing panties to match, I'm willing to sacrifice myself and go out in a blazing inferno." He stepped forward again and bent to run his tongue over the tops of her breasts, tracing the edge of the lace. "Maybe a fiery pyre on the snowy peak of Mt. Olympus."

He slipped the straps off her shoulders, one at a time, pulled down each lacy cup and bent to take one nipple between his teeth. A soft scrape. A lick. A hard suck as he rubbed and rolled the other nipple between his fingers. Then he lifted his head and stood back to look his fill.

"No pyres for you." She began unbuttoning his shirt. Slowly. Tortuously slowly. He was as hard as a Lonsdale stone and thought he might explode every time her fingers brushed his skin. She pulled his shirttail from his jeans and ran her hands up over his chest to push it from his shoulders. He shrugged it off, glad that his sleeves had been rolled up and he didn't have to waste precious seconds unbuttoning his cuffs. Then she was unbuckling his belt, and he was pushing the waistband of her leggings down over her hips, breathing hard as ruby-red, barely-there panties were slowly revealed.

"No pyres needed. I think I've already burst into flames."

She had his belt undone, his pants unzipped, but he dropped to his knees and started in on her boots. He slowly lowered the inside zipper on her right leg, then the left and pulled the leather boots off and tossed them aside.

Then he picked her up, strode to the bed, and settled her on the edge, pushing her on to her back. On his knees between her legs, he removed her socks, stripped off the leggings, and then began kissing up the inside of one leg and down the inside of the other, all the while listening to her every breath and sigh and moan.

All the while, getting harder and harder until he thought the tightening pressure in his balls might achieve critical mass and set off a nuclear chain reaction. He could probably power an entire continent with the potential energy.

Still, he set his needs aside and reached back up with one hand to palm her breast, lightly teasing the pebbled tip until she moaned out his name and arched up against his hand. "Cy."

He pressed his mouth against her, and she said it again. "Cy…"

"Is that yes Cy or a no Cy? A please, Cy? Or just a sigh sigh?"

She huffed out a laugh. "It's a yes, please, do more of everything you're doing, Cy."

"The best kind," he murmured and stroked his tongue against the heat of the damp red silk. Then he pulled the silk aside and put his mouth on her and she nearly shot off the bed. He slipped his other hand under her hip to lift her closer, squeezing, dipping his tongue into her heat, then pressing it flat against her. All the while, circling and pinching and soothing her nipple. Again and again. Deeper and harder as they both moaned in sync.

"That's a nice tune you're humming," he whispered, nudging her legs further apart with his shoulders. "Like we're in harmony."

She moaned and pushed herself up on her elbows to look down her body at him. "We're entangled."

He pulled his hand from beneath her and drove two fingers into her hot core, matching the rhythm and tempo of his tongue on her clit and his fingers on her nipple.

"Seven Sisters, Cy, I'm—" Her fingers tangled in his hair like she was trying to cling to a life raft as she arched off the bed, her body as taut as the string from Odysseus's bow, then collapsed back on the covers in a quivering sprawl, a sated smile on her angelic face.

Hand spread over her heart, he watched her settle and then slid the panties down her legs and hoisted her up, farther onto the bed. Then he shucked his pants, shoes, and socks and climbed up beside her, ready to start charting the curves and crevices he hadn't yet mapped.

She caught his hand, pulled him up to face her, and then rolled on top and started her own journey of exploration. Kisses along his jaw. Down his strong neck to the dip at the base of his throat. She moved to press kisses to both nipples and down the center of his torso, licking along the ridges of ribs and well-defined muscle. Down to his belly button and then lower until she took the heavy length of him in her hand, stroking the silky, hot skin and then running her tongue around the tip and taking him into the wet heat of her mouth. He pushed her hair back so he could see her mouth moving up and down his cock. Groaned as she took him deep and then pulled back, swirling her tongue around him until he swore in English, Spanish, Greek, O'odham and Diné.

"I speak them all, you know." She whispered.

"Figures. I'll never get anything over on you."

"Do you want to get something over on me?"

He huffed out a laugh and flipped her onto her back. "Yes. Me." He stared down at her. "Do we need to use a condom? I mean...."

Her eyes widened in surprise. "Well, this is new. No one has ever asked me that before."

"It's the 21st century. The age of consent ... and disease."

She cupped his face in her hands. "Disease has been around forever, but consent must be a modern phenomenon.

He nudged his hips against hers. "And?"

"No," she said with a shake of her head. "I'm impervious to human diseases and have never borne a child to a human."

"But apparently, I'm not fully human ..."

She let out an impatient laugh. "If the Fates intervene and gift us with a child, it will truly be a miracle for the ages. I think we're good to go, Mr. Bigelow."

"Thank the gods!"

"You're welcome," she whispered as he slid deep into her body. Her eyes went wide as he pushed in until their hips met. "Cy."

"I know."

He could barely choke out the words. His throat felt thick. His chest full, like something big, something monumental, had shifted and cracked open within him, filled him with glowing magma from the very center of the Earth. A fucking ten on the Richter scale. Something volcanic, probably. His own personal Vesuvius. Tambora. Or Olympus. Was that mountain a volcano? He had no idea, but he knew that after this moment, his life would never be the same.

She reached up and touched his lips with a single fingertip. "It's never been like this."

"Like heaven?" He pulled back and pushed in again, watching her face, bending down to touch his tongue to a tear that slipped from the corner of her eye.

"Like home," she whispered, and then wrapped her arms and legs around him, as tight as she could, arched up against him, and held on as he drove himself deeper. And deeper still. Until they were fused. Until they'd entered the boundary layer between a phase change. They had been separate entities before, but now … now they were something new. Something different. Joined body and soul. And no matter what had happened in the past or would happen in the distant echoes of future time, they would neither one be entirely alone again.

As they both came on a roar and the light wavered and spangled around them like fireworks blazing in and out of a wormhole and his ears rang and his mind blanked and as Nemesis wept and held his body close as if it was the most precious thing in the universe and she needed him to survive, Cy blinked back tears and thanked all the gods he'd ever heard of that he was here, in this place, in this moment, with this woman.

This goddess.

His goddess.

40

Nemi stretched out her woman's body, skin still tingling from the last round of lovemaking, and dragged a foot up Cy's leg. He didn't stir. Good. He was, finally, soundly asleep. Demigod or not, he needed serious rest after the night they'd had. And after the last few days of excitement in which he'd been cut open, shot, interrogated, punched and smacked up against a wall. And still, he'd had more than enough energy and stamina to take her to the heights of ecstasy.

Repeatedly.

She smiled at the memory of throwing up a soundproof barrier around them right before they'd both come the first time. Because they had been loud. Rattle the windows loud, set off the alarm system loud. And the noise had not subsided as the night wore on. She didn't think she'd ever been so vocal during sex with a human—or with a god.

She slipped out of bed and went into the bathroom. Took care of her human physical needs and eyed the deep tub and expansive shower. Imagined Cy in it with her, skin soapy and slick. Water dripping down those abs, trailing down those thighs.

Next time.

She looked at herself in the mirror—a sated smile on her face—and hoped the next time was very soon. After not having sex in over a hundred years, she feared Cy Bigelow had unleashed a monster. She wanted him again. Now. But, no, she told herself, he needed to sleep. Instead, she went back out into the bedroom and stood at the end of the bed, studying the man to whom she'd bared her true self. The man with whom she'd *shared* her true self.

He was beautifully made, and in slumber, with one arm resting on the pillow above his head and a white sheet draped low across his hip, looked every bit the son of Apollo. A golden god—skin naturally tawny over hard muscle, hair dark as midnight but with red gold highlights like it was shot through with first-light sunbeams, a mouth shaped to serenade and kiss. The angles of his face sculpted to near perfection. Not absolute perfection. He was half human, after all. And, to Nemi's eyes, the morning stubble, faint shadow of a little scar at the edge of one brow, and his arm and shoulder still wrapped from where Dr. A had treated his bullet wounds, made him even more dear.

The realization nearly blinded her, like the first rays of a new dawn breaking over a mountaintop. *She loved him.* Not loved as she'd cared for countless humans over the millennia, but as one entangled heart recognizes its mate in another.

A pang of longing clutched at her heart and spread through her body, suffusing her blood and bones with a comforting warmth. She would do anything to protect him. To protect those he loved. He was hers and she was his. It should have been startling. And it should've been unnerving that little Sofia had somehow already known. But it wasn't. It seemed inevitable.

Of course, other gods had loved other humans, but it had never happened to her. Ever. Even as the knowledge settled into her mind and into her very essence, he shifted in the bed as if he'd heard her.

She quickly left him to his rest, teleporting into her own suite where she took pains to shower and dress, even blow-drying her hair like a regular flesh-and-blood woman might do. And then she appeared downstairs in the kitchen only to find both Mat and Mason already sitting at the well-worn, plank farm table, drinking coffee, and reading the papers spread out before them.

"Good morning," Mat said with an appraising look.

Mason raised a brow. "Sleep well?" He hid a smile by taking a sip from his cup.

Both men looked at her and then at each other as if they were incorrigible children trying to suppress their giggles on Christmas morning. She pursed her lips, trying to hide her own smile, and then turned and poured herself a cup of coffee.

Dio appeared in the room, looking as fresh and handsome as ever. He stopped. Took in the tableau of smiling faces. "What did I miss?" And then it hit him. "Ooooh. Nice, Nemi. Since the poor man is not down here partaking of morning coffee with you, I take it you wore him out."

She shrugged and Dio winked at her and then pulled open the oven door and peered inside. "I had the cook make a spinach feta quiche." He turned to look at Mat and Mason. "Want any?"

"I wondered what smelled so good," Mason said. "I would ask when and where the cook made the quiche as I've been sitting here for at least an hour, but under the circumstances, the question seems a bit trite."

"The house has been imbued with a bit of magic of its own," Dio said, "but we really do have a cook. You won't see her unless she wants to be seen, though. Not all the spirits and sprites and nymphs and assorted delightful creatures that serve us are comfortable around humans. Some are quite shy, including Hilda. But she makes a mean quiche."

"Smells delicious." Mat stood to get plates and silverware as Dio donned two oven mitts and pulled the piping hot quiche out of the oven.

"We having Hilda's quiche?" A new voice.

"Tisi." Nemi flashed her a knowing smile. "You just getting up or just getting home?"

"Both?" Tisi laughed and looked around the room. "No Cy?"

"Recharging his battery, so to speak," Dio said with a waggle of his eyebrows.

"Ah, good on you." She wrapped her arms around Nemi and gave her a squeeze. "It's about time."

"How's Brooks?" Mat asked, barely suppressing a snort.

A slow smile formed on Tisi's delicate, elfin-like face. "We had a busy night." She took a seat at the table as Mat got out another plate and fork and set a cup of coffee in front of her. "Where's everyone else?"

"Scattered to the four winds." Dio cut into the quiche and plated the pieces. Nemi set the plates on the table and smiled as Mat and Mason each dug in. "Hermes is who knows where," Dio went on. "Asklepios is back in Cambridge. Ali, Meg, Chiron, and Artemis haven't returned. I think they're still dealing with all those kids. Chiron's farm is big, but getting over a hundred frightened children settled and fed and comforted is a big project."

"The world's a busy place right now and the assholes are out in full force," Tisi said. "The Israeli-Iranian war is heating up again, there are more riots in South Africa; a mine owned by a consortium of assholes including Chancellor Jensen collapsed in Mali trapping hundreds, including children; the old Charles Bridge in Prague was damaged by a pipe bomb, and a bomb went off in a marketplace in Ankara killing 37; the prime minister of Egypt was shot while delivering a speech on national television; the highest temperature on Earth, 138.2 degrees Fahrenheit, was recorded yesterday in Australia; and to top it all off there was another earthquake off the coast of Aceh and a tsunami alert has been issued."

"Fuck," Mason said on a sigh. "That's a lot. Maybe we should all just go back to bed."

Running a finger along the rim of her coffee cup, Tisi shook her head. "Can't. Because I have news."

Everyone in the room stopped.

"But I think it should wait until Cy is here. It's about what's going on at his estate."

Mason jumped to his feet, pushing his chair back with a scrape. "What's going on? Is Sybil okay?" Mat shot him a glance. "And Sofia and BoJo?" Mason added.

"They're all safe, but your friend Ken Lane is up to something. Brooks and I are monitoring the situation."

Mason swore under his breath, straightened his chair, and sank back into it, his face a classic study in worry.

"What kind of situation?"

Nemi's heart gave a lurch as Cy walked into the kitchen, strode around the end of the long table, and beelined it straight for her. He was wearing a black thermal Henley, faded jeans, and his feet were bare. His hair, still wet from a shower, looked like he'd combed it with his fingers. He reached around for one of the mugs set out on the counter and bent to whisper in her ear, "I was disappointed to wake up alone."

His warm breath sent shivers across her skin. *You looked too peaceful to disturb,* she sent through their connection.

"Your old pal Ken Lane is up to no good," Tisi said. "We picked up a worrisome conversation between a couple of the guards at your house late last night."

"Worrisome how?" Cy leaned against the counter.

"Apparently, Ken Lane is heading down to that despicable internment camp today to make final arrangements for some sort of shipment going out tomorrow night. The guards said the 'product' will be placed in shipping containers, loaded on trucks, and driven up to the air force base outside of Tucson. There, the containers will be loaded onto a transport plane bound for somewhere. Maybe the guards don't know because they didn't mention a destination. But one did say that he'd 'personally inspected' a few of the items and that the customer would be very happy."

Cy, Mat, and Mason all swore colorfully and loudly. "You thinking what I'm thinking?" Cy asked his friends.

Mason pushed away from the table and stood, his fork clattering to the floor. He looked ready to do violence. "I'm thinking that the only 'product' an internment camp has available to ship to customers is people, and that with this intel, we may finally be able to catch these fuckers."

"I'm guessing Ken's involved in more than just organ trafficking," Mat added.

"And is supplying women and children to work in the sex trade," Cy finished for him.

"Which is largely run off the books by mafioso oligarchs cozy with Jensen and his cronies running the Global Labor Exchange." Nemi added.

"So much for land of the free and home of the brave," Mason growled. "So much for Lady Liberty and human rights." He practically spat the words. "How the fuck did we get to this point? That our leaders are in bed—probably literally, although I don't want that picture in my head—with the worst fucking people on the entire planet." He glared at Nemi, Tisi, and Dio. "And what are the gods doing? Why can't you stop this?"

"I've already explained why we can't stop this on our own." Nemi's voice was even, as if she'd heard this question a million times before—which she had. "Do you want us to don capes and swoop in like superheroes from some movie?"

"No, but—"

"Do you realize how many people we'd have to kill if we wanted to get rid of all the bad guys?"

"But—"

Tisi leaned back in her chair. "Remember Noah and the flood? It'd be that kind of thing all over again." She sighed. "Look, we know it's frustrating, but the gods can't fix everything for you. We can't kill everyone who deserves killing, and we can't save everyone who deserves saving."

"Don't despair, though," Nemi spoke up again. "Rest assured that punishment *is* inevitable even though humans may not see it come to pass. In the King James Version of the Old Testament, Deuteronomy 32:35, Elohim proclaims, 'To me belongeth vengeance, and recompence,' and—"

"Elohim? Seriously? You're quoting the Bible to us?" Mat was incredulous. He couldn't stop himself from thinking of his father, a devout Catholic born on tribal land just south of the border and who'd been deported before Mat had taken his first steps. He'd never been heard from again. And of his church-going mother who was only safe because both she and her parents had been born in Arizona before birthright citizenship had been stripped away. And because Cy had protected her. And of BoJo and how her family had been torn apart by deportations and disappearances. And how Ken Fucking Lane had always parroted the racist line by calling BoJo a mongrel half-breed. Mat wanted everyone who supported this cruelty to pay in the here and now. Not wait for some gods to send their souls to burn for eternity in the fires of hell. Hell, he didn't even believe in hell!

"The gods go by many names," Nemi went on, "and, yes, I'm quoting the book Jews and Christians and Muslims have been told is the actual word of the one true god, and my point is that whether or not humans see that the assholes, as Tisi so aptly calls them, get their due, they *will* receive punishment for their transgressions. For me and the Furies—Tisi and her sisters—doling out those punishments is our very *raison d'être*."

"The point," Tisi chimed in, waving her fork in the air, "is that in the Old Testament, humans are told by Elohim to leave the judgment and the punishment to the gods. In the New Testament's Gospel of Matthew, humans are told to render unto Caesar what belongs to Caesar. Basically, Christians are told to obey the law and leave punishments for lawbreaking up to their governments. But everyone in this room knows that corrupt leaders and their governments enact oppressive laws and use them as a cudgel precisely so the people are bound together before the altar of cruelty."

"Throughout history," Dio spoke up, "human suffering has been legal—even mandated—under human law. From slavery to witch trials, to imprisoning homosexuals, we cannot swoop in and overturn human law without establishing a global theocracy. We need humans to be our front men, so to speak."

"And women," Nemi cut in.

"Exactly," Tisi went on. "Our intervention would only sow chaos. So, when we identify humans who care enough to try to stop suffering and work for justice, we are more than happy to work with them through the Pantheon League. But stepping forward and doing it ourselves in the clear light of day is not in humanity's best interest."

"But in the meantime, innocents suffer when you have so much power." Mason's voice was full of anguish. "It's so fucking ... unfair."

"The world is a fucked up place, my friend," Dio said. "Even though we exist in the real world, humans have always told their own stories about us to achieve their own ends. Just look at the stories that are told about me.

"I'm a completely benign guy going about my business helping people with their harvests and their merrymaking and so forth, but even in the ancient world, I was called a dozen different names and asked for a thousand different favors. On a daily basis. The point is that humans use the gods, rather than the other way around. And as much as you might think it would be great for us to step in and solve all the world's problems, it's impossible because as long as there are humans, there will always be human problems and, in short order, we would be masters and you would be slaves. Not even you would be happy with that."

"Fine. Fine. I get it." Mason's fingers dug into his temples until the tips went white. "But what are we supposed to do? These monsters are cutting people up and selling organs on the black market. They're kidnapping and selling women and children into the sex trade. They're using men as slaves in working conditions that are beyond hellish. We're supposed to be civilized and yet..."

He took a deep breath and blew it out. "I don't feel very civilized at the moment."

"So, then, what's the plan?" Tisi asked.

"We stop them," Cy said. "We go to Arizona, and we stop them."

41

Dio volunteered to stay behind in Georgetown to hold down the fort while Helen and her partner Kemal prepared to fly the Bigelow jet back to Arizona, and Nemi, Tisi, and Hermes headed to the Basement with Cy, Mat, and Mason in tow.

Their trip took less than the blink of an eye, and it was just after six in the morning when Brooks swiveled in his chair and gave them all the stink eye. "A little warning would be nice," he said in his laconic way. "The human heart can only take so much excitement in one 24-hour period. And," he pinned Tisi with a sultry look, "I figured I'd already had my full allotment."

"I fear there's more excitement in store for you today, Mr. Paxon," Tisi said with a sly smile. "We're here to stage an intervention and to shut down whatever your old friend Ken Lane is planning with his shipment of 'product'."

"We don't call him our 'old friend,' any more than I imagine you call Typhon your dear cousin. They're both monsters, although Ken is probably less repulsive looking."

He stood, cracked his neck, stretched out his back, and then waved at one of the screens he'd been monitoring.

"I'm tracking Ken's phone and his truck, and they're both heading south right now."

"How'd you get a tracking device on Ken's truck?" Mat asked.

Brooks laughed. "Your mother helped."

Mat's brows shot up. "My mom installed a tracker? She's resourceful as hell, but—"

"No, she didn't install it, but she did make sure Ken was occupied with freshly baked cookies when Tisi 'snuck' into the garage last night and affixed it under his fender."

Nemi studied the screen with the map where two bright red dots moved down the highway toward SDIC. "Did the guards give any indication about timing? When the product's being transported up to Tucson for shipping?"

"No," Brooks said. "But I'm thinking if it were me, I'd do it tomorrow evening while most of the country is watching or attending state-mandated school Christmas pageants."

"Shit!" Cy exclaimed. "I forgot that's tomorrow. Sofia's going to be an angel in the Bigelow Elementary pageant."

He turned to Nemi, Tisi, and Hermes. "When Jensen's administration shuttered the old Department of Education and closed down public schools because they were 'hotbeds of un-American propaganda,' the kids were all transferred into privately run, state-mandated schools. Using the same tax-payer funded facilities, of course."

"The only things transferred," Mason groused, "were the deeds to the buildings and the land. From local taxpayers right into the hands of Jensen-controlled companies."

"Now," Cy continued, "every school in the country uses "The Jensen Way" curriculum and holds their holiday celebrations at the same time in the same way. For Christmas, it's the whole nativity scene thing. Sofia s going to be the main angel, and I promised I'd be there." He looked at Nemi. "Her costume has a set of wings that flap when she pulls a little string."

Nemi thought her heart might burst at the idea of Cy's little Sofia dressed up like a smaller version of herself.

"Makes perfect sense if you're a fucking asshole," Mason groused. "While everyone's attention is on the cute kids celebrating a story about an immigrant child and his unmarried parents who can't get a room in the local roadside motel, a bunch of sick bastards are loading up human chattel and shipping them off to who the hell knows where."

"May make sense, but I feel dirty even thinking it. Like my brain works like theirs."

"Understanding the enemy doesn't make us like them." Mason's voice was hard. He ran both hands through his hair. Rough. Almost like he wanted to pull it out. "I may have fucked up dozens of times in my life, but Ken ... well, he's made his choices. We've made ours. We're not the same."

"So, when do we stop him," Mat asked, itching to jump into action. "Before the trucks leave SDIC, en route to Tucson, or as they're being loaded onto the plane? And what do we do with the 'product' once we have control of it?"

"I have an idea," Nemi said, reaching out for Cy's hand. "But you all need to remember, we can help make this happen, but we can't be *seen* to be helping."

"No obvious physics tricks?" Cy deadpanned.

"Emphasis on *obvious*," Nemi said with a grim huff of laughter. "We'll need to take on human aspects and," she looked around the room, "we'll need weapons. You have enough or should we bring more in?"

"Depends on the definition of enough," Mat and Mason said at the same time. "Tell us what you have in mind," Mat said.

"And then," Mason offered a devilish smile, "we'll show you our gun closet."

The four Bigelow partners exchanged knowing smiles. "Closet," Cy said with a snort. "Yeah, that's exactly what it is."

It was seven o'clock on the nose Friday evening when the tall, lanky, slightly balding superintendent of Arizona State School District 27 took the stage at the Bigelow Civic Auditorium. The curtains behind him were tightly drawn, the lights were low, and the crowd fell silent as the echo of the high school orchestra's medley of Christmas carols faded.

"Welcome one and all and Merry Christmas to each of you," the superintendent said, stretching his arms wide. "We're so pleased to see a packed auditorium tonight as we enjoy our annual Christmas Pageant along with millions of our fellow citizens gathered in communities large and small across the country."

BoJo leaned over and whispered to Cy. "He gives me the creeps. What do you wanna bet he has a hard drive full of child porn on his home computer?"

Cy snorted. "Not taking that bet." He reached out to take her hand in his and give it a gentle squeeze. He'd received plenty of attention when he'd shown up for the pageant, including expressions of concern and support and more than a few dark, suspicious looks from people he'd known all his life. He, Mat, Mason, and Brooks had done their best to shelter Bigelow from the worst of the Administration's programs and from the cruelty of Jensen's goons, but they couldn't protect everyone. Especially from themselves. Like Ken, too many had chosen to follow the Chancellor into the darkness.

"Don't forget to join us for refreshments in the lobby after the program." With that, the superintendent graciously swept an arm out toward the closed curtains and left the stage.

"You've seemed tense ever since you sat down," BoJo whispered. "Worried about what people are saying about your arrest?"

"I wasn't arrested. Just detained."

"Either way, the people of Bigelow will stand by you." She cast a sidelong look down the row. "Well, most of them."

"Everything okay?" Sybil, sitting on Cy's other side, leaned over and whispered.

"Yeah, you?" Cy whispered back. Everything had happened so fast, he hadn't had a chance to spend any time with his twin. He should've tried communicating with her mind-to-mind so they wouldn't have to whisper. He was sure they could do it. He almost felt her presence, just right there on the edge of his consciousness, but Ken Fucking Lane was sitting on her other side, and he didn't want to give him any reason to be suspicious.

Clad in superfine black wool slacks and a cable-knit black wool roll-neck sweater to match his thick-rimmed black glasses, Ken was, as usual, trying hard to look casually cool. He had his share of admirers in town—he was a surgeon after all—but Cy and his friends had always thought he was a thoroughly venal and ridiculous man. Unfortunately, he was also a dangerous one, and it sickened Cy to see the asshole reach out and take Sybil's hand in his. He felt his sister's body tense. Maybe now would be the perfect time to try to reach her. No, it would be too much of a risk. He couldn't take the chance of making Ken suspicious.

Instead, he cast Sybil a sideways glance and stifled the urge to grab Ken's hand and break every finger, one by one. Maybe he was coming unhinged. He'd never truly wanted to personally do violence before. Or murder. Maybe since he'd killed one man, he'd crossed a line. Maybe it'd be easier to kill again. The idea was appalling, but he knew he wouldn't be satisfied until Ken Fucking Lane was either behind bars—fat chance of that happening in Jensen's New America—or six feet under.

The way Ken kept giving him the nervous side-eye, it was clear the man had no idea how Cy was still alive and kicking. According to Mat's source inside SDIC, Ken had gone berserk when he'd awakened in his surgery with the room in disarray and his drugged and sliced-open patient gone. He'd immediately gone to security to see who had absconded with his patient, but the cameras showed nothing. In his dazed and confused condition, he only belatedly remembered that he'd disarmed the camera in his operating room because he was conducting his little "organ donation" business off the books. And Cy had certainly not been a voluntary participant.

The soft strains of "Oh, Little Town of Bethlehem" filled the auditorium as the orchestra began playing again. Cy looked up to see the heavy maroon velvet curtains—curtains Bigelow Enterprises had paid for to hang in the building his grandfather had originally built—dramatically part to reveal the rustic nativity scene on stage, complete with three donkeys, a cow, and a manger. No angels yet, but he couldn't stop the smile from spreading across his face.

No matter how much he hated what was going on in his country and how the education system had been hijacked by Jensen's and his Christian Nationalist followers—people who would just as soon tie BoJo to a stake and light her on fire as accept her heritage or her sexuality—he would always take time to celebrate the small joys of being a father. Of being a part of a family he loved. A family he would do everything in his power to protect.

Everything on schedule? He sent the question to Nemi.

We're good here. In place and waiting. Tracking the trucks. How's your angel?

It's just starting. The angels haven't appeared yet.

Take pictures. I'd love to see her flap her wings. Someday I might even show her mine.

He smiled at that and both Sybil and BoJo shot him suspicious what-the-hell-is-going-on looks. He hadn't told them anything about what was going on down on Highway

83 or about what they'd learned regarding Ken Fucking Lane's involvement in human trafficking.

He was confident they now knew how dangerous Ken was and he didn't want his sister, his wife, or his daughter to be any more creeped out about his presence than they already were. It was enough that Mrs. C knew they were all up to something tonight. They had to be careful that nothing they said or did around Ken made him suspicious or alerted him to what was about to go down because they couldn't take the risk that he might warn the truck drivers or someone else involved in his disgusting operation.

42

Headlights appeared in the distance. There and gone and there again as the small convoy went up and down the hills and around the curves of Highway 83 North. Standing next to Mat on the left side of the road, Nemi glanced across the pavement at Hermes and Mason, who turned in unison to look back at her.

It was a waning gibbous moon, so none of them were wearing their night vision goggles, not that she, or any of the gods, would need them, but they had to look like soldiers, so they were all kitted up as if going into battle, complete with M7 Carbines, microfiber graphene vests, helmet liners, and tactical gloves, pants, and boots. And masks ready to be pulled up over their faces. They gods had taken on human aspects no one would recognize, but they didn't want to risk one of the drivers or guards recognizing Mat or Mason from around Bigelow.

As soon as they'd finalized their plans to disrupt Ken's convoy, Nemi had deposited Cy back at the Bigelow Hotel where he'd picked up his SUV and headed to Sofia's Christmas Pageant. Chiron and Artemis had arrived soon after that and Artemis, along with Nemi, had taken on a male aspect because women were no longer allowed to serve in the New American military.

Now, Chiron, looming as usual, stood beside an equally looming Artemis in front of flashing barricades and ROAD CLOSED signs behind which were parked four armored trucks blocking both lanes of the highway. Nemi had no idea how Chiron had procured the trucks.

Because they didn't want any innocent civilians getting hurt in case something went sideways, they'd set up one detour/road construction sign at the I-10 exit onto 83 South and another just pass the last scenic overlook so vehicles already on the road traveling north would have a place to turn around and go back south.

Now the road in between the signs was deserted. The only sounds came from the low rumble of the armored trucks' idling engines, the occasional hoot from an owl nesting nearby, and the distant howls of a Mexican wolf pack roaming somewhere out in the hills. It had drizzled earlier, and the air smelled of creosote and petrichor. Nemi inhaled deeply and sighed. She loved the stark beauty and fascinating wildlife of the Sonoran Desert. Always had.

The lights appeared again, and this time the beams held steady. They were getting close. Slowing down. The drivers had obviously seen the flashing barricade. There were seven trucks in the convoy, but only five carried a shipping container. Thanks to some intrepid investigating by Ali and Meg, they'd discovered the identity of the buyer and the destination of the shipment. And they knew that Ken and his criminal colleagues were very explicitly warned to ensure the product didn't arrive in Sevastopol too battered, bruised, or filthy or there would be hell to pay.

So, the "product" had been divided up, five each in five containers. Twenty-five people in total. All bought and paid for by Boris Lushkonokov, a man whose cousin was the new premier of Russia and who was head of one of the most vicious criminal gangs in the world. Although he claimed to be a devout man and often appeared with the same spiritual advisor Jensen relied on, Pastor Erin Knight, he owned a chain of brothels—from luxurious high-end pleasure palaces catering to the richest and most craven men in the world to filthy hovels set up in the ramshackle company towns where impoverished workers slaving away in his Congolese diamond mines were forced to live.

Unbeknownst to the drivers and guards riding shotgun, a Pantheon League drone in the skies above them was blocking both government and commercial satellite imagery and their communications systems had all been re-routed to the Basement where Brooks and Tisi would respond, if needed, to any incoming messages. Tisi, like most gods, was a brilliant mimic who could respond in any language, any accent, any voice. Nothing the drivers or the guards said would reach any of their contacts, but every last word would be recorded. For posterity.

And blackmail.

As for the Pantheon League team members, they were using military grade communications earpieces, enhanced by a few sophisticated tweaks Tisi had come up with. They could practically hear each other's thoughts.

"Ready?" Nemi said, as the first vehicle in the line, a black SUV with dark, tinted windows, slowed to a stop. The semis behind it followed with the grinding squeal of brakes.

"Born ready." Chiron stepped forward to the driver's side of the SUV as Artemis went to the passenger side. Chiron smiled at the driver, all friendly like, and motioned for him to roll down his window.

"What's this about?" The man sounded more put out than pissed. "We didn't get any notice that the road was closed."

"We've got a security situation that concerns your shipment. Step out of the truck and we'll give you the low down," Chiron said. His human aspect was an even six foot six with a stunningly handsome face, a bone structure as fine as cut glass, shoulders for miles, and a voice that resonated with authority—and menace—in the night air.

"What kind of situation? Who are you? Under whose authority are you operating, and why do you have the road blocked?" The driver made no move to get out, and Chiron's gaze flicked to see the guard in the passenger seat unholster his weapon.

"We're on a tight deadline," the driver went on, "and unless you explain this 'security situation' or show me specific orders telling us to turn around, I'm going to have to ask you to move your trucks so we can be on our way."

In a flash of movement, the guard's gun was up and pointed directly at Artemis's face. "We have our orders," the guard said. "And you are interfering with an official transport."

He's fast, I'll give him that, Artemis sent over the comms link. "Unless you have a death wish," she warned the guard, "I wouldn't pull that trigger. You may be fast, but I'm faster, and you may believe you have the advantage, but I can assure you, you don't."

"And I said, step out of the truck." Chiron's voice was as smooth and deadly as a sharp blade slipped between the ribs. "Both of you. Disobey and it's unlikely you'll end the evening on a happy note."

"Or an alive one," Artemis added. She turned to see Nemi and Mat beside the sweeper vehicle, the black SUV at the end of the line. They already had the driver and guard out and were marching them forward, ordering the other drivers and guards out of the semis as they moved. Hermes and Mason stood on the other side of the road, weapons aimed at the tires of the two SUVs. If those vehicles were undrivable, there was no possibility for the five middle trucks to turn around or try to make a run for it. Besides, the road was too narrow for five semis to complete that maneuver. Chiron sent the signal, and the night air exploded with the sound of automatic fire and the smell of burning rubber.

"Holy shit!" The lead driver instinctively put his hands over his head as the guard beside him pulled the trigger. Unfortunately, he was too late as Artemis had already moved out of the line of fire so that his bullet landed harmlessly somewhere in the distant desert shrub just as his head exploded, splattering bone and brain matter all over the front seat—and all over the driver.

"What a waste," Chiron muttered.

"Pity," Artemis said. "I warned him."

"What the fuck? You just shot him! Who the fuck are you?" The driver was shrieking now, frantically wiping his face and smearing the guard's remains all over his skin and hair. His eyes were wide as he yanked at his collar and swiped at the bits of his friend that had blown down his neck.

Chiron opened the door and waved his carbine at him. "Get out or end up like your friend."

The man scrambled to unlatch his seatbelt and climb out, only to fall to his knees and retch on the pavement, barely missing Chiron's boots. "Oh god, oh god, oh god," he choked out as he emptied his stomach on the highway.

Although they'd heard the gunshot, none of the other drivers or guards knew what had happened until Nemi, Mat, Hermes, and Mason herded them forward and they were standing in a little group, hands clasped at the back of their heads and watching in horror as their bloodied comrade knelt on the ground vomiting.

"Any idea why that asshole refused to follow orders?" Artemis asked the group.

"That a rhetorical question?" Hermes said.

"Just wondering if any of his friends had any insights."

None of the other men, drivers or guards, said a word.

Hermes shrugged. "He was an asshole?"

"If I remember from the bios we put together on this gang of lowlifes," Nemi spoke up, so everyone could hear, "that was the guy who beat his wife to a bloody pulp on the regular, so I'd say justice was served."

"Justice?" The lead driver blubbered from his place on the ground. "You just shot him in cold blood!"

"Not in cold blood," Nemi corrected. "Your trigger-happy colleague already had his gun aimed at our friend's face. Despite a warning, he gambled that he could pull the trigger faster and he lost."

"But that's all ancient history," Chiron declared with finality. "Now we're going to tell you what happens next. First, we're going to collect all your weapons. Peacefully, I hope. If that goes well, we'll allow you the dignity of remaining upright while we explain how the rest of the evening is going to play out." He gestured to Hermes, Mat, and Mason and they stepped forward.

"These gentlemen will collect your weapons. Hand over everything visible, along with anything else you have on you. For example," he pierced one of the other drivers with a cold stare, "that gun strapped to your ankle." He looked at one of the guards. "Or the knife in your boot you think we don't know about." And at the driver from the sweeper SUV. "Or the taser you've got in that pocket. Hand over everything or my friends here will strip search you. Your choice."

"I'm not handing anything over until you tell us who the fuck you are." That was the guard from the sweeper truck. The guards were proving to be just as determinedly idiotic as their bios suggested. After Tisi hacked into the SDIC employee database and delivered the suspected participant bios to her sisters, Ali and Meg had verified who was assigned to work the shipment transport and then verified their personal details. None of the men involved were upstanding members of the community. Surprise, surprise.

"We don't want to have to eliminate anyone else, but we will if necessary," Artemis said. "So do as we say, and you'll live to see another day."

"But we have orders to deliver these shipping containers to the Air Force base tonight. We're on a schedule!" One of semi drivers was actually whining. It was probably dawning on him that he wasn't going to get his big payday after all.

The guard from the third semi in line gave Artemis a mean, narrow-eyed glare and let his hand drift toward the holster on his hip—not as if he planned to hand over his weapon, but as if he planned to pull it and shoot it—and Mat flipped his Colt M7 Carbine so fast the guy didn't see it until the butt made contact with his nose with a sick crunch, sending the man to his knees amidst a spray of blood.

"What the fuck!" The driver the guard had been paired with yelled, eyes wide with terror. "He was gonna hand over his gun!"

Hermes laughed and pushed the driver to his knees beside his guard. "You must be under the mistaken impression that we were born yesterday."

"Let's get on with it, gentlemen," Chiron said with an exaggerated sigh. "We've all got places to go, people to see."

Except for the guy still blubbering because his buddy's brain matter was stuck in his hair and the man with the broken and bloody nose, both of whom needed assistance, everyone else handed over their weapons in silence. Mason piled them together and Mat loaded them in a duffel.

"Now, your cell phones," Artemis instructed.

"Fuck." The word came from more than one of the men. But they each pulled out a cell and handed it over to Mason who popped out the sim cards, slipped them into a separate plastic bag, and then tossed them all in with the weapons.

"Now," Chiron pointed to one of the guards. "Open the containers."

"We can't. We don't have keys to the locks."

Nemi nodded to Hermes, who, with Mat and Mason behind him, proceeded to climb up on the flat bed of the first truck.

"I just told you! We don't have keys."

Nemi stepped forward and stared down at the man. "We don't need keys."

Ten minutes later, a bedraggled group of women and children were huddled in the road, facing the drivers and guards.

"One thin blanket and mattress per person," Mat said. "One case of bottled water per container. One toilet bolted to the floor."

Nemi drew in a breath and let it out slowly. She let her gaze travel over the drivers and guards "It's almost 9,000 miles as the crow flies from Tucson to Sevastopol. Flying at 30,000 feet in a cargo hold, it would be freezing, and these children"—she pointed to a boy and a girl who appeared to be twins of about 11 or 12 years of age—have no shoes or socks. I don't see a single coat here."

"At least none appropriate for winter in Crimea," Hermes confirmed with a scowl.

Nemi nodded. "Okay. While I'd like to send you all to Hades right now, I'm going to be merciful. Instead, here's what's going to happen. You are going to take off your shoes and socks," Nemi ordered, her voice sharp as Damascene steel, "and we're going to tie you together, and you're going to walk back to where you came from—"

"What the hell? That's over twenty miles!" One driver protested.

Nemi shrugged. "You all look like you're in fairly good shape. A twenty-mile hike should be no problem. At least you have coats. Or maybe we should take those too."

The questions came fast then: "You want our coats too?"

"In fucking December?"

"Who the hell are you?"

"What unit are you with?"

"Whose orders are you following?"

"Why are you doing this?"

"Ah," Nemi said. "Finally, a good question. *Why* are we doing this? I'll answer that while you divest yourselves of your footwear."

Artemis and Hermes pointed their weapons at them one by one as the men unlaced and toed off their boots and then peeled off their socks. Then Mason went down the line with zip ties. Once they were individually cuffed, Hermes produced a long thin rope made of carbon fiber—difficult to cut through without a fine-tooth carbide blade—and began looping them all together around the waist. They looked like prisoners from an old-fashioned chain gang. Minus the striped prison garb.

"The answer," Nemi said as if giving a Sunday School lesson, "is that we are doing this because we believe human trafficking is a crime against humanity. And we believe that individuals who participate in this crime are among the lowest life forms on this planet. Single cell eukaryotes are more worthy than human traffickers. Preying on other people for profit is despicable. Especially when innocents are involved. Your dead friend in the lead SUV paid the price already, but mark my words, justice will come for you too. You may not know when or where, but it will come. I guarantee it. And the only way you can avoid paying the full price for your crimes is to atone *and* make amends to those you have injured."

Chiron spoke up again. "So, you have two choices to make when you get back to where you came from. One, you can tell those you work for that you refuse to be a party to such heinous acts in the future and then work to expose and hold them accountable for their crimes. Or, two, you can keep callously exploiting your fellow human beings for profit and live out the rest of your days never knowing when or how justice will come for you. But rest assured, we will know what you decide."

He waved his rifle toward the road behind them. "We'll allow you to keep your coats because we want you to survive long enough to explain to your collaborators what happened here tonight. And to make sure they know that justice is coming for them too."

Hermes gave the first man in line a little push in the right direction. "Time to get moving. The temperature is dropping, and snow is going to start falling—" he looked up to see a few flakes fluttering around him—"right about now."

43

"Sofia sure stole the show tonight," Ken told Cy as they stood in the refreshments line. The lobby was decorated with colorful twinkling lights and two giant live Christmas trees probably cut from Bigelow land without permission. Tall windows facing the old town square and county courthouse revealed a quaint scene with old-fashioned streetlamps illuminating the gently falling snow as Ken went on. "She's quite the little prodigy, up there ad-libbing her lines in some made-up language like she was speaking 'Angel' or something."

Ken waited for the server—Sofia's music teacher—to dip the ladle in and pour another cup of punch. He took the cups and handed one to Sybil and then one to Cy, pointedly ignoring BoJo. Cy gave his cup to his wife and smiled at the teacher.

"We'll take one more, Mrs. Moore." Cy waited while the punch was served, clenching his fist so he didn't punch Ken in front of all of Bigelow's fine citizens. "Thank you," he said as he took the cup and then followed Ken down the line toward the baked goods. Cy knew he should keep his mouth shut, but damn it, Ken was such an ass, he couldn't stop himself. "It may have sounded like gibberish to you, but Sofia was actually delivering her lines in koine Greek."

Cy had never heard it spoken before, but he realized immediately that he understood exactly what it was and what it meant. Almost like it was his native tongue. And Sofia's. But what about Sybil? Did she understand it too? He'd felt her stiffen when Sofia started speaking and she'd briefly clutched his hand, but she hadn't turned to catch his eye. Maybe she hadn't understood and thought Sofia was messing up. Or maybe she had understood and didn't want to tip Ken off. It had always been hard to tell with his twin.

As Ken turned to pick up a plate and pile baked goods on it, Cy decided to risk an experiment. Maybe it wasn't wise when there was so much activity going on around them, but as he held his sister's gaze over her cup of punch, he reached out to her mind. *Don't be startled, but it's me. Can you understand me?*

Her eyes widened and she immediately looked down at her punch. Her cheeks flushed and her fingers flexed on her cup. *I hear you. Is this a demigod thing?*

Yes. I don't know if Sofia can do it, but I can do it with Nemesis. She thinks Sofia has inherited Apollo's gift of sight. Did you understand what she was saying up on the stage?

Yes. My god, I almost passed out. I don't know how much longer I can pretend. It's making me crazy! Ken's pressuring me to be with him again. I can't, Cy. I just...

"What the hell is koine Greek?" Ken asked, turning back around and offering the plate to Sybil. She took it and they all stepped out of the refreshment line and gathered around a high-top table. "It sounded like gobbledygook to me."

He barked out a loud laugh, pulled out his phone and looked down at it, brows knitted in confusion. Again. He'd been checking his messages since the last round of applause and was obviously getting antsy that he hadn't heard anything from the convoy.

"You know," Sybil said, casting an innocent look at Ken, "the language the New Testament was written in."

Ken' frowned. And then his expression cleared. "Ah," he said thoughtfully. "Makes sense the schools would be teaching Bible languages, especially since the Chancellor's Executive Order banned Spanish."

Cy could feel BoJo and Sybil tense. "Oh, they don't teach it at school," he said. "Sofia picked it up on her own. She has a gift for languages. Probably inherited from her grandfather." Maybe it was a stupid thing to say, but he couldn't help himself.

"Daddy!" Sofia and the other students poured into the lobby from backstage and Cy swooped his daughter up in his arms as she plowed into him. "I knew you'd come!"

"Wouldn't miss it for the world."

"Did you like the pageant?"

"Loved it. You were the best angel ever in the history of angels." He buried his face in her hair and inhaled. "You even smell like an angel!"

"That's my shampoo, silly." She giggled and then turned serious, her bright eyes shining and rimmed in red as if she'd been crying. "Mrs. Green is mad at me, and I cried a little, but I made a new friend."

Cy feared he knew the answer, but said, "Why is Mrs. Green mad at you? And who is your new friend?"

Sofia looked around and then leaned in to whisper, "Can I tell you when we go home?"

"Absolutely," Cy whispered back, then looked to BoJo. "I think our angel needs a celebratory brownie."

"I think we all do," BoJo agreed.

Sofia twisted in Cy's arm and he put her down. "Look, it's snowing! Maybe we'll have a white Christmas."

"The doctor told us to be thankful for the mattresses and blankets," one of the women said, and Nemi, who had thought her opinion of Ken Lane could sink no lower, felt her skin go cold with fury.

"Where are we?" Another woman asked as the snow began coming down harder.

"Where were they taking us? Do we have to go back to that camp?" A woman who had her arm around a little girl with a delicate face and lank hair the color of honey asked. The girl couldn't have been more than ten.

Standing off by himself with a blanket draped around his shoulders, the corners gripped in a tight fist, a handsome, dark-eyed boy of about seventeen or eighteen spoke up, his voice gritty with anger. "I never want to see that fucking camp again."

Nemi looked into the distance as the linked chain of human flotsam disappeared over the furthest hill in view, then turned to the boy. "We're not taking you back to the camp."

He held her gaze. "They were selling us, weren't they?"

"What's your name?" Nemi asked, her voice soft, comforting.

"Joseph Said. And I'm an American citizen."

Nemi saw Mat and Mason exchange glances. "Any of the rest of you American citizens?" She counted as the hands went up. Eleven. Eleven citizens who had been rounded up and stuck in cages in the desert for who knew what reasons. Speaking out against Jensen? Attending a protest? Loving the wrong person? Having the wrong skin color?

She took a long, calming breath, steadying herself so she didn't sprout wings and take to the skies to hunt down Harold Jensen that very moment. "How did you come to be in custody, Joseph?" she said, instead.

"My father was an physics professor up in Tucson. He is—was—also a Palestinian, born in Bethlehem, of all places. He was declared a terrorist and arrested for just walking across campus to his lab while a protest was going on. He had all his documentation, but they still took him away. We haven't heard from him since. My mother's grandparents are from Nogales, but she and her parents were from Tucson. They met in grad school. Mom and I were arrested last year when we attended a rally against all the disappearances. It was the one where the soldiers opened fire. Three people died and the rest of us ended up down at that fucking camp."

"Where's your mother now?"

"I have no idea."

Nemi swallowed back her rage and swept an arm out to encompass the others in the Pantheon League, all except Hermes who had gone to remove the detour/road closed sign blocking the road to the south. "If it were up to us, that camp would not exist. If it were up to us, no camps like that would have ever existed on the face of the Earth and none would ever exist again. But since it's not up to us, we do what we can, and tonight, our job is to get you to safety and out of the reach of the doctor and his associates."

"So where are you taking us?" One of the women asked.

"See those trucks blocking the road?" Mason spoke up now. "You're going to pile in and we're going to take you to a hiding place. It's underground and, unfortunately, you won't be able to go outside in the open for a while, but you'll be warm and fed and you'll have comfortable beds and there are real bathrooms." He looked at the kids. "And, although you can't just go play outside, we do have a nice big barn and a covered riding ring you can access. So you can help take care of the horses if you want."

"And there are a barn cats and several dogs," Mat chimed in.

"Can I learn to ride?" Joseph Said asked.

Mat and Mason glanced at each other. "I think we can manage that. And for those not interested in hanging out in the barn, we have a library, screens to watch movies, playing cards, and lots of board games. But the most important thing is that you'll be safe."

"And if we determine that the underground bunker is not safe," Chiron chimed in, "we have ways to move you quickly to someplace new."

He'd advocated for flying them all to one of the Pantheon League's places overseas. Greece. Norway. Scotland. Maybe where they'd taken the other kids. They had safe places scattered all over the world, and he'd wanted these people somewhere far away from the corruption eating away at Jensen's New America. But he'd relented in the end, and had agreed that, for now, the Bigelow Basement made sense.

One of the women let out a sob of relief which broke the dam of pent-up emotion and the sound of weeping filled the air.

"Now, Nemi said, trying to be encouraging and even a bit perky, "who votes for getting out of here?"

"I do," Joseph said. "I don't know who the hell you are, but anything is better than going back there." And then the emotion caught up with him and he swallowed hard and shook his head as he turned to stride determinedly toward the armored vehicles as the others followed behind him.

Mason turned to Mat. "Have I mentioned yet this evening that I fucking hate Ken Fucking Lane?"

Mat checked his watch. "Nope. Not since at least breakfast."

44

Cy pulled up in the driveway and pressed the garage door opener button. Since he never stayed at the estate overnight, he usually parked his Lexus outside, but the temperature had dropped to below freezing and the snow was sticking. Up higher in the mountains, they could often get twelve inches of snow or more, but they rarely got more than a few inches at this altitude. Sill, he didn't want to have to scrape his windshield or wait for the defrost to kick in if he had to make a quick getaway.

Especially if he needed to take Sybil, Sofia, BoJo, and Mrs. C with him. And the dogs. Hauling the whole family around meant he'd traded in his ancient Jeep for a nicer 3-row hybrid SUV. Plus, it easily fit his partners and all their gear if they needed to get somewhere in a hurry.

The plan was for him to spend a few nights at the estate so he could celebrate the Christmas Pageant with Sofia and have a rock-solid alibi to prove he had nothing to do with any mysterious activity going on between Tucson and the Sonoran Desert Internment Camp. And, he'd wanted to send the signal that Ken Fucking Lane was not welcome at the house. No way was that motherfucker staying under his roof while he was there. Or parking in his parking space.

Nemi had already let Cy know that all had gone smoothly—save for the one dead guard and the other guard's broken nose—and that the women and children were on their way to the Basement with drones flying above them blocking any satellite tracking imagery. As for the drivers and guards, they'd been sent back to SDIC on foot and the trucks had been abandoned on the highway for someone to eventually come along and discover them. For safety, she informed him, Mat and Mason had turned on the emergency blinkers on each truck. Whoever found the convoy would have no idea what had happened but at least they wouldn't plow into parked trucks in the dark.

Now, BoJo glanced over and gave Cy a parental *I-told-you-not-to-let-her-have-that-last-brownie* look as Sofia climbed out of the backseat, talking a mile a minute. She'd obviously overdosed on sugar and excitement and would probably never get to sleep. Her white-gold curls had come loose from her halo and framed her face with picturesque sweetness, marred only by a smear of double fudge at the edge of her mouth. She skipped to the back door and breezed through as an SS agent opened it wide, looking over the little girl's head to see who'd arrived onsite.

"Aunt Sybil's getting a ride with Dr. Ken," Sofia announced as she swept by the man holding the door.

Pointedly ignoring the agent, Cy and BoJo followed Sofia into the house and through the mudroom to the kitchen. Neither one liked the fact that Ken had insisted Sybil ride home with him, saying he had an early Christmas gift for her. Sybil had tried to feign a headache, but since Ken was a doctor and said he'd give her some pain relievers, and since they'd established that Cy and Sybil could communicate telepathically, they decided to take the risk so they didn't tip their hand. Besides, his phone and his car were being monitored. And Sybil's phone was being tracked as well. She should be safe.

"Can I have—"

"No," Cy and BoJo said at the same time. "It's bath time," BoJo continued. "And then straight to bed. You go on up. I'll be right behind you."

"I'll read you a story after your bath," Cy told her.

"*Twas the Night Before Christmas!*" Sofia squealed, hopping up and down and then darting up the back stairs.

Cy scraped a hand across the stubble on his chin and checked his watch. He tipped his head toward the stairs where he knew there were no cameras. Tisi and Brooks had mapped out all the new cameras the SS agents had added, and it still incensed Cy to his core that they'd taken up residence in his house. That he had to sneak around his own house, and that even though he'd been released from custody, agents were still watching him like he was a crazed killer. He was still under suspicion of something. Or else in danger of doing something. Either way, the agents said they weren't leaving until they got orders directly from their superiors.

"We need to talk about what happened tonight," Cy said, once they were in the stairwell.

BoJo cocked her head and looked at Cy as if trying to read his thoughts. "You know what she was saying up there, don't you. You told Ken it was Greek. Did you understand it? Did Sybil?"

Cy took in a deep breath. "Yeah. And it turns out Sybs and I can communicate telepathically. He tapped a finger on the side of his head. "We're twins. Apparently, it's a demigod thing. I can do it with Nemi too."

"Jesus, Cy. What about Sofia?"

"I haven't tried. I didn't want to scare her. Or have her say something while Ken and the agents are here."

"I hate the idea that Sybs has to pretend to like him," BoJo said. "I want them all out of our house. Out of our lives."

"It was all I could do to not strangle him when he reached out to hold her hand tonight. And the way he ignores you—"

"I'm used to it, Cy," she said with a sigh. "Growing up, his whole family treated us like we weren't fit to scrape the dog shit from the soles of their shoes."

"Well, I hate it. I hate it because it's wrong, and I hate it because it's insulting to you and to Sofia." They reached the top of the stairs, and he checked his watch. Again. "You go on. I need to check in. Text me when Sofia's out of the bath and ready for bed."

BoJo nodded and headed down the hall to the east wing of the house while Cy headed to the west wing, to the master bedroom suite. He knew the agents had installed a new camera in the hallway leading to his room, so he opened the door as if everything was normal, closed it oh so casually, and then opened his arms wide. Nemi, who'd been waiting in the chair by the fireplace, stood and walked straight into his open arms.

Nemi wrapped her arms around him, pressed her face against his chest, and listened to his heartbeat. Strong. Steady. *Hers.* The feeling of possessiveness—and protectiveness—nearly swamped the human emotions that were already in overdrive. She pulled him closer and felt his arms tighten around her. Felt him press his lips to the top of her head, and bend to tuck his face into the crook of her shoulder.

"You are a sight for sore eyes," he said, pulling back to look down at her.

"It hasn't even been five hours." Her voice was soft as velvet.

"I don't care if it was five minutes. I need this," he whispered, and her heart felt like it was expanding faster than light speed, like it might crack a rib and try to break free to fill up the space around them. She'd never, in all her years, felt wanted like this. Cared for like this. *Loved* like this.

He tipped her chin up with a fingertip and pressed his lips to hers. Just a soft touch. And then another. "I need you, Nemi," he breathed the words and then took her mouth again. This time there was nothing soft about it. What had started tender and slow, was suddenly desperate. Demanding.

He palmed her bottom, lifted her, and turned so her back was to the door, her legs wrapped around his waist. He pressed against her, let her feel how much he wanted her.

"I want to be inside you more than I want my next breath, but I'm on bedtime story duty, so..."

"So, what are you waiting for?" Her fingers were already unbuttoning his shirt, then sliding up his chest, over silky skin and warm, hard muscle.

He ground his straining erection against her core, his breathing coming faster. Harder. He grabbed the hem of her sweater and pulled it up over her head, took in the sight of her breasts plump against midnight blue lace. Threw the sweater behind him.

"Too many clothes." With one arm around her waist and one supporting her bottom, he pivoted and stalked over to the bed and deposited her with a little bounce. She reared up and went for his belt buckle, but he gently swatted her hands away, pushed her back on the bed where she rested on her elbows, then bent down to drag her whisper soft leggings and midnight blue panties down her hips. "You first," he said, pulling her shoes off one by one and then tugging her pants off and tossing them aside.

"Now, me." He held her gaze as he unbuckled his belt, slowly pulled down his zipper and pushed his pants down his thighs. Her gaze drifted down his body to where his erection throbbed as if it had a life of its own.

She looked up at him. "Now, both of us. I want to feel you in me. No more dawdling, Mr. Bigelow."

He spread his hands on her legs, just above the knee, and slid them slowly up to grip her thighs. Then he yanked her forward to the edge of the bed, positioned her legs up over his shoulders, and drove himself into her wet heat with one hard thrust.

She gasped and grabbed his wrists, holding on even as one of his hands snaked up to cup her breast, squeezing and kneading as he withdrew and plunged forward again, the pressure building into a tsunami of sensation, rolling through them, engulfing them. He bent over her, his groin rubbing against her as he nudged the lace aside and took her nipple in his mouth, nipping and licking as he drove deeper and harder until they both shot over the edge, tumbling into some new world of dazzling light and sound and wonderment, as if they had discovered a whole universe meant only for them.

Panting from exertion, his heart pounded with a delicious ache as he gently lowered her legs and pulled back to stare down at her. Her eyes were swimming with tears, spilling out of the corners and trickling down the side of her face and into her hair. She reached up to wipe them away.

"I just never knew," she said with a small shake of her head. "The ... emotions are so ... big. I don't know how to hold them in."

"You never need to hold anything in around me. Never. You're a goddess with goddess-sized emotions." He pressed a tender kiss to the corner of each eye, relishing the taste. Human tears. Now it was his turn to shake his head. "Salty. Your body is a wonder," he whispered. "*You* are a wonder, and I can't believe I get to touch you like this. Hold you like this." He held her gaze. "Love you like this."

She let out a little sob, half laugh, half cry. "Never, since my creation, have I loved a human like I love you. Never. You feel like a bloody miracle."

The corner of his mouth curled up in a sultry smile. "What we just did was a bloody miracle." The muffled ding of a text sounded from his pants pocket. "And perfect timing too." He pulled out slowly and watched her as they both began to put themselves back together. He took his cell from his pocket. Story time.

"Something happened tonight at the Christmas pageant," he said, buttoning his shirt. "Something strange with Sofia."

Nemi's face went dark. "What? I didn't feel anything. Nothing like she was in danger."

"Not in danger. I don't know. Like maybe she's coming into her self?"

"What do you mean?"

"She said her lines in ancient Greek. Probably just like they were written."

"She was an angel, right?" Her brows drew together.

"Yeah." He knew she'd put it together.

"You're telling me she said her lines from the Gospel of Luke in koine Greek instead of modern English?"

"Yes. And Sybil and I both understood them. And, apparently, so did some high school teacher."

"Seems like she's inherited more from her grandfather than the gift of sight." Nemi let out a little laugh. "Apollo will be delighted."

He wiped a hand down his face and started buckling up. "I promised her a bedtime story, but I'm going to talk to her about it. She said her teacher was mad. Made her cry backstage."

Nemi nodded. "Go tend to your daughter. I'll be here when you get back."

45

Cy punched the extra pillow on the bed and stretched out. "You brush your teeth?"

Sofia nodded. "Twice."

"Why twice?" Cy said with a smile, picking up the book and opening it to the first page.

"Because Mom said I had twice as many treats as I should have had."

He laughed at that, but then Sofia's brows drew together and her bottom lip trembled. "I guess I was hungry from crying."

He felt like a fist had reached in and squeezed his heart right in his chest. He hated it when Sofia was sad or hurt. He pressed a kiss to his fingertip and placed it on the tip of her nose. "Will you tell me about why you were crying?"

"Well," Sofia looked down at her hands as if she was nervous, "Mrs. Green yelled at me in front of my friends, and that made me cry. But then Mr. Madison said he was proud of me and that made me happy."

"Tell me exactly what happened."

"Mrs. Green gave us printouts of our lines for us to rehearse. Because I was an angel, my lines were straight from the Bible, so I practiced them really hard and had them memorized." She closed her eyes and said them again, this time in English.

"'Fear not: for, behold, I bring you good tidings of great joy, which shall be to all people. For unto you is born this day in the city of David a Saviour, which is Christ the Lord. And this shall be a sign unto you; Ye shall find the babe wrapped in swaddling clothes, lying in a manger.'"

She looked up at Cy, her eyes shimmering. "And then when all the other angels came onto the stage and stood around me, we were all were supposed to say: 'Glory to God in the highest, and on earth peace, good will toward men.'"

"But that's not what you said." he prompted.

"Well, it is, but it came out all different. It was strange because I felt like I was saying it just like in rehearsal, but when I went backstage Mrs. Green told me I messed up my lines on purpose because she knew I had them memorized and had said them right in rehearsal. She said I stood up there on stage and just spouted gibberish because I wanted to be special and wanted extra attention because you were arrested by Chancellor Jensen and that you might be a terrorist and a murderer.

"So, I started crying. Because she said all that right in front of the other angels, but then one of the high school teachers came over—the donkeys and the cow belong to him—and he told Mrs. Green that she was a ridiculous old crone and that if she had a lick of sense, she'd be very proud of me because I said the lines exactly the way they were written. In Greek! He said he knew that because he teaches Greek and Latin, and he asked me how I learned the lines in Greek. But, Daddy, I don't know how I did it. I didn't know I could speak Greek, but I think I can."

Cy's fingers were gripping the edges of the book. "What did Mrs. Green say to the other teacher?"

"She told him she didn't care what he thought. That you and your friends had always been troublemakers, and that I think I'm special because I'm a Bigelow and I'm too big for my britches. That you probably deserved to be arrested and that Bigelows had too much power in this town anyway."

Sofia sniffed and wiped her nose with her sleeve. Then she brightened. "But the high school teacher, Mr. Madison, said he was proud of me and that maybe I should visit his class one day after Christmas and we could talk in Greek together."

Cy didn't know Saul Madison personally, but he knew he'd moved to the area some five years ago and that he'd bought a small farm and opened a little petting zoo just east of town. "That sounds fun. Going to a high school class? Learning a whole new language? Good for you."

Sofia eyed him. "You understood it too, didn't you? The words. In Greek."

He nodded. "And so did Auntie Sybil. It's another thing we need to keep a secret. For now."

"Like your friend is a secret?"

He nodded and tried an experiment. *Exactly like that. Can you understand me? When I talk to you like this?*

Sofia's eyes widened. She sat up on her knees and took her father's face in her hands. *It's like you're in my head.*

I'm not in your head, silly goose. I'm right here. Beside you, propped up on your pillows. But I'm glad we can talk to each other like this. It's another very cool secret, right? But one we have to be careful to hide.

Can I talk to Mom like this?

I don't think so. But maybe Auntie Sybil. I think it's a Bigelow thing. We can test it out with Sybil tomorrow, okay?

She nodded thoughtfully, taking it all in as if telepathic communications was normal. Then she curled up beside him. "Now let's read the book together. Out loud. And not in Greek."

"Definitely not." He wrapped one arm around her and pulled her close. "Okay, sweet pea. You start."

"I don't like it," Brooks said, his voice a low growl.

"What?" Tisi had her feet propped up on one of the desks in the communications center and was swiveling back and forth in her chair as she typed away on her laptop. "Something up with your new guests? Looked to me like they were settling in. The women helping the children. Mason getting sleeping arrangements sorted out. That Said kid helping Mat make spaghetti."

"It's not that. Ken and Sybil aren't moving. They've been at the same location for twenty minutes."

"That doesn't seem very long."

"It's not the length of time, it's the place. St. Margaret of Scotland Catholic Church. It's Thursday night. Almost ten p.m. So, what are they doing there?"

"Who's where?" Hermes said, appearing out of the blue.

"Sybil and Ken Fucking Lane," Brooks said. "They're at a church in the middle of the night."

"It's not the middle of the night," Hermes scoffed, with a wave of his hand. And then he went still. "Wait." He closed his eyes. Nodded as if in conversation with someone else. Then opened them. "We've got trouble."

Mason strolled in the door with a cold beer in hand. "Well, the good news is that I've got everyone assigned rooms, and I handed out bedding and toiletries. A couple of the kids went straight to bed while most of the women are taking turns in the showers. Mat and Joseph are in the kitchen making Mat's 'famous' spaghetti sauce." He stopped. Saw the grim look on Brooks' face. "What?"

"Sybil," Brooks said.

Mason froze, beer halfway to his mouth.

"I think she's in trouble," Hermes said.

"Tell me." Mason set the beer down carefully on the nearest table.

"The drivers and guards got a ride. After you all came back here, I followed them as planned. They had a little more than eight miles to go on their hike back. Some yahoo in a long-bed truck with a double gun rack gave them a ride back to SDIC and dropped them at the guard house. I followed them until they went inside, then ran an errand for Chiron, and then came back here." He turned to Tisi. "Show us inside the camp. See what's going on."

"What are you thinking?" Mason demanded as they watched the screens fill with differing views of the internment camp's interior. Their gazes tracked to the screen where a couple of men wearing lose jumpsuits were snipping off the men's zip ties and sawing off the carbide rope linking them together.

"I'm thinking they've had enough time to find a phone and warn Dr. Lane and whoever else is giving the orders."

"He needs a hostage, so he's kidnapping her." Tisi said.

Hermes shook his head. "But why take her to a church?"

Mason's face went grey. "Church? Where are they?"

"St. Margaret's on Mountain View Road," Brooks waved at one of the screens and zoomed in on the map. Their trackers show them stationary. Been there for over twenty minute."

"Godfuckingdamnit!" Mason checked his watch. Then the gun on his hip. "That's his church. He's going to force her to marry him. Probably roofied her like he did Cy."

Brooks scraped his fingers through his hair. "Fuck."

"He's asked her before. Back in college. Over and over, but she always said no. But now he knows he's fucked because Lushkonokov doesn't play games. He'll need hard cash to compensate Lushkonokov for failing to deliver his 'product.' He's gonna fucking marry her and then blackmail Cy for the money and then Sybil will be tied to him because divorce is illegal. Then he'll hand Cy and the rest of us over to Jensen on a silver fucking platter and be Jensen's hero."

"Ken doesn't know we know what he's up to with the trafficking," Brooks said, his voice tight. "He has no idea how Cy got out of that damned operating room and away from SDIC, but since Cy's was with him tonight, my guess is he doesn't think Cy remembers. So Ken knows his operation has been blown, but he doesn't know how or by whom."

"Which gives us the advantage of surprise." Mason pointed at Hermes. "Can you get me to the church?"

"I'll talk to Cy," Brooks said, grabbing his cell off the desk.

"I already told Nemi," Hermes said, reaching for Mason's hand. "Cy's with his daughter, but she'll get him. They'll meet us at the church."

46

Am I dreaming?

Sybil didn't remember going home and getting into bed, but her vision was wavy at the edges and everything felt and sounded as though she was swimming underwater. Her limbs seemed disconnected from her body. Like they were floating separately from the rest of her. She'd had flying dreams before, but never a floating dream. It wasn't an unpleasant feeling, but still, something didn't seem right.

She tried to open her eyes, but her lids felt weighted down. Tried to sit up, but her stomach lurched, and she choked back the bile. She put her hands out to steady herself. Opened her eyes again. Looked down. A wooden seat. A long bench. *Where am I?* Not home in bed, that was certain. At a picnic table? No. She was inside. She turned to look around her. The room spun. She swallowed hard. Was she sick? Moved her head slowly, as if it were fragile. As if she were fragile. Realized she was sitting in a pew. In a church. *Why?* It wasn't Christmas Eve. Was it? No. Not yet. She'd just been to Sofia's Christmas Pageant. She was an angel. Sybil smiled. Her precious little niece was an angel. It seemed fitting. It was nice. It should all be nice … but it wasn't.

A wave of fear swept over her. Something was wrong. Very, very wrong.

"You don't have a choice, *Father Nez*," a voice said. It was a mean voice. A *hissing* voice. And yet familiar. It made her go cold. Like a creeping fog swirling around her, alighting on her skin. She shivered and fought the urge to close her eyes again. Lay back down on the pew. Take a long nap.

"Why are you doing this? You'll destroy us. We've never done anything to hurt you."

A different voice. A man begging. His voice a scrape against Sybil's consciousness.

"You're fucking deviants, that's what you've done to hurt me. Hurt the whole community. Two priests fucking each other's brains out in the house of the Lord when you know it's against the law."

"You broke into the rectory, stormed into our bedroom! That's breaking and entering, and you're accusing us of breaking the law? What is wrong with you?"

Sybil registered that last as a different voice. A third person. Another man. A very angry man.

"You're not only breaking the law, but you're sinning in the eyes of God."

"The Bible never says—"

"I don't care what the fucking Bible says! Jensen says it's a sin, and I can call the authorities and send you both to prison for a decade of hard labor—if you live that long—or you can do what I say."

"How did you find out about us?"

Sybil couldn't follow the conversation, but she could tell this voice was furious, even though the tone was even, calm.

"People talk, Father Nez. When they go under anesthesia, sometimes they tell all sorts of stories. Some of them may even be true. Like the one your church secretary told me when I had a colonoscopy camera up her ass. She saw you kissing. Holding hands. Thought it was sweet how you love each other despite everything."

"Please, Dr. Lane," the begging man said. His voice was soft. Pleading. "Don't make us do this. It's not right."

"I need this wedding performed right here, right now."

Wedding? Who's getting married? Did I miss an invitation? Maybe Cy knows. If I'm here, my brother must be here too. Sybil blinked, rubbed her eyes, and looked around, but the church was empty. *Cy? Where are you?*

Ken put a hand under Sybil's armpit and yanked her to her feet. "Come on, darling. We're about to be married. I may not be the groom you've dreamed of, but I'm here and he isn't."

He steered her toward the altar. "One of you say the words, the other can be the witness."

"I donwanna…" Sybil mumbled. "Where's my brother?"

That's when something snapped in Father Adam Nez. If Ken had been paying attention, he might have had second thoughts because at that moment, Adam looked more like a warrior than a priest. His eyes were dark with intent, his voice sharp as a blade. "I don't think your bride is eager to pledge her troth to you."

"My bride has simply over indulged tonight, right darling?"

"We cannot marry you. The state requires two witnesses."

"Why don't you just forge your secretary's signature? I'll be a happy man, and you'll both live to see the sunrise."

"Can't marry you." Sybil's tongue was thick and felt like it was covered in wet moss. Or coated in concrete. Maybe moss covered concrete. What was wrong with her brain?

She wobbled sideways, but Ken caught her in his arms. Held her upright. *Damn it.* In his haste, he'd misjudged the dose.

"Not you," she whispered. "Don't love you." Her head flopped forward, and she mumbled into her chest. "Gonna marry Mason."

Ken's face went purple. He grabbed her by both arms and shook her, jerking her head back and forth until Father Nez rushed forward and grabbed his arm. "Stop. You're hurting her!"

But Ken pushed him away, his fingers digging deeper into Sybil's arms as he bent over her, swore in her ear. "You may want Mason, but he's not here, is he? He doesn't want you like I do."

His voice was like burning cinders on her skin. She flinched, tried to move away, but her muscles refused to be a party to any deliberate movement.

"He was long gone when you needed him. But I was there. I took care of you." He shook her again. Harder this time. "Have you been fucking him again?"

It was barely a whisper, but the words were like acid on her skin and she heard herself gasp out a sob. "Leave me alone!"

"Let her go, Ken." Mason's voice rang out in the empty sanctuary. He stood in the narthex, gun drawn and pointed at Ken, center mass. He was laser-focused on the scene in front of him even as he was also aware of the beauty around him. The air in the church practically shimmered. Fresh garlands scented the air with spruce and pine. Votive candles glowed in neat stair-stepped rows along both walls. Ornate chandeliers hanging from the soaring ceiling cast faceted shadows on the tall stained-glass windows.

Ken swiveled toward the back of the church, dragging Sybil with him, holding her body in front of his like a shield. She flopped forward, but he held her tight, his arm banded beneath her breasts. And then he pulled his own weapon. And placed the barrel of his pistol against Sybil's temple.

"Good evening, Mason. How did you know we were here?"

"Put a tracker on your phone and truck. Old law enforcement trick, you know?"

"But you're not law enforcement anymore, and I'd wager you didn't have a warrant for that. I could report you. Lock you up and throw away the key. You and these faggot priests."

Mason took a step forward. Gun steady. "You're going to call in a report about an unauthorized tracking device while you've got a gun to the head of an innocent woman? How do you think that's gonna go for you?"

"I'll tell you how it's gonna go, Mason. These fine, upstanding priests are going to perform a wedding ceremony. You can be our second witness because if you care about this woman at all, you will not want me to put a bullet in her brain."

Mason took a deep, calming breath. Ken obviously knew his shipment had been intercepted. Knew the Russian client would be unhappy with his failure. Knew he was at the end of the line. That he had no good choices left. And Mason knew that men without choices were willing to kill. And willing to die.

He had to keep Ken talking. Keep him occupied until he could get to Sybil. She wasn't in real danger because Hermes would never let Ken pull the trigger. Or Nemi would stop the bullet. Or something. The gods could not let Ken win. They just couldn't.

"Why are you in such a hurry to get married tonight? I figured a man like you would want a big wedding, not a secretive ceremony in the shadows. I figured you'd want the whole county to attend. Choirs of angels. The biggest cake in Arizona. Maybe invite Jensen himself, because that's how important you are, right? A big man. Up and coming. You just need a little more money. A little more prestige. A little more influence. That's why you're selling human beings, women and children, to sex-trafficking monsters like Boris Lushkonokov, right?"

"I *knew* you had to be behind stopping the shipment. You and your fucking high ideals. But what you've never understood is that the world doesn't run on ideals. It runs on money and power. Cy has both, but he won't use it. If I had control of Bigelow Enterprises, I'd wield it like a weapon. And my wife would be one of the most admired and celebrated women on Earth."

"Seriously?" Mason scoffed. "That's the story you've been telling yourself? You know Jensen's fortune dwarfs Cy's. Hell, we barely made a profit last year. And Jensen would never let you share the limelight. Look at how he treats Julian Valentine. The president of New America and Jensen treats him like shit." Mason huffed out a laugh and moved forward. Slowly, but knowing every step took him closer to Sybil. "Still, it explains why you tried to kill Cy."

"What are you talking about?" Ken glanced around the room as if Cy would appear at any moment.

"But you wanted to make a tidy profit off his organs first, right? Go for his kidneys, maybe his heart. Even his eyes. And then throw him in the SDIC incinerator. Comfort Sybil and marry her. Take over Bigelow Enterprises. That was the plan, wasn't it?"

"I don't know what you're talking about."

Ken's hand was shaking now, even as he pressed the barrel of the gun harder into Sybil's temple.

Out of the corner of his eye, Mason saw Cy and Nemi appear in the shadows to his right, behind a pillar and out of Ken's sight. He could only imagine what was going on in his friend's mind as his twin was slumped in the arms of a maniac who held a gun to her head. Mason dared not acknowledge them. Didn't want to give Ken any additional reason for insane behavior, and if he knew Cy was in the building, who knew what he'd do. The only thing Mason was certain of was that between the four of them—he and Hermes, Cy and Nemi—Ken would be dead before he could pull the trigger.

"Do you seriously think Cy will just welcome you into the family, even if Sybil is your wife? When the only reason you want her is political power?"

"No! I *love* her! I've *always* loved her even when she was obsessed with you and you were too cool and cocky to pay her any attention. And I was her first, so I'll always have that on you. *I. Fucked. Her. First.*"

For a fraction of a second, Mason's vision went black. And then his sight cleared, and Ken was in even sharper focus. Christ. A bullet was too fucking good for this motherfucker. He'd never *not* paid attention to Sybil, but she was Cy's twin and she was as delicate and beautiful and fragile and unique and special as a snowflake. And he was a brute, a brooding, awkward lummox who towered over her and felt like he would hurt her even if he looked at her too hard. And looking too hard at her hurt him. Down to the marrow. So, he'd never allowed himself to do more than that—for both their sakes. And whenever she turned her gaze toward him, he'd been too flummoxed to know what to do. He'd told himself that she just had a schoolgirl crush on her brother's buddy. She was Sybil and he was just a guy who liked to climb up cliffs and fire a gun and drive too fast. Someone like her couldn't really like someone like him. So he'd tried to stay away from her. During high school. During college. She was temptation personified. Then he'd been in law school and it was her turn to avoid him. Wouldn't even look at him. Then they'd had that one night together just after the grad school convocation, and it was glorious. But then he'd left for the FBI Academy and everything went to shit, and when he came home, she wouldn't even be in the same room with him. Fine. She was better off without him, anyway.

She may not want him, but he wasn't gonna let Ken force her into marriage. All Mason cared about was making sure she was safe. The rest could wait.

"Cy won't hurt me if I'm a member of the family," Ken was still talking. "Family is everything to him. You and your band of brothers. You all suck off the Bigelow teat."

Mason was still moving, still carefully placing each foot in front of the other in steady, even treads so he could fire in an instant. But he was also watching the man standing behind Ken, one of the priests, as he took two quiet, cautious steps back. And then two more. Angling for the side wall.

"So why don't you tell me how you did it," Ken went on, his voice edged with tension. With panic. "How you stopped my shipment. Was Mat with you? Former FBI agent and former Navy SEAL. What a joke. So high and mighty until you both quit in disgrace. But guess what? I'm *still* a surgeon. Still serving my country. I'm not a cowardly quitter! I was always the better man, and you never even saw me. Never considered me good enough. But the Russian saw me. When Lushkonokov toured the camp, he recognized my superiority and knew I could deliver for him. And he always pays by the pound."

Behind Ken, Father Adam Nez stole a glance at his fellow priest. He was disgusted by the talk of human trafficking and murder, but he was more disgusted by the fact that Dr. Ken Lane—a man admired throughout Bigelow—was threatening the life he and Eric had built together. Eric von Hollen. The love of his life. A man he'd first met in seminary. A man he would die for. A man he might be dying for at any moment.

Adam took two more steps and then slowly reached his arm around the doorway to the sacristy where they kept his father's old Sig Sauer 938 on a high shelf. Just in case. These days, they never knew who would come knocking on their door to drag them away. Or worse. If that time ever came, Eric would plead their case and beg for their lives, but that wasn't the way Adam had been raised. That wasn't the way he operated.

Adam gripped the pistol. Stepped back toward the altar. Toward the madman who threatened everything. Slowly. Barely breathing. Moving like a whisper on the wind, just like his grandfather had taught him when they'd gone hunting before their Diné land was stolen. Moving ever closer even as Dr. Ken Lane continued blathering on about how unfair it was that the Bigelows had everything and how he deserved more and how Mason Cox was never going to put his filthy hands on the woman he loved.

And then everything happened at once. There and gone in an instant, a circlet of gold and silver flame wrapped around Ken's throat like an otherworldly garrote. The light in his eyes flashed and went out. Dead. But still on his feet as Sybil fell sideways like a rag doll and two shots rang out in unison. From behind, Adam's bullet hit center mass, punctured Ken's heart and knocked him forward just as Mason's pierced the man's throat, blew through his trachea, and exited out the back of his neck, severing his spinal column with a fine spray of red mist and white bone.

Then Nemesis was there, crouching next to Sybil's limp form. Cy at her side. But Mason didn't stop moving until he had Sybil in his arms. Her head lolled against his chest. He pressed two fingers to the pulse point in her neck. Almost wept at the strong thrum of life. She was alive. *She was alive!* Just passed out. Drugged. Just like Cy had been the day Ken Fucking Lane had tried to separate him from his kidneys.

In the chancel by the communion altar, Adam still held the gun as he and Eric stood looking at each other, oblivious, at first, to the tumult around them. And then, the nave was suddenly full of people. *Where had they come from?* Mason Cox cradled Sybil Bigelow as her brother and a fine-featured woman who moved like lightning and glowed like starlight crouched beside them. An absolutely gorgeous man they'd never seen before—a man with broad shoulders, burnished silver hair, and dark silver eyes—stood over them, looking as radiant as if he had just descended from heaven on silver wings. He surveyed the room and stepped toward the priests in an easy, confident gait.

He gave them a short bow. As if his manners had been forged in a different age. "That was a fine shot, Father…"

"Nez. Adam Nez." Adam was amazed his voice was steady after shooting a man in the back. "And this is Father von Hollen."

"Hermes the Herald, at your service."

Adam's eyes narrowed while Eric's went wide. Their mouths dropped open.

"Do you have any security cameras on the premises?"

"No. The diocese sent us cameras for the parking lot and the front doors, but we never installed them. In this day and age, we refuse to monitor who comes to us for refuge."

Hermes nodded at that. "I could wipe your memories, but I think you'd like to keep this night close to your hearts. A memory of what one does for love."

"Love?" Adam shook his head. "The only thing that man was in love with was himself."

"I was talking about you. And Mason Cox."

"Oh." Eric and Adam's hands found each other and their fingers twined.

"I doubt the authorities will show up, but if they do come asking questions, assure them that you were in the rectory and never saw anyone enter the church. I'd put your gun somewhere safe, not back where you were keeping it. For now, if the two of you would ensure the church is locked up, we will take care of the rest. Make sure the sanctuary is good as new. There is nothing more you need do or worry about."

He gave them another little bow and turned to go. Then stopped. Turned back toward them.

"I will say one more thing, though." Hermes offered them a brilliant smile that nearly lit up the church. "In the course of human events, justice is always served. Sooner or later. And in the meantime, the most courageous thing anyone can do is to turn away from hate and choose love. As men of faith, you may find taking a life to be a terrible tragedy. But in this case, you did the right thing."

Even though his hands were now shaking and he spoke through gritted teeth, Adam squared his shoulders. "I'm not a bit sorry."

"Good," Hermes acknowledged the statement with a nod. "As Seneca said all those years ago, 'All cruelty springs from weakness.' Tonight, you were strong. You are a good man, and your parishioners are lucky to have you." And then he strode back toward the others.

The two priests watched, speechless, as the strange visitors conferred, apparently deciding their next course of action, and then, suddenly they were gone. All of them. Adam and Eric both blinked. There was no evidence of a shooting. No dead body sprawled face down. No blood pooling on the slate tiles. No woman collapsed on the floor. No bullet hole in the pew or blood spatter on the steps to the chancery. The whole place was quiet as a held breath.

"Holy mother of God," Eric finally said on a soft exhale. And then he turned to Adam and they wrapped their arms around each other and held on tight.

47

"Move, goddamnit," Cy growled at the SS agent breathing down his neck as he yanked the front door open wide.

"What's wrong with her?" The agent said with a sneer, looking on as Mason barreled into the foyer with Sybil in his arms. "She have a bit too much to drink?"

"She's not drunk, asshole," Mason said. "She's been drugged and left for dead."

"What are you talking about?"

"Why don't you ask your buddy Dr. Lane?" Cy shouted, his temper long past the boiling point. "He was supposed to bring her straight home after the Christmas Pageant."

Mason headed for the stairs. "Did you call your doctor?"

"He's on his way," Cy said, knowing full well that Dr. A was already upstairs, ready to check Sybil over and then, if all was well, ready to 'call in' and apologize that he wouldn't be able to get there after all. "God, I'm so sorry I missed your texts," Cy went on, performing for the SS agent's sake. "I must have fallen asleep in Sofia's room while reading to her. I can never repay you for finding her."

"Let's just get her to her room," Mason said, already half way up the stairs.

"Where's Dr. Lane now?" The guard called after them.

"Who the hell knows?" Cy yelled. "He drugged my sister and left her to freeze to death at a fucking cemetery!"

Mason paused at the top of the steps, holding Sybil close to his chest, and glaring daggers down at the agent. "She called me when she couldn't get a hold of Cy. Said Ken tried to rape her. That he'd drugged her. That she'd escaped and was somewhere near the cemetery on Mountain View Road. I found her passed out in the snow, and if you don't do your job and find Ken Lane, I'm going to fucking do it for you."

"But—"

"Why don't you start by tracing his cell phone!" Mason didn't have to draw on any acting skills. He was ready to shoot the motherfucker all over again. "Find out who called him and when. Maybe then you can figure out why he drugged a woman he claimed to love and left her for dead in the snow."

"Why didn't you take her to the hospital?" The agent would not let it go. They'd all been told that Dr. Lane was one of the good guys. A man climbing the Administration ladder with his medical work down at SDIC. And conversely, the agents camped out at the Bigelow estate had been primed to be suspicious of anything and everything the Bigelows did.

Cy stared at the agent as if he was the dumbest motherfucker ever born. "There's always an hours-long wait at the ER, and as long as her pulse was strong, we prioritized getting her warm to prevent hypothermia. What would you do if it were your sister? Sit for hours in a cold, sterile hospital waiting room?"

"Okay, okay." The guy raised his hands in surrender. "Fine. I'll track down Dr. Lane and get his side of the story."

His side of the story? Mason wanted to march back down the stairs and lay the agent flat. Instead, he climbed the rest of the stairs, hurried down the hall to Sybil's bedroom, and laid her gently on the bed.

Dr. A leaned over to open and shine a light in her eyes. "How long has she been out?"

"Not even ten minutes," Mason answered. All business.

"We got her out of there as soon as we could," Cy said as Dr. A moved on to checking Sybil's pulse and temperature.

"I take it this isn't her blood."

"It's not hers," Mason said.

"We had to figure out the logistics since the house is occupied and being watched," Cy said. "Hermes talked to the priests, then conjured Mason a car so he could get Sybil back here the old-fashioned way. He and Nemi magically cleaned up the church, and sent for you, then got me back here since I supposedly never left. Then they both left to dispose of the body. And it all happened so fast, my head is still spinning."

Dr. A's brows knitted together in a frown. "Where are they taking the deceased?"

"They're leaving him as a gift for his client," Mason said, scrubbing both hands down his face in relief, frustration, and disgust. "At Boris Lushkonokov's fancy, high-end brothel in Sevastopol. Stripped naked. No identification. No cell. No money. No nothing. If they care enough, they'll eventually be able to ID him through facial recognition software, DNA, or dental records. But that's okay. We figure Lushkonokov will consider it some sort of power play in one of his turf wars. And he'll have no idea how the man got from southern Arizona to Crimea so quickly— unless, of course, Jensen had something to do with it."

"So, the mobster will suspect the Chancellor," Dr. A said, pulling off Sybil's shoes and tucking her feet under the covers.

"The timing all depends on when the body is discovered." Mason stepped up and took the edge of the covers from Dr. A and pulled them up over Sybil's shoulders. He could feel Cy watching him as he tucked the quilt under Sybil's chin and smoothed her hair away from her face.

"She's going to be fine," Dr. A said. "I'll draw some blood and test it when I get back to my lab, but I suspect she was given the same thing you were, Cy. Not the general anesthetics, but the flunitrazepam."

"I'd appreciate it," Cy said. "He's not going to bother her anymore, but I'd still like to know."

Dr A procured the necessary tools, quickly swabbed Sybil's arm, drew a vial of blood, bandaged her arm, and marked the vial. He put everything in his bag and went into the bathroom to wash his hands. "I don't think you need me anymore tonight, so I'm heading home. Do you mind if I run some of the tests on her blood that I'm running on yours?"

"No. That's fine," Cy said, knowing it was the right thing to do, but dreading the definitive answers the tests would reveal about their futures—and their pasts. "Nemi should be back soon. She'll let you know if we need you."

"Thanks for coming, Doc," Mason said, extending his hand. "It's nice to have the most famous physician in history make a house call."

"Anything for Nemi," he said with a smile. Then looked at Cy. "And for my brother and sister. Now, you both get some rest. We'll talk soon, I'm sure."

As soon as Asklepios disappeared, Cy and Mason locked gazes. "You love her, don't you." Cy said after a long moment.

"Jesus, Cy." Mason drew in a long breath and exhaled slowly. Drew a hand down over his face. "I can't do this tonight."

The corner of Cy's mouth kicked up. "It's okay if you do. And it's okay if you don't. I'm not getting in the middle of it, but you should know I think she's always had a thing for you. Ever since she invited you to that Sadie Hawkins dance. When was that?"

"We were fifteen."

Cy huffed out a laugh. "I think you broke her heart. I remember trying to explain to her, but she cried all night."

Mason let out a disgusted sigh. "And the next day, she invited Ken Fucking Lane, and he said yes, and then ... Christ. I've been a fucking idiot for so long."

"Look, brother. I love you both more than I can express. And you're both adults now, so I refuse to interfere. I just want you to know that—"

Mason put both hands up. "Please, don't say anything more. I'm not sure my delicate sensibilities can take you giving me advice on my love life with your sister. Not after that scare."

Cy drew two fingers across his compressed lips. "Fine. I get it. Now, it's 10:45. I assume you're staying in here? Keeping watch?"

"Do you mind?" Mason held his breath.

"Of course not. You know where the linen closet is if you want to get an extra blanket and sleep in the chair. Or not."

Mason nodded. Unable to speak.

"See you in the morning?"

Mason swallowed. "Cy."

"Yeah?"

Mason swept a hand through his hair. "That whole time, I kept telling myself she'd be safe. That Nemi would never allow Ken to hurt your sister. That she'd be able to do something to save her if I couldn't. And I'm not sure whether she strangled him with that magic flaming garrote thing or the priest killed him or I killed him. I don't really care. But please tell Nemi I'm glad she was there. Glad she got you there."

Cy smiled at that. "Don't worry. I'll definitely be thanking her. All night long."

48

The pounding on the bedroom door sent both Cy and Nemi bolting out of bed, covers flung to the floor as they evacuated their deliciously warm cocoon as if the house were in flames around them.

"Cy! Get up!" It was BoJo, pounding on the door, rattling the locked knob. "She's gone! Oh my god! Cy! She's gone!"

"Hold on!" Cy hollered, jumping up and down, nearly falling over, as he struggled to put a leg through the pair of flannel pants that had been thrown over the back of a chair last night after Nemi had finally arrived. He glanced up to see Nemi, already dressed, pull open the door.

He cinched the drawstring at his waist as BoJo reached out to grab his hand. "She's gone, Cy! Her room's empty. She's not in the house."

"Is it Sybil?" He let BoJo drag him into the hallway. "Where's Mason? What's happened?"

"Sybil and Mason?" BoJo stared at him for a moment. "No! No! It's Sofia!" BoJo dragged Cy by the hand toward Sofia's room. "I went in to wake her to see if she wanted to help me make Christmas Eve French toast, but she's not there!"

They were both running now. Down one long corridor, racing around the landing, and rushing headlong down the other corridor to his old bedroom. Sofia's bedroom.

"See?" BoJo said, her eyes wide with panic as she followed Cy into Sofia's bedroom. It was a big room made warm and cozy by the bookshelves and stuffed toys, the fluffy rugs and the bean bag chair in the corner. "You know how I have to nag her to make her bed. And there's a note on the pillow. And a golden apple. I didn't touch it in case the police—"

Suddenly Nemi was beside them. "A golden apple?"

BoJo jumped. Blinked, then went on. "I didn't touch it."

"She was here last night," Cy said as they all stared down at the perfectly made, perfectly empty bed. "I looked in on her before I went to bed."

Nemi picked up the apple, hefted it in her hand as if weighing it. Then held it up. "My sister, Eris. It's her calling card."

"What does that mean? What does the note say?" BoJo waved at it as if it were a rattlesnake curled up on the pillow.

Nemi picked it up, unfolded it and read it silently. Then handed it to Cy. He skimmed over it, then read aloud.

> *My dearest sister,*
>
> *Rumor has it you've fallen in love with a human. Since you refuse to see me—you never call, you never write—I thought I'd take this little treasure with me and see if you can track us down. It'll be a fun game! Like the hide and seek we played when we were young. Remember that time I hid in the depths of Tartarus and you couldn't find me for a thousand years because you were too scared of the dark to venture so deep? It'll be like that.*
>
> *Hope it doesn't take you a thousand years this time. I think this sweet treasure has a limited shelf life.*
>
> *—Always, Eris*

"Shit." Cy handed the note back to Nemi.

BoJo reached for the note, but it suddenly disappeared. Nemi had sent it directly to Pantheon League HQ in Georgetown. Instead, she grabbed a stuffed Pegasus with shiny, multi-colored wings from Sofia's bookshelf and clutched it to her heart.

"What the hell's going on?" Mason strode down the hall, still wearing the clothes he'd had on last night, clothes he'd obviously slept in. "You're all making the kind of racket that will bring the SS agents running up here. " He stopped at the threshold and looked in the room. Grabbed the door frame. "No, Cy. God, no."

"Goddess." Nemi's face was a storm cloud. "My sister. I would call her my evil twin, but we're not twins. She's all about manipulation and mind games. Causing strife and discord just to watch everyone flail around in the aftermath. She's not above targeting innocents, but she'd be a fool to harm Apollo's granddaughter, so I doubt she's aware of the connection." She looked at BoJo. "I will fix this. I swear to you, BoJo. We will find her."

Nemi started to disappear, but Cy's arm shot out to grab her. "Should you tell Apollo? Can he help?"

"Yes, and probably." Then Nemi did disappear.

And BoJo fainted. Cy caught her just before her head hit the bedpost.

"I brought you a gift."

Harold Jensen nearly fell out of his chair. Slapped a hand over his heart. "You!"

"You seem surprised to see me."

"I haven't seen you in weeks!" He looked around his office, now thoroughly cleaned from any debris or evidence of the bombing. The banquet hall was a floor above and everything in his space had been covered with dust and debris from the ceiling. And his windows had to be replaced. Small price to pay even if it wasn't as successful as he'd hoped. Now, pale sunlight filtered through the grey winter's morning cloud cover to illuminate his space. It still smelled of dust and cleaning fluid. But she smelled divine and looked like an answered prayer.

She was the most beautiful woman he'd ever seen. Dressed like any other woman you might meet on the street, but he knew she was so much more than that. She was everything. All dark eyes, sable hair, luscious curves, and a mouth that could suck him dry. He got hard just thinking about her. "You come and go with no warning. I try to summon you, but you ignore me. Sometimes I think you're just a dream."

More like a nightmare. "You've watched me preach hellfire and brimstone from the pulpit," she said. "I've been by your side for every one of your Executive Orders. And in your bed for more nights than you can count. How can you think I'm a dream when you've been inside me?"

The man stood and leaned forward, fingers pressed on his desk, a leer on his face. "Is that why you're here? Are you giving me the gift of your body once again? It's been too long."

She wanted to wipe that lecherous grin off his face. Seriously smite the smarmy bastard. It had been fun for awhile, but Harold Jensen bored her now. Disgusted her, was more like it. He was too easy to manipulate. To easy to convince he was the most brilliant man in the world. Perhaps even in history. After all, he was the richest, so he must be the smartest. What a fool.

"There's always time for that," she said, "but that is not the gift I brought today. Do you want to see it or not?"

"Did you really bring me a gift?"

Orion's Belt, some humans were slow. Fun for toying with, but not very interesting. "Have I ever lied to you?" she said, rustling her ink-black wings, extending them wide until they blocked out the pale sunlight and his pupils went wide with fear. And unbridled desire.

"You wanted power. I gave it to you." Her voice was like a song. A beautiful, terrible, hypnotic song. "You wanted wealth. I gave it to you. You wanted children. I gave them to you. Now, I'm bringing you a gift that can shift the balance of power again. Do you want it?"

"Yes, yes." He practically slavered over her. "I'm no fool. Of course, I want it. Where is it? Show me!"

"Patience. It's somewhere safe. But I'll give you a peek." She waved a hand as if she were a witch conjuring a magic mirror, an image appeared, suspended amidst the motes floating in the air. A child sitting cross-legged in what looked like a prison cell.

Jensen's eyes narrowed. "You brought me a child? I have dozens of my own. Why do I need someone else's?"

"Oh, but this is not any child. This is Cyrus Horatio Bigelow the Fourth's only daughter."

And then, Jensen's eyes went wide. He slapped a hand on the desk and barked out a laugh. "And I bet he'd agree to anything to get her back. Safe and sound. Or not."

"I knew you'd catch on." Eris purred. "You told me copper is king. Now, you're the king."

"He's always refused to entertain an offer to buy his mining interests. But now ... I already had the power to *ask*. I already had the power to *take*. But that would have been too public and could have provoked an ugly outcry from other landholders. Now, I have the power to *demand*. In secret. And no one will ever know why he caved."

"And never forget I'm the one who gave it to you. As long as you proclaim Pastor Erin Knight as a prophetess of the New Life Eternal Church, I will give you everything you deserve."

Eris tucked in her wings, disappeared them, then walked around Jensen's vast desk, her eyes glowing like bright stars reflecting the velvety deep of an ancient abyss, hips swaying like a mesmerist's watch. "What else do you deserve, Chancellor?"

"Everything," he breathed out, grabbed her by the arm and pushed her face down onto his desk. He yanked her pants down, hearing the zipper rip and a button pop, then slapped her round ass until it was glowing red with heat and his palm stung. With one hand, he gathered her hair in his fist and yanked her head back. With the other, he unbuttoned his pants and pushed them down his thighs. Then he pushed himself in to the hilt with a grunt. Every time she let him use her like this, he was sure he'd died and gone to heaven. Fucking a divine prophetess. Having power over her body. It was a narcotic. An addiction. And now, it built and built and built until his mind blanked.

Eris closed her eyes to her surroundings. The man pounding into her sounded like a rutting pig. He was an animal. No better, no worse. But he was her animal. For now. Until she was ready to lock him away in a zoo. Or put him down.

In the meantime, her human aspect needed a shower. She was going to take a little trip home. Swim in the sea. Bask in the sun. Wash the stink of Harold Jensen off her skin. Fuck someone worth fucking. Get away from everything human and start renewed and refreshed in the new year. The girl had a bathroom and enough food in her room to last her a few days. She didn't need a babysitter too. She'd be there when she got back, and then the fun would really begin.

Jensen pushed in one last time and held, his orgasm exploding with a roar, nearly sending him to his knees. He collapsed on top of her, gasping for air, feeling her power settle in his blood like an energy reserve. Taking her was like injecting jet fuel straight into his veins, and he vaguely wondered what life would be like if she left him. He was at the pinnacle of the world. If she abandoned him, how far would he fall?

49

Sybs, I'm about to go out of my mind. I keep trying to do this telepathy thing, but Sofia isn't answering. What if she's...

She's not dead, Cy. You'd know it. Right? Your goddess would know it.

We're up against another goddess though. Eris is apparently the opposite of Nemesis. But just as powerful. The whole fucking Pantheon League is trying to find Sofia and they can't. No one can feel her presence. It's like she's in some black hole or something.

It'd been over twenty-four hours and Cy was pacing again. Back and forth in front of the wall of screens. Along with Cy, Mat, and Brooks, they were all there. Every core member of the Pantheon League was in the room in Georgetown—Nemesis, Alecto, Megara, Tisiphone, Chiron, Artemis, Dionysos, Hermes, and Asklepios. Of course, there were hundreds of other creatures of divine lineage or varying magical abilities who helped the gods do their work, but these were the main players. These were the gods who worked together to balance the scales of justice for humans the world over.

And they were furious because despite all their power, they couldn't find one little girl.

They are furious a lot of the time, honestly. Wouldn't you be if you knew the potential of humans to create great art, compose beautiful music, give of themselves with compassion, love with abandon, and yet watch them, millennia after millennia, century after century, year after year, day after day, light their own hair on fire and rejoice when their brains boiled?

Humans are killing each other at alarming rates and with alarming cruelty. One leader, enabling the bloody carnage with weapons, disinformation, and deceit, declared empathy a lead weight hung about the necks of humans by crybabies who could not get ahead on their own merits—even though his wealth was utterly dependent on Jensen's largess. *Empathy is the enemy of progress*, he'd pronounced. Even those with an abundance of empathy did not mourn when his super yacht was mysteriously lost at sea. Some joked that the orcas must have taken him out, and they were right. But the gods knew it was Poseidon—infuriated at the increasing water pollution from this man's companies—who'd directed the operation.

It wasn't only the gods and the orcas who were disgusted by human behavior. There were many humans who cared deeply. As Nemi had told Hermes, the Pantheon League had always been able to find honorable humans with whom they could work to do good in the world. Hermes was right, however, that too many humans simply turned a blind eye to the growing devastation. If the wreckage wasn't in their own backyards, they couldn't be bothered to care.

Unfortunately, humans are not only killing each other, they are killing the other species with whom they share the planet. And killing the beloved Earth itself. Oh, Earth will survive as a rock with a molten iron core—much like Venus or Mars or countless other planets home to countless other failed civilizations—but it will never be the same if the humans keep up their ruthless campaign of environmental devastation.

So, yes, the gods in that room were angry. For many of us, our immortal lives are tied to the Earth. It is the only home we'll ever know. Unfortunately, there are other gods—i.e., Eris—who, like the billionaire taken down by pods of orcas, simply don't care. She has zero empathy. Toward humans, toward other species, and toward other gods. Toward the Earth itself. She is an emotional void.

But most of the gods do have emotions. Emotions as vast as the universe. As deep as the deepest levels of Tartarus. We *feel*. And we *hate*. And we *love*. And, as I mentioned in the prologue to our story, these gods have favorites, and it is unwise in the extreme to interfere with those favorites.

Nemesis definitely has a favorite and his daughter was now missing. The gods had rejoiced when they realized that Nemesis and Cy had found in each other a love for the ages. And now Nemesis' own sister had stepped in to rip Cy's family apart. To rip Nemesis's new family apart.

And there was Artemis whose great niece, whom she had yet to meet, was the missing little girl. Artemis who had two nephews in that room, one she'd loved for nearly three thousand years and one she had respected since she and Chiron had recruited him, and had now learned to love in the span of a single week.

And Asklepios had a half-brother and a missing niece. And Tisiphone's current favorite, Brooks, was just as frantic as Cy. As was Mat, who was pacing and cursing and hoping Helen Cross was safe and that whatever connection she had to this group of gods did not put her in danger. And Mason who watched from afar because, as you might expect, he had stayed back in Arizona with Sybil and BoJo.

As soon as the reality of Sofia's kidnapping had sunk in, Mason packed up Sybil, BoJo, Mrs. C, and Sofia's dogs and took them out to stay at the Bigelow homestead cabin. In reality, he took them to stay in the Basement where the connection to the

Pantheon League was secure and where the women and children rescued from Ken Lane's thwarted human trafficking operation were staying.

After Mrs. C arrived and had been apprised of the situation regarding the women and children taking refuge there, she immediately took charge, leaving Mason time to spend monitoring comms with the Pantheon League and taking care of Sybil and BoJo. And Sofia's dogs, who sensed that something was very wrong. Both Cricket and Pixie Dust were nestled in BoJo's lap and had barely left her side since they'd arrived.

The facts were this: Sofia Bigelow had been discovered missing at 6:47 a.m., Arizona time, a golden apple and a taunting note left on the little girl's pillow, written by Eris, goddess of strife and all-around eternal pain in the universe's ass. And that was it. That was all they knew for sure.

Eris could have taken Sofia anywhere on the planet. But chances were high that she was indeed playing with her sister instead of trying to start a war among the gods, so she was probably not in some secret lair on the other side of the planet.

At least that's what they hoped.

It was now around 5:00 a.m. the following day. None of the humans had slept since Sofia was discovered missing. Desperation filled the air like heat from a raging fire and tempers were growing short.

"As many of you know," Dr. A said suddenly, looking up from where he'd been writing in a leather-bound notebook. "I've been paying regular visits to Jensen's personal physician, Dr. Geoffrey Hunt—he thinks I'm some sort of ghost of Christmas past, or something—and I've been 'encouraging' him to give Jensen higher and higher doses of a benzodiazepine to slow the man down. Lessen his paranoia. Stop him from doing even more damage than he's already doing."

"I don't think it's working," Mat quipped.

Dr. A huffed out a grim laugh. "It is working. The banquet bombing was not nearly as devastating as the campaign of terror he had planned."

"Well, that's at least something," Mat groused. "But go on, sorry I interrupted."

Dr. A nodded and continued. "I have long suspected that the reason Harold Jensen transformed himself from a relatively benign billionaire philanthropist into a multi-trillionaire, violent, power-hungry dictator in such a short amount of time is that he had help. He was egged on. At every stage of his descent into the madness of absolute narcissistic tyranny, he had a little voice in his head saying *more more more*."

"Eris," Nemi said, her gaze fixed on her old friend.

"Eris," Dr A confirmed. "Anyway, while Dio was making the millionth pot of coffee, I paid an early morning visit to Dr. Hunt—he is particularly forthcoming when I 'haunt' him in the early morning hours. Hunt has apartments near Jensen's in his underground bunker, and he admitted Jensen's been muttering about a dark angel guiding him to greatness. He says this angel is his spiritual advisor by day and by night she visits him like a succubus. She fucks him. Lets him do anything he desires to her. Bondage. Pain. Whips. Chains. Whatever makes him feel powerful. And then she whispers ideas into his ear. Pushing him to consolidate more power. Confiscate more wealth. And to punish anyone who opposes him. Men who refuse to bend to his will. Men like Cyrus Bigelow."

"Fuck." Cy sank into a chair and let his head fall back to stare at the ceiling.

"Do you think Eris knows I'm Alexander Whitelaw?" Nemi asked. "I've always tried to keep that identity hidden from her."

"I'm not sure," Dr. A said. "But she somehow knows you've had your eye on Cy. And that Jensen is interested in Cy's mineral rights. And that Cy suddenly befriended Whitelaw."

"So," Artemis cut in, "Jensen is one of Eris's pet projects. Cy is one of Nemesis's favorites. Jensen wants Cy's land so what better way to get what he wants than to blackmail him with the safety of his kidnapped child."

"So," Chiron picked up the thread. "Eris gifts Sofia to Jensen and makes him a happy man while also 'playing a game' with her sister. If this is the case, it makes sense that she plays her game in Jensen's domain."

"Exactly," Dr. A said. "It didn't take too much persuasion for me to convince Hunt to tell me about Jensen's bunker, and I can assure you Jensen is paranoia personified. Even the good doctor has never been to the lowest levels."

"If I had an evil goddess whispering in my ear, I might be a little paranoid too," Brooks muttered.

"The problem is that because of Jensen's paranoia, Geoff has never seen the plans for the bunker. He has no idea how big it is or how deep it goes."

"While we were confined to the Waldorf, I had a chance to speak to several Administration lackeys," Helen said, walking into the room to the utter surprise of everyone there.

"What the hell are you doing here?" Mat demanded. "You're supposed to be in Arizona."

"Mason told us Sofia was missing and to be on standby. We decided we couldn't do anyone any good in Arizona, so we flew back last night."

"You know you're always welcome here, Helen," Ali and Meg said in unison as Tisi stood to give her a hug.

"Thanks." She bent to press a quick kiss on Ali and Meg's cheeks. "But let me tell you what I learned about the bunker. It's insider gossip mostly. Guys sitting at the bar, trying to impress a pretty woman. Talking about the fact that Agent Bill Reynolds is one of Jensen's favorites and always knows where he is and how to get to him, and the second in command on his team, a man named Jack Dennehey, hates Reynolds with the heat of a thousand exploding suns. And hates Jensen more. They both know the bunker inside and out. They have to because their job is to keep Jensen safe."

Nemi looked at Cy. "Jack Dennehey is the one who told us we weren't alone when we were taken into custody."

Cy stood. "We need to find him. Bring him here."

"I'll do it," Hermes volunteered. "I'm getting antsy. Need to move."

"Hold on," Tisi said, her fingers flying on her keyboard. "I'll get you an address."

"Get us one for Bill Reynolds too," Chiron said. "If we know where he is, we can make sure he doesn't get in our way when we do whatever it is we're going to do."

"On it," Tisi said with a nod.

"By the way," Brooks asked. "Where is Governor Guerrero? Is he part of all this?" He waved his hand around the room.

Chiron and Artemis looked at each other. "Yes and no. He's safe and he's working with us, but he's not ready to step out into the open just yet."

"There's more," Helen said. "Jensen's living space is rumored to be five stories below the ground floor of the New America building. The lowest level of the bunker is five stories below that. The whole place is a maze of rooms built with steel-reinforced concrete walls that are three-feet thick with some rooms lined with lead. There are air shafts that could be accessed by humans if we needed a back door in. And the place is apparently stocked for one hundred people to survive up to a year without surfacing."

"Home sweet home," Mat muttered.

"Sounds like the Basement," Brooks quipped.

"The problem won't be accessing it," Artemis said. "Any of us could gain access in a heartbeat. The problem is knowing *where* to access it. Eris has the same capabilities as every god in this room, but she's also a devious bitch who loves to play games. We could spend eternity popping in and out of rooms and never find Sofia. And there's no guarantee she's even there."

"I'm basically useless here," Nemi admitted. "Worse than useless. Eris and I have a sister bond, which means she can lead me on a wild goose chase and shield herself from me. I've certainly spent most of my lifetime shielding myself from her and look where that got us."

Cy, I've got an idea.

Cy held up a finger. "Sybil," he told the group. She says she has an idea."

Mat stared at him. "You're talking to Sybil right now?"

Cy nodded, looked at Mat and Brooks. "Because of our bond, Nemi and I can communicate mind-to-mind. Sort of like quantum entangled communications."

"Exactly like quantum entangled communications," Nemi said.

"And turns out I can do it with my twin too. I've been trying it with Sofia, but she's not responding."

"Cy ..." Nemi said, standing up, running her fingers through her hair. "I've been trying to feel her too, but I can't. Or at least I haven't felt anything from her that signals she feels like she's in danger. Maybe she doesn't have this capability."

"Not all demigods or children of demigods, have the capacity for quantum communications," Dr. A said. "You may not be able to reach her simply because she isn't wired that way."

Or, Sybil sent to Cy. *She's only seven. Maybe she needs more than a nudge.*

Say it outloud, Sybs. Get Mason to put you on screen.

A moment later, Sybil appeared on the big screen in Georgetown. Mason sat in a chair in front of the bank of computers, and BoJo and the dogs were curled up on one of the couches in the room. She looked haunted.

"I can't *see* Sofia, but I think she's being held somewhere that has some sort of cage around it. Preventing any communications."

"A Faraday cage can shut out some electromagnetic fields, but not quantum," Brooks said.

"But a goddess can create an impenetrable shield so it can't be accessed by other gods. It's how we protect our minds from each other," Nemi said. "Otherwise, my sister would've hacked my brain millennia ago."

"So," Sybil said, "my idea is that we should harness all our collective power and try to penetrate the cage. Stage a family intervention."

"Time to bring in my brother?" Artemis asked.

"Past time, if you ask me." Chiron said. "While you all deal with Apollo, I'm going to track down Security Service Agent Reynolds."

"And I'll find Dennehey," Hermes said.

They were already gone by the time Dr. A fished a coin from his pocket and turned to Artemis. "Heads you go get Apollo, tails I go get him." Artemis nodded. The coin flashed as it rose into the air, flipping over and over and then coming down into his palm.

He looked down and smiled, held it out to Artemis. "Have fun."

50

Sofia sat on the rug, back up against the bed. She rubbed her eyes. She didn't have a watch, but she knew that she'd been asleep for a really long time. She'd had too many brownies after the pageant, but she was really hungry now. How long had she slept? She had no idea.

She also had no idea where she was, but she now knew for certain that her new Auntie Eris was not to be trusted. When the woman had shown up in her bedroom asking for help with a secret Christmas present for her sister, Nemi, and her new boyfriend, Sofia had jumped at the idea. She thought it would be exciting. A secret present for a secret friend. Sofia knew her mother and father did not live together like her friends' parents, and she wanted them each to have someone special. And the moment she first saw Nemi in her dream, she'd known Nemi would be her daddy's special person. So, if she could help make that happen, it would be the best Christmas present ever.

And it was exciting, at first. She was so happy to have such a big secret. And why should she be scared? The house was crawling with guards who, although she didn't like them, were supposed to be keeping her safe. Her mom was just down the hall. Auntie

Sybil down there too. Her dad was over in his rooms. And it was almost Christmas!

She even thought it was exciting disappearing out of her room. Being transported somewhere new—even though her parents always told her to never go anywhere with a stranger. But surely Nemi's sister would be safe. Right?

Now, she knew she'd been tricked. She wasn't stupid, but boy oh boy had she ever acted stupid. And now she was locked in a room by herself. Somewhere.

She stared down at her hands. What had she been doing when she'd first seen the vision of Nemi? First known she was coming? She'd thought it had been in a dream, but now she wasn't so sure. Maybe she hadn't been asleep at all. Maybe she'd been daydreaming. Yes. Standing at the sink, filling the dogs' water bowl, thinking of ... *what?* She couldn't remember. But she knew she'd been staring down into the water. And maybe if she looked into water now, she could see Nemi again. The bad lady—she refused to call her Auntie Eris anymore—had left her a bowl, some dry cereal, milk in a little refrigerator, and bottles of water.

She hopped up and opened a bottle of water and poured it into the bowl. Then she sat back down cross legged, bent her head, and looked down at the water. She felt a little silly, but somehow it seemed natural to look into the water. To talk to it. She rested her arms on her crossed legs and took a deep breath. "Let me see Nemi," she whispered. "Where is she? Show me."

Nothing. She tried again. Nothing. Then she tried a new tactic. Tried talking to the water in her head. Somehow that felt right.

Let me see my daddy. Where is he? What's he doing? Is he looking for me?

There! A flicker in the bowl of water.

Water, please help me. Can you hear me?

A ripple on the surface.

Water, please! Show me Cyrus Bigelow the Fourth.

A bigger ripple.

CAN SOMEONE HEAR ME?

And then it happened! The water shimmered and then settled. She could see a big room.

DADDY!

Her father's head snapped up. He was sitting at a table in a big room and there were other people with him. People she'd never seen before. Except for there! Uncle Mat and Uncle Brooks. They were with him. In her mind, she yelled to them. *Mat! Brooks! Can you hear me? Can you feel where I am?*

Nothing.

She concentrated on her daddy again.

Cyrus Horatio Bigelow. This is your daughter speaking. Sofia Bigelow. Can you hear me? Daddy? Daddy! Please! Can you hear me?

He looked around, searching. His expression hopeful. Focused. She could see his lips moving. Saying her name. But she couldn't hear him. Couldn't reach him. And she could tell he couldn't really hear what she was saying. Couldn't even see her. How could she tell him she was okay? How could she tell him where she was?

She couldn't. Because she didn't know herself.

51

"Have you come to wish me a Merry Christmas?"

"Merry Christmas," Artemis said, stretching out her long legs on the chaise lounge on the top deck of Apollo's yacht. The weather in Delphi had been so cold and dreary recently, he'd taken advantage of the clear day to bask in the sun and forget about everything and everyone. Just the sky. The golden rays warming his skin. And a glass or two of a favorite wine. Maybe he'd find a willing woman later, but for now he was content to be alone on the water. Relaxing on the gentle waves of the wine-dark sea.

And yet, it wouldn't be a terrible thing to talk with his sister. She usually had interesting news. So, he cracked open an eye and waited.

"I've been spending a lot of time with your son lately."

"Indeed? Which one?"

"Cyrus Bigelow."

"Never heard of him."

"He'd never heard of you, either, as it turns out. Well, of course he knew about the myth. But that's different, isn't it? No, he was completely clueless as to his parentage. Believed himself to be the only son of a cattle and copper king from the American state of Arizona."

"I may not travel much anymore, but I do know where Arizona is."

Artemis nodded and waited. She knew deep down he was proud to be a father of so many children. Gods or demigods, many of whom were fine people. Not all of them, certainly. But many of them.

Apollo took a sip of wine. Licked his full, handsome lips. "You said he *was* completely clueless. Past tense."

"He's heard of you now. Apparently, he and Nemesis have fallen in love."

"That always ends well," he said with a snort. "And why do you believe this Cyrus Bigelow is indeed my son?"

"Aside from the fact that he was born eight months after you slept with his mother after giving her an 'insider's tour' of the museum that lasted an entire week. And that he can apparently understand Greek. Without ever having studied it. He heals quickly. Has lightning-fast reflexes. And recently survived a stabbing, a bombing, and two bullet wounds with nary more than a bit of fatigue and some interesting scars. In sum, he has demigod vibes pouring off him in veritable tidal waves. And he has a twin sister that looks just like you."

"Doesn't prove anything."

Artemis raised an eyebrow at her brother. She knew she had him hooked.

"Her name was Madeline Marquez. She was a beautiful archaeologist. Just graduated from college. Engaged to be married to a man she hardly knew. And you took advantage. Seduced her. Then she went home, got married, and bore you a set of twins."

Apollo shrugged, but a definite smile had formed on his lips. "I have lots of children. I always thought Asklepios was your favorite nephew. Has this Cyrus Bigelow usurped his position?"

"Oh, Dr. A likes him too. We've all been working together. Pantheon League stuff."

"Ah," Apollo let the word hang in the air. He had little patience for such do-gooders. He wasn't opposed to their work, but he wasn't much interested in it, either. He shifted in his lounge chair, squinted into the sun. Held up his wine glass. "Want some?"

"No, but there is something I do want."

He waited.

"I want you to help us find your granddaughter who, we believe, has been kidnapped by Eris."

Apollo choked. Spewed his wine. Coughed. Sat up. Speared his twin with a dark look. "Eris has a child of mine?"

"She's not *your* child. She's Cy's child. And she's an innocent seven-year-old who, Nemi says, has the gift of sight and can speak and understand Greek without ever studying it."

Apollo stood, looked down at his sister. "Where are they? Where did that bitch take my granddaughter?"

"We don't know. We have an idea of where she is, but that's why I'm here. We need your help. We're staging a family intervention, and we need as much firepower as we can get. We need you, brother. Your son needs you."

"Let's go."

"Um, Apollo? These are humans we're dealing with. You probably should put some clothes on?"

Sofia stared into the water. In truth, it was making her thirsty, but she didn't dare move. Barely dared breathe. She was watching when her dad got up and started pacing. When Uncle Mat and Uncle Brooks began to pace with him. The three of them charging around the big room like ... well, she didn't know what it was like. But she was glad they were together. She knew they were scared. She was scared. She tried again.

Daddy. Please can you hear me? Please come find me!

And then another man appeared. With a woman who looked so like him they could be twins. Like Daddy and Auntie Sybil. Only Daddy was dark and Aunti Sybil was fair. All her life, she'd thought she looked more like Auntie Sybil than either her Mommy or Daddy, who were both dark. But this new man was like her and Sybil. White gold hair with lots of curls. Bright eyes. Handsome like some king out of a picture book. She thought he should be wearing a crown.

She watched as her father's eyes went wide. As the new man stood there, just looking at him. And then as the new man stepped forward and wrapped his arms around her father.

The water rippled as she realized a tear had plopped into the bowl. And everyone in that far away room stopped. They all cocked their heads as if listening for something. Or as if trying hard to hear something.

The man turned to Nemi and said something and she disappeared. Just like that day at home. And then Sofia began to cry. And realized she was thinking in another language.

Λυπάμαι που πήγα με την κακή κυρία. Έρις. φοβάμαι. Κλειδωμένος, αλλά δεν ξέρω πού. Βρείτε με παρακαλώ. *I'm sorry I went with the bad lady. Eris. I'm scared. Locked up, but I don't know where. Please find me.*

She watched as more tears fell into the bowl. More ripples formed. The new man waved his hand and suddenly there was a large silver bowl on the table. It was huge. Bigger than a bird bath. Or a fountain. Then the man motioned to everyone else in the room. And she realized there was water in their bowl too. She gasped out a sob. Then Auntie Sybil and Mason and Mommy appeared and everyone gathered around the bowl. Then the man dipped his fingers in the water. And everyone else in the room did it too. They all dipped their fingers in the water. They were going to look for her. Through the water!

She stared down at her bowl. Put her fingertips in the water. Stared harder. Another tear fell. And she saw the water ripple in the far away bowl. Was it her tear? Or someone else's? Someone was crying. Daddy! His tear hit the water again and she could see more clearly. Another tear. She was crying harder. Leaning over the bowl. She could hear them now!

Daddy! I'm here! Do you hear me?

"God, baby, yes! I hear you. Where are you?"

I don't know! In a room. It's locked. Eris left me here.

"Περιγράψτε το δωμάτιο," The new man said that. Who was he? "Describe the room," he repeated in English.

She took me from the house like a magic trick, but when we got here, she made me walk down a long hallway. The lights only came on when you got close and then they turned off behind us. It was like she couldn't decide what room to put me in. It was scary! And it all felt too quiet, muffled. Like everything is under a thick blanket.

"Do you think you might be underground?"

That was a different man talking. She'd never seen him before, but her daddy nodded at him like it was a good question, so she concentrated extra hard. Tried to feel what was outside the room. Outside the hallway. Outside the walls.

Yes! I think I can feel the dirt. And the roots of the grass and the trees. I can feel it surrounding me. Pressing down on me.

"Don't be afraid, Little One. The roots are alive and can lead us to you," the man said. "Imagine reaching through the walls until you can touch them. Talk to them. Think of how they're connected. How the roots of one tree connect to another and another and another. They're looking for you. Tell them where you are, and they will tell us how to find you."

She concentrated and imagined her mind reaching out to the world around her. It felt like the soil itself was paying attention. She tried to think of herself as a little pin on a map, like on the nav system of a car.

"Keep thinking of the roots," the man talking about the dirt smiled at the water in their bowl and she smiled back. "Keep thinking of everything that's alive in the soil," he said. "The seeds and the little grubs and the earthworms and all that will bloom and grow in the springtime. Tell them to wake up and tell Dionysus where you are."

Little grubs and bugs and worms and roots and seeds and everything else, my name is Sofia and I want to be your friend. Wake up and help me find my way home.

She closed her eyes and repeated that over and over and over, reaching her mind out to everything in the dirt around her and imagining herself sitting and talking to a little beetle and a long worm as a seed sprouted and a tendril wrapped itself around her finger and she imagined she was a pink pin on a big map, and said, *tell them I am right HERE!*

Everyone in that faraway room jumped. As if her voice had shouted through the water.

"Oh my god! We can all hear you, baby! Stay right there," Daddy said. "If the bad lady comes, try not to let her move you from that room. Keep your water with you. If she makes you leave the room, take a bottle of water with you. This is our connection. We're coming for you."

52

Protected from security cameras by the shielding fields of nine gods, thirteen heavily armed 'special ops agents' and one deeply hypnotized man strode through the main doors of the New America Building and confronted the Security Service agents at the metal detectors and body scanners.

"What's this all about, Reynolds?" One of the familiar guards manning the security station asked, coming to attention because obviously this was an important op since both Supervisory Security Service Agent Reynolds and Agent Dennehey were leading the group.

"We'd tell you, but then we'd have to kill you," Dennehey joked. He pulled out an order that looked like it had been signed and sealed by Chancellor Jensen himself. "Seriously though, you need to shut down access to the building immediately. This is an elite group of the COSO, and agent Reynolds and I are just here to accompany them on a highly classified mission."

"COSO?"

"The Chancellor's Own Special Operators," Dennehey said, as if the guard was an idiot. "This is need to know, so you all better keep your fucking mouths shut."

"But—"

"All I can tell you is that information has just been surfaced about a mole inside the Chancellor's staff and this team has been tasked with finding him and taking him into custody."

The guard looked back at his comrade, then quickly scanned the official-looking papers. He looked up at Reynolds. "This is all highly irregular."

"Of course, it's irregular. The infiltrator poses a direct threat to the Chancellor's welfare." Dr. A put the words in Reynold's mouth. "Jensen's being sequestered right now for his safety, so we need to move. Now, before it's too late."

Reynolds sounded a bit like an AI version of his own voice, but they hadn't wanted to substitute a simulacrum since they needed him for a retinal scan to access secure sections of the bunker below the building. They could have just teleported in and bypassed all the security. And they could have simply hypnotized the guards, but Nemi and the Furies said no. They wanted it all on tape. They wanted Reynolds and everyone who kowtowed to him held accountable in the end.

"The bombing was irregular too," Dennehey said, voice hard, channeling how Reynolds treated everyone on his team. "You want to be the one to stand in the way of Jensen's men doing their job?"

"No! Of course, not. What do you need? What can we do to help?"

"I told you. Shut down the building and stay out of the way," Dennehey ordered.

"Will do, sir." He nodded at his security colleagues, and they stepped aside as Dennehey led the group through the lobby toward a secure elevator situated beyond the central bank. He stepped aside as Dr. A walked Agent Reynolds forward and pushed his face toward the retinal scanner until it beeped. A green light came on, and the elevator door opened.

The heavily armed contingent of gods and humans stepped inside the oversized elevator and Dr. A told Agent Reynolds to push the button for U10—Underground, 10th floor—while upstairs, on the 13th floor of the 14-floor building, in his expansive office overlooking the National Mall, Harold Jensen thrust his cock through his lubricated fist, imagining it was Pastor Erin Knight's throat as she knelt at his feet and moaned in ecstasy.

In the deep underground, the overhead lights in the otherwise dim corridor blinked on as the group stepped out of the elevator just like Sofia had said. Dr. A instructed Agent Reynolds to walk ahead of the group, leading the way as they turned left and strode down the hallway, all invisible to the cameras except for Reynolds.

They passed door after door until they all heard Dio's voice in their ears—or earpieces.

"Stop! It's here. The door on the right."

"I can't feel anything," Nemi, back in her Alex Whitelaw masculine form, said. "Eris has completely blocked me."

"Shit," Dennehey said after he tried the door knob. "Honestly, I didn't know these rooms locked. I thought this was all just storage and mechanical systems." He cocked his head toward his boss, standing immobile in the middle of the hall, eyes blank. "I doubt he can open it either."

Artemis looked from Cy to Apollo. "Just because Eris has locked out humans and blocked Nemi's access, doesn't mean we can't get in."

Apollo looked at the son he'd just met and held out his hand. Then he looked to his other son, Asklepios, and to his sister. "Eris is powerful, but she's not more powerful than our blood tie to little Sofia."

Cy put one hand in his father's and one hand in his brother's. Apollo and Asklepios completed the circle with Artemis and then they were gone.

A few heartbeats later, the door opened from the inside and Cy, holding Sofia in his arms with the others behind him, stepped out into the hall. Still clad in her Christmas pajamas, her arms encircled his neck as she sobbed against his shoulder and whispered, "I wanna go home."

Nemi stepped forward, rested a hand on Sofia's back and held Cy's gaze, full of love and wonder, as he inhaled the sweet scent of his daughter's hair. He pressed a kiss on Sofia's cheek and hugged her close. "We've got one stop along the way, sweet pea, and then we'll go home." He checked his watch. Not even noon.

Nemi walked past him into the small room and looked around. Moved forward and bent over the bed. Placed something on the pillow and headed back to Cy and Sofia.

Then the gods encircled the humans, reaching out to make contact. And suddenly the hallway was empty—except for a dazed and very confused Agent Reynolds who meandered his way to the elevator and headed back up to the lobby alone.

Down on Floor U10, the hallway went dark.

"Agent Dennehey!" The agent opening the front door of the Bigelow Estate said in surprise. "What are you doing here?"

"I hope you're glad to see me, because I've come with orders straight from the Chancellor. He's got a plane waiting up at the Air Force Base in Tucson to get you all back home in time to spend Christmas with your families."

The agent blinked. "Um ... well, that's great, but that doesn't sound much like—"

"Don't say it," Dennehey warned. "And don't look a gift horse in the mouth."

"Okay...." The agent turned around as one of his colleagues stepped into the foyer behind him.

"Suffice it to say that the situation on the ground in D.C. has changed, and you've all been called back. You've been rewarded with some time off for the holiday, and will report back for duty on January 1. SSS Agent Reynolds will be emailing your orders, but he asked me to come personally in case there were any questions. I'll stay behind to wrap up any last details and interface with the Bigelows."

If Reynolds survived the next few days, Dennehey would be the one surprised. With his signature on forged orders, his retinal scan on the secure elevator bank, his body the only one visible in the hallway of the lowest level of the Emergency Executive Retreat Bunker and his reappearance in the lobby alone, he wagered Reynolds and his entire extended family would be in custody before the last bite of Jensen's Christmas ham was eaten.

As for his own family, they were settling into their quarters in a place called the Basement. He didn't know exactly where it was located—Bigelow and his amazing friends trusted him, but not quite that much. Yet.

But he would be transported back there this evening to spend the rest of the Christmas holiday with them. He didn't care if they blindfolded him and tied his hands behind his back. He just wanted out from under Reynolds and as far away from Jensen as possible. And he couldn't believe that the doctor who'd hypnotized and controlled Reynolds, Dr. A, they called him, even volunteered to treat his father's cancer. It was strange how the world could change in just a few days. He finally, after so many years, had hope.

"Thank god," one of the agents said. "These are nice digs, but we haven't exactly been welcomed with open arms here. And it'll be good to get back home for at least part of the holiday."

"Go ahead and pack up," Dennehy said. "The plane's waiting."

53

"Good riddance."

Cy stood on the front steps, BoJo at his side and Sofia in his arms, and watched two black SUVs turn out of his gate and headed down the road toward the highway.

"What happens next?" BoJo asked.

"Next, we have some dinner, and then we prepare for the best Christmas ever. We'll have a full house."

"Mrs. C wants to stay at the Basement. Says she's more useful there than here. Taking care of those children. And with most of the women helping too, the place is going to be transformed from a utilitarian hideaway to a home away from home."

"As long as they all stay out of sight up top and don't mess with the comms center, we're all happy for them to be there and safe. I'm sure Mrs. C will keep them in line."

"That one boy, Joseph, the oldest of the kids, wants to help Brooks and Tisi with the Pantheon League technology. He seems very bright. Said his father was a professor before he was disappeared, and he used to help him in his lab."

"He'll fit right in," Cy said, taking a deep breath of the cold, dry Arizona winter air. He was beyond glad to be home and to have those watchdogs out of his house. So much had happened over the last week and a half, it was almost unbelievable. Actually, it was unbelievable. Still completely and totally incomprehensible.

The whole crazy story unfolding around him—the gods, demigods, new relatives, new friends. A new father. It was unreal. But after almost losing both Sybil and Sofia, he knew it was most definitely real. No matter how skilled he and Mason, Mat, and Brooks were, they'd have never been able to save his sister and his daughter without help from Nemi and her friends. Without help from the Pantheon League.

"They've all got a lot of healing and readjusting to do." Cy opened the front door and stepped into the house. He gave Sofia a squeeze and set her on her feet. "We *all* have healing and readjusting to do. And Mrs. C's right. Those people need her help more than we do. Anyway, I have the feeling we'll have plenty of help around the house now that Nemi's here."

"And Dio." Sofia said. "He told me he can cook and bake and make me anything I want."

"Great," Cy and BoJo both said with a laugh. "Just don't ask him for too many triple fudge brownies," BoJo warned.

Sofia squealed and took off for the kitchen as BoJo turned to Cy. "We haven't been able to really talk since you dumped all this magic woo woo stuff on me. Are you and Nemi really a thing? I mean are you really in love with an immortal goddess?"

Cy smiled and looked down at his wife and friend. He shook his head in wonderment. "Yeah. I really am. You'll love her too when you get to know her."

"If you and Sybs are demigods, does that mean you're immortal too? And what about Sofia?"

"I don't know. Dr. A's doing some blood tests, but I'm not sure I want the results. Not yet anyway."

"And what about Sybil and Mason? After you left us at the Basement, Mason told me what happened with Ken at that church. I can't believe that asshole was going to force Sybs to marry him! Plus, I'm her best friend, and had no idea she still carried a torch for Mason. I thought she was over him years ago."

"I promised I wouldn't get in the middle of whatever that is. We'll just have to see what happens. Same with Mat and Helen. She's flying back to Bigelow later tonight. I suspected something was going on there, but ..." He laughed and shook his head. "Did you see the way they were circling around each other after we got Sofia back?"

BoJo laughed. "Like they're getting ready for a cage fight?"

"Yeah, the sparks were definitely flying."

"Brooks seems pretty tight with that tech goddess too. Tisi. She's actually one of the Furies? Like in the myths?"

"Incredible, right? They're kindred spirits, I think. Probably gonna get matching tattoos and piercings next."

None of the guys had been in an actual relationship in what seemed like years. Probably longer than that. Maybe since college, back when they were young and had hope for the future. And even then none of them had long-term girlfriends.

Still, they'd all believed in the possibilities of love and the promise of a better tomorrow back then. They'd all believed they could do something good, make a difference in the world. Even Cy, though he'd still missed his mom, his dad was a fuck-up of colossal proportions, and Sybil sometimes felt like a ghost making diaphanous appearances in and out of his life as though she was smoke slipping through his fingers. Some family. That's why Mrs. C and the guys meant so much to him.

"Jeesh. It's all so hard to swallow." BoJo bit her lip and huffed out a soft laugh. "I, well, all of this craziness has made me hungry. Let's go see what Dio is making for dinner."

"You go ahead," Cy said. "I'm gonna find Nemi." He bent to press a kiss to the top of BoJo's head and then headed up the stairs.

With every step, he moved further away from the past. From his doubts. About who he was and what he was supposed to do with his life. Away from his long-cherished grief over his mother's death, grief that both he and Sybil had clung to as if it defined them. Grief about their father losing it, closing in on himself, ignoring his children—or blaming them—and throwing himself into an increasingly erratic lifestyle. First the lovers. Then the foolish investments. Then the reckless behavior. Dying on a mountainside in Switzerland, of all things. Then the shock of finding out that he and Sybil had inherited nothing but debt, the house, an old hotel, and the Bigelow Enterprises building down the street. And a lot of seemingly worthless land.

But he'd persevered. Through Sybil's withdrawals and breakdowns. Through an unexpected pregnancy. Through marriage to a woman he loved like a sister but could never love like a wife. Who could never love him like a husband. And then fatherhood. All with his friends at his side. All without ever knowing his biological father was an immortal being who never even bothered to find out if the woman he'd seduced all those years ago had born a child. Or two.

With every step, he moved away from the grief and confusion and anger of all that.

And closer to his destiny.

Nemesis, Immortal Goddess of Divine Retribution and Vengeance. Hallelujah Delphinium Jones. Alexander Whitelaw. And every other aspects she could take on. She was a mystery and a marvel, and she was his. And he was hers. For however long they had together. For whatever purpose the Fates decreed.

Tonight, they would share a meal with family—with gods and demigods, and humans. And then he and Nemi would retreat to his suite—the one he'd never really felt at home in—and make it their own.

He'd decided to keep the penthouse on the top of the Bigelow Hotel, but he was going to make this house his home. He knew his sister and his friends all had lives of their own and someday (maybe soon!) they'd all have loves of their own, but he was never going to take Sybil or Sofia or BoJo or Mat or Brooks or Mason for granted again.

So, for the next few days, they would celebrate the holiday and all that meant—love and togetherness and giving and sharing and accepting each other for who they were in all their various incarnations. And they'd open presents and toast to the future—and, no doubt, to the past—and they'd laugh and sing and make music and stuff themselves until they couldn't eat another bite.

And then, they'd get up and face the future. The Pantheon League. Working together to see justice done. He couldn't wait.

He reached his suite, and the door opened wide before he could turn the knob.

"Finally," Nemi said with a smile that seemed to promise the sun and the moon and the stars. She crooked a finger at him. "I've been waiting forever."

He slipped inside, kicked the door closed behind him, and stepped into her open arms.

"How lucky we are that our forever starts now."

 EPILOGUE

Christmas Day

Eris materialized in the dark corridor on the lowest level of the New America Building. Her vacation had been everything she'd hoped for, and she hadn't given a single thought to Jensen or Nemesis or Cy Bigelow's little brat.

The lights blinked on. She stood there. Unmoving. The door was open. The girl was gone. After a long moment, she stepped into the room. Walked slowly to the bed. Stared down at the pillow where her golden apple rested, now impaled by an elegant diamond dagger glittering blue under the flickering fluorescent light.

Her sister hadn't even left a note.

ACKNOWLEDGMENTS

Fiction may be the product of an author's imagination, but that imagination is fired by creative conversations inspired by countless other storytellers and poets and filmmakers and artists. To all these other creators and for all these countless interactions and inspirations, I owe my deepest thanks.

For this particular work—which started out as a much different story—I owe my thanks, as always, to Jason and Amira and Elena who listen patiently, read critically, and always have my back.

I also owe my thanks and gratitude to my sister Karen (a voracious reader and giver of devious plot points and delicious twists and turns), my long-lost cousin Eric (a thoughtful reader and enthusiastic champion), my sister-in-law Kathy (who reads my work even though it's definitely not her cup of tea), and my friend and fellow editor, Nancy (whose critical eye is, well, critical).

Real life is also an inspiration, and I am deeply troubled that many of the plot points I envisioned for this series have already come to pass. I hope with all my heart that more of these remain in the realm of fiction.

ABOUT THE AUTHOR

With degrees in government and education, and a career in writing, communications, marketing, and design Marie K. Savage (a.k.a. Kristina Makansi) dove into publishing by starting Blank Slate Press in 2011 in St. Louis, MO, and then by cofounding Amphorae Publishing Group in 2014. Since then, as editor and designer, she's worked with amazing authors on 160+ book projects including many award winners, books with major publication starred reviews, and books that have moved her to revisit them time and time again.

Today, she focuses on her own writing while living in the Sonoran Desert with her husband and two ridiculous chiweenies. *Nemesis in Love* is the first book in the Pantheon League Series. Stay tuned for *Helen Unleashed, Tisiphone Unbound,* and *Sybil Empowered.*

To learn more, visit kristinamakansi.com.